THE DARKEST HEART

Dan Smith

An Orion paperback

First published in Great Britain in 2014
by Orion Books
This paperback edition published in 2015
by Orion Books,
an imprint of The Orion Publishing Group Ltd,
Carmelite House, 50 Victoria Embankment,
London EC4Y 0DZ

An Hachette UK Company

1 3 5 7 9 10 8 6 4 2

A CIP catalogue record for this book
is available from the British Library.

ISBN 978-1-4091-3745-0

For Divya

Acknowledgements

My novels all start right here, at my keyboard, but before they reach you, they sail through the hands of many experts. I'd like to take a brief moment to thank my agent, Carolyn, who always offers the best advice, and my editor, Laura, who has done a fantastic job of steering *The Darkest Heart* in and out of the shadows. Thanks also to everyone else at Orion who has helped this book along its winding journey. And what would I do without my wife and children to support me? I would, of course, be lost; somewhere out there in the darkness ...

1

There were times I felt I would always be death's passenger. It moved one step ahead of me wherever I went, letting its shadow fall across me. It carried me on; shaded me from the world other people lived in. Whenever I tried to step into the light, it shifted, slipping its arm around me, draping its black cloak over me and bringing me home like an old friend. We were inseparable. Partners. I could never leave it behind.

I walked in death's shadow that morning – the morning I saw Costa's men across the street – and I knew it was going to be a bad day as soon as I laid eyes on them. They weren't the kind of men who brought good news. Standing out of the morning sun, watching my place, they hadn't come to pass the time of day. They were there for a reason.

I'd had nothing to do with Costa for at least six months but I'd always felt his presence. Just like that shadow, Costa was always there. You work for a man like that, you can't just walk away. And now he'd come calling again.

I stopped at the edge of the road, pretending to adjust my shirt, touching my fingers to the handle of the knife tucked into the back of my belt. I watched Luis and Wilson just a few metres away on the other side, considering my options, while they considered theirs.

Nothing passed on the dusty red road. The morning was quiet.

Luis shifted his weight and pushed back the peak of his cap. The early sun was already warming the day but there was more than just that to put sweat on his brow. He knew me, and he'd be wondering what I was going to do.

I

Somewhere to my right, a car door slammed with a tinny, hollow sound. An engine started up, but Luis and I continued to watch each other. Behind him, Wilson looked in the direction of the disturbance. A small shift of his eyes and then he was looking back at me again.

A pickup came into my field of vision, gathering speed, passing between us, blocking our view for a moment and then it was gone, moving away, leaving a cloud of dust in its wake. The dirt swirled, rolling out, falling, settling around my feet. I waited for it to subside, then crossed over to meet them.

'Costa wants to see you.' Luis started speaking straight away, stepping back so he was just beyond my reach. He looked like a foreman, the way he wore his cap and stood like he was in charge, drawing himself to full height. He was at least a head taller than me, but I wasn't worried about that. What concerned me was that he had one hand in his pocket, his fingers probably curled round the handle of some old revolver.

Wilson stayed behind him and stared at me for no longer than a second, then ran his fingers over his moustache and glanced about, checking the street and alley, taking everything in. He was shorter than his partner, the beginning of a pot belly pushing at the cotton of his T-shirt, and he wore a straw hat pulled low against the sun.

'I don't want to see Costa.' I stared Luis right in the eye. 'Anyway, I'm late for work.'

'You're working now?' he asked. 'What kind of job you got, Zico?'

'You know what kind of job. You people are always watching.'

'Don't need to watch you to know what work you're doing. Just have to take a sniff. You stink like Batista's place.'

I put one hand on my hip, fingertips close to my knife. 'What does he want?'

'Ask him yourself.'

'I'm busy. I haven't got time.'

'Maybe you should make time.'

'And if I don't? What did he tell you to do *then*?'

2

Luis shook his head like he didn't know what I was talking about.

'He tell you to use that?' I nodded at his pocket, his hand stuffed hard inside.

'Use what?' Luis showed me his smile; thin-lipped and tight-mouthed. He still had yesterday's growth on his chin and there was a patch around the chest of his T-shirt where yesterday's sweat had dried. It made him look road weary. Behind him, Wilson moved, his hand dropping out of sight.

'You think you could pull that pistol out of your pocket before I ...' I shrugged at Luis and patted my hip. 'You know.'

Luis narrowed his eyes.

'And with Wilson getting ready behind you,' I said. 'Nice and close like this. Who's standing right in the middle?'

Luis swallowed and I could see it all playing out in his mind. He was imagining his partner pulling his pistol, putting holes in his back just to get to me. He took a deep breath and his expression betrayed his feelings.

'All right.' He took his hand from his pocket and spread his fingers. 'No trouble,' he said, turning to shake his head at Wilson. 'No trouble. Costa just wants to talk.'

'Sure he does.'

Somewhere out there, Batista would be cursing me for being late, thinking I was just what everyone said I was; a waste of time and only good for one thing.

And right here, death's shadow grew a little longer.

2

Luis and Wilson walked a few paces behind me, making my skin crawl. Even with the growing heat of the day, it made me cold to know they were there.

When I came to the building on the corner, I paused to look back at them, then pushed open the heavy wooden door. The blue paint was cracked and flaking, some of it coming away on my fingers. I dusted it off as I went into the stuffy stairwell and climbed to the office above. Loose tiles rattled on the steps.

The room at the top was drab and had a temporary feel to it. It had been that way since I first saw it a couple of years ago, and God knows how long before that. Nothing on the walls but stains left by age and neglect. There were drawers in one corner, a filing cabinet, and a broken fan hanging its head. A pile of boxes without lids had spilled their contents of papers and no one had bothered to pick them up. Some of the papers were yellowed, the corners curled in the incessant heat. There was a simple desk with an old, dusty computer, and an even older secretary – a woman who might have been a hundred years old. Her face was fissured like a dry lakebed.

Costa was in the room, too, leaning over the desk, holding a sheaf of paper in his thick fingers. Fair skinned, maybe fifty years old, coarse black hair touched with grey at the temples. He was dressed like a city businessman – dark trousers and a white shirt – but he'd pulled the patterned tie loose and unfastened the top button.

'Ah.' He straightened and waved the other two men away. 'Good to see you, Zico, come in, come in.' He dropped the paper in front of the secretary and held open the door to his office.

I hesitated, approached, and he put his arm around my shoulder as if we were old friends.

He walked me into his office and closed the door, sealing us from the others before moving round to the far side of the desk.

There were documents on the scratched surface but Costa made no attempt to cover them. He knew I couldn't read them even if I wanted to. I had never spent a full day in school and couldn't even write my own name.

'Sit, Zico.' He pointed to the only other chair in the room. 'I have something for you.' In the silence after his words, there was only the sound of his laboured breathing, as if the warm air was too thick for his lungs.

I shook my head. 'No, Costa—'

'Something much better than pig farming. A man like you shouldn't work with animals – not that kind, anyway. I have something much more suited to your talents.' When he spoke, there was an air of authority and education in his words.

'I haven't done anything like that for a long time. Not for you, not for anybody.'

'But it's in your blood, Zico, it's what you do best. Men like you are rare. You can look a man in the eye and feel his last breath on your face, walk away and sleep like a child. It's a rare talent.'

'I'd rather have another talent,' I said. 'An artist, maybe. Or a farmer.'

Costa smiled and dabbed sweat from the back of his neck with a handkerchief. 'I can offer you something better than that.'

'I don't do this any more.'

'I know, I know. You say that, but you've said it before and—'

'This time I mean it.'

'But *this time*, the pay is more than you might think.'

I looked away and thought about walking out. If I didn't hear what he had to say, I wouldn't be tempted.

'A thousand,' he said.

'Reais?' I turned to look in his eyes; to see the lie. It was more than I'd ever been paid for anything.

Costa shook his head. 'Not reais.'

'*Dollars?*'

He nodded and grinned.

'A *thousand dollars*? American?'

Costa's eyes narrowed, becoming small and dark. He could read my indecision; my need for money. 'Why don't you listen to what I have to say?'

His chair creaked as he lowered himself into it, then he waited for me to do the same. I let out my breath without realising I'd been holding it, then yielded, and sat down. If there had been any doubt in Costa's mind about my willingness to work for him again, it was now gone.

We remained still, studying one another, each knowing what the other could do – I had my skills and he had his connections.

'Who is he?' I sighed, knowing I should have walked out. 'What's his name?'

'Not he. *She.*'

I blinked hard and stared at the surface of the desk.

'Zico?' Costa's voice intruded.

'Hm?'

'You still with me?'

I looked up at his serious face, his eyes shining like glass. 'OK,' I said. 'Who is *she?*'

'Dolores Beckett.'

I took a deep breath to clear my head and leaned back in the uncomfortable wooden chair. 'I've heard that name. Why do I know it?'

Costa averted his eyes. 'I have no idea.' He started to say something else but I wasn't listening. The name had triggered a memory.

Dolores Beckett.

'Wait.' I held up a hand. 'I *do* know that name. I've heard you complaining about her. But it's not just Dolores Beckett, is it? It's *Sister* Dolores Beckett.'

6

Costa stopped and looked at me, his mouth open.

'Isn't it?'

'Yes.' The word was short. Tense.

'The American nun.'

'Yes.'

'The *Indian rights* nun.'

Costa nodded.

I put a hand to my chin, felt the day's growth already beginning.
'You want me to kill a *nun*?'

3

I didn't know exactly how many people I had killed, but at least eleven of them had been close enough to blow their last breath in my face, just like Costa had said.

All of them had been men, though – or male, if not yet men – and I had never lost a moment of sleep over any of them. They were all made from the same mould and they had all deserved it. But my life was changing and it was time to leave certain things behind. The work I did for Costa was one of those things, but I was tempted by the money, and I might have done it one more time for him. But this? A nun?

'She's well known, so it needs to be quiet.' Costa took out his handkerchief again. '*Very* quiet. No connections coming back to me or... well.' He wiped the sweat from his forehead and made a show of almost letting something slip, but he was just reminding me he had knowledge I didn't. Costa had city sophistication and links to people who gained him respect in a town like ours. He was more important than me, and he didn't want me to forget it.

'It's even better if no one knows she's dead,' he went on. 'If you can make her disappear, that's the best thing.' He wiped the beads of moisture from his upper lip. 'And you've always been so good at that.'

'Foreign nuns don't just disappear.'

'I'm sure a man like you can—'

'Not even a man like me, Costa. Get someone else to do it.' But he'd mentioned money, a *lot* of it, and a small part of me was tempted, drawing me back into the shadow.

'Is it because she's a nun? Or because she's a woman?'

'Neither. I'm finished with this.' I was more than just a killer. I had other things now.

Costa raised his eyebrows and gave me a knowing look. He'd heard me say it before and sometimes I felt like I'd been saying it or thinking it most of my life. I was going to leave the shadow behind, find honest work; let the blood fade from my hands. But the shadow was always close, and people like Costa had a way of seeing how it followed me. He was willing to pay for the kind of work I could do and, no matter how much I wanted to get away, there was always something to entice me back. I could tell myself the people deserved it one way or another, that none of them was a good person and any one of them would do the same to me or to someone like my sister Sofia.

Sister Dolores Beckett, though; she was different.

'What if we were talking about a man?' Costa asked. 'Some cruel landowner who needs shifting from his land? The kind of work you've done before? What would you be saying to me now?'

'That I'm finished with this.'

'Zico.' Costa shook his head. 'That's not true. You wouldn't think twice.'

I wondered if he was right; if he knew me better than I knew myself.

Costa looked away, tightening his thin lips. 'I need to get the air conditioning fixed in this office. I keep telling that woman to get it sorted but she's damn useless. I don't know why I keep her on. It's hotter than hell in here.' He stood and went to the window, staring out at the street.

Sweat patches grew under his arms as the perspiration leached into the material of his shirt and darkened it. There was a fan in the corner of the room, its head rotating back and forth in a lazy arc, but it had no effect in the enclosed space.

'You know I can't get anyone else to do this,' Costa said.

'I don't want to hear it.'

'Of course you do. That's why you're still in your seat. You want to know how much I need you; how much I can offer you.' Costa turned around, face glistening. He'd never got used to the heat.

9

All the time I'd known him, he'd been like that. He'd had his hair cut short, shaved off the moustache he wore when I first met him, and the way he smelled, you'd think he bathed in aftershave, but nothing worked.

'You know I can't afford for some local *pistoleiro* to screw this up,' he said. 'Times are changing. People are watching now and they write things in the newspapers. Even about things that happen in shit-hole, middle-of-nowhere places like this. It's not so easy to get away with things any more. *That's* how much I need you.'

When I was growing up in Rio, the few years of real childhood I had, my sister Sofia and I used to blame the *saci pererê* for anything that went wrong. We used to believe he was right there in the dust devils that swirled on the street in the *favela*, a one-legged *mulatto* ready to cause all kinds of mischief. If the milk soured, it was the *saci pererê*. If the meat was bad, or the keys were missing or the sole came off your shoe, it was him. Later, when Sofia was gone, if the knife's edge was dull, or the cartridge misfired, the boys blamed the *saci pererê*.

Right now, looking at Costa, feeling him draw me in, I saw something like the *saci pererê* trying to trick me with flattery and promises and clever games. Except there was something more cruel in Costa's heart. The *saci pererê* was a creature of mischief. Perhaps Costa was more like Anhangá.

The Indians said Anhangá was a shape-shifter who could look like a caiman as easily as he could look like a man. He was a protector of the forest but loved to torment humans, filling their heads with mistrust and misery and horrific visions of hell. When the Catholics came to evangelise the Indians, Anhangá was the name they chose for the Devil.

The old man, Raul, said he knew people who had seen it in the forest, and some of the fishermen swore they'd seen men who walked to the river's edge before transforming into a caiman and sliding into the murky waters. Some of them were afraid to take their children on their boats because they thought Anhangá would steal them in the night.

My sister Sofia would have liked the stories just as she did when we were children and we sat on the steps to listen when the women talked about the *orixas* – the gods of the Candomblé religion. Once our father was dead, Sofia found comfort in Candomblé and its rituals, while I turned to more worldly things.

When I thought of those things now, though, I remembered the shadow in which I had walked since Sofia had gone. Perhaps she would have known a name for that shadow. And I couldn't help wondering what she would say about me now; about the temptation I was feeling.

'You know I need *you*, Zico,' Costa said. 'That's why you're still sitting there. Because men like Luis and Wilson lack your subtlety. They can be effective in their own way, but for something like this?' He shook his head. 'Luis and Wilson are like a hammer but you are like a filleting knife. They can move a man from his land or ... deal with a difficult worker.' He let that idea hang in the air for a moment. 'But they're too heavy-handed and loose-tongued.'

'And they're on your payroll.'

Costa looked surprised that I'd even thought about that. 'This can't come back to me,' he said. 'That's one of the things you're so good at. You keep it to yourself. There's no proof you ever worked for me.' He shrugged. 'If you get caught ...' He turned around again and opened the window. The sound of samba music eased in from the street below, where the café was serving up breakfast. He took a lung full of air and came back to the desk, drying his sweaty palms on his trousers and sitting down.

'So who wants this nun dead?' I asked him. 'The Branquinos?'

'You know I can't tell you that.'

I was sure I was right, though. Costa was discreet, he never mentioned the Branquinos by name, but everyone knew they owned all the land round here. Some of the older people in Piratinga remembered when the Branquino brothers lived on their *fazenda* not far from Piratinga, but they had people to run their businesses now, they were too important to live in a place like this. Heat and sweat and the stink of cattle wasn't their style any more. Now they lived the good life in Brasilia or Manaus or some other place that was far away, passing their orders down to men like Costa in towns all over this area.

'And what's she done to upset them?' I asked. 'She causing some kind of trouble?' I didn't know much about land ownership or Indian rights but I knew there were people trying to bring some balance – little people who could put a barb into the big man's fingers when he tried to grab more territory.

'Does it matter?'

'Not really. Like I already told you, I don't do this work any more.'

Costa smiled again. Always the same expression of knowing, as if he saw things I couldn't. 'Maybe if you say it enough times, you'll believe it.'

'What?'

Costa waved a hand, then eased back in his seat and fanned himself with a folder from the desktop. 'You haven't done any work for me for six months at least. You must be hard up, needing the cash.'

'I'm all right.'

'Of course. Because now you do ... what? I heard you were working at Ernesto's one time, the soya place, odd jobs for that old boatman you spend so much time with, and now you're shovelling shit at Batista's pig farm, is that right?'

He dug a packet of cigarettes from the top drawer of his desk and took one out. Throwing the packet towards me, he reached for a lighter. 'That's what happens when you meet a woman,' he said, thumbing the wheel a few times before sparking a flame. 'That's what they do to you, Zico.' He breathed his smoke into the tepid air. 'They take what you are and strip it away. Change you into what they want. Next thing you know, you're shovelling shit on some pig farm.'

'What are you talking about?'

'I watch, Zico, I listen too, just like you do; only I listen better. I listen *deeper*. I know you're friends with the old boatman. You have a girl, too. The one who works in the store. She's very pretty.'

'You're threatening me?'

Costa held up his hands. 'I don't want it to come to that. I'm just saying they stop you from doing what you do best. Women, I mean.'

'No one stopped me. I stopped myself. I don't want to do it any more. I have a different life.'

'No money? No real job? No place to call your own? Not much of a life, Zico – which is why you're still sitting here, right? You need money. I could never persuade you to come and work full-time for me, but I could always call on you when you needed the money. For those special jobs.'

'It's different now.'

'Is it? I can see you need money, Zico. I can see it in your eyes. If you weren't considering it, you'd be out that door already.'

'You don't know me as well as you think—'

'I've been instructed to go to two thousand.'

For a moment the office was silent but for the swirl of the fan and the lilt of samba music from the street.

'*Dollars?*'

Costa smiled. 'It's a lot, Zico. More than ever before. Probably more than you ever saw in your whole life. Think about it. You could treat your girlfriend. Do something nice for her. Or how about that old boatman? Raul, isn't it? Just think, Zico, you could fix up his boat for him, give him a better life.' He sighed and rose from his seat again, leaving a trail of smoke as he went to the flask that stood on a table by the fan.

Costa pumped coffee into his cup and drained it, wiping the back of his hand across his lips before speaking again. 'Two years ago a tenth of that money would've got me the bishop. And you would've organised it.' He pointed at me, the cigarette wedged between two fingers, both adorned with wide bands of gold.

'That was two years ago,' I said. 'Things are different now. And you're talking about killing a nun. A *foreign* nun. From what I've heard, she's practically a saint.'

'She's a pain in the—'

'Whatever she is, she's obviously worth more than a thousand.'

Costa smiled. 'Ah, now we're getting to it.'

13

'That's not what I meant.'

'Of course it is, Zico. How much, then? How much is she worth?'

'I don't do this any more.' I watched his lips moving, hating him and everything he stood for. I hated being in this impossible position. I hated having no choice but to do what Costa wanted. Most of all, though, I hated the part of me that didn't need to be threatened by this man. I could see a positive side to this and I wanted his money. I thought it would give me the life I hoped for with Daniella.

'We both know you're going to do this,' Costa said. 'So let's stop pretending you have a choice.' His forearms were on the desk, across some loose pieces of paper, the cigarette smouldering between two fingers. 'The only reason I'm allowing this game to go on is because I want to find a price that will make it agreeable to everyone. That way we all get what we want.' He lowered his eyes for a moment, then looked back at me, his expression dark. 'I can see you're struggling with this, Zico.'

'I—'

'You want the money but you don't want to admit it to yourself. You want to be noble, to do the *right thing*. You want to leave here and have nothing to do with me or Dolores Beckett. You think you want a different life where you're someone else. Maybe a happy farmer with his wife and kids or whatever the hell it is people like you dream about. So let me make this easy for you, Zico. I'll take the decision away. I'll make you an offer you can't refuse.'

He spoke slowly and clearly, the words carrying such weight that I could almost feel them.

'If I were so inclined, Zico, I could make you do this for nothing. I couldn't have done that a year ago, but now? Now you have ties. This girl. The old man, Raul. You have something more important than money to think about. There are people who matter to you. People who—'

'Don't threaten me, Costa.' I put my hands on the desk and leaned forward so our faces were close and the smoke from his cigarette drifted around us.

'Or what? There's nothing you can do, Zico. You have too much to lose. If anything happens to me, there are people who will take action. And if I'm dead, who would protect the old man? Who would keep Daniella safe? You? *Alone?*'

I leaned back, knowing he was in control.

'So let's sort this out together,' Costa said. 'You can save yourself a lot of pain and make something out of this. Make it swing in your favour. Just name your price and I'll see what I can do. I'll have it waiting for you in that safe.' He pointed to the corner of the room over my left shoulder, but I stayed as I was, staring into him, feeling the frustration build in me.

'Come on, Zico. Name your price.'

I sighed and shook my head. 'Something like this won't be easy. She'll have people round her—'

'She doesn't have security, she's a nun, for Christ's sake. This'll be easy for you, Zico. Just another job. How much?'

'Ten thousand.'

'Ten thousand dollars?' He stubbed the cigarette into a full ashtray. 'You're serious?'

'Ten.' I kept my expression set, my eyes directly on his, daring him to smile again.

'You really *are* trying to sway this in your favour.'

'And I want a piece of land with my name on it. Nothing big. Just enough.'

'Ten?' he repeated, his expression becoming serious. 'And you want land?'

'With my name on it. Signed over.'

'Enough for you and the girl from the shop ... what's her name?'

'None of your business.'

'You drive a hard bargain, Zico, I like it. You've grown since you first worked for me.' Costa smiled a grin that showed me teeth straighter than any dentist in Piratinga could have made them. 'I'll have to check with my employers,' he said. 'See what they say.'

'OK.' It wouldn't be easy. The people he worked for were not well known for their generosity. Rich people don't stay rich by giving away their land and money, and it would hurt for them to have to give anything to a man like me. I was nothing. We both knew they wouldn't give me ten thousand dollars but if I went in high I stood a better chance of getting enough to make some choices. With enough money, Daniella and I could get married, get a place of our own or even leave town. Leave the shadow here. And the old man could move away to Imperatriz like he always wanted.

I moved to the door, eager to escape the smell of tobacco and aftershave. The years of sweat and smoke ingrained into the soft walls. I pulled it open and turned to look at Costa sitting behind his desk. 'You can find me when you have an answer. I'll be around.'

'Where?'

'It's a small town,' I said. 'You'll find me.'

Costa nodded. 'And let me save you a trip. Your job at Batista's farm is gone. It's all been arranged.'

I stared at him for a moment, angry at how easily he had backed me into this corner; angry at being *owned* by this man. He was no better than the men I had killed, and I would find it as easy to take his life as I had taken theirs, but there would be consequences; he had made that clear. I had more than just myself to think about now, and Costa had used that to his advantage.

'I'll see you soon, Zico.' He smiled and then looked down at something on his desk, as if I weren't even there.

I slammed the door and made my way down the stairs and out into the sunlight.

Outside, I stopped and leaned against the wall beside the door. I took a deep breath of warm air and watched a pickup pass on the road, tailgate rattling.

I closed my eyes and, for a moment, I was somewhere else. I wasn't on the street in Piratinga, standing outside Costa's office. I was nineteen years old again, hiding in Father Tomás's room at the back of the church, listening to the pounding on the door, the boys looking for me the day I left the *favela*. Somewhere further up the hillside, in a small house occupied only by boys and drugs and guns, a body lay stiff and dead, and right here, right outside, right now, the others had come looking for me.

Father Tomás's footsteps were soft on the concrete floor of his small, empty church where no one came any more. I pictured him walking the length of the room, his robe rough and old around his thin ankles, his hands together, his back straight, his hair grey against his black skin. I heard him draw back the bolt, the sharp words of the boys outside, the sudden and familiar sound of gunfire defiling this place of worship forgotten by people with a terrible emptiness inside them.

Wherever I went, whatever I tried to do, that shadow always slipped over me. And here it was again, smiling its wicked smile, a knowing glint twinkling in its dark eyes as it welcomed me back.

4

I went straight to the grocery store, hoping to see Daniella, but her mother was outside, in the plastic seat, waiting for customers. She was sitting under the awning, out of the sun, her thighs splayed out over the seat of the chair, her forearms flattened across the armrest.

'Zico,' she said, looking me up and down. 'You keeping out of trouble?'

'Always, Doña Eliana.' I gave her my best smile. 'How are you? Business good?'

She sagged and made a noise like escaping air. 'Ah, you know how it is. Why aren't you at work?'

'Is Daniella inside?'

'She's busy. Working hard. You shouldn't disturb her.'

'I won't be long.'

'And why aren't you at work? You ...'

I missed the end of her sentence and went into the shop, allowing my eyes to adjust from the brightness outside. It was cooler in here, where it was dark and the air was being turned by a couple of floor-standing fans with red ribbons tied to the cages. Everything smelled of dry and fresh goods.

The shop wasn't much, just a square room with three or four aisles of shelves filled with tins and bags and tubes and packaging. Near the entrance, there were sacks of rice and beans and, at the back, by the counter, there was a fridge with Coke and a couple of brands of beer. There were cigarettes in a rack, and jars of sweet things for the children. Even a small section for hooks and lines and folding knives that could be used to cut and gut a fish.

Antonio was there – the man who lived in the room above mine at Juliana's. He was older than me, maybe in his late forties. The muscles in his arms and neck were tight and sinewy and his features were lined with experience. Dark skinned and grey haired, he moved as if life had been hard on him. He had drifted into town a few weeks ago, taken the room at Juliana's and started working a few days at one of the *fazendas*, rounding up cattle from the back of a borrowed horse. Today must have been a rare day off. Or maybe he'd lost his job and was getting ready to move on.

He was coming away from the counter with a plastic bag full of beer cans and acknowledged me with a nod of the head. 'Oi, Zico.'

'You having a party?' I asked, pointing at the cans of beer. They were already sweating in the bag so I could see the brand label through the plastic. Skol.

'Just a few to get me through the day.' He raised the bag a touch and showed me an almost toothless smile.

I clapped him on the shoulder and told him to take it easy, but when he moved out of the way, I saw who else was in the store.

Wilson.

As soon as I laid eyes on him, I felt my rage come to life, like a snake that had been sleeping inside me. My stomach went cold and my heart thumped and a surge of adrenalin flooded my muscles so they trembled in anticipation. It had been different when I had seen him waiting outside my place this morning. He had come for *me*, then, but now he was here, standing at the counter, talking to Daniella, while Costa's threats were still fresh in my mind.

'What are you doing here?' I could hardly disguise the tension in my voice.

'Hm?' Wilson turned around and leaned back against the counter. 'Oh. It's you.'

'What are you doing here?' I asked again, but I knew he was here to remind me who was in control.

Wilson shrugged and lifted a hand to show me a packet of cigarettes. 'I was running low.'

'Well, you got what you want, now get out.'

'Zico?' Daniella asked. 'What's going on? You can't—'

'Outside.' I tried to stay calm.

Wilson gave me a lazy smile and tucked the cigarettes into his pocket. 'On second thoughts, maybe there were some other things I needed.' He started to turn back to the counter.

'No.' I reached out and grabbed his wrist. 'I think you have everything.'

Wilson tore free of my grasp and stood straight. He moved towards me so his nose was no more than a hand's breadth from mine.

'Don't touch me.' His rancid breath washed over me, and flecks of his spit peppered my face. I could feel the heat coming off him and smell the stale sweat on his shirt.

'Everything all right, Zico?' Antonio had stopped in the doorway and turned to watch what was happening. 'You need some help?'

Wilson raised a hand and placed it on my chest, fingers spread. 'Out of my way.'

Allowing him to push me back, I watched him saunter along the aisle, knowing there was nothing I could do. Nothing.

When he reached the door, Wilson shoved past Antonio and stalked out into the sunlight.

'You OK, Zico?' Antonio looked back at me.

'Who *is* that?' Daniella asked. 'What was that all about?'

'No one. It doesn't matter.' But I couldn't just stand by. I had to do something.

My head was filled with a vision of the last time I had seen my sister Sofia. I saw her dull eyes and her twisted expression of pain and anger and fear. It couldn't happen again. I would not allow it to happen again.

'I'll be back in a minute.'

Daniella called after me as I left the store, Antonio too, but I didn't hear the words. There was only one thing on my mind now.

The sun was blinding when I moved from the darkness inside, and I lifted a hand to shade my eyes as I scanned the street for Wilson. He was only a few metres away, strolling along the street, opening the packet of cigarettes. He had dropped the wrapping into the red dirt, and was putting a cigarette between his lips as he passed the narrow alley between Rui's café and Josalino's hardware store.

I jogged to catch up with him, my flip-flops slapping the soles of my feet and kicking up dust behind me. It wasn't quiet, but I didn't care if he heard me. He was too arrogant to think I would follow him; too sure that I was under their control.

A couple of paces behind him, Wilson heard my approach and turned in surprise, but he was too late to stop me. I shoved him hard towards the alley and followed him in, hitting him once in the kidneys and then pushing him up against the wall.

I gripped my left hand around his throat and slipped the knife from the back of my waistband, pressing the tip into the soft flesh beneath his chin. 'If you go anywhere near her I'll—'

'No one's going near her.'

I turned to see Luis standing just inside the mouth of the alley.

'Not yet, anyway,' he said. His pistol was in his hand, but he hadn't felt the need to raise it.

'Where the hell did *you* come from?' I spoke through gritted teeth.

'Lucky for both of you, I just got back from running an errand for Costa. Someone told me Wilson had come to the store and I saw you push him in here and ... well, here I am.'

'Keep away from her,' I said.

'Whatever it is Costa wants from you, his orders are clear,' Luis told me. 'Your girlfriend is safe, but the moment he gives the word ...' He drew his finger across his throat. 'And you know what? She's a pretty girl. Whoever gets the job will probably have some fun. But if you press that knife any harder, I'll shoot you dead right here, right now, then go round to the shop and find Daniella. That's her name, right? Daniella?'

'Costa wouldn't be too happy about that,' I said.

Luis shrugged. 'Then we're stuck, aren't we? We can't hurt you; you can't hurt us. So what are we—'

He stopped mid-sentence as Antonio grabbed him from behind. One hand came around to slap against Luis's forehead and tip his head back, then another came from the other side to put a blade to his exposed throat.

'Drop the pistol.' Antonio put his mouth close to Luis's ear and spoke in a quiet whisper.

Luis didn't attempt to struggle. He remained perfectly still except for the movement required to open his fingers and drop his pistol into the dust. It landed with a dull thump and Antonio kicked it towards me.

'What do you want me to do with him?' Antonio asked.

Luis swallowed hard, his Adam's apple rising and falling against the taut skin of his throat. When it moved, it came close to the gleaming blade of Antonio's knife.

'Let him go.' I kicked the pistol further along the alley so it was out of reach.

'You sure?' Antonio asked.

'I'm sure.' I nodded. 'Just go, Antonio, you don't need to be part of this.'

Antonio hesitated, turning to look at Luis, their faces close together. Then he nodded to me, withdrew his knife and moved away.

Luis turned to stare at him.

He didn't speak. He just stared.

'I'll be all right,' I told Antonio. 'You can go. I'll see you later.' I still had the knife at Wilson's throat, my knuckles white as I gripped the handle.

'Come with me,' Antonio said. 'We'll leave together.'

I stayed as I was for a moment, then released Wilson and stepped back. I stared at him, seeing the face of the first person I had ever killed. I had another glimpse of Sofia as I last saw her, and I knew that both Luis and Wilson deserved my blade just like the others had deserved it.

'You should go now,' Luis said.

I turned slowly and pushed past him, heading out of the alley, swallowing the rage brought on by my helplessness.

'Oh, and I went to Batista's this morning,' he said as I stepped out into the street. 'Lost you your job, but I probably did you a favour. If it weren't for me, you'd be shovelling shit on the pig farm right about now.'

'But instead, you're in a different kind of shit.' Wilson laughed at his own joke. 'You *and* your girlfriend, eh?'

I left without another word.

Antonio collected his plastic bag of beer cans and walked alongside me as we returned to the store, asking, 'Do you want me to hang around a while? I can—'

'I'm fine,' I told him. 'Thanks for helping but you need to stay away from those men.'

'I can handle myself,' he said.

'I reckon you can. Thanks for your help.'

'Anytime.' He shrugged and grinned, showing me the gaps in his teeth. 'Hey. You want to come drink a beer?' He lifted the bag to show me the cans perspiring against the plastic.

'Sure. I'll meet you back at Juliana's. There's something I need to do first.'

'I can wait.'

'No, you go on. I'll catch you up in a while.'

'My place?' he said, starting to move away.

'Your place,' I agreed.

As I watched him go, swinging the bag, my mind was filled with a dust storm of cruel images and thoughts fighting for attention. I kept seeing my sister Sofia, cold and violated, but I didn't want to remember her like that. Not like *that*. So I tried to picture the day we had sat on the hillside and watched the sea. The day we talked about what we would do if we could get onto one of the ships and sail away to find somewhere better. It was *always* about finding somewhere better. Some*thing* better. Even now, that's what I wanted. It's what had brought me to Piratinga in the first place, and now maybe Costa's money would give it to me. I just had to hold my nerve, do what he wanted, and then everything would be different.

Better.

5

Daniella and her mother were outside when I came back to the store. They were standing side by side watching me approach. Doña Eliana had her hands on her wide hips and she was shaking her head.

'What was that?' she asked as soon as I was close enough. 'I saw you—'

'It's nothing,' I told her.

'I know what sort of man you are.' Doña Eliana pointed a finger at me. 'Never holding down a job, mixing with the wrong people. If I had any control over my daughter, she wouldn't look at you twice.'

'Shush, Mãe.' Daniella gave her mother a serious look before turning to me. 'What's going on, Zico? Who was that?'

'No one. Just some guy who wants to cause trouble.' I put my hands into my pockets so they wouldn't see my fingers trembling as the aggression subsided.

'*You're* causing trouble.' Doña Eliana pointed again.

'Come inside.' Daniella took my arm and turned to her mother. 'And you stay here.'

'Don't keep disturbing my daughter when she's working,' Doña Eliana said, still watching me. 'She's busy.'

Daniella led me into the store, taking a can of Coke from the cooler and putting it down on the counter. She leaned back against the scratched plastic surface and crossed her arms over her chest. 'You going to tell me what's going on?'

On the counter beside her was a fashion magazine with dog-eared pages, the paper soft and creased from the attention she'd given to things she could never afford. Things *I* could never afford to buy for her.

'Some guy who owes me money,' I told her. 'Look, I don't want to talk about it; it's not important.'

Daniella's hair was tied back in a loose ponytail and secured with a pink rubber band. She was lighter skinned than I was – *canela* we called it – a rich cinnamon colour against my darker *chocolate*, but Daniella loved the beach, so she lay in the sun until she was almost the same colour as me. Doña Eliana hated that – they were shopkeepers, she said, not peasants.

Like mine, Daniella's hair was brown and nondescript, but while mine was cut short for convenience, she had dyed hers a shade lighter and allowed it to tint in the sun with an underlying darkness of its natural colour. It looked good against her skin tone and emphasised her honey-coloured eyes that watched me from beneath dark lashes. Her cheekbones were high, giving her a good smile when she showed it, and hidden beneath a thin layer of cheap make-up, her skin was faintly marked with the spots of her youth. Her temperament could swing both ways, from calm to storm in a flash, but the calm always made it worth riding out the storm.

The old man told me if you want to know what a woman is going to look like when she grows older, take a look at her mother, but it was hard to believe Daniella would ever turn out like the woman sitting outside on the plastic chair. Doña Eliana was like a diseased tree. A husk of what it once was. Rotten on the inside and gnarled on the outside.

'Your mother hates me,' I said. 'She thinks I'm worse than a dog.'

'My mother hates everyone.' Daniella shrugged. 'I think she even hates herself.'

'But she hates me most of all. Should I be honoured?' I turned the magazine to look at the face of a model wearing too much make-up. 'She said you're busy. This is what she meant? Busy reading beauty magazines? You don't need them.'

Daniella smiled and I moved closer, putting my arm around her waist, pulling her to me and kissing her lips.

Daniella glanced over at the door then returned the kiss, pulling my lower lip in her own as she broke away. She pushed the magazine out of the way and turned to lean her forearms on the counter, cracking open the Coke and taking a sip.

'You have a good time last night?' I asked.

'At Kaiana's? Yeah.' She swallowed and put a hand to her brow. 'Feeling a little fuzzy.'

'You drank too much? Meet anyone?'

Daniella smiled. 'Manuela met a man. He was nice, I suppose. Good-looking. Maybe I could have fancied him for myself.' She watched for my reaction.

'Well, I know what you're like when you're drinking with your friends. I've seen the way you flirt.'

'You jealous?'

'Should I be?'

Daniella fluttered her eyelashes at me. 'I only have eyes for you, Zico.'

'Good. So who was he?' I took the Coke and drank, the bubbles fizzing around my teeth.

'Some guy.' She shrugged, deciding not to tease me further. 'I don't know. Passing through, maybe. He seemed OK, though.'

'They always do.'

'Don't worry, they're never as handsome as you. Not my Zico.' She pulled a sympathetic face and stroked my cheek as if I were a child. 'All my friends think so, too.'

'Yeah, yeah.' I brushed her hand away and we looked at each other for a moment.

'So why aren't you at work?' She straightened and removed the rubber band from her hair. She combed her fingers through it, revealing the darker strands growing beneath the blond.

'That job,' I said. 'You can't ask a man to do something like that. Shovelling—'

'You lost your job, Zico? Again?' She scraped her hair tight, tying the rubber band back in place, then taking another sip of the Coke. 'What happened this time?'

'I was late.'

'Late? Why were you late?'

I couldn't tell her about Costa, so I just shrugged and raised my eyebrows.

'Oh, Zico.' She picked up the magazine and slapped my shoulder with it before putting it down again. She lowered her voice and came closer. 'How are we ever going to get a place of our own if we don't have enough money?'

'I'll find other work,' I said.

'Where? Where is there other work? You lost so many jobs already. In the six months we've been together, how many jobs have you had, Zico?'

'You sound like your mother.'

'Screw you.'

'And there's always the old man.'

'He pays less than anybody.'

'At least it's money.'

'And he hardly ever works these days.'

'I'll find something.' I reached out to touch her, pull her close. 'I'll find something, I promise.'

I held her to me, putting my hand on the back of her head and pressing her into me, before kissing her again. I didn't care if her mother was watching us. Right then I wanted to be with Daniella more than I wanted anything else in the world. And that feeling was one of the only two things stopping me from leaving this town.

'You'd better go,' Daniella said, looking over my shoulder to where her mother's small, squat silhouette was standing in the doorway. 'We're closing for lunch.'

'Sure.' I counted out a couple of notes onto the counter and took four cans of Skol from the fridge. 'I owe a man a drink,' I said, thinking about Antonio waiting for me. The least I could do was buy him a beer.

I drained the Coke in a long, fizzy gulp that made my eyes water. 'Can I see you later?'

'Not today.' She tilted her head towards the door. 'Mãe made me promise to go to Valdenora's this evening.'

'You know she's trying to set you up with her idiot son, don't you?' I whispered.

'Valdenora's?'

'Uh-huh.'

'If you don't get another job, maybe I might think about it,' she said with a smile.

I left the store feeling a little better for having seen Daniella. She had a good effect on me. But the shadow hadn't finished yet. It still had more to show me.

6

The smell of blood leaked out on the warm air as soon as I opened the door.

The room was much like my own, except Antonio had not lived here long enough to make it a home. The only furniture was the unmade bed and a small chest of drawers with an open can of beer on it. There was a page from a magazine on the wall – a picture of a dark woman with naked breasts – and beside the door there was a pair of flip-flops and the same plastic bag he had been carrying when I last saw him. The beer cans were still in it.

Antonio was slumped in the far corner of the room, beneath the shuttered windows. His legs were extended in front of him and his arms were splayed to either side as if he had come home drunk and collapsed there. He was not resting, though.

He was dead.

His head was tipped back so his face was angled towards the ceiling, and his throat was open, punctured with a sharp knife. It wasn't cut from side to side, but had been pierced. Antonio's murderer had slipped the narrow blade of a knife in and out, the same as I had seen Batista do to the pigs on his farm.

Already the room was filling with flies, buzzing in their frenzied delight.

The front of Antonio's shirt was dark with blood that still glistened in the slats of sunlight cutting through the shutters. It had pooled around the place where he sat, collecting in a large puddle on the concrete floor. Small particles of dust had alighted on the surface of what was left of Antonio's life.

I remained at the door and stared at the body, feeling my anger rise as the shadow wrapped itself around me. However much I tried to turn my back on it, death was always there. Always. It was there in the shape of Luis and Wilson. It grinned at me from Costa's eyes as he tricked me with his clever words. And it was in my heart, desperate for release.

I had hardly known Antonio, but he had come to my aid when he thought I needed it, and this was the fate he earned for himself. When he had needed my help, though, I had not been here, just as I had not been there for Sofia when she had needed me.

I closed my eyes and tried to crush the feelings that threatened to fill me, but all I could see was Luis and Wilson, coming into this building, to this door. I saw them knock and force their way in. I saw them push and punch and I saw Antonio's fear grow as he realised he was alone.

I felt his fear now. It welled up inside me like a paralysing drug as Luis drew his knife and raised it to Antonio's throat.

Only it wasn't Antonio now, it was Sofia. My sister. She was the one who was dying. She was calling for my help. Terrified and alone, she was pleading for me to help her, but there was nothing I could do. She was gone. She was ...

I opened my eyes and shook the image away, trying to rid myself of the guilt that rose to mingle with the anger and fear. Blood was thumping in my ears, my whole body paralysed by those crippling feelings. And one thought pierced those emotions, just as the blade had pierced Antonio's throat.

I wanted to punish whoever had done this.

'Luis and Wilson,' I said under my breath, and then I turned and headed back down the corridor.

I didn't know where they were but it wouldn't be difficult to find them. Killing a man the way they had killed Antonio was a messy business. His blood would be on their clothes, in their hair, between their toes. They would have had to go home to wash themselves.

I would find them.

*

The flick and slap of my flip-flops was hollow in the cool passageway as I walked to the far end and descended the concrete stairs.

Letting myself into my room, I went to the lopsided chest of drawers and yanked out the bottom drawer. The old man had helped me build the piece of furniture using wood from the forest and ancient tools that he kept on his boat. The saw blades had been as black as the Devil's heart from use and oil, but they worked well enough. The same couldn't be said for our carpentry skills, and the wood had warped so now the drawer caught on the runners and came out in spasmodic jerks.

I put it to one side and reached into the vacant space to remove a bundle of oilcloth. I unrolled the cloth on the bed and looked at the two revolvers wrapped in oiled plastic bags. Taking the smaller pistol from its bag, I checked it was loaded, then slipped it into a slim nylon holster, which I clipped to the left side of my belt and hid beneath my shirt alongside a pouch containing a speed loader. The other revolver, this one much larger, I rolled back into the cloth and put away before forcing the drawer back into place.

Sitting on the bed, I tried to gather my thoughts; to put some order to the guilt and anger. I was so filled with the need to punish Luis and Wilson that everything was muddled. The shadow had reached right around me and was shrouding my mind, confusing everything.

I put my head in my hands and tried to concentrate. I forced myself to think through the consequences of what I was about to do.

There was no doubt in my mind that Luis and Wilson deserved to die. Even before they had murdered Antonio, I knew they deserved it. And killing them would protect Daniella and the old man from them.

That was it. I had to protect them.

I stood and went to the door. I put my fingers on the handle.

I had to protect them.

I stopped.

For every Luis and Wilson, there were two more men Costa could call upon. Men who would be just as ruthless.

Daniella and Raul would not be safe. If anything, they would be in more danger. Costa would feel the need to make a point and he would know just how to do it.

Perhaps he would take one life to show me that the other was in need of saving.

For a moment, I imagined him driving the point home, giving me the chance to choose for myself. Raul or Daniella. Who would live and who would die?

I punched the door in frustration, then returned my revolver to its place beneath the drawer. There was nothing I could do. Costa owned me. Wherever I turned, he was there, grinning like Anhangá, in league with the shadow, twisting my life to his own means.

Costa was sitting at his desk when I pushed my way in. The old woman who filed his papers and answered his telephone barely even had time to lift her backside from her seat before I was at the door. She called out to me but I didn't hear what she was saying.

Costa looked up in anger but his expression changed the moment he saw me. His eyes widened and there was a moment of indecision before he reached for the pistol on the desktop.

My hand was on it before his.

I pinned it to the desk and placed my other hand a shoulder's width apart from it, leaning over to stare into Costa's eyes. 'His blood is on your hands.' But even as the words left my mouth, I knew Antonio's blood was on my hands too. He had tried to help me. If not for me, Antonio would never have crossed paths with Luis and Wilson.

'What are you talking about?' Costa leaned away from me and his words came with quick, sharps breaths.

'Those men are out of control.' I straightened and picked up the pistol. 'They're ... out of control.'

'You can't do anything to me Zico ... People will—'

'I'm not going to do anything to you.' I removed the magazine from the pistol and tossed it back on the desk. 'I'm not going to do anything.' I wanted to, though. I wanted to shoot him dead and, if not for Daniella and the old man, I might have done it.

'What's going on?' Costa pushed his chair away from the table, trying to put as much distance as possible between us. 'What's happened?'

'Your men Luis and Wilson,' I said. 'They murdered Antonio. He tried to help me so they followed him home and stuck a knife in his throat.'

'Antonio? Who is that? Is he a friend of yours?'

'Yes.' But I hadn't even known his last name or where he was from. He wasn't my friend, he was just a man who had tried to help me and been swept away by the shadow.

'I'm sorry, Zico, I don't know who he is or why they—'

'It doesn't matter,' I said. 'Just tell them to clear it up.'

'What?'

'He's lying up there in his room with his throat cut. Tell them to clear it up. He deserves better than that. And so does Juliana.'

'Who the hell is Juliana?'

'My landlady,' I said. 'How do you think she's going to feel when she goes up there to clean his room and finds him like that? Or what if her niece goes in there? She's just eleven years old; what will that do to her?'

Costa stood and held his hands in front of him. 'Calm down, Zico.'

'Calm down? You're lucky I *am* this calm. You're lucky I *am* calm.' I turned and walked to the door, stopping with my fingers on the handle. I paused and looked back at him. 'Clean it up,' I told him. 'They're your men. Control them.'

Costa nodded and I pulled open the door.

'Zico,' he called, making me look back at him once more. 'You're right about them.' He watched me for a long moment, our eyes locked together. 'If you do this job right for me,' he said, 'they're yours.'

'What?'

'You heard me. Do this right, and those two are yours.'

7

I weighed my options for the rest of the day, but they felt light, so I headed down to Ernesto's on the waterfront, keeping in the shade as much as possible. The sun was reaching its highest point now and it was unbearable to be under its angry glare for longer than a few minutes. Even the stray cats and dogs had left the street.

The bar smelled of stale beer and tobacco, with a hint of fresh lime lying over it, and there was only a handful of people in there. Three or four of the boatmen drinking beer straight from the bottle, or sipping sweet *caipirinha*. They said Ernesto made the best *caipirinha* in town.

Ernesto was leaning across the counter, laughing with another customer, but broke off his conversation and came over, taking a beer from the fridge.

'Zico,' he said, snatching the cap from the bottle in one movement. He clinked it down on the tiled surface of the bar, beside the wooden board he used to cut limes. There was a single fruit on the board, sliced in half to expose the soft flesh. Looking at the knife, though, the steel shining in the sun, I couldn't help thinking about Antonio.

I fished the fold of small notes from my pocket and counted a couple from the top. 'Let me know when this runs out.' I pushed them towards him and poured the beer into a glass that was mostly clean.

'How's things?' he asked, looking at the cash sitting on the warm white tiles.

'Not good,' I replied and raised the bottle. '*Saúde.*'

Ernesto wiped his hands on the cotton towel that hung from

his pocket and watched me take my drink to one of the plastic tables on the small terrace outside. It wasn't anything special; faded terracotta tiles that were loose and broken, rusted metal railings that were tired of the constant sun and rain, the paint bubbled and split.

The old man was at the table, under an umbrella advertising Brahma beer. Raul Perreira had the tranquil look of a labourer at rest after a hard day. Everything about him was weathered and seasoned like the bark of a savannah tree, as if he were part of the land. He had skin that was dark and furrowed, with deep lines running around the back of his sun-beaten neck; thick, strong hands, armoured by dry and cracked calluses. Grey hair was cropped right down, almost to his scalp, and there were heavy creases at the corners of his eyes from a lifetime of squinting against the sun. A slight upturn to his mouth suggested he was always on the verge of breaking into either a smile or a growl.

He was leaning back, dusty feet up on an empty chair, hand around his glass, brown eyes staring out at the road. There was nothing in the street of any interest, though. There wasn't much of a beach here, no shops to speak of, so there wasn't any reason to come here unless you had a boat moored on the river, or were looking for someone who did. Further up, there were white sands and bigger, more comfortable bars. There would be people drinking, sitting in the sun, but here it was calm so this was where the old man liked to come. It was a second home to him and the other boatmen.

I watched him for a while, thinking he looked as if he'd crashed right there at the table, his brain shutting down, but then he blinked. A long, tight blink, and when he opened his eyes again, he was looking right at me. 'Zico,' he said. 'Arthurzico Alves.'

The dog lying in the shade at the next table lifted her head and thumped her tail on the concrete terrace before snapping to her feet and coming over. She was about knee height to me, with dirty brown fur and a white patch on her chest. The scar across her muzzle made her look tough, but it wasn't a war wound; it was the result of getting it stuck in an old tin when she was a pup.

The old man was drunk when he found her like that; just a ball of skin and bone, whining because her nose was trapped in a half-crushed can of chickpeas. He took her home and called her Rocky, and it wasn't until he sobered up the next morning that he realised she was female. It didn't matter, though, he liked the name so it stuck.

They made a good pair.

'Rocky.' I crouched as she came over and turned in an excited circle in front of me, lifting her face to mine. 'You been looking after the old man?' I rubbed her head and looked up at her owner.

'You've been to see that snake Costa.' The old man's voice was raw, deep and raspy from a lifetime of heavy smoking. But there was a different quality to it today. He sounded more tired than usual.

'Nothing escapes you, does it?'

The old man nodded. 'He has work for you?'

'Maybe. Maybe not.'

'Is that right?' he said, glass of beer in one hand, cigarette in the other, sitting so that the street was to his left and if he turned to look over his right shoulder he would see the river and the boats that were waiting for their owners. He put the cigarette in his mouth and squinted against the thin smoke which rose to his eyes and made them water. 'Anything for *me* to do?'

'No. I mean, it's not really your kind of work, but I might need the boat, who knows?'

The old man took his feet off the empty chair and pushed it away from him, the legs scraping on the bare concrete.

'You look tired,' I said, coming to sit down. 'You feeling all right?' Rocky put her chin on my knee and I reached down to scratch her ear.

'I have a job for tomorrow.' The old man ignored my question. 'To collect something from upriver, you want to come?'

'Maybe.'

'If this other thing doesn't get in the way, you mean? The thing for Costa.' The old man leaned forward on the table, sitting up as if he was making himself ready for an important conversation.

'What's the pay like for this other thing? This new job you might or might not have?'

I took a deep breath and met his eyes. 'Good. *Very* good.'

'Ah, but what's the price, I wonder?' He shook his head in disapproval. 'I remember the day you first came in here. You remember that? What was it? Two years ago?'

'Two.'

'Just a kid, and now look at you. It's like you became a man without me ever noticing.' He coughed and wiped his mouth with the back of his left hand. The tip of the smallest finger was missing above the first knuckle – a fishing accident that had stripped the flesh right off. The local doctor had clipped the bone for him, sewn the end up and waited for it to heal.

'Took you under my wing,' he said, telling it the way he always did. 'I could see it in your eyes, the kind of shit you had in your past.' He raised his hand, pointing the crooked index finger and using his thumb, bringing it down like a pistol hammer. 'You smelled of violence – still do from time to time – but you told me you wanted something different, you remember that?'

'I don't think you'll ever let me forget it.'

The old man drained his beer and called to Ernesto for another, holding up two fingers and throwing a questioning look at me. Ernesto didn't wait for me to nod, he just went to the fridge for the bottles.

'"That's not the kind of thing I'm looking for", isn't that what you said, Zico? You wanted something honest.'

I liked his direct nature, the way he saw straight through me. It made me feel like I was confessing my sins without having to speak them aloud. 'Yeah, something like that.'

'But that's the road you took. Someone pointed you in Costa's direction and—'

'I needed to live.'

'You worked for *me*.'

'I worked *with* you, old man, and the pay was crap.'

'At least my money was *clean*, Zico.'

'Not exactly. Your work's not always the honest kind.' I made a show of thinking hard. 'In fact, not ever.'

'But not as dirty as the Branquinos and their snake Costa. He saw what you were the same as I saw it, only he nurtured it. And once you'd done that first job for him, he had his hooks in you.'

But his grip was tighter than ever now, and one of the reasons was sitting right in front of me. I knew the old man better than I had known my own father; I wasn't going to let Costa hurt him.

'You don't know what I did for him,' I said.

'I know the *kind* of thing. And how many times did you do it?'

I sighed and nodded, wafting away a fly that was taking too much interest in Rocky. 'I changed, old man. I'm a farmer now.'

'At Batista's place? You lost that job like you lost all the others.'

'You know about that, too?'

'I know everything.' The old man watched me with red-ringed, watery eyes. 'And now?'

'Now?'

'What are you looking for now? Going back to Costa? What you going to do for him that pays so well, huh? Blood money again? You're better than that, Zico.'

Blood money. For killing a nun. It gave me an ugly feeling that made me hate Costa and his people more than ever. Sure, I wanted the money, but for *this*?

Raul stopped talking as Ernesto approached, bringing the smell of limes with him as he placed another two bottles on the table. Rocky had grown bored with my attention, so she went back to her spot in the shade at the next table and collapsed with a grunt.

'Talk about something else,' I told him and he nodded his understanding, crushing his cigarette into a misshapen foil ashtray before refilling his glass. He pushed the other bottle towards me and when both glasses were replenished, we touched them together. Old friends.

'*Saúde.*'

Two beers became three, three became four, and we spent the afternoon talking, neither of us drunk because the sun was so hot it sweated the alcohol out of us before it had a chance to make us

39

woozy. We just drained our glasses, called to Ernesto each time they needed refreshing.

Ernesto was pleased for the business and put a samba tape in the player behind the bar and let us get on with drinking.

'You never did move on,' Raul said.

'I never made enough money. When I have enough, maybe I'll move on. Just like you keep saying *you're* going to do.' But that wasn't why I had stayed in this town. It wasn't just about the money. It was *him*. I liked him. And now there was Daniella, too.

Before coming here, I'd been through Belo Horizonte, Uberlândia, Goiânia, Brasilia ... so many cities, so many jobs. And after those places, there hadn't been much more than small towns and villages for me to wander through, and not one of them had anything that made me want to stay. Piratinga was the last town on the road. Small and quiet, sitting in the dust by the river.

'You decide where you want to go?' the old man asked. 'Maybe back to Rio?'

'No. Not there. Maybe I should go to Imperatriz with you.'

Raul sniffed and took a sip of his beer, a wistful look falling across his face. 'You know, I once heard about a man in Imperatriz who was killed by a Brazil nut. You ever seen one of those things fall from the tree? Tallest tree in the forest, and that great thing like a rock coming down onto you? Split his head right in two, is what I heard. Must've been something to see.'

I smiled. 'If I come to Imperatriz, then, I'll remember to keep away from Brazil nut trees.'

We sat in silence for a while before the old man sighed and shook his head. 'Don't do it.'

'Hm?'

'Whatever it is Costa wants you to do. Don't do it. It feels like ... like something bad is coming.'

I looked out at the river, narrow here, at just five hundred metres from one bank to the other. The brown water was flowing past, always moving, always going somewhere. I wondered where it would end up; whether it would be better or worse than this particular stretch of the Araguaia.

It felt like a lifetime ago that my sister and I had talked about moving on. We had sat on the hillside in Rio and watched the sea and thought about the things lying beyond our weary *favela*, Sofia saying there was something better out there.

The old man, he dreamed too – about more money, moving on, a new life. I wondered if Antonio had dreamed about that; if he had come to Piratinga on his search for a better life but ended up lying dead in a rented apartment with his throat cut. Sofia's dreams never came to anything either.

I couldn't let the same thing happen to the old man, or to Daniella. I didn't want to be alone again. I would have to do what Costa wanted.

8

Late afternoon, the sky grumbled somewhere over the open savannah that lay beyond the forest on the other side of the river. Rocky sensed the oncoming storm and took refuge inside the bar, but the old man and I shifted our seats and watched the dark grey thunderheads rolling in across the trees and water.

It was like the end of the world unfolding before us as the sky grew blacker and blacker and the gloom reached across Piratinga.

When the rain finally broke, it came down as hard as I had ever known it, soaking into the dry land, releasing a warm earthy smell. It churned the river into a murky froth and battered the umbrella over our heads. It pummelled the tiles and the concrete and the road with such violence that the world was filled with white noise. It came at us from all directions but we stayed as we were, enjoying its ferocity.

The cool air and the rain washed away my frustration and I tried to find something positive in everything that had happened that morning. Daniella was disappointed I'd lost my job at the farm, but mucking out pigs for Batista wasn't ever going to give me the life I wanted for us. And I thought about what Costa was doing right now, who he was talking to, and what kind of deal he would bring back to me. I had to take something good from this.

When the rain had passed, we went to the old man's place, further along the river, at the edge of town. Rocky trotted ahead, moving from shade to shade now that the clouds had gone. There was still a touch of lingering freshness brought by the storm, but the sun was uncompromising and had started its work. The rainwater was already evaporating and the misty air was growing hot again.

'Look.' Raul stopped and pointed. 'See?'

Ahead, his small house stood close to the beach. Now the rains were here, though, the river would start to rise and soon the water would be almost at his doorstep.

The house was made of brick, most of it built by the old man himself, and painted a bright green because that's the colour his wife chose. The roof was tiled rather than covered with tin, so it didn't rattle in the hard rain.

Four vultures were hunched over a large dead fish at the water's edge, squabbling and screaming at one another, jostling for the best place at the banquet. A fifth was sitting on the roof of the old man's house, back curved and wings folded.

Rocky ignored them and made for the shade of the porch.

'That's bad,' the old man said as he bent to pick up a stone. 'Not on the house. Not on my roof.' He took aim and threw the rock as hard as he could. It sailed up and up, a black speck against the blue sky, before it clattered down on the tiles, startling the scrawny bird.

The vulture hopped on one foot and screeched.

'Get off, you devil!' The old man threw another rock, and this time the bird spread its wings and took to the sky, sailing out over the water, before turning back and settling with the others over the carcass of the fish.

'Calm down, old man, you'll crack your tiles,' I said as Carolina came out from the house and looked up at the roof before spotting us.

'It's bad luck,' he told me. 'Especially *there*. A vulture on my house? You know what that means?'

'You're too superstitious,' I said, raising a hand to his wife. 'It means the bird wanted somewhere to rest, that's all. Come on – I think all this heat and beer is going to your head.'

As we headed over the scrub to his house, though, I couldn't help glancing at the birds huddled round their meal. Dark and ugly and smelling like carrion, it was hardly any wonder people saw them as an omen of death.

*

Carolina had prepared boiled rice and *feijoada*, made with black beans and a few thin strips of dried beef. My sister Sofia used to make it that way, though we didn't always have the beef. Sometimes it was chicken, sometimes nothing at all. Doña Melo, the woman next door, taught Sofia to cook when we were growing up because our mother was already buried and she felt sorry for us. Whenever I smelled *feijoada* now, it reminded me of Sofia.

Carolina placed a bowl of *farinha* on the table – coarsely ground manioc flour – and invited me to sit with them. There wasn't much so I ate just a little, telling them I'd repay them. The old man waved a dismissive hand and Carolina shook her head, telling me there was no need. I was always welcome to share what they had.

Carolina was Xavante Indian; *A'uwe Uptabi*. The True People, they called themselves, coming from further south, past Piratinga, on the Rio das Mortes. The River of Deaths. She hadn't lived in a Xavante village since she was seven or eight and couldn't even remember her real given name. She never went back, never mixed with her people, but showed no sign of regret. Life had put her and the old man together and she was happy that way.

Carolina wasn't beautiful and her face was hard, but her eyes carried a warm look every time they met her husband's. And Raul's smiled in reply. Seeing them together made me think that Raul had everything he needed right here in Piratinga. He didn't need Imperatriz and Imperatriz didn't need him. There was no reason to suffer the despair of always chasing something he would never catch.

The old man had talked about it so many times, telling me how the money was so important. He needed enough to buy him and Carolina a place in Imperatriz, close to their son Francisco; a place where they could make a better life. Francisco had done that – gone to find a better life – because he hated it here. He hated the slow pace and he resented his parents for not taking him away from it. He was married now, a wedding that Carolina and Raul had seen only in photos, and he wrote once a year, asking them to come. A year ago he had sent them a picture of their first granddaughter, Luziene; a child they had never seen in the flesh.

When we had eaten, Raul and I sat on his narrow porch, a glass of *pinga* each, a cigarette for him and a bottle of mosquito repellent for me. I spread the Autan on my arms and face as we spoke, and Rocky came to curl up on the cool concrete floor beside the old man's chair.

The sun had dropped now, the last of its light was shimmering over the forest on the other side of the river, and soon it would be gone. The cicadas chirped with an unnoticed monotony, and the frogs were beginning to call their own tune.

'You don't look so good, old man, you feeling all right?' His eyes were bloodshot; the bags underneath were bigger and darker than usual. The deep tan on his lined face was pallid and drained of colour.

'It's the beer,' he said, coughing as if to prove himself wrong. 'And the *pinga*.'

'I've seen you drink more beer than that, and chase it down with *pinga* and cigarettes and God knows what else.'

'The heat then. It's so damn hot today.'

'Just like every day. No, you look like you're getting sick.'

'You tell, him, Zico.' Carolina had come to the door. 'He won't listen to me. Old fool never listens to me.'

'If I always listened to you, woman, I'd never listen to anything else.' Raul chuckled and blew a kiss at his wife before turning to me. 'I don't get sick, Zico. When have I ever been sick?'

I could tell he didn't want to talk about it. Men like Raul don't like to admit they're feeling weak, so I nodded and let it pass, changing the subject. 'So what's this job you've got tomorrow? Delivery or collection?'

'Both. Something to collect and then we have to deliver it.'

'You shouldn't be working,' Carolina said as she came to sit beside him. 'Look at you. You're in no state for it.' The plastic chair creaked and Rocky shifted, looking up, then letting out a long sigh and settling again.

'There's nothing wrong with me,' Raul said. 'Stop fussing.'

45

'You need to get well.'

'I need to *work*.'

'Then promise to take Zico with you.'

'Of course I'll take Zico with me.'

'So where are you collecting from this time?' I asked. 'São Tiago? Further north?'

The old man shook his head. 'Further south.'

'South? How far?' There wasn't much down that way and the river was only navigable a few hundred kilometres in that direction. Once we got to a certain point, the water was laced with rapids, falls and rocky canyons. 'Anywhere I know?'

'Just the river. We're meeting a plane. It's going to land on the water.'

I whistled. 'They tell you what's on it?'

Raul shook his head, then sipped his *pinga* and stared out at the river, watching the last splinter of sun disappear. 'When do I ever ask? That's why people come to me. All I know is I'm meeting a plane, taking on cargo, and heading to Mina dos Santos.'

'That's a long way.' We'd been once before, a gold mine three or four hundred kilometres west on the Rio das Mortes. Maybe further. 'And you have no idea what the cargo is?'

'I don't need to.'

'It's too far to go in your state,' Carolina told him. 'This sounds too dangerous, Raul. It's too much for you.'

I looked across at the old man sitting with Rocky at his side and I remembered the bird perching on his roof that afternoon. I was too practical to be superstitious like he was but it bothered me anyway and I wanted this day to be over. Tomorrow would be better. A fresh start.

'It'll be fine.' The old man spoke to his wife, reaching out to take her hand in his own. 'Money for nothing.' Then he turned to me. 'Cargo for Mina dos Santos is all I know. A man came to Ernesto's this morning, gave me half the money up front, the rest when I get to the mine.'

'What man?' I asked.

'Said his name was Leonardo.'

46

'What's he like?'

'Like any other man.'

'And he gave you money?'

'Half.'

I nodded. The *Deus e o Diabo* wasn't the fastest boat on the river and it wasn't the biggest, but it would carry anything that was asked of it, and its captain always delivered. She was big enough to carry a good cargo and put about fifteen, twenty kilometres of river behind her in an hour, depending on the conditions. Raul had been carrying people and contraband up and down the Araguaia since he was a young man and he knew the rivers like he knew the contours of his own wife.

There were other boats, other captains, but taking the wrong channel when the river split or turned could lead to narrowing passages blocked by the forest and a nest of tributaries that writhed about each other like snakes. In there, surrounded by the dense forest, the heat and the pounding rain, there were a thousand deaths waiting for every man who lost his way.

Raul knew the channels, the sandbanks, how to recognise the change in the water. If the riverbed had shifted and risen with the rains or droughts, Raul knew how to spot it just by looking at the surface of the water.

His knowledge of the river wasn't the only reason why people came to him, though. He had a reputation for discretion and always turned his eyes when he took the money. He didn't care what he carried, as long as the money was real when it touched the palm of his callused hand.

'And this guy Leonardo?' I asked him. 'He paying you much?'

'Not much,' Raul said. 'But it all goes into the pot. And when we have enough, Carolina and me ...' Raul made a blowing noise and tilted his head while lifting one hand like it was taking off from his knee.

Like everyone else, Raul had plans. When he had the money.

Always when he had the money.

9

Around ten o'clock, the old man stood up and said he was tired. He rubbed a hand across the back of his thick neck and stooped a little as he went inside, bumping his shoulder against the doorframe.

'Too much *pinga*,' I said.

'Or maybe not enough,' he replied as the door swung closed behind him.

Rocky stayed where she was, chin resting between her paws as she watched him go, but Carolina followed him, coming back out after ten minutes or so with a shawl draped over her shoulders to combat the night's chill.

'He's not well,' she said, pouring more *pinga* into my glass.

'Just tired is all. Tired and drunk.'

'No, it's something else; he's just too proud and stubborn to admit it. I worry about him.'

'We both do, but whatever it is, it'll pass.'

Beside the old man's chair, Rocky lifted her head and looked out into the night, a low growl rumbling in her throat.

'Come here,' I called to her. 'What is it?'

The dog rose to her feet and slinked over to me, her head low, eyes watching the darkness. She continued to growl, lifting her lip just enough to show a flash of teeth.

Putting one hand on her, I squinted to see beyond the glare of the bare bulb that hung over us. 'What is it, Rocky? What's out there?'

She responded with a long, low, snarl.

Then movement in the darkness. Close to the river's edge.

'You see something?' Carolina asked. 'Is there something there?'

'Not sure.' I pushed myself out of the seat and stepped down onto the grass. Rocky followed on my heels. 'Stay with me, girl.'

Having the light at my back made me feel exposed. Whatever was out there would have the advantage.

I took a step forward and slipped the knife from my waistband, holding it at my side, blade pointed towards the ground.

Rocky stayed with me but I sensed her tension. She stood with her front legs taut, splayed to either side, and her head was down. She lifted her lips to show her teeth, then the growl heightened and she barked at the silhouette that materialised as my eyes grew more accustomed to the darkness.

'Stay with me.' I reached down to grab the scruff of Rocky's neck in my left hand. I didn't want her racing off into the night until I knew what was out there.

'What is it, Zico?' Carolina whispered.

I kept my eyes on the figure standing just a few metres away.

'*Boa noite,*' I called out, waiting for a reaction.

'*Boa,*' came the reply, but the figure remained as it was.

'Is that you, Luis?'

'Luis? No.' It was a man's voice. 'You got hold of that dog?'

I tightened my grip on Rocky but she continued to bark.

'Who are you?' I asked. 'What you doing out here?'

'Been fishing,' came the reply. 'On my way home. You sure you've got hold of that dog?' The man shifted, as if he might be lifting a hand to point at us.

'It's a bit late for fishing.' I tilted my head, trying to see who it was, and wished I were better armed.

'I lost track of time. Put my boat up too far along the shore, that's all. Just keep that dog away from me.' In a brief moment of quiet between his last word and Rocky's barking, I heard the unmistakeable click of a pistol being cocked.

'The dog won't hurt you.' I pulled Rocky back and told her to be quiet. She stopped barking straight away but remained tense in my grip. I didn't think the man intended to shoot me – if that

49

was his intention, he would have done it already. He was afraid of Rocky. The pistol was for her.

'I've got her,' I told him. 'You don't need that.'

'I'll be on my way, then.' And now the figure moved again. An arm reached up as if to push back a cap, then the man sniffed and moved away, feet scuffing on the sand.

'Who was it?' Carolina asked as I came back to her. 'Is everything all right?' Her voice was tight, and when she put a hand on my arm, it was hot and damp.

'Fisherman.' I sat down.

'At this time of night?'

'It's nothing to worry about.' But I kept my eyes on the spot where the man had been, and I rested the knife on my thigh.

Rocky sat beside me, but didn't settle. She remained upright, ears pricked, twitching at every sound.

After a moment, Carolina spoke, saying, 'Eloiza has been ill. Someone said dengue fever. There's been a few people with it.'

I scanned the darkness for any sign of the man, wondering how many people would risk fishing on the river at night. I didn't believe he had lost track of time, it was too late for that. Whoever had been out there, he was no fisherman. He had been watching us.

'Zico?'

'Hm?'

'Something wrong?'

'No.' I reached out and rubbed Rocky's ears. She grunted and started to relax. 'What was that you said about dengue fever?'

'Eloiza told me a few people have had it.'

'Not Raul.' I shook my head. 'He's too strong. But look, if you're worried about him, you should make him stay at home. I'll do his job for him.'

'I've tried but he won't listen to me. Maybe he'll listen to you.'

'He never did before.'

'Then look after him, Zico.'

'I always do.' I glanced out at the darkness once more but everything was still and Rocky had eased back into a half sleep on the floor beside me. Somewhere in the river a fish jumped and splashed, but Rocky was so used to that sound, she didn't even stir. 'I won't let anything happen to him. If he looks bad, I'll bring him straight home.'

'You promise?'

'I promise.'

By the time I had finished my drink, Carolina said it was too late and I was too tired and drunk to go home, so she made up a bed on the sofa. Falling asleep, I wondered how many nights I had slept like this since coming to Piratinga and meeting Raul; how many times I had accepted his hospitality and eaten the food from his table.

The small room I rented was just a dusty box in a house with other workers. It was no place to return the old man's kindness; no place to invite Carolina. I did what I could to earn enough to buy a proper home of my own, maybe even get a small piece of land if there was one to be had, but work was thin and the pay even thinner. Money was so meagre it was worthless almost as soon as it was in my hand, but a job like the one Costa had talked about today might be enough to give me a start. Maybe his offer was an opportunity for me. Maybe he was right.

The alcohol spread itself across my thoughts and feelings, and let me see a good side to this. A place to live with Daniella; something to make me worthy of her and my friends.

For a moment the shadow was forgotten. For a *moment*, I imagined myself with a home and a wife.

Then I remembered the vulture on the roof, and the old man's reaction. I wasn't superstitious like he was but now, in the quiet and lonely hours of darkness, I shivered as I pictured its shabby feathers and curved neck. I had to open my eyes and stare at the ceiling so I didn't see the bird's hooked beak and hear its ominous scream. I saw blood, too, and Antonio lying dead in his apartment, with no one to ask about him or care that he was gone.

I was afraid of being like that; of having nothing and no one.

I was afraid of being forgotten.

51

10

I didn't sleep well, my mind was filled with images of vultures and forgotten dead men, so I rose before dawn and let myself out of the old man's place. Rocky thumped her tail on the floor and hurried out to relieve herself before following me part of the way into town. I was halfway home when I told her to go back to the old man. It took her a while to understand, so I clapped my hands and shooed her away and she turned in disgust and trotted back.

Nothing stirred in the street. The cicadas creaked their chorus, but theirs was the only sound. Out on the *fazendas*, the *vaqueiros* would be taking their first coffee and mounting up, but Piratinga was like a ghost town as I passed through it.

When I came to my building, I caught myself checking the roof for vultures and had to tell myself to stop thinking about it. It was the old man who believed in signs and omens; I should leave that thinking to him.

Juliana the owner would still be asleep and wouldn't thank me for waking her, so I crept through the front door, keeping as quiet as I could, then eased it shut behind me with a gentle click. The windowless corridor inside was dark and still.

There were four doors, two on either side of the passage, and a flight of stairs leading to the other floor. Juliana occupied one of the apartments, while men like me rented the others. Men without families and belongings. Men without futures. Men like Antonio.

I took off my old, worn flip-flops and headed to the far end of the passage, liking the way the floor cooled the soles of my feet. When I reached the door to my room, though, I was surprised to find it already unlocked. The key refused to turn any further but the door still stood firm.

Even when I applied a little pressure with my shoulder, it wouldn't budge.

The only way it could be locked was if someone had pulled the bolt inside.

I tried the handle once more, growing frustrated and shoving a little harder, but there was no doubt someone had bolted it from the inside.

I stood back and glared at the door in confusion, feeling a hint of anger building. I told myself to relax, there had to be a reason for this. Maybe something was jamming it. Maybe Juliana had done something because I was late with my rent.

Or perhaps there was someone in there.

Someone like Luis or Wilson.

Someone like the man who had been watching the old man's house last night.

That thought made my skin tingle and the hairs on my arms prickle. It suddenly felt colder inside the passageway and I found myself reaching for the knife.

I would go outside. Head round the back and look through the window. It was safer that way.

But a noise from inside made me stop. Someone was moving inside my room, coming towards the door.

The handle turned, a twisting and scraping as someone tugged to draw the bolt. I took another step away and drew my knife from its place at the small of my back, holding it so the tip was pointing at the tiled floor.

When the bolt finally gave and the door swung open, I raised my right arm, the blade of the knife coming up, my whole body twisting, lifting the weapon towards the silhouette.

'Zico? Where the hell have you been?'

I dropped my arm, the air coming out of me in a long breath. 'Daniella? What are you doing here?' I whispered, glancing along the corridor, checking I hadn't woken Juliana.

53

I stepped inside, closing the door behind me, pushing the bolt back in to place.

'Where have you been all night?' Daniella looked down at the knife in my hand. 'And what are you going to do with that?'

'I was at the old man's place, where else would I be?'

'I don't know, Zico, where else *would* you be?'

I put the knife on the chest of drawers and rubbed my face, shaking my head. 'We drank too much. Carolina fed me and I slept on the sofa. How did you get in?'

'Juliana.'

I nodded and looked at her standing in front of the window, the first light of the day creeping around the shutter and settling over her, shining through her tousled hair.

Daniella was wearing one of my T-shirts, the white cotton falling to the top of her thighs. It was big on her, the material at the front falling loose around her breasts, the sleeves baggy and to her elbows. Her legs were naked.

'You slept here?' I asked. 'How come?'

Daniella threw a hand in the air and sat down on the bed. 'My mother.'

Taking off my own T-shirt, I tossed it into the corner of the room and went to the sink. 'Your mother?' I splashed cold water onto my face, my chest, across my shoulders, not caring that it was falling on the floor. 'What did she do this time?'

'You're not the only one who had too much to drink last night.'

'Oh yeah,' I said, taking a towel and drying myself. 'You went to Valdenora's. She was trying to set you up with her son. What's his name?'

'Paulo.'

'Yeah. Paulo. How did it go?'

'Awful. All night she was telling me what a nice boy he is, what a clever boy he is, what a good husband he was going to make for someone, not like—'

'Not like me?'

Daniella nodded.

54

'So what did you say?'

'I left.'

I sat down beside her. 'You mean you just got up and left?'

'Yes.'

I couldn't help smiling. 'Well, good for you. I bet that pissed them off. You tell them you were coming here?'

'Yes.'

'Even better.' My smile broadened and I turned to her, pushing her hair from her face. 'Maybe we should make the most of it, then.' I lifted the hem of the T-shirt. 'Maybe we should take this off.'

Daniella was still for a moment, then she crossed her arms and pulled the shirt off, shuffling away, lying back on the bed and waiting for me.

I took off my trousers and looked down at her shadowy form, the darkness beneath the swell of her breasts, around the bones of her hips, her stomach, the place between her legs. 'At least this way you can go to work with a smile on your face.'

'Work? I'm not going to work.'

'You'll have to.'

'I don't want to talk to her.'

'She's your mother.'

'So what?'

'OK, then don't talk to her. But you still have to go to work.'

Daniella giggled.

'What?'

She began to laugh now.

'Shh. You'll wake Juliana. What's so funny?'

'You,' she said, controlling the laugh. 'Standing there like that, naked, talking about my mother. Can you imagine her face?'

'Don't,' I said. 'Don't make me imagine that. Not now.'

She laughed again and reached up to pull me down on the bed, burying her face in my neck, the laughter subsiding as I ran my hands over her skin, our lips coming together, her fingers on my back, our bodies joining.

*

Daniella stayed for a while afterwards, lying on my arm, drifting in a sleepy haze. I stared at the ceiling and listened to her breathing, trying not to think about Antonio in the room upstairs. I concentrated on Daniella instead, feeling the way her chest rose and fell against me with each breath, the way her skin was warm against mine. I looked at her, moving my head to get her in focus, seeing her eyelashes against the top of her cheek. It was a good moment and I thought about how it would be to have this every morning, every night, and whether it would feel stale or if it would change. But I would need a place and money. I wasn't a farmer. Like Costa said, I had other talents. I could provide if I needed to. If I *wanted* to. I was trying to escape that shadow, but if I let it smother me one more time, maybe it could be the last.

Just one more life.

Something at the back of my mind was telling me it was *always* the last time, though; that Costa was a trickster who used his words to twist my thoughts and play games. He was like Anhangá, but instead of provoking me with terrible visions of hell, he was taunting me with visions of what could be heaven.

I put my hand on Daniella's shoulder, cupping the bony part in my palm, and tried to decide what I really wanted. A long time ago, in another life, my sister Sofia and I had talked about moving away, and I had always imagined a piece of land for myself, something open and clean and wide, a million miles from the dirty cramped constraints of the *favela*. That was the dream that might now be in my grasp, but it would be tainted by the very thing I had to get away from if I wanted to be completely free. Blood and death.

Costa was forcing me back into the shadow, and the person he wanted me to kill made it even harder. I knew it wasn't right, but I couldn't see a way out.

I kissed Daniella's forehead and she made a soft noise in her throat, opening her eyes and looking up at me. 'What are you thinking about?' she asked.

I shook my head. 'I was thinking about the first time I saw you. In Ernesto's. You were with your father.'

'And it was love at first sight?'

'Not exactly.'

'Lust, then?'

'I thought you were beautiful.'

'And now?'

'You still are.'

There were other beautiful girls, I'd been with a few of them, but there was something about Daniella that drew me to her. She had a spark, a kind of unpredictability that kept me on my toes. She could be soft or she could be fun, but she was tough, too.

Those first weeks, she flirted with me, touched me when she talked to me, but she did that with others, and I wondered for a while if she was interested in me or not. Even now she sometimes liked to make me jealous by saying this boy was good-looking or that one had a good shape, and I still hadn't got used to it, but it was just part of who she was.

'You ever thought about leaving Piratinga?' I asked. 'We could go now. Just leave town this morning and never come back.'

'Is everything OK?' she asked.

'Sure,' I said. 'Everything's good. I was just thinking that—'

'What about Raul and Carolina, wouldn't you miss them?'

'Sure, but—'

'And what about my parents and my friends?'

'I wouldn't miss *them*.'

'*I* would.' She gave me a playful slap and sat up. 'We can't just leave. My whole life is here. I want us to get a place here and...' She shrugged one shoulder and smiled. 'You know.'

'I thought you hated your mother.'

Daniella sighed and flopped back onto the pillow. 'I don't *hate* her, I just... don't like her sometimes.'

She was right. Her life was here and I couldn't take her away from it. If I wanted to be with Daniella, it would have to be here in Piratinga. And I had the old man to think about too. Costa had threatened him just like he'd threatened Daniella. If I disappeared, Raul and Carolina would not be safe.

11

When the time came, I propped myself on one elbow to watch Daniella dress. She kissed me, the long kiss of a lover who didn't want to leave, and then closed the door behind her, going out to face her mother at work.

For a while, I lay there and listened to the creak of a loud and irritating cicada that had landed on the mosquito netting behind the shutter. He stopped only when there was a loud bang from somewhere on the street, but it wasn't long before he started again so I opened the shutter and tapped the green mesh to make him fly away.

I washed and prepared myself for the oncoming day, retrieving my revolvers from beneath the drawer and clipping one to my belt. The other, I secured in a small canvas backpack which I kept under the bed along with a good knife and replacement cartridges.

I put the backpack on the floor by the wall and took a warm can of Coke and cracked it open. Sitting on the end of my bed, I listened to the town come to life and waited for Costa's men to come, as I knew they would. Costa wasn't a patient man, he wanted this job done, so he would be back with his offer. He'd have people standing over him – powerful people who needed to be pleased.

About nine thirty, I heard voices in the corridor, Juliana talking fast and loud, footsteps approaching. She was still talking when there was a knock at the door.

'Costa,' I said, opening up and doing little to disguise my distaste as I looked him up and down.

'Zico.' Despite the heat and his inability to cope with it, Costa was wearing a pressed shirt and a tie.

'I'm honoured. You want to come in?' I pulled the door wide and looked over his shoulder at Luis and Wilson. 'Those two can wait outside; there's something they need to do. Upstairs, I mean.' I let my eyes meet theirs so they would know I was not afraid of them.

'We'll get to that when we're ready,' Luis said.

Costa put out a hand to stop me as I took a step forward. 'Enough,' he said. 'We've got things to talk about, Zico. Luis and Wilson will clear up their mess.' He turned to look at them. 'Won't you?'

The two men had more to say, but they tightened their lips and nodded like children.

'Right.' Costa cast his eye around my room then turned up his nose. 'You know what?' he said. 'Maybe we should talk outside. Your place stinks even more than my office.'

'So,' I asked as we left the building and headed towards the waterfront. 'You got some news for me?'

Luis and Wilson walked a few metres behind us, out of earshot.

'She's pretty, your girlfriend. Daniella, right? She stayed the night.' After just a few steps, Costa's face was shining.

'So now you're watching my place?'

'Just keeping you safe.' He grinned like a devil.

'More like making sure I don't leave town. Just keep those idiots away from Daniella,' I told him, glancing back at the two men shadowing us. 'And any other idiots you have.'

Costa smiled. 'They'll check on her from time to time, that's all. They've been told not to harm her until I allow it.'

The thought of Costa having that much power threatened to overwhelm me. I wished I could take my friends out of Piratinga and I wished I didn't want his money. If those two things were different, I could settle this right now. 'And who was that last night? By the old man's place?'

'Last night?' Costa looked surprised.

59

'Have you got someone watching the old man?'

'No one was there last night.'

I stopped. 'You sure about that? Someone was there and if it wasn't one of yours, then—'

'I haven't come here to talk about ghosts in the night, Zico.' Costa came to a halt and turned to face me. There was an impatient edge to his voice. 'Do you want to hear the offer or not?'

'Sure,' I said.

'Then walk with me.' Costa scanned the road but there was hardly anyone about. Just a few cafés and shops opening up, their owners winding out the awnings.

I stayed as I was, thinking about the man on the beach. Maybe he *was* just a fisherman returning from the river, but something about it didn't feel right. It had been too late, and he'd been afraid of Rocky. All the fishermen knew the old man and that meant they all knew Rocky.

'Zico?'

'Yeah. OK.' I picked up my pace, letting my flip-flops slap in the red dust that had piled at the side of the road. We passed the whitewashed buildings, the smell of coffee and fried steak drifting out from a café, making my stomach groan.

Luis and Wilson continued to follow, always a few metres behind so they couldn't hear what we were saying but would be on hand if Costa needed them.

'They won't go to ten.' He lowered his voice. 'It's too much.'

'I thought you wanted this to be agreeable to everyone.'

'Don't get ahead of yourself, Zico. I said they won't go to ten, that's all.'

We were walking past the school now, the whole place quiet because all the kids were in class, doing things I never did.

'How much then?' I thought about Daniella – about how much money I'd need to marry her, build or buy a place of our own.

'Five.' It sounded almost painful for him. 'They'll go to five.'

'They can afford it. Five thousand dollars is nothing to them.'

'And they'll give you a piece of land. Just outside town, close to where the old man lives.'

I stopped again and looked at Costa, trying not to show any emotion. 'A place? Of my own?'

'There's an old house there, it's not much, needs fixing up, but you can have it.'

'They must really hate this nun.'

Costa widened his eyes and glanced over at Luis and Wilson. 'Keep your voice down, Zico, nobody can know about this.' He stepped closer to me. 'If this gets out... if anybody but you and I know about this, and I mean *any*body, then everything changes.'

'Meaning what?'

'Just keep it to yourself.'

'OK.'

'So you'll do it?'

On the other side of the road, a horse ambled past, hooves thumping in the dirt, its rider swaying in the saddle. I watched them and thought about Costa's offer. It was a lot of money, the land and the house meant more, but it was nothing if something went wrong; and God knows there was enough that could go wrong.

I looked at him, his face dotted with perspiration, his nose moving as he pursed his lips, sucking them together.

'You already know I'll do it. You knew it from the moment you made the offer. I don't have any choice and that makes me so damn angry with you, Costa.'

'But the money's good, right?' He grinned.

'Yeah.' I had to agree. 'The money's good.'

'You're a smart man, Zico.'

'Not smart enough,' I said. 'Not by far.'

Costa put his arm round me and I could smell his aftershave. His familiarity with me, his dominance, came only from the protection his employers offered him and from his understanding of what this place meant to me.

We walked for a while in silence, before he started telling me the detail, saying, 'She's coming in by plane the day after tomorrow.'

'To Piratinga?'

'Um-hm. Gets here early. Seven o'clock. She's going to meet with the bishop and then she's taking a boat down Rio das Mortes.'

'Rio das Mortes?' It was the same place the old man was headed. Costa looked at me and nodded. 'Is that a problem?'

'No.' I shook my head and thought for a moment about the mysterious cargo the old man was to collect. He didn't know anything about the man who had chartered his boat. 'And she's taking the river? Why not take the road?'

'I don't know, maybe she likes the water, what difference does it make?'

'And what's she going there for?' I wondered if there was some connection with the job Raul was doing. Sister Beckett coming in by plane, taking a boat along Rio das Mortes; cargo coming in by plane, taking a boat up the same river. Maybe they were supposed to meet somewhere in the middle.

'She's visiting reservations on the *cerrado*, some shit about working with the American companies to put animals back on the land. Teaching the natives to look after themselves. Or maybe she's complaining about agriculture again, who knows.' The way he shifted his eyes when I looked at him, I thought he was lying. He knew something he wasn't telling me.

'Which reservation?' I asked. 'There must be at least four.'

'I don't know, but she's going to Mina dos Santos first.'

'The gold mine?' The same place the old man's cargo was headed. It could have been a coincidence or it could have been planned that way, I had no way of knowing for sure, but I might be able to make it work in my favour. 'Is she staying there? At the mine?'

'One night at Fernanda's.'

'What boat?' I asked. 'Whose boat will she be on?'

'Santiago's. The *Estrella do Araguaia*.'

I was already thinking I'd go out with the old man today, do his pick-up, make the delivery. We'd be on the river ahead of Santiago, which would be better than following; the old man's boat would never keep up with the *Estrella*. If we tried to follow them, we'd lose them and the money would slip away from me. But if we were ahead of them, things would be different. We were leaving today which meant we could be in Mina dos Santos before them. We could wait for them there. Last time we went there we stayed a day before returning, so it wouldn't be unusual. Mina dos Santos would be a good place to do it.

A good place for her to disappear.

Just one more life.

I could see it already in my mind. The old man and I could rent rooms at Fernanda's. It would be easy enough for me to slip from one room to another in the early hours before sunrise and take the woman in her sleep. No one would ever know. And there are many places in a gold mine for a body to disappear like it was never there. Except, the way it played out in my head right now, when I put the knife to her throat, my hand hesitated.

'You're planning it already,' Costa said. 'I can see your mind working. I knew I could rely on you.'

We were coming to the river, walking alongside the pastoral centre where the bishop lived, and it was clear that the Branquinos weren't the only people in this area who had money.

These were the largest buildings in Piratinga, two of them, whitewashed like almost everything else, but clean and new. I could smell the fresh paint and wood shavings as we passed. Between them, the church stood tall and proud, the bell tower rising from the red-tiled roof. There was a wall around the area, with welcoming gates at the front, facing the river; gates that were open for anyone who cared to go inside and accept the church's charity. In the constant battle for souls, the church was pushing deeper into the country, opening its arms to Indians and sinners. And though the church was not so involved in the fight for land, there were still those who worked hard to redress the balance of distribution.

Sister Beckett was one of those people, and I suspected that the price on her head was connected to that in some way.

'So why do they want her gone? What's she done?' Perhaps if I had a reason to think she deserved it, my blade would not pause at her throat.

'She causes trouble wherever she goes.'

'For who?'

'For the people who're going to put money in your pocket and a roof over your head.'

We stopped and Costa waved his hand out at the river. Mocha water, white sand protruding here and there, then trees on the other side. Nothing but trees and water and sand. It was as if we were standing at the edge of the world.

'Make her go away, Zico. Somewhere out there, make her go away. But no one can know.' He took a piece of folded newspaper from his top pocket and handed it to me.

'What's this?' I unfolded the clipping, slightly damp with his sweat.

The words on the paper were of no use to me at all, but they surrounded a grainy picture that Costa tapped with his finger. The gold from his ring glinted in the sunlight. 'That's her.'

I looked at the picture and then at Costa. 'Tell me something,' I said. 'Why are you here in Piratinga? Anyone can see you're not suited to it.'

'We've all made our mistakes, Zico. Mine landed me here so I end up working with idiots like those,' he glanced back at Luis and Wilson, 'and manipulating good people like you. It should be the other way around.'

'The Branquinos put you here as some kind of punishment?'

'Something like that.' He started to walk away, leaving me standing there, the newspaper cutting in my hands.

'What did you do?' I asked.

'Just make sure you get the right person,' he said without turning round.

'I will,' I told him. 'I always get the right person.'

When Costa was gone, I stared at the clipping for a while. Sister Dolores Beckett's face was just a collection of grey and black dots, and I didn't know much about her other than her name and reputation, but already I could feel her presence. She wasn't just some violent rival of the Branquinos, she was something different and, once again, I found myself thinking about the priest from the small church in our part of the *favela*.

When our father was still alive, he would take Sofia and me to church at least once a week. We washed and put on our best clothes – me in a shirt and faded trousers passed down from another family, Sofia in her green dress that made her look so pretty. I could picture her now, checking herself in the mirror, turning this way and that to see from every angle. She had the deepest brown hair, dark and long so it fell past her shoulders, and she would hum some tune or another as she brushed it. At the church, the women would all smile and tell her how pretty she looked and then we would say our prayers and make our confession.

When Pai started to drink, though, everything changed. Sofia was a cleaner by then, working for some rich people who lived in a different world. She came and went in their house like a ghost, all of them pretending she wasn't there. If the *senhora* was in the room when Sofia walked through, neither of them even acknowledged each other. She made their beds for them, washed their clothes and cleaned their toilets, but the only time they couldn't pretend she didn't exist was when they had to pay her.

We used to talk about a better life, leaving the *favela*, but she knew we'd never have enough money to go anywhere if we tried to do it on her wage. I brought in more money than her just standing on a street corner watching for cops or rival soldiers from another *favela* coming in to steal our drugs. That's what I had turned to for money, because there was nothing else for a boy like me to do.

Sofia moved away from the Church and found happiness in Candomblé. It made more sense to her and she liked the ritual. I thought God had abandoned me, so I abandoned him. It had never made much sense to me anyway. My life was hard and I never believed there was someone watching over me.

Sofia died when I was seventeen. She was nineteen. I spoke with Father Tomás that day, not long before finding her, and he asked me why I never came to church any more. I joked with him, telling him God had given up on me and that I was beyond saving.

He told me everybody could be saved.

Just a few minutes later, I had found Sofia lying in her own blood.

Now I looked at the picture of Sister Dolores Beckett one more time, then folded the newspaper cutting and put it into my shirt pocket. I wandered along the water's edge towards the old man's house, passing Ernesto's, and coming to the spot close to his home where he moored his boat just offshore. Putting my bag on the ground, I squatted down in the dry grass to wait.

I took the clipping from my pocket once again and looked at the picture of Sister Dolores Beckett, wondering whether or not I would be able to do what Costa had asked. When he had mentioned her name, my immediate instinct was that this was wrong and I was forced to consider why. Until now, I had always been able to carry out my job and collect the money that was offered, because there had always been a secondary element; the belief that the person somehow deserved what I was going to do to them. But this was different. The nun was not a common *pistoleiro*. She was not a cruel landowner or a brutal enforcer, and when I looked back at all the people I'd killed for money, they all led to one man. The one who deserved it more than any other.

And it always came back to my sister. Sofia.

12

'There's my baby,' said Raul, coming beside me and looking across at the *Deus e o Diabo*, lazing where the water was more than deep enough to take her draught.

To me, the old man's boat was a floating scrap heap, assembled from bits of junk. The paintwork, cream above the water and burgundy below, was faded and split. In some places the bare wood of the keel showed through, threatening to rot and let in the river. The lettering which gave the boat its name, painted on both sides of the bows, was barely legible in some places.

At just over twelve metres, the *Deus* wasn't small, but she wasn't as big as some of the other vessels that came past this way. The three or four metres at the stern was taken up by what might have been called a hut if it were on dry land. This enclosed section, which provided an area for storage away from the elements and gave access to the engine, was bolted on with rusted rivets. In some places the brown-red corrosion had eaten through the metal skirting. I wondered how old the boat was for it to have rusted like that, in a place where the water was taken by the sun almost as soon as it touched any surface, and even the torrential rains of the wet season dried quickly.

I'd asked Raul many times how old she was, but he had no idea. He'd bought the boat from a man just like him, nearly fifteen years ago, and even then, the *Deus* was ancient. No one knew who had built it, who had first owned it, nor when its name was given to it.

Deus e o Diabo. God and the Devil.

Further forward, beyond the centre of the boat, there was a

small wheelhouse that was open on all sides but above. The entire vessel was roofed by a series of blue and green tarpaulins rigged across a frame running from the rear housing right up to the wheelhouse. The covering gave some shelter from the sun, and tinged everything with a green hue, but provided little protection from the violent rains that arose almost without warning and sheered in from all sides.

Her bow was turned up, higher than the stern, giving the impression that she was sitting back in the water, tired and in need of a rest.

'Keep meaning to clean her up,' Raul said, 'but... well, you know how it is.'

Rocky trotted past me and splashed in the water at the edge of the river.

'You always say that, old man.' I stood up, shouldering my backpack and turning to greet him. 'Tell you what, when I have enough, I'll clean her up *for* you. Maybe even buy you a new one.' I raised a hand to Carolina who was at the back of the house, fifty metres away, carrying a plastic basket of washing.

Raul laughed. 'And you always say *that*.' He slapped one hand on my back and coughed, bending almost double. He was still pale, his watery eyes ringed red.

'Old man, you look like shit. You feeling worse?'

'I'm fine.' Raul waved a hand to tell me not to worry about it, but he stooped as if he were drawing himself in. His bullish shoulders were tight, his head lowered, his body constricted.

'You sure you're up to this? I can go alone, I don't need you.' I liked being with the old man, but things could work out better this way. If he wasn't with me, navigating the river would be harder because I didn't know it like he did, but I wouldn't have to keep anything from him. I wouldn't have to lie, and moving about in Mina dos Santos would be easier if I were alone. 'Go home to your wife and let me deal with this.'

'Not today, Zico. You're not going to take over my boat just yet.'

I sighed and looked over Raul's shoulder at a man coming

68

across the grass and onto the sand. Young, thin and clean-shaven, he waved and called out Raul's name.

When the man smiled, I saw a pleasant face the girls would like. His skin was the colour of the river, his eyes like tarnished emeralds. He wore a long-sleeved checked shirt unfastened to below his chest, and faded brown trousers rolled up at the cuffs. His cap was tipped back and twisted to one side in a subtle display of arrogance. Hanging on a silver chain around his neck was a carved *figa* pendant – a good luck charm in the shape of a small hand with the thumb tucked between the first two fingers. There was a cigarette behind his ear, a backpack similar to mine slung over one shoulder and something under his shirt, a knife or maybe a pistol.

'You know him?' I asked Raul.

'This is Leonardo,' he said, as the man came to join us. 'Leonardo, Zico.'

I nodded, waiting for more information.

'He's the one paying for this trip.' Raul winked at me. 'Remember I told you about him?'

Leonardo reached up to tip his cap even further back on his head, sniffing as he did it, and I immediately knew who he was.

As if to confirm it for me, Rocky barked once and tore up from the water's edge, coming to a sudden halt at the old man's side. She splayed her front legs and lowered her head, baring her front teeth and growling.

Leonardo took a step back and put his hand to the front of his shirt.

'What's the matter, girl?' Raul crouched and put his arms around her. 'It's all right.' He looked up at Leonardo. 'She's pretty friendly really. Just takes a while to warm to new people.'

'Keep it away from me,' Leonardo said.

Raul let his gaze linger on Leonardo for a moment, then he nodded. 'Go on,' he told Rocky. 'Go.' The old man pushed her away, encouraging her back to the water's edge, but she wasn't keen to leave him. Instead, she moved just a few paces to one side and sat on the sand, keeping her eyes on Leonardo.

'You were watching us last night,' I said to him.

'I wasn't watching, I was *passing*. I saw you outside, wondered who you were, that's all. Protecting my interests.'

'Protecting them from what?' I looked at Raul for a second before turning my attention back to Leonardo. 'And why didn't you stop when I called out?'

'It was late.' Leonardo slouched, tried to look indifferent. 'You'd been drinking. I didn't want it to turn into trouble.'

'Why would it? You were the one who was armed.'

'I thought the dog was going to attack me.' He took the cigarette from behind his ear and rolled it between forefinger and thumb. 'And I don't know you. You might be trouble.'

I stepped back from Raul, freeing up the space between Leonardo and me. 'So you've come to wave us off?' I asked.

Leonardo's pleasant face darkened, just a flash, but long enough for me to spot it. He held out both hands and glanced at Raul. It was a questioning look that required some kind of confirmation.

'He's coming with us,' Raul said.

'Coming with us? It's a simple collection and delivery. Why does he need to come? Does he not trust us?'

Raul looked surprised. He lowered his voice and came closer to me. 'Is there a problem with this, Zico?'

'You two want to take a moment?' Leonardo asked, tucking the cigarette back behind his ear.

I looked the man over one more time, then pulled Raul to one side. 'You didn't say we were taking passengers.'

'What's the problem? It's not the first time we've carried passengers.'

'You know anything about this man? Anything at all?'

'I know he gave me half the money yesterday,' Raul replied. 'I know that the other half comes straight on delivery from someone at the other end. And I know that what he gave me feels good in my pocket.'

'You still have it on you?'

'No, of course not, you think I'm stupid? Come on, Zico, I know you look out for me but I've been doing this for—'

'I know how long you've been doing this, old man, but how many times have I saved you from landing in the shit? I mean, what's to say this guy isn't going to try to rip you off? Get us out there, make his delivery, pull that *pistola* he's got tucked away and make a few holes?'

'*Pistola?*' Raul looked back at Leonardo. 'He's armed? See. I knew there's a good reason I take you along.'

I softened a little and forced a smile.

'Is something making you edgy?' Raul asked. 'Is something the matter?'

'Maybe you forgot about your vulture yesterday,' I said.

'It would be easier if you didn't keep reminding me.'

Leonardo had moved closer to the water but was keeping some distance from Rocky. Hands on his hips, he was looking out at the *Deus e o Diabo*, a slight shake in his head like he was thinking the boat would never get us to where he wanted to go.

'This got something to do with the Costa job?' the old man persisted. 'You want to tell me about it?'

'I didn't take it.'

'Really? They let you say no?'

'Forget about it. Come on, we need to get going if we're gonna make this collection.'

'You don't say no to people like Costa. Is there something on your mind?'

'I turned him down. That's it. Stop talking about it.'

Raul watched me, his eyes scouring my face. He was only a touch shorter than me, an inch maybe, so we were more or less eye to eye. 'You sure there's nothing you want to tell me about, Zico?'

'I'm sure,' I said, hefting my pack on my shoulder. 'Come on.'

'So what about him?'

'He has to come?'

'Part of the deal.'

'OK. Leave him to me.' I left Raul standing where he was and went over to Leonardo, watching him turn around as I approached.

I offered him my right hand and he glanced at it before taking it, both of us shaking with a firm grip.

'You all done?' he said.

'Just like to know who everyone is,' I told him.

Leonardo nodded.

'And you're going to have to give me whatever you got under there.' I reached out with my left hand and touched the handle of the revolver hidden under his shirt. I pressed it hard against his waist, so he couldn't reach for it, and I kept his right hand occupied within my firm handshake.

Leonardo's free hand hovered for a moment as he decided how he was going to react, then he relaxed, and nodded, fixing me with those green eyes.

'Good choice,' I said, taking a second to glance around before I slipped my hand under his shirt and removed the *pistola*. I kept my movements hidden, seeing that Carolina was still behind the house, hanging washing on the line. She had her back to us, pinning one of Raul's shirts.

'You always this nervous?' Leonardo spoke close to my ear. 'Mind you, looking at that boat we're going on, I'm starting to get a bit nervous myself. Will it even get there?'

'You got anything else I should know about?' I asked, tucking the weapon into my waistband.

Leonardo shook his head but I wasn't going to take his word for it, so I kept hold of his right hand while my left felt for all the usual and unusual places a man might hide a weapon.

'You country people really know how to make a man feel wel-come,' Leonardo said.

Satisfied he was no longer armed, I released his hand and stepped back. 'The only people allowed to carry weapons on this boat are me and him,' I said.

'OK by me,' he replied with a shrug.

'Good. Then I think we'll get along just fine.'

'So.' Leonardo cocked his head and stared at me. 'Are we going to stand around all day touching each other or should we get going? If we're not there when that plane arrives, then it's bye-bye money. For all of us. And there are people who will be very upset about that.'

13

We loaded everything onto the aluminium boat which Raul kept tied to a dry mooring on the shore, and pushed it into the water.

'After you,' I said to Leonardo.

'You can't bring the big boat closer?' he asked.

'It's safer out there,' Raul told him. 'Harder to steal.'

'Who'd want to steal that?'

'Just get in,' I said. 'Time's wasting.'

He paused, touching the *figa* around his neck, then waded into the river, threw his backpack into the boat and tried to look casual about climbing in after it.

Gripping the near side of the small boat, he steadied it as he lifted one leg.

'I'm guessing you're new to this,' I said as the boat tipped towards him and he stumbled backwards, only just keeping upright. 'Let me help you.'

I held the small boat with both hands while he climbed in, but even then, his face was set firm with concentration and his body reeled with the tiniest sway of the vessel. He stood with both arms outstretched for balance, then bent at the waist to hold the sides and prevent himself from tipping into the water.

'Just sit down,' I told him.

Leonardo wobbled a few more times, his legs stiff, not rolling with the movement, then he dropped onto the seat and stared at me.

Rocky came into the water, wading out until the surface was lapping at her chin, so I scooped my arms under her and lifted her into the boat.

She was moving right away, the water pouring from her coat before she stopped to shake it off. The sun shone rainbows through the fine spray that misted the air, then she was moving again, excited by the activity.

Leonardo pushed back in his seat, torn between wanting to get away from the dog and being afraid of the boat tipping over.

'What's the matter with you?'

'Get the dog away from me.'

'Rocky always comes with us,' I said. 'She's part of the crew. What's wrong? You got a thing about dogs?'

'I don't like them,' he said.

'Don't be such a coward.' I looked over at Rocky who had gone to the other end of the boat and was sitting upright, watching Leonardo. 'And guess what? I don't think she likes you either.'

I stepped back and moved to one side to let Raul go next, turning my head, catching sight of movement up on top of the bank. Someone was jogging towards us, a hand in the air.

'Zico,' Daniella called as she came. 'Zico, wait!'

She was wearing a skirt that fell short of her knees, ruffled around the hem. A white T-shirt without sleeves. Her hair was tied back in a ponytail like it had been yesterday when I visited her in the shop, and she was carrying a bag over her shoulder.

When she reached me, her cheeks were flushed and she was breathing heavily but she wasn't out of breath. 'Zico, Raul, I'm glad I caught you.' She looked upset.

'What is it? What's happened?'

'My mother,' she said. 'It's my mother.'

'What's happened to her?'

'What's *happened* to her?' Daniella dropped her bag to the ground. 'What do you mean what's *happened* to her? Nothing's happened to her.'

'Well, what's the matter, then?' I looked at the old man standing close by. Outside his house, Carolina had put down the washing and was watching, one hand on her hip, the other raised to her brow to shade the sun.

Leonardo was sitting in the aluminium boat, his attention shifting from me to Rocky and then back again.

'She's a bitch, that's what's the matter with her.'

'What now?' I took Daniella's arm and led her further along the shore. Leonardo didn't have to hear any of this. My business was not his.

'I can't live with her any more ...' Daniella was saying, and I nodded, only half listening as I made sure we were away from the others.

'OK. You want to tell me what this is about? I thought you were going to go talk to her.'

'Have you heard anything I've just said?' She pulled her arm from my hand; a sudden movement, sharp and forceful without needing to be.

'Well, I—'

'For God's sake, Zico, listen to me. I *did* talk to her, at least I tried, but she wouldn't let me say anything. She was waiting at the shop, standing on the step, yelling at me the moment I came close. Calling me a *puta*, saying I'd be punished for staying at your place, for sleeping with a ... She called you ... Well, it doesn't matter what she called you.'

'You're right,' I told her. 'It doesn't matter, so I don't know what you're angry about. Your mother's always saying things about me, you should be used to it by now.'

'I can't work for her any more, Zico, and I won't live with her. I want to stay with you.'

'My place is so small. It's not good enough for—'

'It's good enough for *you*.' She came closer, trying to soften her manner, but there was a fire burning behind her eyes. 'If it's good for you, it's good for me.' She took my hands and looked up at me, working her charm.

'You need something better, cleaner. I don't even have hot water.'

'So I'll use cold.'

'You say that now, Daniella, but—'

76

'Zico, I want to stay with you. It's what I want. And then we'll look for somewhere better.'

'That's not so easy. I'll need money for that.' An image of the woman in the newspaper cutting came to mind; a collection of grey and black dots that was worth five thousand dollars and a piece of land. We'd need the money even more now that Daniella was saying she'd quit her job.

Just one more life.

'Please,' she said.

I sighed and closed my eyes. She knew she'd beaten me. She always did. She could get what she wanted from me every time. 'Here.' I fished a key from my pocket and held it out to her. 'If Juliana asks, tell her it's only for a couple of days. I'll be back soon and we'll see what happens then.'

Daniella looked at the key, not understanding.

'Take it,' I urged her.

'A couple of days?' She still didn't take the key. 'But we're supposed to be going out tonight. The *festa*.'

I sighed. 'Shit. Look. I'm sorry. There's a job. I can't turn it down.'

'You forgot.' She stepped back and put her hands on her waist, dropping one hip, her head tilting the opposite way. 'I leave my home, my job, I tell my mother she can rot in hell and now you're going to piss off and leave me on my own? Where are you going?'

'A long way.' I glanced at the old man.

'Don't look at him,' she said. 'Look at me and tell me why you forgot about me.'

'I didn't forget about you ... Well, about the *festa*, yeah, but I need the money, Daniella. *We* need the money. It's for *us*. So we can be together.'

Daniella sighed and looked down. She was swallowing her temper, dousing the flames. She must have sensed that this time she might not get her way if she didn't try a more sensitive route. 'I don't want to be on my own, Zico. What am I going to do on my own?'

'You'll think of something. It's not for long.'

77

Her expression softened further and she reached out for me. 'Stay here,' she said, taking my hand but not the key. 'With me. Forget about the money, we'll have some fun.' She ran her fingers along my forearm.

'I can't just forget about it, it's too much money.'

'How much?'

'And anyway, Raul needs me.'

'So do I.' She stepped closer, looking up at me, one hand on my chest.

'Come on, Daniella, I have to go.' I looked at my watch again. 'I'll be back in a few days, a week at the most.' As soon as I said it, I knew I shouldn't have.

'A week?' I felt her hand tense on my chest.

'No. It won't be that long. *Shouldn't* be.'

And then an idea came to her. I watched it light up her face, her eyes widening, a smile touching the corner of her mouth. 'I'll come with you,' she said. 'It'll be—'

'No. You can't come with us.'

'Why not? I've been out with you before. I can fish.'

'We're not catching fish, Daniella, this is work.'

'That's OK, I know what kind of work you and Raul do. I can keep quiet, you know that.'

There was a fraction of a second when I imagined saying 'yes' to her. I could see us on the boat together and something about it felt good. To be with Daniella, on the river, away from Costa and his people, away from her mother and my need for money. A surge of emotion welled in me and I knew I loved her and wanted to be with her and would do anything to make that happen. That's why I was doing this job for Costa – so that Daniella and I could be together. But that was also why she couldn't come with us.

Hiding the killing from the old man would be easy enough, but not from Daniella. She would be with me every moment, and she would see a side to me I didn't want her to see.

'What about all your things?' I said. 'We're going to be at least four or five days. You won't have—'

'Everything I need is right here.' She toed the bag by her feet.

'Daniella, it's not safe.' I lowered my voice. 'You know the kind of stuff Raul carries. There are people up and down the river who might try to take it. And that man back there? He's a killer.'

Daniella turned around to see Leonardo sitting still in the boat.

'I know him,' she said, thinking for a second. 'Yeah. That's the guy Manuela met at Kaiana's the other night.'

'What?'

'Seemed all right to me,' she said. 'And Manuela liked him. In fact, she liked him a *lot*. He's actually quite good-looking, in a rough way. Doesn't look like a killer.'

'And what does a killer look like?' I asked her.

'Like you, maybe.' She let her eyes linger on mine for a moment, speaking without words.

'Zico, we need to go,' Raul said, coming over. I could see he didn't want to interrupt, but he knew better than I did how long it was going to take us to get to the place where we were meeting the plane. And if we weren't there at the right time, Leonardo had made it clear the plane would leave without us.

'It's OK,' I said to him. 'Daniella's—'

'I'm coming with you,' she interrupted.

Raul threw me a questioning look and I shook my head at him. 'No. I already told her it's not a good idea.'

'You're right,' he agreed. 'Zico's right, Daniella, this is no place for a woman.'

Immediately I touched a hand to my forehead. Of all the things Raul could have said.

'No place for a woman?' Daniella turned on him, making him take a step back and hold up his hands. 'You saying I'm not strong enough?'

'And your parents will worry,' Raul back-pedalled. 'They don't know where you are.'

'Let them worry.'

'You don't mean that. That's not like you.' Raul looked to me for help, but I gave none. I was glad that she had turned on him for a moment, giving me space to breathe. Daniella's passion was

79

one of the things I most liked about her, but when her temper was changing like this, I always found it best to step away.

'Carolina can tell them where I am. And what exactly did you mean "no place for a woman"? I can fish. I can lift. I can probably even shoot a rifle straighter than you can.'

Raul held up his hands. 'All I'm saying is that... Oh, you know what, Daniella? If you want to come, you can come. We haven't got time for this.' He looked tired. The bags under his eyes were fleshy half moons of dark, wrinkled skin. His eyes were red like he'd been drinking. 'It's your call, Zico. But either way, we've got to go now. You stay here if it makes it easier. I can manage without you.' He wiped moisture from his eyes and yawned.

'No, old man, you're sick. You're not going anywhere without me. In fact, maybe *you* should be the one staying here.'

'You're sick?' Daniella looked concerned.

Raul shook his head. 'Tired is all.' He started walking back to the boat, seeing Leonardo becoming agitated, tapping his finger on his watch, saying something I couldn't hear.

'Take me with you, Zico,' Daniella persisted. 'I can keep an eye on Raul for you. And I might be able to make your journey more exciting.' She reached forward with her right hand and pressed it against my crotch.

I backed away, looking over to see if the others had spotted it. Carolina was hanging washing again and Raul had his back to me, but Leonardo had seen. He raised a hand and waved his fingers at me.

'You don't want to leave me alone over the weekend, do you?' she said. 'I'd have to find someone else to take me to the *festa*.'

'That's cheap.'

'I can be as cheap as you like.'

I turned around and walked away from Daniella. I took off my cap and ran a hand over my head, looking up at the bank and seeing something that made the decision for me.

The trip would be dangerous and I had no idea what kind of cargo we would be carrying. There was something about Leonardo that made me nervous and I didn't want him on board. Daniella would see a different side to me, too. When I was on the river with the old man, I had to be focused – I was his protection. There was Costa's job to think about too.

So many reasons for her not to come.

But up there, on the bank, standing in the wide-leaved carpet grass, there were two reasons for me to take her with us.

'OK.' I turned back to her. 'OK. But you have to promise to do whatever I tell you, OK? No matter how pissed off it makes you.'

She nodded.

'And stay away from him.' I looked across at Leonardo.

Daniella stepped back and saluted. '*Sim capitan.*'

I nodded and glanced up at the two men standing on the bank.

It would be dangerous on the river, but at least Daniella would be safe from Luis and Wilson.

'Come on,' I said. 'Let's get you in the boat.'

But as we headed back to the water, Luis kicked off his flip-flops and began to make his way down onto the beach.

'Wait here,' I told Daniella and turned to meet him halfway.

'What do you think you're doing?' Luis said as he came closer. 'She's not going anywhere. And who the hell is that other guy?'

'Have you got nothing better to do than follow me around?'

'A job is a job.' He squared up to me and I glanced over his shoulder at Wilson, still on the ridge of the bank. His hand was under his shirt, no doubt gripping the handle of a pistol.

'Is that what Antonio was?' I moved closer to him so our noses were almost touching. 'A job?'

Luis grinned. 'No, that was just fun.' He reached up and put a hand on my chest to push me away.

I stepped back and worked hard to control my urge to hurt him, reminding myself what Costa had said. When I came back, Luis and Wilson were mine. I couldn't help Antonio, but I would avenge him.

'Costa won't like this,' Luis said. 'Other people on the boat. Taking your girlfriend and the old man with—'

'Costa can go screw himself. I told him I'd do what he wanted.

81

All he has to do is wait for me to come back and have my money ready.'

'You think you'll keep them safe if they're with you?'

'Safer than if they're here with you.'

Luis thought for a moment then looked over at the old man's house. 'His wife's ugly,' he said, leaning to one side and spitting in the sand. 'I think we'd just burn her inside the house. We could do the same to the store. Burn your girlfriend's mother. Find her father and—'

'I'm coming back,' I said. 'You're not going to burn anyone.'

'We'll be waiting.'

'I'm looking forward to it.'

I watched him walk up the beach towards his friend and wondered what I would come back to when we returned to Piratinga. Whatever it was, I knew it wouldn't be good.

14

I rowed out to the *Deus*, nudging the hull of the larger boat, the two vessels making a hollow sound as they knocked together. The old man helped me hold us against the *Deus* while Daniella climbed aboard, then waved me away when I tried to help him. I watched him struggle over the gunwale, then passed up the few things we had with us.

'Is she your *namorada*?' Leonardo asked as I took Rocky in both arms. 'Not the dog. The girl.'

I ignored him and lifted Rocky up onto the deck. She was glad to be on the larger boat and immediately began rushing around, rediscovering familiar smells.

'She's nice. Pretty. Just the right amount around the hips for me. Her friend was a bit too fat. If she's not yours, then maybe I could—'

'Just stay away from her,' I said, looking him in the eye.

'What's her name?'

'Doesn't matter. All you have to do is sit and be quiet. We make the collection, we make the delivery, you pay us, and then we're done.'

'Just trying to be friendly.'

'We don't need to be friends.'

Leonardo stood and reached out for the *Deus*, clinging onto the tyres fixed to the hull. 'You got something against me?'

I looked at him standing there in his wet trousers and his shirt, his cap skewed at an angle, and I wondered what it was about him that I didn't like. It wasn't the way he wore his cap. It wasn't the way he smiled or the look in his eye. It wasn't the lazy slouch to his shoulders, nor was it that he had tried to bring a pistol on board. It wasn't a single one of those things, but it was all of those things. All of those things made him a man I knew I could not trust.

'I bother you, don't I?' he asked.

'I don't want you here.'

'It's the only way you're going to get paid. I *have* to be here. We should try to get along.'

'Just get on the boat.'

Leonardo laughed and pulled himself up onto the deck. He was young and fit, and it came in one swift movement. The larger boat didn't dip in the water like the other one had done, and the stability made him more confident.

I followed him up, keeping hold of the rope tied to the bow of the smaller vessel.

'Leonardo,' he said, making straight for Daniella, the rolled bottoms of his sodden trousers scraping together at his ankles. 'I remember you. You were with the girl in the club. Marisa.'

'Manuela.'

'Yeah.' He reached out to take her hand, kiss each cheek, but I hurried to step between them, letting him see my expression before taking Daniella to one side where the old man was organising the supplies.

'He seems OK,' she said under her breath. 'Nice eyes. Good-looking.'

'He's not OK,' I told her.

'You know him?'

'I know people like him, and I know not to trust him. You agreed to do as I say, remember.'

'Listen to him,' Raul said. 'Zico has an eye for people. If he says Leonardo's bad news, then we should listen to him.'

Daniella nodded. 'OK. Whatever you say.'

'Your boyfriend isn't very friendly,' Leonardo said, coming to join us. 'Not half as charming as you are.'

Daniella looked at me, then back at Leonardo, opening her mouth as if to reply.

'Help me with these.' Raul handed her a coolbox before she could speak, and encouraged her to follow him towards the wheel-house.

When Daniella was out of sight, I hauled the small aluminium boat from the water and used a rope to secure it to the stern of the *Deus*. Leonardo leaned against the gunwale and folded his arms as he watched me struggle with its weight.

'You need some help?' he asked. 'You want me to call the old man over? Or maybe your *namorada*? I'd like to see her help with something like that.'

When I'd finished tying it off, I came around the enclosed section at the stern of the vessel and onto the main deck, telling Leonardo to sit on one of the narrow benches that ran along either side.

Daniella and Raul had stowed the supplies and were standing on the prow, beyond the wheelhouse. Raul was pointing south, as if he were showing Daniella which way we'd be travelling. Rocky had her front paws up on the gunwale and her mouth was open, her tongue hanging out.

'You just get comfortable.' I looked down at Leonardo. We were at a good angle now for the canvas cover to provide shelter from the sun but it trapped the heat and the air smelled of the old material.

'Is there anything else to do on this boat?' He took the cigarette from behind his ear and put it in his mouth.

'You're a paying passenger. All you need to do is sit back and relax.'

Leonardo fished a match from his top pocket and scraped it along the empty bench seat beside him. When it flared, he cupped it with both hands and touched it to the tip of the cigarette. He took a long drag and blew it up at me, squinting against the smoke. 'Is the old man up to this?' he asked, glancing over at Raul and Daniella. 'He looks sick.'

'We'll make your collection *and* your delivery,' I said. 'Just make sure you're good for the money.'

'A sick old man and a girl for a crew? I hope you know what

you're doing.' He looked past me at Daniella who still had her back to us. She was leaning forward, her skirt tight around her backside. Leonardo made a contented noise, low in his throat. 'Mind you, I could get used to that view.'

'Just stay right here,' I told him. 'And keep away from *her*.' I knew I shouldn't have said it. I was admitting my weakness to Leonardo but everything about him put me on edge, and already he was picking at me, working his way under my skin.

Leonardo sniffed hard and leaned back to spit into the water.

I resolved not to let him bother me so much, and the only way to do it was to avoid him. So I left him where he was and went to the wheelhouse, checking I was out of his line of sight. I squatted and pulled up a loose board, reaching into the darkness to remove a wrap of black plastic containing a rifle and a revolver that belonged to Raul. I removed the wrapping and stuffed it back under the board before replacing it and ensuring it was unnoticeable.

Crouched like that, I slipped the pistol under the dash where the wheel was, then came out on deck, the rifle in one hand, the shoulder strap hanging against my thigh.

'What's that for?' said Daniella, with a half smile. 'You planning on shooting someone?'

I looked along the deck at Leonardo who was sitting and smoking, watching us. 'Doesn't matter what we carry on this boat,' I said. 'Might even be nothing at all, but there are some people, they see a boat like this on the river, they think maybe there's something worth taking. Maybe they know us; know that we carry stuff for people.'

'Pirates,' Leonardo told her with a smile, leaning back, his arms stretched out either side of him along the top of the gunwale.

'Call them whatever you like.' I shrugged and lifted the rifle a fraction. 'This is for your protection.'

I went to the bow and stowed the rifle and Leonardo's pistol in a box seat with a lid that creaked and needed oil. It was my spot. The place from where I could keep watch.

'No reason for you to go up that end of the boat,' I told Leonardo as I came back towards him. 'You just stay right here.'

'And my pistol?'

'You can have it back when this is all done.'

Raul came alongside me, slapping my shoulder. 'What would I do without you to look after me?' He allowed a short raspy laugh to escape, then went aft and eased down to his knees where there was a hatch on the deck. It was an effort, making his breath come hard, and I could see the moisture glistening on the back of his neck.

'I'll do that,' I said, going to him.

'No need.' He held up a hand without looking at me. He paused to catch his breath, then took the recessed ring and lifted the hatch saying, 'Spanner?' and waggling his fingers.

I took a rusted spanner from a box of tools and handed it to the old man who leaned into the hatch. He stayed there for a minute or two, effort showing on his face as he did something with his hands in the darkness of the boat's belly. When he eventually sat back and closed the hatch, he passed the spanner to me and wiped the palm of his hands down his trousers, adding to the grease patches that were already there.

'You really think someone would want to steal this piece of junk?' Leonardo smirked.

'You'd be surprised,' said Raul. He tapped the side of his nose with one finger. 'But until I work my little bit of magic, no one else can get her started.'

I leaned over the side and pulled up the anchor.

'She isn't much,' Raul called back as he took his place behind the wheel. 'But she's mine, and she gets the job done.' He turned the key and the motor started first time. A raw thumping beneath our feet that made the deck vibrate and the water bubble and churn behind us.

A waft of blue smoke drifted from one side of the boat, floating across the surface of the water and thinning. The air smelled of diesel.

Raul looked at me and raised his eyebrows, a smile touching

his cracked lips. 'Let's get moving, then. There's some stuff we need to pick up.' He turned the wheel and steered us into the main channel.

15

Standing forward on the bow, one bare foot on the gunwale, I lifted a hand to shade my eyes from the sun and looked back at Raul, sitting with Rocky at his side. I wondered if he would ever get what he wanted from life. All the time we had known each other, we both thought we wanted something different. Raul always talked about saving up and moving to Imperatriz, while I was always on the cusp of earning enough money to get what I wanted. It gave us something to talk about when the journeys were long and the sun was cruel, but now I was beginning to wonder if either of us would ever find our balance, or if we would die right here on the river, side by side, in the place we knew best.

'I should have made him stay at home,' I said to Daniella who was sitting on the deck close to me. She was leaning against the gunwale with her legs drawn up so her knees were against her chest.

The river was more than a kilometre from one bank to the other here, both sides thick with forest that hummed, vibrant with life. All around us, white sandbanks rose from the silt-laden water like pale-boned monsters. The surface of those ever-moving islands was untouched by man and rippled as if water had been imprinted upon it. Here and there, sunken trees reached up, breaking the surface of the river like the hands of drowning men grasping for rescue.

A pair of *anhinga* snakebirds dried their plumage in the branches of one of those trees, watching the water with fixed stares. Another was swimming, only its long neck visible above the surface. I watched it disappear under and turned back to look at the old man behind the wheel.

Raul noticed me watching him and he nodded once in acknowledgment. A brief smile showed around the bent cigarette clamped between his lips. He shifted on the bench which was fixed to the deck behind the wheel, straightened himself for a moment, then allowed his back to hunch over the wheel once more.

His entire body looked tired, the fever taking hold. Despite the intensity of the sun, he shivered from time to time, and I could almost feel his headache, the fuzzy discomfort in his old joints. I imagined the pain behind his eyes and how it would hurt to smile. But Raul would ignore it just like he had ignored so much distress and inconvenience in his life. If he thought of something else, he could make the fever less acute; dull it with the strength of his mind.

We'd come about sixty kilometres south past the mouth of the Rio das Mortes. Just over an hour ago, we passed the remnants of a small gold-mining operation that had dried up many years ago and been more or less abandoned to the forest. A few ramshackle buildings close to the water, the trees and undergrowth advancing to reclaim them. There had been a couple of Indian canoes there, the occupants looking up from their fishing lines to watch us pass, but we hadn't seen anything else other than trees and water and sky.

Another couple of hours and we'd meet the plane. We could make it back to the Rio das Mortes before nightfall, then moor somewhere until morning. After that it would be a day's travel to Mina dos Santos. The old man would be thinking he had three or four days on the river and he'd be with his wife again. He'd have to admit his illness then, and she would take him into the cool darkness of their home and care for him until the fever passed. She was a strong woman; she would force the sickness to leave him. The way I saw it in my mind, she would shout and beat it into submission until it left his body like an exorcised devil. She would take it in her hands and squeeze it until it gasped for breath.

'If he gets any worse,' I said, still looking at him, 'maybe we should drop him back at Piratinga before we go on to Mina dos Santos. I don't know if he'll manage the rest of today, let alone three or four days. You can get off, too. It was a mistake to let you come.' But I couldn't be sure that would be the best thing. The old man might die here on the boat if his fever worsened, but Daniella might just be safer.

'Am I in the way?' she asked.

I shook my head and raised a hand to the old man. 'I just have a feeling,' I said. 'Things haven't started out well today.'

'Then they can only get better.' Daniella stood and came to me, putting an arm around my waist and letting the breeze brush her face. A few strands of hair came loose from her ponytail, moved in the wind, one of them catching on her lip and sticking.

I reached out to brush it away as I scanned the river. 'No, we should go back. It's out of our way, but it's the best thing to do. We'll get what we came for and then we'll go back to Piratinga. I'll go on to Mina dos Santos alone. Just me and Leonardo.'

Even as the words were on my lips, though, the *Deus* shuddered beneath us, an abrupt and violent motion that shook right through me. The boat lurched a second and third time before the engine cut out and died.

I held onto the gunwale and caught Daniella as she fell against me, seeing the last tongue of smoke wisp away behind us while the boat coasted in silence, losing its momentum to the river. All I could hear was the sound of the bow cutting through the water, slowing, coming to a stop.

The silence that followed was stark and empty.

In the wheelhouse, Raul and Rocky were recovering from the jolt. The old man looked dazed and all he could do was raise a hand to let me know he was all right. Rocky was scrabbling to her feet, indignant at having fallen from her place on the bench beside her owner.

'I'd better go see what's wrong,' I said to Daniella. The sound of my voice was flat and strange in the vast openness of the river. 'You wait here.'

When I reached the wheelhouse, the old man had recovered

and restarted the engine. When he tried to put the *Deus* in gear, though, the familiar whine and chug was cut short by a grinding as the boat shuddered and failed. He tried one more time, then sat back from the wheel and showed me a blank look.

'What is it?' Leonardo said, coming forward but stopping short when he saw Rocky. His eyes lingered on her for a moment, then he looked up at Raul. 'You know we have a collection time, right? And if we're late, no one gets paid.' There was a slight tremble in his voice that might have been fear.

I put a hand on the back of the seat and leaned in to speak to Raul. 'What do you think, old man?'

'Not sure. Did you feel anything? We hit something maybe?'

Leonardo raised his voice, but couldn't hide his nervousness. 'Hey, if we're not there when that plane—'

'You know how to fix boats?' I turned on him.

He pursed his lips and watched me.

'I didn't think so. From what I've seen, you're more roads than rivers, so you want to let us figure this out or you want to swim to meet your plane? If you know how to fix boats, then that's good, but if not, why don't you sit down and shut up?'

Leonardo stared at me, his eyes fixed on mine for several seconds, then he nodded once, slowly. 'OK,' he said, pausing a moment longer before returning to his seat. He was showing me that he wasn't afraid of me. He would not be intimidated by me. If I hadn't taken his gun before he came on board, there's a good chance it would be in his hand by now.

I watched him go, then told Raul to try the engine one more time. As soon as he put us in gear, though, the *Deus* convulsed. The old man swore under his breath and stood up. 'I'll have a look.'

I followed him to the stern, going into the covered section at the back where the engine was housed. I held a torch for him while he checked it over, all the time breathing heavily, grunting with effort.

'You see Leonardo's reaction?' I spoke to Raul's back.

'Uh-uh.'

'He looked scared.'

92

'Just gave him a shock, that's all. He's not the scared type.' Raul straightened up and put his hands on his lower back.

'Anything?'

He looked at me and scratched his cheek, leaving an oily mark amongst the grey bristles. 'Nothing. You'll have to go in.'

'In the water? You think maybe the propeller?'

'I think maybe we hit something.'

I switched off the torch and came out of the housing, glad to be in the fresh air again. Inside, it was dark and close; hot and smelling of diesel.

'Going for a swim?' Leonardo asked when he saw me taking off my shirt.

'Unless you want to go?'

He held up both hands.

'I didn't think so.'

'Is it safe here?' Daniella asked, looking over the side of the boat, then raising her eyes to the distant shore. 'We're a long way out.' It was half a kilometre to each bank, and maybe the same distance to the bottom of the river. 'There's things in there that—'

'It'll be fine.' I waved away an insect that had come to buzz around my face, attracted by the sweat. 'I've done this before.'

Daniella nodded, but looked worried.

'And if I don't go in, we'll be stuck here for a while.'

'We can't get closer to the shore?' she asked.

'Maybe,' Raul told her. 'But it's not easy. We have to try this first.' He looked at me with a serious expression, knowing I wouldn't go into the river unless I had to.

The *Deus* drifted, turning sideways as the lazy current took us back downriver. Here, more sandbanks lifted from the water, creating a maze of channels. We couldn't risk being washed against one and wedging into the soft sand, so I dropped the anchor, hoping it would find purchase. We had moved a little closer towards the left bank, coming within four hundred metres of the tufts of marshy vegetation that grew there. Beyond them, on the beach, a huddle of dark shapes lay like damp, rotting driftwood.

I flicked at the insect that had returned to land on my shoulder, and stared at those shapes on the beach. It wasn't driftwood, though, it was a group of caiman enjoying the sun.

'*Jacaré*,' I said, not liking the idea of being in the water near a large group of armoured reptiles with mouths full of sharp teeth.

The old man thought for a moment. 'They won't bother you. Too far away.'

'And if there's a big one down there?' I looked over the gunwale and stared into the opaque water. 'Right here? I heard there's *jacaré* that grow up to four metres.'

'I never heard of them attacking a man.'

'I don't want to be the first.'

The old man smiled.

'All right, hold onto these.' I took him to one side and handed him my pistols.

The old man stared as if he didn't know what to do with them, then sighed and clipped them to his belt.

Leonardo's eyes went to them straight away, like a bird drawn to a shiny object.

'Look after the old man,' I said, squatting to rub Rocky's head. 'Daniella too.'

I stepped out of my trousers, so I was wearing only a pair of cotton shorts, and swung one leg over the gunwale. I beckoned the old man closer and spoke quietly. 'Don't worry about me,' I said. 'Just watch Leonardo. I don't trust him.'

Raul glanced behind him and then looked back at me. 'Sure. No problem.'

'And don't let him get too close to you. He has a chance, I think he'll try for those.'

'Why?'

'Because that's the sort of person he is. Just don't show him your back.'

The old man nodded and moved away as I swung my other leg over and dropped off the side of the boat with a splash.

The water was warm and I was a good swimmer but there was something about being in the river that prickled at the back of my mind. Something that wondered what was down there in the darkness.

Countless creatures glided through that water; a thousand things that could kill a man in the most terrible ways, and once I was submerged, I was at their mercy. I would be blind, swimming with my eyes closed against the silt that swirled in dense clouds through the waters. If anything were there, I wouldn't see it. If anything came for me, I would be unprepared. It would snatch me away and drag me into the darkness.

With those terrible thoughts in my head, I took a deep breath and went under.

16

Feeling along the rough underside of the boat, I tried to find the propeller while keeping track of the hull above me. It was disorientating in the darkness, and even though I tried to keep my eyes closed, the silt-laden water found a way in and felt grainy under my eyelids.

Something brushed past my cheek and I fought hard not to panic. It was nothing more than a fish, I told myself, or a twig caught in the current. I focused on the task and continued feeling around the hull until my lungs began to burn and I turned to kick for the surface, breaking out and taking a deep breath.

'Anything?' I heard the old man say and I looked up to see his face peering over the gunwale.

I held onto one of the tyres hanging from the *Deus* and wiped the water from my eyes. 'If there's something, I'll find it,' I told him. 'Don't keep asking. And don't keep turning away from him. Watch *him*, not me.'

'Don't worry about him, he's fishing.'

'Fishing? I don't want any hooks down here.'

'No,' the old man said. 'Not anywhere near here.'

I shook my head at him and moved a little further along, then took another deep breath and dived.

Slipping under the hull, scraping my scalp as I felt for the prop shaft, my fingers touched something unexpected.

A smooth object.

My immediate reaction was to pull away, to get away from whatever it was, but I hardened my resolve and forced myself to continue.

I couldn't tell what it was and I traced its outline, not wanting to touch it, not wanting to be down there in the darkness, and I was surprised by a sudden movement when it jerked in my hands.

An abrupt spasm that startled me, making my chest hitch, bringing water in through my nose.

The water irritated my nostrils and my involuntary action was to cough, expelling my breath and sucking water into my mouth.

Fear welled inside me as my body reacted and my mind raced. All thoughts of anything other than death and survival were now gone. I pushed up against the hull, banging my head, swimming and dragging myself along the underside of the boat, following it round until I kicked up to the surface and broke out into the fresh air, coughing and retching.

I grabbed the tyres that ringed the *Deus* and pulled myself out of the water. Panic still raged in my blood, and I scrambled further up the tyres, dragging my legs and feet from the water, not knowing what was below; what it was that had moved beneath my touch.

'What's going on?' Raul was looking down at me again. 'You all right?' Rocky was beside him, with her front paws on the gunwale, barking as if she didn't recognise me.

Raul hushed her while I waited for the coughing to subside. 'There's something down there,' I said once I had started to recover.

'Caught in the propeller?'

'Yeah. Could be.' And now that he said it, I knew it must be so. Something was jammed in the propeller – something living. Or, rather, something dying.

'You tell what it is?'

I took a moment to think about what I had felt. 'A fish maybe. Big. Christ, it scared the shit out of me.'

'Can you get it out?'

'Maybe.' I didn't like the thought of going back down there, though, the sudden movement had put a fear into me. Blind and beneath the water was no place for any man. I didn't know what was stuck in the propeller, and I didn't really want to find out, but it was the only way we would be able get moving again.

'Be careful,' he said. 'If it's bleeding ...'

'It's stuck in the propeller, of course it's bleeding.'

'Then you'll have to be quick.'

'No shit.' I looked up at the old man and shook my head before slipping back into the water. I took another breath and went under.

Feeling once more for the smooth surface of the creature, I was better prepared for what I would find. My main concern was that it had teeth or barbs or venom or that if it thrashed too much, the excitement would attract other predators. Everything in the river is preyed upon by something else. Everything is part of the food chain, and I didn't want to join them.

I didn't want to be in there when others came to feed.

I reached out, fingertips making contact with the creature. This time there was no movement, so I ran my hands along it until I felt the place where it was stuck. I couldn't tell what kind of fish it was, but it was large, with a strong spine that was now wedged in the blades of the propeller. I put my hands on either side, braced my feet against the hull and tugged several times, pulling hard, sensing my oxygen burning away. I tried once more before resurfacing, filling my lungs and looking up at the old man.

'You get it?' he asked.

'Not yet.' I didn't wait for more conversation, I dipped back under the water again and went straight to my task, determined to finish it this time.

Once again, I braced my legs against the hull, took the creature in both hands and pulled with as much strength as I could manage. I tugged once, twice, and then felt bones crack as they gave in to my strength.

The animal twitched as it came out from the propeller, and I floated away with it, releasing it and swimming for the surface once more. I should probably have gone under again, to check for damage to the boat, but I had caused enough movement in the water, and there would be blood, so I wanted to be back onboard when the predators arrived.

I came up a few metres from the *Deus*, and the river dolphin popped up close to me. An adult with pink-grey skin. It managed a few feeble movements from its tail as the water around it began to splash, just one or two ripples at first, then more violently.

The coffee-coloured river darkened as the animal's blood mingled with the silt.

'Get out,' Raul called to me. 'Get out now.' But he didn't need to say it twice. I knew what those movements in the water were, and I put as much distance between myself and the increasing agitation as I could.

Rocky was barking at all the excitement now. One moment she was up on the gunwale and the next she was gone. Then she would appear a little further along the boat, still barking.

'Faster,' the old man called. 'Come on, Zico.'

As I swam, I saw Daniella and Leonardo come either side of Raul. Daniella was calling to me and there was worry in her expression, but Leonardo watched without any emotion other than interest and the occasional nervous glance at Rocky.

As soon as I was within reach of the boat I grabbed hold of the tyres, and hauled myself out of the water, pulling my legs up in panic, twisting my waist to bring them out of the river.

The old man and Daniella leaned down to grab me, Raul getting hold of my shorts and Daniella taking my arm, helping me up over the gunwale.

I tumbled onto the deck and Daniella came down beside me, putting her arms around me. 'Are you all right?' she asked. 'Did you get hurt? I was so—'

'I'm fine.'

'You sure?' She broke away and looked me up and down as if searching for damage.

'I'm sure.' I got to my feet and turned to watch the commotion in the water. Not a froth but more like a hundred splashes all at once, as the smaller fish snatched and grabbed, their tails thrashing, their bodies twisting, their red bellies flashing at the sky.

It was as if the water were boiling in just that once place.

'What the hell is that?' Leonardo asked.

'Piranhas.' Raul sounded as if he needed to clear his throat.

'Eating what?'

'*Boto*,' I said, hearing my own voice, thinking how lucky I was to get out in one piece. No cuts. Not even a scratch. 'That's what was stuck in the propeller. We must have gone over it and ... I don't know. Maybe it was old. Maybe it was deep and came up for air right underneath us.'

'A *boto*?' Leonardo said, making me look up at him. 'That some kind of fish?'

Raul and I looked at each other.

'Where're you from that you don't know what a *boto* is?' I asked.

'I look like a fisherman? How the fuck would I know what—'

'It's a dolphin,' Raul said.

'No shit. Well, it had bad luck,' Leonardo smiled.

'Bad luck for us,' Daniella said. 'Everyone knows it's bad luck to kill a *boto*.'

'We didn't kill it.' Raul dismissed her with a wave. 'It ... killed itself. The river killed it.'

Leonardo looked around at us. 'Well, whatever it did, it gave me and Daniella a chance to get to know each other.'

I turned to stare at him. He was standing close to Daniella, a smirk on his face.

'She's been teaching me how to fish,' he said. 'We got bored waiting for you and—'

'Stay away from her.' I stepped up to him, our faces close to one another. 'Don't talk to her. Don't *look* at her.'

'We were just fishing,' Daniella said.

I grabbed her arm and took her to the bow, almost dragging her with me as she protested. 'You told me you'd do as I asked when you're on this boat.' I was still high from what had happened in the water, my whole body was wound tight and now I was unravelling.

'Zico.' She snatched herself away. 'You're hurting me.'

I let go and shook my head at her. 'Please. Just do as I ask.'

Daniella's face tightened, her upper lip raising just a touch, her nose wrinkling. 'What the hell is the matter with you? It's like you turned into someone else.' She glared at me. 'Telling me what to do, where to go, who I can talk to.'

'You promised me. You said you would do as I—'

'I know what I said, but I didn't ask him to come over. I was bored, so I cast a line. I didn't ask him to come, but he did. And he was being friendly. He even made me laugh, Zico, which is more than you've managed since we got on this boat. I liked being with him, I couldn't tell him to leave me alone.'

'You should. He's dangerous.'

'Dangerous? Like you?'

'What?'

'He's not the one grabbing me and pulling me around. Right now, Zico, I'm wondering who *you* are.'

'I—'

'Maybe my mother was right,' she said and turned away, heading for the bow.

I let her go, knowing that behind me, Leonardo would be watching the way her hips swung in the short skirt, seeing her dark shoulders, her bare feet on the deck.

It took everything I had not to go to him right now, to vent my anger and frustration.

'Everything OK?' Raul was beside me, holding out my trousers.

'Apart from nearly getting eaten by piranhas, you mean?' I took them from him and pulled them on, my skin already dry, but my shorts still wet.

'With Daniella, I mean.' He took my holsters from his belt and handed them back to me.

'I know what you meant.' I watched her standing at the very tip of the bow, one arm on either side, her chin resting on her forearms.

'Talk to her,' Raul said. 'I'll check the engine.'

He turned to walk away but I stopped him, saying, 'Hey. You believe that superstitious stuff about the *boto*?'

I knew the fishermen told stories about the *boto*. Some said they were *encantado*, and could turn into a handsome man at night and seduce young women; others, that if you looked into their eyes, you'd have nightmares for the rest of your life. They all agreed on one thing, though – it was bad luck to kill one.

The old man looked at the deck and took off his hat. He ran a callused hand over the top of his head, the grey hair was short and bristled so that it flicked up a fine spray of sweat.

'Yeah,' I said. 'Of course you believe it. Vultures and *boto*. We're doomed.'

When he was gone, I took a deep breath, giving myself time to swallow my anger at Leonardo and settle the creeping sense of dread beginning to smother this whole trip. Feeling calmer, I draped my shirt over my shoulder and went to Daniella, leaning on the gunwale beside her and looking out at the river. 'I don't want to fight.'

'Then don't.'

'I'm sorry. I was worked up from being in the water, and seeing you with Leonardo... I'm just not used to having anyone else on the boat. You said I was like a different person, and maybe you're right. Maybe I *am* when I'm on here. Sometimes I have to do things that need me to be different. I have to think in a different way.'

'That's why you need those?' She glanced down at my pistols.

'Yes.' And for the first time in a few hours I thought about something other than Leonardo. I thought about the newspaper cutting, folded in my pocket, and I thought about what I intended to do to the woman in the picture.

Daniella sighed and raised her eyebrows. 'He's not that bad, you know. Maybe you've got him wrong. Maybe he's like you.'

'He's not like me.' I pushed the image of Sister Beckett from my mind. There would be time to think about her later. For now, Leonardo was my concern. 'You have to believe me, Daniella. He's not like me.'

Now she turned to look at me. 'He was only talking to me.'

'Did he touch you?'

She rolled her eyes and turned away.

'OK, OK, I'm sorry. Maybe he *is* all right. But I don't know him and you don't know him. We don't *need* to know him, we just need to collect his cargo and then... well, I'm not sure what then. But, please, I don't want to fight about this. All I want to do is keep you safe.'

Her body language softened. Her shoulders were less hunched, her arms less tight, her back more relaxed. 'I don't like being told what to do.'

'I know.' I reached out to brush back her hair. 'I know. But please, you have to listen to what I tell you. Here, on the boat, that's all I'm asking. I want you to keep away from him. Please.'

She thought about it, her mouth tightening, then she looked up at the sky and nodded. 'OK.'

17

We'd been on the river five or six hours when Raul dropped the throttle and the boat slowed in the water, drifting shoreward.

'This the place?' I asked him.

'Somewhere round here.'

We were on a long, straight stretch of the Araguaia, leading to a sandy fork up ahead. It looked to be a good spot to land a plane if you didn't want anyone to know about it. The trees on the near bank were thick and there weren't any settlements on this stretch other than a *fazenda* five or ten kilometres further south. Even if someone from the *fazenda* noticed the plane coming in low, it would have touched down, unloaded and left before they could investigate.

The old man looked at his watch. 'We've still got a few minutes.'

I crouched beside him so my face was level with his. 'When this is done, I'm taking you home.'

Raul looked at me as if I were insulting him.

'You're sick, old man, and you know it. So why don't we collect the stuff and head back to Piratinga? I'll take the cargo to Mina dos Santos first thing in the morning.'

'Leonardo won't like it.'

'I have to get you home to Carolina.'

'Tell you what,' he said. 'Let's meet this plane, load the cargo, then we'll decide what we're going to do, how about that?'

I watched him, sensing it was going to be hard to persuade him. 'OK. It's a deal.'

Raul cut the engine dead and the world became silent but for the buzzing in my ears left by the perpetual hum of the *Deus* over the past few hours. He turned the wheel so we coasted nearer the shore, away from the centre of the river, and as the boat drifted, the lilting incantation of birdsong came across from the trees.

'*Uirapuru*,' said the old man.

Carolina told a tale about a young Indian warrior who fell in love with the chief's daughter. The chief was so angry he asked the god Tupa to turn the boy into a bird they called *uirapuru*. But the bird came to sing his beautiful song to his beloved every day until the chief gathered his best warriors and ordered them to hunt and kill him. The girl persuaded the bird to fly away, to save himself, but it was good luck to hear his song, and if you could catch him, he would give you a wish.

She told other stories, too, about the creatures that hid in the forests and rivers. Creatures both real and unreal. For every jaguar or anaconda, there was a Corpo Seco – a man so rotten that even the devil would not take his soul – or *mapinguari* – the beast that moves among the trees without sound.

I stared into the forest as we slipped into the place where its shadow darkened the water and cooled the air close to the bank. I was not a superstitious man, but looking into that dense darkness made it easy to believe that such creatures might be real. If they were to exist anywhere in the world, this would be exactly the right place.

Yet, alongside those terrors, was the beauty of the gentle splash of a fish in the shallows and the happy lilt of the *uirapuru*.

Then a *piha* wolf-whistled in the forest, breaking the moment, and I turned to see the old man watching me.

'What?' he said. 'You suddenly get lazy?'

I smiled and went to the side of the boat to pick up the anchor. I lifted it and turned to look at the old man. When he nodded, I threw it over into the water and waited as the boat drifted for a moment, taking up the slack, then the rope tightened, flicking water as it sprung taut.

'It's like we're being watched,' Leonardo said, coming to stand beside me and scan the forest.

'You *are* being watched.' I nodded towards the wheelhouse,

where Rocky was sitting. She was on her haunches, mouth open, tongue out to one side, staring at Leonardo as if she trusted him even less than I did.

'I swear that dog doesn't like me.'

'She knows you're afraid of her,' I said.

'I'm not afraid.'

'Of course you are. And she sees it better than the rest of us. She can smell it on you like I can smell your sweat.'

Leonardo watched her for a moment, the two of them trying to stare each other down. Only when Rocky got to her feet and closed her mouth did Leonardo look away.

'We made good time,' he said, trying to ignore the dog. 'I was worried we wouldn't make it. The plane won't stay long.' He leaned forward, putting his forearms on the gunwale beside me and looking out at the trees lining the shore. 'Can I ask you something?'

I glanced at him but didn't answer.

'Why did you take my *pistola*? What do you think I'm going to do?'

'You don't need a gun on this boat.'

'But if there's trouble, wouldn't two guns be better than one?'

'If I need your help, I'll let you know.'

Leonardo nodded. 'There's not just your boat to protect now, though, is there? There's her as well.' He inclined his head towards Daniella still standing by the bow. 'She's nice. Nicer than her friend I met the other night. I mean, she was good, but Daniella's got something else. She's got fire in her.'

'Don't.' I stared at him.

Leonardo opened his mouth to speak but I turned my back on him and went to Daniella.

Rocky trotted behind me, panting hard from the unrelenting heat, but decided not to join us. Instead, she slipped into the wheelhouse and jumped onto the seat beside the old man. She turned once and collapsed with a grunt.

Standing with Daniella, watching the water, it occurred to me that there was no sight like it anywhere else on earth, no sounds to match those that drifted across from the forest. The sun was comforting on my back and I tried not to think about how Leonardo was using Daniella to work his way under my skin. For a moment I pretended he wasn't on the boat with us. For now it was just Daniella and me.

'Beautiful, isn't it?' I said to her.

'I suppose so.' Her brow was furrowed, her lips tight. She was still a little angry with me.

'I remember a time, sitting with my sister on a bench high up in the *favela*, looking out at the sea. I was twelve, thirteen, and from the hillside, the sea looked calm, and I wondered what it would be like to sail away on it. I thought it would make me feel like a different person.'

Daniella turned to me. 'I didn't know you had a sister. Older or younger?'

'Older by two years. Sofia.'

She thought about it. 'I've known you for months and you never mentioned her. Where is she?'

I shook my head. 'She died.'

Daniella stayed quiet for a moment, her eyes on me. 'What was she like?'

'She was … my sister. She was my friend, too. She always tried to keep me out of trouble and her temper could flare up like yours.' I looked at Daniella and found myself smiling. 'And she took care of me as much as I would let her.' I put back my head and let the breeze cool my face, remembering my sister as she lived rather than as she had died. I remembered the flick of her hair, the contagion of her laugh and the arguments we had about the company I kept.

'So what about your *mãe* and *pai*?'

I hadn't told Daniella much about my life before I came here. She had asked, but I always felt as if I wanted to leave it behind me. Something felt different now, though. Something was changing.

'They moved from the country looking for a better life and ended up in the *favela*,' I said. 'I didn't really know Mãe; she died from cholera when I was five years old. The "dog's disease" they used to call it. Pai worked for the *prefeitura*, picking up litter while kids ran around the streets with money in their pockets from drugs. They wore the best clothes and laughed in his face at his uniform. When he came home he drank and fell asleep. One day he just didn't wake up.'

'What happened?'

I shrugged. 'He drank himself to death, I suppose.'

'That's awful. How old were you?'

'Twelve.'

Over by the edge of the river, something splashed close to the bank. A hollow sound, a muddle of froth on the water and then nothing but ripples, reaching out for us.

After Pai was gone, Sofia wanted to get away from the *favela*, but we just carried on. There was nothing else we could do. She worked hard for some rich people, cleaning their house, doing what they asked, but I wasn't going to do anything like that. I wasn't going to work like Pai to get laughed at and earn barely enough to stay alive. I started working for the older boys instead, watching for the police. We used to shoot rockets into the sky when we saw them, so the others could hide, and I earned enough money to buy clothes and shoes with labels on them. Sofia said I should be ashamed of myself, but I didn't see it like that.

'I never believed I'd be in a place like this,' I said, 'with someone like you.'

Daniella put her hand on mine.

I felt her touch and for a moment I was on the bench again, on the hillside in Rio, with the sea in front of me and Cristo Redentor watching over us, welcoming everyone into those outstretched arms. From his perch on Corcovado mountain, he could see the wonders of Rio de Janeiro spread below him like a carpet of colour. Sofia said he saw the rich hillside real estate just as he saw the dilapidated and makeshift *favelas*, slumped, rusting and decaying on the hillsides.

A few years later, though, Sofia was gone and I sat alone on that bench, thinking maybe I could find the life we had talked about. And that's why I had taken that last job, because I thought it would give me enough money to get out. But all it had given me was more trouble and a reason to run. It occurred to me now that I was still doing that one last job; over and over, always trying to get away.

Just one more life.

I took my hand from Daniella's and touched my fingers to the shirt pocket containing the newspaper cutting. I pictured Sister Dolores Beckett and felt that doubt again. This was not what I wanted.

'You hear that?' Daniella said, breaking the moment.

I tilted my head.

Raul came out from behind the wheel to join us as we scanned the blue sky. Not a cloud. Nothing at all to mar the perfect blue sheet above us.

Daniella shaded her eyes as she looked up and pointed, saying, 'Is that what we're waiting for?'

I followed the line of her finger to see a dot of white and silver, the fuselage catching the sun as it descended, the drone growing louder as it approached.

18

Within minutes, the Catalina seaplane was low enough to touch the treetops with its white belly. The stifling day was filled with the buzz of its propellers as it came down, skirting across the forest on the far side, then banking so it was in line with the river. It dropped and dropped, skimming the water, the ridge on the underside of the plane slicing into the ripples created by its draught on the river. The plane lifted once, as if the pilot were having second thoughts, then touched down again, frothing the surface and pushing a wake out behind it.

The twin propellers, attached high on the wing that spanned the fuselage, slowed to a monotonous drone as the plane continued past the spot where we were anchored.

Its old paintwork was faded and rusted, its white body stained and in need of attention. The only livery markings were the red and blue stripe coursing from its upturned nose to its rounded tail.

'They must be brave,' I said to Raul. 'Flying in that thing.'

It reminded me of a flying version of the *Deus*, and I was glad I was on the water and not in the air. At least if a boat went down, there was a chance of swimming, but if a plane fell out of the sky, it meant certain death – especially here. Last year, *vaqueiros* on the *fazenda* east of Piratinga watched a light aircraft come down in the forest, and sent men out to find it, but it was too far into the dense vegetation. There was no way to get to it. A couple of days later, a second plane came, circling over the trees, and then a helicopter, but they were too late. The only thing they took out of the forest was bodies and, even then, the story was that there wasn't much left of them.

The forest is cruel.

Rocky trotted up and down the deck, excited by the activity, then put her paws up on the gunwale and barked at the Catalina as it turned and headed back. Eventually, it came to a halt in the centre of the river, the engines still running, the props still chugging.

Rocky continued to bark, so Raul grabbed the scruff of her neck and pulled her back, telling her to be quiet.

'We'll have to get alongside it,' he said, heading back to the wheelhouse and starting the boat again. 'Take care of the anchor, Zico.'

I took Daniella by the hand and led her to the back of the *Deus*, opening the door to the rusted covered section. 'This is one of those times I want you to do as I ask,' I said. 'Stay out of sight. Please. It's better no one knows you're here.'

'It stinks in here,' she complained.

'Engine oil,' I told her. 'You'll get used to it.'

'Not just engine oil,' she said, using her foot to slide out an old plastic bucket. The rest of us had been able to relieve ourselves over the side of the boat, but it hadn't been so easy for Daniella. The bucket had been the best solution.

'It'll only be a few minutes. That plane's not going to stay long. Props are still running, so that means they want to get away fast.'

'Why?'

'I don't know. Please, just ...' I motioned towards the door.

She frowned and looked like she was going to resist, but rolled her eyes and went into the small room.

'It's safer this way,' I told her, closing the door and going to the anchor.

I pulled it up and hauled it onto the deck while Raul turned the boat and puttered out to where the plane cooled its belly in the river.

The bow of the *Deus* slipped beneath the wing, passing the blistered window that protruded like an insect's eye behind the yellow-tipped propellers.

Raul nudged us closer to the Catalina's fuselage and the plane door opened, a man leaning out to take the rope I threw to him.

Rocky hurried over, ignoring Raul's calls, but she had stopped barking and the man hardly acknowledged either her or me as he secured us together. He kept his head down, and when he was finished, he pulled his cap low and stepped aside for Leonardo to climb aboard.

The two men shared a few words, then Leonardo disappeared into the darkness of the plane's interior.

I waited, watching the dark space, glancing up at the pilot sitting in the cockpit, headphones around his neck. The window was open beside him and he was smoking a cigarette, drumming his fingers.

He lifted his large sunglasses and winked at me.

'What's taking so long?' Raul called from his place behind the wheel. I shrugged then glanced over at the section where Daniella was keeping out of sight. Rocky had lost interest in the plane and was sniffing at the crack in the door as if she were missing Daniella's company.

'Come here, girl,' I said, beckoning her over. 'Come away from there.'

She looked round at me, then at the door, as if deciding what was more interesting, then trotted over to me, toenails clicking on the deck.

When she was at my side, I rubbed her head and watched the plane, wondering if I should go after Leonardo. Maybe he needed my help. Just then, though, he reappeared, dragging a wooden crate across the floor of the plane.

About the size of a coffin, the box was constructed from rough-hewn wood and carried no markings or distinguishing features other than a coarse rope handle at either end. When it was close to the plane's door, the other man slid forward a wide gangplank to bridge the gap between the boat and the plane.

Leonardo took the far end of the crate and pushed it across the plank towards me so I could grab it and heft it onto the boat. Rocky stuck close to my legs, sniffing at the box, until I shooed her away.

Between us, Leonardo and I manhandled the crate onto the deck and stacked it beside the store cabin where Daniella was keeping out of sight.

'How many more of these?' I asked as Leonardo climbed back onto the plane, jumping over the gunwale and through the cargo door.

'Four,' he said, disappearing from sight again.

The top of the crate beside me had been prised open, so I guessed that's why Leonardo had taken so long. He'd been checking the contents.

Not caring that he would see me, I leaned down and pulled up the corner of the lid, shifting it to one side. Underneath was an oiled covering which I lifted to look at the weapons beneath.

Rocky came close, putting her nose in for a quick sniff then backing away as if she didn't like the smell.

'I wonder what these are for?' I said to her.

They were rifles, but not the kind used for hunting.

These guns were designed for killing men.

Five assault rifles were nestled together in a formal line, and I estimated from the depth of the crate that there would be at least another three layers of weapons in there.

Five crates containing twenty rifles each.

I closed my eyes for a moment, making the addition, using my fingers.

'A hundred?' I put a hand on Rocky's head. 'What the hell does anyone want with a hundred of these?'

They were the kind of weapons I hadn't seen since leaving Rio. Back then, boys bought weapons like these from corrupt policeman selling them from the boot of police vehicles, but they had been used. They were damaged and worn, just as likely to go off in your face as shoot a hole in your enemy.

These ones looked new and it made me wonder how they were connected to Sister Dolores Beckett. It was too much of a coincidence that she was headed to Mina dos Santos at the same time as a shipment of weapons like this. There were enough rifles here for a small army, but not an army led by a nun who fought for Indian rights. Perhaps an army, led by men who wanted to occupy more land; an army that would be glad if a woman like Sister Beckett were to disappear.

Her name was a reminder of the clipping folded in my pocket and, without intending it, my fingers felt for it nestling against my heart. That soft paper with the grainy picture and the illegible words had become a presence just as the shadow was a presence, the two of them fighting for space in my thoughts.

Sister Beckett was with me during the quiet moments of our journey and I was struggling over whether or not I would be able to do what Costa wanted. There was no obvious way out of it, though, and every time I imagined myself putting a knife to the nun's throat, I saw Sofia's face. I was ashamed of what I was going to do, and she would have been ashamed too.

Maybe if it had been someone else. Someone who deserved it.

I glanced up when I heard scraping from inside, then Leonardo came into view again, pushing another of the crates. He stood and put his hands on his hips. 'You like them?'

I shrugged.

'Maybe if you make this delivery on time I can do some kind of deal for you. A good price for one of them.' He grinned and there was something different about him. He seemed energised, and I put it down to having met the plane on time. Maybe there were consequences for him if he failed here.

'I have no use for one of these,' I told him.

Leonardo raised his eyebrows. 'I've seen men like you before, Zico. I *know* you could find a use for one of these.'

'But for a hundred?'

Leonardo looked confused for a moment, then smiled. 'Eighty,' he said. 'The last crate is for something else.'

'Ammunition?'

He raised both hands and pretended to sight down the barrel of a rifle at me. 'They're not water guns, Zico.'

'What're they for?'

'Killing people. What else?'

19

It didn't take long to load the remaining crates onto the *Deus*, and once it was done, Leonardo stayed on the boat, leaning across to speak to the man who had opened the cargo doors. I couldn't hear them over the sound of the idling engines, so I took a step back and looked up at the pilot.

Something had agitated him. From having been almost motionless, he was suddenly animated as if struck by an unexpected urgency. He grabbed the earphones, pulling them back on and twisting in his seat to shout to his partner. As soon as he did this, the man standing in the doorway looked in his direction, an expression of concern and surprise beneath the peak of his cap. There was a fraction of a second when he decided what to do, then he reacted, taking a step back and throwing the tethering rope onto the *Deus*. He dragged the gangplank back onto the plane with a couple of hard yanks, mock saluted Leonardo, then slammed the door just as the engines throttled hard.

'What's going on?' I asked Leonardo, but all he could do was shake his head as the seaplane moved away from us.

As soon as it was past the boat, gathering speed on the straight, flat stretch of the river, I saw what had sent them away in such a hurry.

Coming from the right fork in the river, maybe four hundred metres away and approaching with speed, a boat was skimming across the water. It was a small craft, much smaller than the *Deus*, and it must have been equipped with a good motor because it was gaining quickly. The old man gunned our engine and started to turn the *Deus*, but there was no way we were going to outrun the boat. If the people on board intended to catch us, there was no doubt they would.

'Police?' Leonardo turned to me.

'No,' I said, my eyes going from the approaching boat to the plane that was now gaining speed. 'Not here.'

Rocky sensed our tension, and mirrored it, pacing the deck beside me, stopping every now and then to watch the activity. She alternated between whining and barking, pushing against me one moment, then jumping up on the gunwale the next.

Leonardo kept an eye on her while trying to concentrate on the river as the plane's nose began to lift, the impossible bulk of its bloated belly rising out of the water, the sun glinting on the hull.

Further away, the boat approached.

Nearer and nearer by the second.

'Pirates?' he offered.

'Could be. They would have seen the plane land. There's always a chance.'

The Catalina lifted into the air, water cascading from its underside, engines droning as it climbed into the sky. It tracked away from us into the blue, rising to safety before banking as it slipped over the trees.

Leonardo pulled a pistol from beneath his shirt, a more sophisticated weapon than the *pistola* I had taken from him. He racked the slide on the automatic and held it loose in his right hand, obscuring it behind the gunwale, before meeting my eye and shrugging. 'I felt naked,' he said. 'And they had a spare on the plane.'

'Well, make sure you keep it cold for now,' I told him, pointing at the pistol. 'You don't know how things work out here. They might be anybody. Curious fishermen, locals looking to make a trade. Don't shoot anybody.'

Leonardo grinned and shrugged. 'Whatever you say, boss.'

I couldn't tell if he was excited at the prospect of a fight, or if he was just pleased that he'd had the chance to show me he was armed, but he was more animated than before. And when Rocky came between us, he put his foot on her and pushed her away, making her yelp in pain.

'Keep the damn dog away from me.' He pointed the weapon in her direction. 'I'll shoot it.'

Rocky turned on him, baring her teeth, so I grabbed her by the scruff and took her back to the wheelhouse, telling the old man to keep hold of her. 'Something's got into him,' I said. 'He's different.'

'Leonardo? Different how?'

'I don't know exactly. Excited. Revved up.'

'He was worried about missing the plane, maybe he's just pleased to pick up.'

'Those boxes are full of guns,' I said. 'You have any idea why they need eighty assault rifles at Mina dos Santos?' I couldn't help wondering whether Sister Beckett was connected to this delivery of weapons. Something was happening along the Rio das Mortes; that much was clear.

The old man shook his head.

'You look like shit,' I told him. 'Feeling any better?'

'I'll survive.'

'Sure you will.' I looked out at the smaller boat. It was two hundred metres away now, the sound of its motor coming to us across the water. Leonardo was waiting, watching with interest. 'I'd better get over there.'

I jogged back along the deck, reaching the gunwale just as Daniella emerged from the housing. The metal door squealed and she stepped out saying, 'They gone? Can I come out now?'

'Not yet. Stay inside.'

'Why? What now? It stinks in there.'

'You'll get—'

'I haven't got used to it yet,' she said.

'Please.' I gently pushed her back inside. 'Please. Just for a while longer.' I left the door ajar, so that some fresh air might find its way into the hot, dark interior, and turned my attention to the boat which was now almost upon us. I took the revolver from its holster on my hip, and stood beside Leonardo, hiding the weapon behind the gunwale.

*

The boat wasn't big, perhaps twice the size of the one secured to the back of the *Deus*. It was light and low to the water, skipping across the surface as it skimmed around the sandbanks, but it wasn't a long-range boat. There was a chance it could have come from Piratinga – sometimes the locals used them to come upriver and fish for a couple of days – but it would have to be carrying spare fuel, otherwise it would never make it back.

There were two men on board. One sitting at the stern, operating the tiller, a red cap on his head, and the other at the centre of the boat, a rifle across his knees.

'That a shotgun?' Leonardo said without looking at me.

'Yeah, they look like hunters. Fishermen, maybe.'

'Only one shot in that thing.'

I looked at him. 'Stay calm. They're probably nobody.'

As they came near, the driver slowed the engine and the other man stood up, resting the butt-plate of the shotgun against his hip and raising his left hand as he shouted, 'Oi!'

I waved back and smiled. *'Tudo bem?'*

'Bom,' the man nodded. He had a serious face beneath the straw hat and he shifted his shotgun so he was holding it in both hands. If he wanted to, he could raise it and aim it in just a few seconds.

When the driver cut the engine, the smaller boat drifted towards us, skewing in the current, so that it knocked against the tyres on the hull of the *Deus*. He threw up a rope which I wrapped around a cleat on the gunwale, then he sat back down and watched us.

For a moment, no one spoke as the smaller boat twisted in the current so that it was at a right angle to the *Deus*.

'We saw the plane,' said the man with the shotgun, breaking the silence. He was skinny, all angles and bone. His T-shirt hung off him like it was still on the hanger.

The bottom of their boat was flooded with four or five inches of water, reels of fishing wire washing from side to side. There were four jerrycans at the back, so I might have been right about them coming from Piratinga, but I didn't recognise their faces.

There was a catfish in the bottom of the boat, too, a big one.

'Pirarara,' I said. 'Good catch. That was you?'

He shook his head and pointed with his thumb at the man sitting by the motor. 'Took him close to an hour to bring it in.' His eyes flicked from me to Leonardo and back again. 'Thirsty work.'

'You planning on shooting the next one?' Leonardo asked, drawing the man's attention.

'Eh?' He looked confused, then glanced down at his shotgun and raised it a touch.

I sensed Leonardo's tension beside me.

'It's for the *paca*,' the man said. The large rodent had good meat and it was a treasured prize for hunters. 'Maybe a boar.'

'Not many of those on the water,' Leonardo said.

The man showed us a nervous smile and shrugged. 'Maybe in the forest.'

'Well, it was good to meet you.' I was eager to end the conversation. Leonardo was winding tighter and tighter, becoming twitchy beside me.

'Water,' the man said. 'You have water?' The sinews in his arms loosened a touch and the shotgun hung a little lower as he showed us an embarrassed grin, full of stained teeth. 'My brother came past about an hour ago and took our water.'

'We haven't seen anyone else on the river,' Leonardo told him.

'Maybe he went a different way. There's channels and ... which way did you come from?' the man asked.

'Which way did he go?' Leonardo replied.

I could feel the tension crackling around him like electricity and when I glanced down, I saw his fingers wrapped around the butt of his automatic. His knuckles were white, as if he were squeezing the handle hard enough to crack the grips.

I had to make him relax. He was starting to feel more dangerous by the second.

'We have water,' I said to the man before turning to Leonardo. 'Why don't you get them some? There's bottles in the cooler box.'

I thought it would diffuse the situation, give Leonardo something to do, but instead he stared at me and shook his head. 'You get the water.'

As we glared at each other, I caught movement out of the corner of my eye. Leonardo spotted it too, and we turned to the man standing in the boat. But what I saw and what Leonardo saw were two different things. I saw a man stepping forward to come closer to the gunwale of the *Deus*. I saw a man coming to accept our gift of water. Leonardo saw something else.

He saw a man who was preparing to attack us.

'Stay where you are.' Leonardo lifted his pistol, gripping it with both hands as he pointed it at the nervous, angular man.

I put out a hand to stop him, reaching over the pistol and pushing it down, but the fisherman flinched back in surprise, lifting both hands in a natural act of self-protection. As he stepped away, though, he caught his left heel on the snout of the catfish lying dead in the bottom of the boat. He slipped backwards, his legs collapsing beneath him, the barrel of the shotgun lifting.

His weapon discharged with a loud, flat boom.

Out there in the silence of the river, it was like thunder.

Both Leonardo and I ducked behind the gunwale and there was a sound of heavy rain as the swarm of shot flew high and wide of us, peppering the treetops on the bank behind the *Deus*. We stared at each other for a fraction of a second, assessing the situation, then we both popped up, into the cloud of smoke, weapons trained on the boat.

A small group of blue macaws, startled by the commotion, had taken to the sky with harsh calls that faded as they distanced themselves from us, and then everything was mute. Even the insects were dumb.

We looked down at the man lying back in the boat, his partner white eyed and open mouthed. As soon as he recovered from the shock, he dropped the shotgun and held up both hands to show it was an accident. He hadn't meant for this to happen.

I allowed myself to breathe, lowering my pistol.

'Sorry,' he said. 'Sorry. I didn't mean to ... Please don't—'

Leonardo fired four times.

His first two shots struck the man with the shotgun, pushing him against the slatted seat. Holes appeared in his white T-shirt, right over his heart, and blood puffed from the wounds, soaking into the material and spreading as his life evaporated into the scorching afternoon.

The unarmed man operating the outboard hardly even had the chance to begin to stand before Leonardo's third shot hit him in the face.

The lead caught him at an angle across the bridge of his nose, knocking his head back and to the side as it gouged through the cartilage and collapsed his right eye, shattering the bone around the socket. He screamed once in pain before Leonardo's fourth shot silenced him.

20

The gunshots didn't echo. They didn't linger or call their triumph. They just sank into the water, rose to the heavens and vanished into the hot air around us.

The smell of cartridge propellant hung above the gunwale in the dissipating cloud from the shotgun and the wisps of spectral smoke from Leonardo's pistol. The blue tendrils twisted in the stillness, breaking up, drifting, and becoming nothing. My ears rang with a high-pitched mosquito whine, and my head was filled with a million thoughts as I looked down into the boat where the men lay dead.

I stared in silence for what felt like a long time before I turned to Leonardo, seeing the way his eyes grew wide and then narrowed again, his pupils dilated, his Adam's apple rising and falling in his throat.

His mouth opened a touch, the tip of his tongue snaking out to wet his lips then darting back in again, and I knew that he had enjoyed the killing.

The moment had given him a feeling of power and I could see in him the surge of the thrill, the rush of pointing and squeezing. For him, there had been a moment of joy in taking those lives – ending them in a twitch of time so brief it was impossible to measure.

I had seen people before who enjoyed it the way Leonardo did; people who took more from it than just a feeling of power.

Taking a deep breath sucked the gunsmoke into my nostrils, and I tasted it in the back of my throat. 'He slipped,' I said. 'That's all. He slipped. He slipped and you killed them.'

Raul remained behind the wheel, waiting for the next move. I willed him without words to hold onto Rocky and keep his hands away from the revolver tucked under the dash. I didn't want this to escalate. No more blood needed to be spilled here.

'What the hell did you do that for?' I was controlling my anger. There was nothing I could do now.

'He nearly killed us.' Leonardo's dry mouth clicked. 'Nearly blew our damn heads off.'

'He slipped,' I said again. 'It was an accident.'

Beside us, the door to the covered section scraped open. The squeal of the rusted hinge was like a scream in the calm. Shrill and sharp.

'What happened?' Daniella's words were tentative and softly spoken.

I held out my left hand, fingers spread wide, signalling for her to stay where she was. 'You didn't need to do that,' I said to Leonardo.

He sniffed, turning his head to look at me. His hands were still raised, the automatic still pointed at the boat on the water below us.

'There was no reason to kill them.' I spoke through my teeth, desperate to stay calm. My fingers were tight around the handle of my pistol.

'Kill who?' Daniella asked. 'What—'

'What's done is done.' Leonardo snorted hard and turned towards me. He lowered his weapon, but both hands still gripped it, ready to raise it again in a heartbeat. 'We going to have a problem about this?' he asked, not taking his eyes from mine.

'You're a liability,' I said. 'Those men ... You didn't need to do that.' I glanced down at his pistol then looked back at his eyes once more. His pupils were still dilated and he had a crazed appearance. Something about Leonardo felt even more dangerous and unpredictable than before. It wasn't just that he had shot the men in the boat, it was something else. His movements were more exaggerated; his words were spoken more quickly.

Beside us, Daniella shifted, as if to come and look, but her movement alarmed Leonardo and he jerked in her direction, the pistol raising.

She stopped and flinched away, surprised by his sudden reaction.

'It's all right.' I held up a hand. 'It's all right. Daniella's not going anywhere.'

Daniella took a step back and Leonardo nodded. He closed his eyes and took a deep breath as if trying to collect his thoughts.

'So,' he said, looking at me again. '*Are* we going to have a problem about this?'

'No. What's done is done.' I repeated his own words, keen to calm him down. The way he was, I was worried he might try to kill the rest of us.

'Then it's time to go, right?'

'Not yet.' I swallowed away the bad taste in my mouth. 'We need to clear this up. We don't want someone coming past here and finding this.'

'No time. We need to make our delivery by—'

'We have to make time,' I said, keeping my voice steady. 'Or we deliver late. Either way, we need to clear this up. We don't want someone following us, looking for murderers.'

'There's no one out here. Look at this place.'

'We don't know that.'

He thought about it, eyes shifting to look at Daniella, then back at me again.

'And I'm going to need your weapon,' I told him. 'No one carries on this boat but me.'

Leonardo drew in a deep breath, his nostrils flaring. He tilted his head to one side as if he had an itch but didn't want to take his hands from his weapon in order to scratch it.

'We'll clean up,' he said after a moment. 'Maybe you're right about that, but if you want this gun, you'll have to take it from me. And the only way that's going to happen is if I'm dead.'

I relaxed my right arm, tightened my finger on the trigger of the pistol. I could try it. I might be quicker. I might be able to raise my weapon high enough to hit him somewhere below the waist. His feet, his knees, maybe his groin. But he might react too quickly. He might see it in my eyes, see the movement of my arm. And then I would be gone and Raul and Daniella would be alone with him.

'I can see what you're thinking, Zico. Don't do it.'

'OK,' I nodded. 'Together.'

'Together.'

I began to raise my revolver, slowly, turning it to the side, pointing it away from Leonardo. He did the same thing, lifting his pistol until both our weapons were pointing at the sky. Together, we placed our thumbs over the hammer, releasing and easing them back into position.

'We done with this?' he asked me.

'You tell me.'

'OK,' he said. 'We're done with this.' And, as if nothing had happened, he tucked away his pistol and turned to lean on the gunwale. 'We better get this mess cleared up, then.'

'Yeah,' I said, holstering my revolver. 'Let's do that.'

21

Daniella was paler than I'd ever seen her. Paler even than the time she'd had food poisoning that kept her in bed a week. The colour of her skin was leached of all its beauty. She had started to shake as she stared down at the boat, but was unable to look away. Human nature is human nature. We subject ourselves to things we know we might not be able to endure. We do it to test ourselves, to scratch an itch, to punish ourselves. Whatever the reason, we can't help but look at atrocity. Even if it's only to reassure ourselves that our own life could always be worse.

I pulled her away from the gunwale, away from the tableau of death on the small boat, and buried her face against my shoulder.

'Don't look at them,' I said. 'Go up there with Raul and help keep Rocky out of the way – I don't want her making Leonardo angry. The way he is, he might go off again at any moment.'

She stayed like that, breathing against me. Her whole body was trembling, and I tried to imagine what she was feeling. For me, this sight was not new. I had seen all manner of death. Daniella, though, would not be accustomed to it and the image would be burned into her mind. Perhaps she didn't know *what* to feel. Revulsion, fear, sadness, anger. Maybe she felt all those things at once.

'Can you do that for me?' I asked. 'Stay with Rocky?'

Daniella leaned back. 'Did you ... is this what you ... ?'

'I didn't do this.'

Daniella nodded, an almost imperceptible movement, and reached up to touch my face. Her fingers paused against my cheek before she snatched them away. It was as if she had connected

with my skin and seen what was in my head. I had not done *this* –
what she had seen today – but she knew I must have done things
like it. The old man brought me on the boat to protect him. I was
armed. There were whispered rumours in Piratinga that linked me
to men like Costa and the Branquinos, so Daniella knew this kind
of violence was not beyond me. I wanted to reassure her; to tell her
I had never done it like this. I wanted to explain that I didn't gun
men down for the enjoyment of it, that I had never killed a man
who didn't deserve it, but there were no words that could diminish
the horror she had just witnessed. And there was a newspaper
clipping in my shirt pocket, giving presence to a woman whose
death would make me just like Leonardo. Perhaps worse.

'Go with Raul,' I said to her. 'Sit with him a while.'

The old man extended his hand and took Daniella's, encouraging her to follow him. He led her past the wheelhouse, going to
sit at the bow and look out across the river. Rocky sat with them
as he spoke to her, his voice a low murmur in the quiet air. I
couldn't hear what he was saying but the sounds were temperate
and soothing.

I watched them a while, sitting together, the old man stooped
in sickness, Daniella rigid with shock and revulsion.

Beneath us, the boat moved gently with the current of the river.

'It's difficult for some people,' Leonardo said. 'They're not like
us. This doesn't bother us like it bothers them.'

'You don't know anything about me.' My words were whispered
over a dry throat and formed by a dry tongue. I was filled with
concern for Daniella and anger at Leonardo. There was a frustration at the hopelessness of my situation; that I could have done
nothing to prevent him from his murderous actions. It was the
same feeling that had burned in me when I found Antonio. The
same I had felt when I found Sofia.

'I know you've killed people,' he said. 'I can see it in you.'

'We are not alike.'

'You've done this before,' he prodded. 'You've killed people.'

'I never killed a man who asked me for water.' My lips hardly
moved as I spoke.

'What difference does that make?' Leonardo shrugged.

'Don't compare us,' I said. 'We're not alike. These men ... didn't need to die. They were thirsty, that's all.'

'They're not thirsty now,' Leonardo smirked.

'Don't joke about the dead.'

'That some country superstition?'

'And don't try to piss me off more than you already have.'

Leonardo's face fell, the smile dropping from his lips like an unwanted annoyance. 'You sure we're not going to have a problem about this?' he said, moving a hand towards his waist.

'No,' I told him, staying his hand and looking him in the eye. 'We're not. There's money coming our way, so we're going to get this job done and you're going to pay us.'

His smile edged back.

In his mind, he was in charge now.

My mind was on other things, though. I was wondering how long Leonardo and I could be together on this boat before one of us killed the other.

22

Out there, in the middle of the river, it was like no place on earth. It was an inferno. A place of suffering. There was no sound but the gentle wash of the water against the two boats. The occasional knock as they came together and separated. Came together and separated.

Without shade, the sun was almost unbearable. Even with the day beginning to wane, it was hot and without mercy. Heat like that could drive a man to insanity. It seared the skin and tortured the mind. No one could survive long in a place like that.

Already, the insects had come. It was impossible to know how they had sensed it or where they had come from, but they had caught scent of what had happened here and had gathered to take their nutrition from it.

Flies blackened the patches of blood, as they had in Antonio's apartment when I found him yesterday. They rose in annoyance when I jumped down into the boat and disturbed them; the lazy buzz of their wings was quiet only when they settled back to their meal.

Other creatures had come to investigate too, drawn by the spray that had misted across the water. They had taken the few pieces of the driver that had settled on the surface, and now dark shapes drifted, half unseen in the murk of the river. There was an occasional flash of fish close to the boat as they searched and squabbled, and a few metres away something larger broke the surface and slipped back under before I could identify it.

Waving away the flies once more, I grabbed the dead man by

the motor and dragged him towards me, glancing over at the *Deus*, making sure Daniella was still with Raul.

'You going to come down here and help?' I said to Leonardo, who had made no attempt to move. 'This is your mess.'

'You want me to come in there?' He frowned.

'You got some kind of a problem with that? You scared?'

'No.' But he hesitated and his face was set like stone when he lifted a leg to climb down. His grip was tight on the gunwale of the *Deus* when he lowered himself.

'This is going to delay us,' Leonardo said, trying to keep steady in the smaller boat.

'You should have thought about that before you pulled the trigger.' I hauled the man further along, rocking the boat and leaving a shining trail of blood as I lay him beside his friend.

'*Filho da puta* nearly blew my head off.' Leonardo flicked his chin at the dead man. 'What do you—'

As he spoke, something large thumped into the underside of the boat, rocking us to one side in a violent motion. Leonardo flinched, losing his balance and dipping the boat first to one side and then the other as he tried to remain upright.

'Keep still,' I hissed at him. 'You'll turn us over.'

'What the fuck *was* that?' He squatted, putting his hands on either side of the boat, snatching them away when he felt how hot the metal had become.

'I don't know,' I said. 'A fish maybe. Or something else.'

'Like what?'

'A *boto* like before?' I suggested. 'Or maybe Anhangá?'

'What?'

'It's a devil,' I told him. 'Maybe it saw what you did.'

'Devils don't swim,' he said, but he put his hand to the *figa* around his neck without realising he had done it.

'Anhangá can be anything he wants to be,' I said.

Leonardo looked into the water, watching for shapes moving down there, then scanned the distant shore and shook his head. 'There are no devils.' He glanced down at the dead men. 'And these two deserved it anyway.'

I looked at the man who had asked us for water. His shirt was soaked red and his eyes had rolled back so that only the whites were visible.

'Have you calmed down now?' I asked.

Leonardo looked up at me as if he didn't understand.

'Something got into you,' I said. 'What was it?'

He shrugged. 'Maybe one of your devils.'

'Well, if we see anyone else, I want you to keep that gun under control. We can't leave a trail of—'

'Don't give me orders.'

'I'm not giving you orders, I'm just ... Look,' I sighed, 'we need to secure them to the boat. I'll get a rope.'

As I climbed aboard the *Deus*, Leonardo collected the shotgun and set about searching the men's belongings for spare shells and anything else worth taking.

When I came back to him, he was loading the shotgun and laying it to one side.

'Give me a hand,' I said, wrapping the rope around the men, securing it to the slatted seats of the outboard. 'We need to make sure it's tight. We'll sink the boat with them tied to it, but we want them to stay down there. After a few days, there won't be anything left of them.'

'I knew you'd done this before.' Leonardo looked at me, our faces just a few inches apart, both of us sweating from the exertion in the afternoon heat. 'You could be a useful man to know if you weren't so bad tempered.'

'Just keep tying.' I lifted the hem of my T-shirt to wipe my brow.

Behind us the forest had returned to life after the sudden intrusion, the birds settling and feeling safe to sing again. The *uirapuru* bird began its cheerful lilt and I looked down at the dead men, thinking that if they had heard it, perhaps they would have had better luck today.

When we were done, I called Raul, waiting for him to come to the side of the *Deus* and look down. Rocky left Daniella and followed on his heels. She sensed that things were not right on the boat and she was sticking close to her master.

The old man's eyes were bloodshot, and perspiration formed beads on his brow.

'How is she?' I kept my voice low, not wanting Leonardo to hear.

'Fine.' He took off his hat and fanned himself. 'She's strong. We don't breed weak women out here, there's no room for them.'

I took a deep breath and wiped the sweat from my face. 'She knows this wasn't me, doesn't she? You told her ...'

'She knows,' he said. 'But she knows your reputation and she knows why you're here—'

'What?' For a moment, I wondered how they could know why I was here. How did they know about Sister Beckett?

'To protect the boat.' Raul looked confused at my reaction. 'That's why you're here, Zico.'

'Yeah. Sure.'

'She's always known you've probably done things, and she's lived with it and ignored it because it's a part of life here. You're not so unusual. But this?' He shifted his eyes to the bodies in the boat, tied together, face to face, ready for an eternity beneath the silt-laden water. 'Knowing is one thing, Zico, seeing it is another. It's ugly.'

'But she'll be OK.'

'Of course.'

'And you?' I asked. 'How are you feeling?'

'I've been sick before, Zico.'

'But not like this, right?'

The old man lowered his eyes. 'Maybe not.'

I wanted to do or say something that would make Daniella better and make Raul's sickness leave him, but in the past few days I seemed to have lost control of everything. There was nothing I could do to put anything right. 'We need to sink it,' I said. 'Where's it deepest?'

Raul looked out across the river. 'On this stretch? Just exactly where you'd think.'

'No sandbanks under there? Nothing shifting?'

'Do it right in the middle.' He pointed. 'If you sink it there, it'll be gone for ever.'

I followed the line of his finger and contemplated the terrible blackness below the water.

There was so much life and death even in the places where light can never reach.

23

'You really think all this is worth it?' Leonardo said as I steered the outboard into the centre of the river. 'You ask me, we should've just left them to rot.'

I looked back through the wisps of smoke from the engine, seeing Daniella with her hands on the gunwale, watching as we moved away from them.

'Leave a boat on the river with bodies in it?' I said, raising my voice over the sound of the outboard. 'Men who've been shot?'

'Anybody could've done it.'

'And if someone comes this way in an hour? They find this and catch us up? If we're the only boat on the river, they'd know it was us.'

'And if they come round that fork now? They find us like this?' He indicated the bodies at our feet.

'Then we deal with it. But this way, we may not have to.'

'You worried about the police?' Leonardo had unbuttoned his shirt so it blew open in the breeze as we moved quickly across the river. His pistol was tucked into the front of his waistband like the boys in the *favela* used to carry them when they were strutting about the streets, maybe going down to the *baile* to make some sales. There was a *baile* most nights, everyone coming out into the square to dance and drink. The air was filled with the smell of frying *bolinhos de bacalhao* and *acarajé* and the girls would shake their backsides and the boys would try to chat them up. I used to go with my friends, Sofia with hers, even when I was just twelve years old and she was fourteen. She always found me and dragged me home, though, before the trouble started.

'There's worse things than police,' I said. 'If you kill a man, you have to be worried about more than the police. If someone killed *your* friend, what would *you* do?'

'I don't have any friends.'

'A brother, then. A sister. Mother or father? There's always someone.'

Leonardo looked away, his eyes glazing for a moment, becoming unfocused.

'That person,' I said, pointing at him. 'The one you're thinking of right there – what would you do if this happened to *them?*'

'I'd find the man who did it and I'd kill him.'

I nodded. '*That's* why we have to do this.'

Before reaching the centre of the river, I cut the engine and we drifted the last few metres. A gentle breeze had risen now that the afternoon was growing old, and it rippled the surface of the water, lifting the fumes from the engine and blowing it around us.

I looked up at the sky so I didn't have to see the bodies by my feet. There were a few clouds there now. Tendrils of white like the spider webs I'd seen stretched from tree to tree in the forest.

'So who was it?' I asked.

'Hm?'

'The person you were thinking about just then. Who was it?'

'No one you need to know about.'

Leonardo was a man uncomfortable in his surroundings. He didn't like where he was and was probably here for money, like I was, and because he didn't know how to do anything else. Like I didn't.

It troubled me to think there might be something of Leonardo in me and, if there was, then it was a part of me I wanted to cut away and throw into the river. It was the shadow I had been unable to leave behind; the darkness that Costa wanted to nurture in me.

And now I wanted to lose it more than ever before. Sitting in the boat with Leonardo, seeing what kind of person he was, I wanted more than anything to be *un*like him.

I cast my eyes across the river, seeing the ripples in the places where the currents moved, and the eddies caused by the *Deus* as it caught up with us.

As soon as it was near enough, I went to the stern of the outboard and reached into the water slopping about in the bottom of the boat. I felt for the bung and unscrewed it. The river immediately began to wash in so we climbed aboard the *Deus*, Leonardo taking the shotgun with him, stamping his feet at Rocky when she came too close.

'Keep the damn dog away from me.' Leonardo pointed at her and I exchanged a glance with Raul.

The old man nodded and took hold of her, going to join Daniella at the bow, out of sight.

When they were gone, Leonardo and I turned to watch the motor boat fill with water.

'Throw the shotgun overboard,' I said. 'If someone sees it, recognises it, they'll put this together. You don't want anything to get in the way of your delivery.'

He looked at the shotgun for a moment then dropped it over the side.

I shook my head at him, wishing we hadn't brought him along. Things would have been so much simpler. With just Raul and me on board, everything was uncomplicated. He did his thing and I did mine. A partnership in which each of us knew our standing. With Leonardo and Daniella on board, though, everything was harder, there was more to think about; more that needed attention.

Raul had moved into the wheelhouse now and was sitting hunched over the wheel. Daniella was at the bow, standing with her back to us, her face lifted to the sky as if she were praying.

I needed to get her home.

I glanced at Leonardo, then looked back at the motor boat again, the two of us silent as we watched the river rising up to claim it for its own. We stayed like that until the bodies were covered and the boat skewed and tipped backwards. The heavy motor dragged it down and soon the boat disappeared from view under the murky water.

There was no sign of it but for a few bubbles.

'You think that's them?' Leonardo said.

'Hmm?'

'The bubbles. You think that's what they had left in them?'

I shrugged. 'Does it matter?'

'Not really. I just never saw anyone drown before.'

'They didn't drown,' I reminded him. 'You shot them.'

'Yeah,' he nodded. 'That's true.' He turned to look first at Daniella standing on the bow, then at the old man sitting in the wheelhouse. 'But maybe that's something I should see. Someone drowning, I mean.'

24

The old man throttled the engine and pushed us back downriver with our cargo of death on board and the last of the bubbles from Leonardo's victims still rising to break the surface of the water.

I watched our unwanted passenger settle into his seat and turn his face to the wind, and I contemplated his presence for a moment before clearing my mind and going to Daniella's side.

When I touched her arm, she drew it away as if from something she was loath to acknowledge, then she softened and allowed her fingers to brush mine.

For a while we didn't speak. We stood side by side in silence, only the slightest caress from the callused skin at the very tips of our fingers.

'What he did...' I broke the spell, my throat dry, my voice insignificant. 'What he did—'

'It's OK,' she said. 'I just... need a moment. I've never seen anything like that.'

'It's ugly.'

'But *you* have. You've seen it.'

I nodded. 'Yes.'

'And done it?'

My heart shrank and tightened like a dry sponge. I closed my eyes. 'Yes.'

'I know it, Zico. I think I've always known it. I just... I pretend I *don't* know it. It's not you, it's not who you are, but it *is* who you are. It's like you're good and bad at the same time, does that make sense?'

I didn't answer.

'I'm sorry I didn't listen when you told me about him. You're not like him, though, are you?'

'No.' She *couldn't* think that. I was nothing like Leonardo. Nothing at all.

'What is it that makes you different?' She looked at me now, her eyes narrowed against the falling sun. 'I need to know.'

'He enjoys it.'

'Then why do you ... How can you—'

'Because I feel nothing.'

She swallowed as tears glistened in her eyes. 'Not ever?'

'Only for this. Not other things. Not *you*, Daniella.'

She watched my face, then looked away to the breeze. 'I don't understand.'

'Nor do I.' I didn't want to talk about it with her. I didn't want to talk about the fact that I had killed other men. I didn't want her to know the anger I felt at them when I pulled the trigger. I didn't want to talk about what happened to Sofia. 'Maybe it's because I've always seen it,' I said. 'Because it's always been there.'

'Always?'

I nodded. 'Maybe something switched off inside. Maybe it switched off a little bit each time I saw something that stayed in my head and wouldn't come out. Maybe it's how my soul decided to deal with my life.' I put out my hand and wiped a tear from her cheek. 'This is the first time you've seen something like this. It'll stay in your mind, if you let it. You'll see it in your sleep, in each face you look at, in every dark moment. You have to push it away.'

'That's what *you* did?'

'I don't know.' I took her hand and encouraged her to sit beside me. 'Maybe.' But I hadn't done that with the image I still carried of the last time I had seen Sofia. I had let it haunt me.

'Tell me about it.'

'Hmm?'

'The first time you saw ...'

I shook my head. 'You don't want to hear it.'

'Please,' she said.

I ran my tongue over my teeth and wondered if this could ever be a good idea, but Daniella put her arm through mine and waited.

I sighed. 'I was nine years old. Sitting on a step with a girl I knew, called Alicia. I remember her face. It's still right here.' I tapped my forehead. 'Except maybe it isn't her I remember at all. Maybe it's just my mind making it up. I remember her dark brown eyes, the way her hair came forward onto her cheeks, the light brown tinted with ginger streaks from the sun or from not eating properly, I don't know which. She was always dirty, but we all were.'

'Who was she?'

'Just another kid. Eleven or twelve years old. She was a lookout for a bunch of boys selling drugs, but I knew she made money in other ways, doing things for people who liked children.'

Daniella looked up at me, but I didn't meet her eyes.

'We talked about kid's stuff, mostly; sitting on the step drinking from a Coke can we'd stolen. Always the same place, my spot. It's where I set up every day, calling to people as they passed, hardly even looking down at me sitting there.'

'You asked them for money?'

'I polished their shoes. Pai didn't earn much, so I polished shoes and Sofia helped in the bakery. Things changed after Pai started to drink, though.'

Daniella waited for me to go on.

'One time, sitting there, not working, she went quiet and looked down the street at a man who was coming towards us. He was wearing a suit, which wasn't so unusual, all kinds of people lived in the *favela*, not just people without jobs, but I remember it, that's all. A brown suit. And as he came towards us, I thought I recognised him. I might have cleaned his shoes sometime, and found myself looking down at his feet to see if they needed a polish. He had his eyes on us, as if he was coming over, and I thought he was going to ask for a shoe clean, but the girl beside me started to stand and I realised he was looking at her, not me. They seemed to know each other so maybe she'd done things for him. The kind of things that happen in narrow alleys, where the houses are close together and the roofs almost join. Dark places.'

Daniella's expression was a mix of sadness and horror, but she didn't say anything. She just shook her head and waited for me to go on.

'My friend knew how to take their money. She knew how to give them what they wanted. I saw her smile at him, drop her hip like a *puta*, flick her hair. And the man? He came closer, pulled a gun from his pocket and pointed it at her, almost touching her. He fired just once.

'She fell onto me, sitting in my lap, her head dropping back onto my shoulder, blood coming out of her, and I stared up at the man and he stopped to look at what he'd done, then he spat on us and walked away. I never knew why he did it.'

Daniella puffed her cheeks and breathed hard, shaking her head. 'And you were nine years old?'

'Maybe ten.' I shrugged and looked away, remembering that Sofia was the only other person I had told about this.

Daniella put her hand on the side of my head, her smallest finger brushing my ear, then she pulled me towards her. She kissed me with lips still damp from tears and eased my face into her shoulder. 'You poor thing,' she whispered.

'I survived.' My words were muffled.

'Yes,' she said. 'You survived.'

25

'How you feeling, old man?' I was coming back from the bow, raising my voice over the sound of the engine. 'Still bad?'

He lifted a hand to pinch the bridge of his nose. 'It's like someone stuck their fingers in my brain and twisted them around.'

The whites of his eyes were shot through with tiny rivers of burst vessels, and he was having trouble focusing on me. His skin was pale and his shirt was soaked with perspiration. His breathing was heavy.

He forced a smile, as if to reassure me, but I was afraid for him. His fever was worsening.

'You want me to take the wheel?' I asked.

'No. You need to watch Leonardo.'

'You're a stubborn old man.'

'And you're a cheeky boy.'

I let his comment rest and watched the way he scanned the vastness of river. Where we were now, the water stretched as far as I could see and the banks were a blurred dark line, shimmering in the heat haze.

The muscles in the old man's face twitched and contracted as if he were in pain. I wanted to do something for him, but I knew he wouldn't let me. The best I could do was let him keep his dignity.

'You know what's in those crates, right?' I said, trying to think about something else. 'All those guns back there? All that ammunition? What do you think they're for?'

'Not my business.'

'Looks to me like someone's starting a war.' A nun who fights for Indian rights and a payload of guns both heading to the same place? It had to mean something and I was desperate to ask the old man's opinion but I couldn't tell him about Sister Beckett. I would have to explain how I knew about her and he would connect it to Costa. 'Why do they need weapons like that at a mine if it's not to make some kind of trouble?'

'It's better not to know.'

I nodded and took the cap from my head. I held it by the peak and slapped it against my leg. 'How long d'you think you can keep doing this?'

'This?'

'Working like this.'

'Don't know,' he said. 'As long as it takes, I suppose.'

'And then Imperatriz. Be with your son.' I pulled the cap back onto my head.

'*Sim*. And then Imperatriz.'

Looking at him now, though, it occurred to me that maybe too much of a man's life is taken up looking for something else, something *better*, and too little is passed with the understanding of what he has, and what he really wants.

I looked up at Daniella sitting on the bow and wondered if this was how it was meant to be. Maybe I didn't need more money, more work, more of anything. Maybe I *already* had everything, right here on this boat.

'We've got about an hour of sunlight left,' the old man said. 'We should find somewhere to stop.' Already, he was nudging the *Deus* towards the western bank.

'No, we should keep going. We need to get you home.' The thought of the old man spending the night out here was a worrying one.

'We'll never get there before sundown,' he said, 'and I don't want to be on the river then.' Daylight ended with suddenness out here, and once the night came, the darkness was total.

'We've done it before. We'll take it slow and—'

'I'm tired, Zico. We all are. We've got no business being on the river at night in this state. If we hit something and go down in the dark, there's no escaping it. No one will even know we were there.'

'We won't hit anything, we'll—'

'Please.' He put a hand on my shoulder. 'I need to rest. Let me rest. I'll be stronger in the morning.' His chest wheezed with each breath as the fever spread through him and when he looked at me, the desperation was clear in his eyes. He was exhausted and he needed me to support him. He was right to think he was in no state to be on the river at night, and I didn't want to navigate the darkness on my own.

'All right.' I nodded.

He showed me a weak smile of relief. 'We can land over there.' He pointed to a gentle inlet on the river, a place where the bank had fallen away into a beach of white sand dotted with bleached driftwood and tufts of dry grass. A pair of caiman was there, lying with their mouths open to catch the last of the day's sun.

The old man moved the wheel with the palm of his hand and allowed us to drift towards the shore, aiming the bow towards the white sand that lounged at the water's edge.

The caiman on the beach snatched their jaws shut and darted away as we approached. They disappeared beneath the water with little more than a ripple.

Raul cut the noisy engine, so the propeller would be motionless if it made contact with the riverbed, and he let the momentum of the boat take us forward. The gentle vee bottom had a shallow draught and allowed us to move close to the bank.

'What's going on?' Leonardo came up from the stern, where he'd been sitting with the cargo. 'What are you doing?'

'We have to stop.' Raul's voice was weak. 'It'll be dark soon.'

'What is it with you? We haven't got time to rest. I need to get this delivered by—'

'What's the hurry?' I said. 'What are the guns for, Leonardo?'

'Not your concern. All you need to know is that if they're not delivered on time, you won't get paid.'

'Well, we can't travel at night,' Raul told him. 'It's just how it is.'

Leonardo came right to the wheelhouse and looked down at the old man. 'Then we'll stop when it gets dark.'

Sensing the threat in his voice, Rocky growled and jumped to her feet, making Leonardo step back. His hand dropped towards his waistband, where the pistol was tucked away.

I moved between him and the old man and saw Leonardo think about it. He slipped his hand closer to his waist. His finger and thumb rubbed together as he considered drawing the weapon.

I kept my eyes on his and shook my head. 'Don't.'

He bit his lower lip and held my stare.

'This is a good place to stop.' I tried to break the tension. 'There might not be others.'

Leonardo swallowed. 'When it gets *dark*,' he insisted and I understood that he didn't want to back down. I had to give him a good enough reason.

'I know you want to keep going,' I said, 'and so do I, but it gets dark quick here. It takes you by surprise. You don't want to be on the river in the dark.'

He took a deep breath and clenched his teeth. His mind was working hard, trying to decide if we were tricking him somehow. He was determined not to look weak.

'If we touch the wrong part of the river, we could end up on a sandbank and be stuck out here,' I said. 'There'd be no chance of getting your guns to Mina dos Santos then.'

Leonardo blinked and I saw the first hint that he was trying to relax. He dropped his hand a touch.

'It's the best thing,' I said. 'We can set off again at first light.'

He dropped his hand further and slapped it on his thigh. He nodded and looked at Daniella who came to stand on the other side of the wheelhouse.

'There's logs, too,' she said, putting a hand on Rocky's head.

'Logs?' Leonardo looked her up and down in a way I didn't like. 'What are you talking about? What logs?'

'The loggers use this river,' Daniella said. 'Cut down in other areas, float the logs on the smaller rivers until they come here. Load them onto boats and take them to the sawmills.'

'I never saw that.' Leonardo watched her.

'You're not from around here,' she replied. 'Why *would* you have seen it?'

'I've been on this river enough hours today to see there's no logs on it.'

Daniella shrugged like she'd said enough, and asked the old man for a cigarette, but she had hit a nerve. Leonardo was afraid of the water, I was sure of that, and I wondered if Daniella had noticed it too.

'Just last year a boat hit a log further north of here,' I told him. 'It cracked right through the hull and the people were standing in water over their ankles in just a couple of minutes.'

'That's just a story.'

'No, it's true. Most of them managed to get to shore but the captain had to break the window of his wheelhouse to get out. He cut himself on the glass and the blood attracted the piranhas. When they pulled him out, one arm was stripped clean and his face was eaten right down to his skull. And that was during the day. Imagine what it would be like in the dark.'

Daniella accepted a cigarette from Raul, took a light and dragged on it. She held the smoke for a long time before she let it drift from her nose, the smell of it coming to me in the hot, still air. I didn't smoke, but I liked the smell of it in the air like that.

Leonardo watched us, suspecting a conspiracy, then shook his head and took the cigarette from behind his ear. He put it in the corner of his mouth and popped a match alight with his thumbnail. He flicked the match into the river and lifted his hand, forming the finger and thumb into a make-believe pistol.

'We leave at first light,' he said, pointing at Raul. 'And keep that fucking dog away from me.' He moved his arm so he was aiming at Rocky, and he pulled the trigger.

26

'He's getting worse,' Daniella said. 'I'm worried about him.'

The old man was asleep on the sand, with nothing more than a thin sheet to cover him. The night was cold and there was a light wind blowing in over the water, carrying the scent of the river. Somewhere in the darkness, a *boto* surfaced to take a breath. The way it sounded, it was as if someone was out there. It was no wonder people believed the river dolphins could take human shape.

Beside us, the fire crackled, sawing in the breeze. Raul had come close to it because it kept the insects away, but it also added to the heat of his fever. His body was damp with perspiration and he turned and fretted as he slept.

Rocky was anxious, as if she knew something was wrong with her friend. She wouldn't settle and had sulked when we moved her away from him. She tried to curl up beside him, but we were worried her heat would make him worse, so had chased her away. Now she was lying against a piece of driftwood with her chin on her paws, watching.

I put a hand to the old man's neck and he shifted and moaned as if it caused him pain.

'He's so hot.' I looked at Daniella, seeing how kind the firelight was to her. The orange glow reflected on her skin and the shadows danced around her cheekbones. Her eyes glittered. Strands of her hair had come loose and framed her face, twisting in the breeze.

'He's going to die,' Leonardo said. He hadn't wanted to leave his cargo unguarded, but when he saw the rest of us coming

147

ashore, he followed. I guessed he was afraid the boat would break its mooring and float away into the darkness.

He had sat apart from us, doing nothing while Daniella and I gathered firewood, but when we cooked rice and beans over the fire he was happy to share it while the day fell behind the trees. Red and orange ripples had streaked the sky above the forest, glowing in the wisps of cloud that hung there.

'He's not going to die,' I said. 'He just needs to rest.'

Leonardo was standing behind me now, poking the fire with a long stick. 'You want me to make it quick for him?' he asked. 'You can have the money for yourself that way.'

'Don't be such an animal,' Daniella told him, but it only made him smirk.

'This man is my friend,' I said, looking back at him. 'Keep your gun tucked away and your mouth shut.'

'Doesn't have to be my gun. I could hold him under the water if you—'

'You won't touch him,' I said, getting to my feet and facing him. 'You don't even need to come near him.'

Leonardo threw the stick down in a shower of sparks and turned to face me. He held up both hands. 'I'm joking,' he said. 'Just joking, that's all.'

I shook my head at him. 'Just keep away from him.'

Leonardo thought about it, then shrugged. He moved to the other side of the fire and sat down facing the river. He took the pistol from his waistband and turned it over in his hands, removing the magazine and checking the load.

'I need to get that weapon off him,' I whispered once I had sat down again. 'I don't trust him.'

'Is there anything I can do?' Daniella asked. 'I could try to—'

'No.' Just the thought of it made my stomach turn to ice. 'Don't do anything. He's even more dangerous than you think. Promise you won't do anything.'

'OK,' she said. 'I won't.'

I hoped she meant it. Daniella was fiery and headstrong, two things I most liked about her, but also two things that could get her into trouble. I was afraid that if she saw an opportunity to do something, she might take it. I would have to keep her and Leonardo apart.

'We need to get the old man home,' I said, keeping my voice quiet. 'When we get back on the river, we have to head for Piratinga first.'

'*He's* not going to like it.' She tilted her head in Leonardo's direction and I looked over my shoulder to watch him.

'I'll work something out,' I said. 'I don't think the old man will make it to Mina dos Santos. If we try to get there with him like this ...' I shook my head and looked over at Leonardo.

I thought about killing him.

I could probably do it now.

I could draw my revolver, turn, point and shoot. It was dark, but I was a good shot and didn't think it would take more than one bullet. I would be able to take Daniella and the old man home without Leonardo getting in the way.

But then Daniella would see the shadow that cloaked me.

She would see the ugly side of me that I didn't want her to see.

There was the old man's money to think about, too. His dream of moving to Imperatriz and buying a better boat. If Leonardo was dead, I could try taking the guns on to Mina dos Santos, but there was a strong chance I wouldn't leave that place alive. The old man would lose his money and I would lose my life.

I also wondered if Daniella would be any safer in Piratinga with Luis and Wilson than she was here with Leonardo.

I rubbed my face and clenched my jaw with frustration. Whatever I did, whichever way I turned, there was no way out. I was trapped on this course of events and there was no way for me to escape. Daniella had to stay with me and Leonardo had to stay alive. The only two things I might be able to gain some control over were taking the old man home and disarming Leonardo. But I didn't know how I was going to arrange either of those things.

After a while, we lay on our backs and stared at the stars, listening to the old man groaning in his sleep. Rocky forgave us for sending her away and came to lie between us, pressing her back against me. From the water's edge, the night stretched out across the river and into the eternity of the forest. Behind us, it crawled over the shrubs and molasses grass, encircling the *buriti* palms that stood sentinel on the bank, and it flowed on through the savannah, wrapping everything in its darkness.

We were a hundred kilometres from the nearest town, a thousand from the nearest city, and my best friend was fading away. There was nowhere I could take him. Nothing I could do to help him.

Daniella's breathing grew deeper as the night pressed on, but I tried to keep awake. I checked on the old man, soaking a cloth in river water and putting it to his head in a weak attempt to keep him cool.

Leonardo remained in his spot, sitting up and watching. I wasn't sure if he was afraid of me or the night, but he kept his pistol in one hand and a torch in the other. He flicked it on from time to time, scanning the bank behind us and playing its light across the ripples in the river. I ignored him, tending to my friend, wishing there was more I could do for him.

'There's something out there,' Leonardo said.

I stopped, one hand pressing the cloth against the old man's forehead.

'Out there.' He stood up. 'On the water.'

'There's nothing there,' I told him.

'You think I'm lying? Come and look.' He lowered his voice, as if whatever was out there was going to hear him.

I paused, dropped the cloth in the pan of water and went over to where Leonardo was standing.

He shone the torch onto the river, moving it back and forth until he caught them in the beam. There were a dozen of them. Eyes. All staring back at him.

'What the fuck is it?' His voice heightened and he raised his pistol at them.

'Maybe it's Iara,' I said.

'What?'

'You don't know about Iara? She lives under the water.'

'What are you talking about?'

'The fishermen talk about her all the time. She sits on the bank and sings to them, but if she really likes you, she casts a spell on you with her song. She makes you go to her, and when you do, she takes you down into the river and drowns you.'

'And that's her out there?'

'No. That's the *jacaré* watching you. This is their beach and maybe they want it back. Maybe they have eggs here. *Jacaré* are much worse than Iara,' I said. 'She sings to you; they eat you.'

Going back to the old man's side, I sat close to the fire and reached into my shirt pocket to remove the newspaper cutting.

There was more on my mind than what was here on the beach.

The old man's sickness, Leonardo's threat, and Daniella's company had all been more immediate, but there was another presence on the boat; a woman who was not here in person, but whose existence still played on my mind.

I opened out the cutting and looked at the photograph of Sister Dolores Beckett. A spattering of grey and black dots that shifted in the flickering firelight as if they were alive. 'Just one more job,' Costa had said, but I heard *Just one more life.*

I stared at the picture until I couldn't see it any more. It became a blur as my eyes lost their focus and I wondered what it was that Sister Beckett had done to make her life worth five thousand dollars to a man like me. Costa had said that she deserved it, but that didn't mean anything and when I remembered how the boys in the *favela* had killed Father Tomás, just as Costa wanted me to kill Sister Beckett, I still felt the loss of his death. I felt the guilt and shame of it as surely as if I had killed him myself.

I had to think about the money, though. I had to think about Daniella and the old man. Taking one life was a small price to pay for the safety of theirs.

In the newspaper cutting, Sister Beckett was wearing trousers and a T-shirt and didn't look much like a nun. I tried to imagine her wearing a habit, sandaled toes poking from beneath the hem, but somehow it didn't look as if it would suit her. She was coming out of a building that might have been mentioned in the words, but their undecipherable meaning was lost to me. She was surrounded by people and everyone's focus was on her, as if they were intent on knowing her thoughts.

Only one person who was close to her was looking away. A woman who was striking because of both her height and her posture.

Costa had said that Sister Beckett would not have any security, but seeing the tall woman made me think he might be wrong. The woman looked as if she were there to protect Sister Beckett and I suspected there might be someone standing between me and my money, after all.

I returned the clipping to my pocket and lay back, closing my eyes and wishing life wasn't so complicated. Close by, the old man grumbled in his fever while Rocky had slinked back to press against him and fall asleep. Beside me, Daniella breathed heavily.

Eventually, sleep took me, too, but it was broken and troubled and filled with disturbing images. Flashes of me standing over Sofia while she begged me not to kill her. Leonardo leering over Daniella. The old man slipping away to a fevered death.

And in the early hours of the morning, I woke to the sound of chaos.

27

Rocky was barking. But this was no ordinary warning bark. It was a savage and primal sound that turned my blood cold. She was snarling and growling like a wild animal.

My muscles ached from lying on the beach, and my head was woozy with half-sleep, so the effect of her vicious noise was multiplied a thousand times, and it took a moment to remember where I was.

Opening my eyes, I sat upright and grabbed the pistol tucked into the pack beside me.

Close to my feet, Rocky was moving from side to side, continuing to produce that dreadful sound. The hair on her neck bristled, her tail sprung out behind her and her eyes rolled up. Her lips were pulled back to bare her teeth, and saliva hung from her mouth.

There was another sound breaking into the dawn air.

Leonardo.

His voice was shrill but there were no words, just a scream full of fear and pain.

Beyond the corpse of last night's fire, Leonardo writhed in the sand, screaming for my help. It was hard to tell exactly what was happening, the day was still only preparing itself, and the sun had not yet begun to rise over the trees. The grey light gave a strange hue to everything, and all I could see of Leonardo was his frantic movement and the commotion of the sand.

He shrieked, his voice rising in desperation.

Rocky continued to snarl and bare her teeth like a forest devil.

Pulling my revolver free, I jumped to my feet, but stopped

myself from rushing to Leonardo's aid. I didn't know what was happening and I would be a fool to hurry into the fray. It was better to know what I was dealing with. The commotion had shocked me, my heart thumped hard, my breathing was erratic and my whole body trembled.

'Get it off!' Leonardo finally managed to shout, and once the words had formed, he repeated them over and over, desperate for my help. 'Get it off! Get it off!'

I moved closer, squinting in the grainy light, seeing Leonardo twisting and kicking in the sand. With one hand, he was hitting at his leg, raising his arm over and over again, pounding at something. A dark shape that shouldn't be there.

A young *jacaré*, maybe a metre and a half long, had sunk its teeth into Leonardo's right calf and was trying to drag him to the water. The creature's teeth were not designed for much more than grabbing, and its prey would usually be small enough to swallow whole, but as they grew bigger, these river monsters would take larger and larger prey, which they would drag into the river and drown. Twisting and rolling, they would disorientate their victims, fill their lungs with water, then wedge them somewhere beneath the surface until the flesh was rotten enough to eat.

This particular *jacaré* had decided to punch well above its own weight, because although it was strong, it was too small to be much threat to a human. Anyone with enough experience of the river would have known that, but to Leonardo it must have been terrifying. This creature had slipped out of the water while he was asleep and clamped its jaws around his calf. Its teeth were big enough to cause considerable pain, and it would take a hard man not to be alarmed when he woke to find a *jacaré* trying to drag him into the river. Perhaps if it had been a little bigger, or had another to help it, it might have succeeded.

'Get it off me!' Leonardo yelled as he continued to writhe and hit at the animal with one hand, while stretching for his pistol with the other. His weapon was just beyond reach, his fingertips brushing the grip.

'Do something!' The pitch of his voice heightened in panic as the *jacaré* tugged at him in jerking movements, trying to pull him towards the water. 'Kill it!'

There was something fascinating about seeing Leonardo battling the *jacaré*, struggling in a storm of limbs and sand. It was almost mesmerising, like some bizarre dream come to life, and as I watched, I considered turning away and leaving them to it. Perhaps it would solve my problems if the animal dragged him into the water and drowned him. Maybe he deserved such a death. I even found myself wishing the creature were larger, or wondering if I should just kill Leonardo myself.

'Help him.' Daniella woke me from the trance. It was she who spurred me into action. She was a better person than I, and she saw only that we should help Leonardo. We couldn't allow him to die like this.

And we had come a long way – the old man needed his money.

I took a step closer, raised my revolver, and shot the creature through the eye.

'You hesitated,' Leonardo said. 'You thought about letting it have me.' He was sitting on the sand, with his left leg extended in front of him and his foot up on his backpack.

'It wasn't big enough,' I said, wrapping his calf with a bandage. 'And these aren't much more than puncture wounds.' I glanced back at the dead *jacaré* lying a few feet away. There was more than just one hole in it now.

Leonardo's rage had overcome him once he had recovered from the shock of waking up to find a *jacaré* attached to his leg, and though he had lost his grip on his pistol during the attack, he made up for it afterwards. He had emptied his pistol's magazine into the dead creature before reloading.

I might have done the same thing. The thought of being in the water was still fresh in my mind; the fear I had felt when I was under the boat, trying to free what remained of the *boto*. All kinds of thoughts had come to me then; of being dragged down into the darkness.

'Well they hurt like fuck,' he said.

'You'll live. Just be thankful the *jacaré* wasn't any bigger. Some of them are as big as four metres long. If it had been one of those, you'd be wishing you were dead.'

I used my teeth to tear the bandage, then ripped it a short way down the middle and tied it off before putting everything back into the first aid box I'd taken from the *Deus*. 'You going to say thank you?' I asked, standing and looking down at him.

Leonardo scowled. 'All right. Thank you.'

The sun was peering over the top of the trees in the distance, and the morning was still fresh. On the bank behind us, the cicadas creaked in the molasses grass and a pair of magpie tanagers played in the closest *buriti* palm. The black and white birds hopped from frond to frond, their heads turning in jerky movements as they picked insects from the leaves. They were undisturbed by our presence.

'How about you?' I asked the old man. 'Any better?'

He was sitting up now, drinking water from a plastic bottle, and tried to smile in reply to me, but it hurt his head too much, so he let it go halfway. He saw the worry on my face before I could disguise it. 'It'll pass,' he said. 'It's nothing. Flu, maybe, something like that.'

'There's been dengue in Piratinga; you know that.'

'Dengue passes, Zico. I've seen it before.'

'So have I. But it doesn't always pass. Sometimes it gets worse.'

'I don't want to talk about it.'

I raised my eyebrows. 'Sure.'

Raul stood up and stretched his back, pretending not to feel the pain in his joints, then walked to the river and put his toes into it. They disappeared under the silt-laden water.

'Be careful,' I told him, thinking about what had happened to Leonardo, but he made a dismissive sound and waved a hand.

'On Tocantins, the water is much clearer than this,' he said without looking back at me.

'Then your job will be easier when you get to Imperatriz.'

'I like it muddy,' he replied. 'I like it that you can't see what's down there. It's like we're not supposed to know. There are things down there we shouldn't see.' He paused, worn out from the effort of talking, and I watched him, thinking about what we'd left beneath the surface yesterday, and what had crawled out of the river and attacked Leonardo this morning.

'You know,' Raul went on, 'I heard about some *gringos* came down this way, brought some fancy gear so they could get a good look at all our fish. Scientists, they were, coming down here with diving suits and cameras, spending all their *gringo* dollars on equipment to study our river. And you know what they saw?'

'What?' asked Daniella, her voice lazy, the increasing heat sapping her strength. 'What did they see?'

'They saw *shit*, that's what they saw. It was too damn dark and dirty for them to see anything. Went home with pictures of sand and mud and dark.' He waved one foot from side to side in the water, feeling the gritty sand settling between his toes, then he stopped and turned to me, saying, 'How long have we been doing this, Zico, you and me? Up and down this river?'

'Two years?'

Raul nodded. 'Two. And before that I was doing it alone, sometimes with Carolina, for fifteen. Things have changed a lot since then. For one thing, I feel old.'

'You *are* old. You can rest when you get to Imperatriz. Take it easy on your new boat.' I knew that Raul would never have enough money to do it, that maybe he didn't even really want it, but I allowed him his dream of escaping Piratinga. 'You got something else lined up after this?' I asked, saying it for no other reason than to make conversation, but the old man just grunted and waved a hand, making me want to say something else. 'I'll get us work,' I said, knowing it might not be that easy.

'You want to hear something funny?' he said.

'Sure.'

'I don't want to go to Imperatriz. I couldn't give a shit for that place or for its river.'

'What about joining Francisco?' Daniella said. 'What about being with your son?'

'And buying a boat,' I added. 'Tourists ... that whole thing. You've been talking about it all the time I've known you.'

'Talk,' he said. 'Talk is just talk. I never wanted to go there. We make dreams to pass the time, and we pretend that we want to be somewhere else; it's what men do. Maybe we do it for our women or maybe we do it because it's expected of us, I don't know, but we're all supposed to have dreams, Zico, we're not supposed to be content.'

I waited for him to go on.

'I mean, my son ... sure, it would be good to see him from time to time, but time to time would be enough. I don't need to live in his pocket.' Raul reached for a cigarette, looked at it for a moment and put it back into the packet. 'And what do I want another boat for? I got one already.'

'So you can do the tourist thing on Tocantins,' said Daniella. 'That's what you always said you wanted. You want to work there, you'll need a bigger boat, one with beds, a kitchen.'

'Beds and a kitchen.' Raul let the words fall from his lips like they had numbed his mouth and left a bad taste. 'Who needs beds and a kitchen on a boat when you've got the shore right alongside you? You want to eat, you make a fire. You want to sleep, you make a bed. What's wrong with eating under the open sky? What's wrong with sleeping in a hammock? Or on the beach?'

'A hammock's OK for you and me to sleep on, maybe even Daniella,' I winked at her, 'but these tourists, they want something different. They're soft. They're used to beds.'

'Then let them stay in their beds. What do they want to come here for anyway? Why do they want to live like us when they're nothing like us? They have no idea how we live.'

I smiled at my friend. A sad, understanding smile. I knew him better than I had known my own father and probably loved him more. I would do almost anything for him, including help him lie to himself, it seemed, because now that I thought about it in light of what he had just said, I knew he didn't want a better life. He already had it. And, in my heart, maybe I knew the same was true for me too. 'You belong here,' I said. 'This is your river, it's where you need to be.'

Raul removed his hat and ran a hand across his head. The cropped grey hair as rough as the bristles on his chin. 'Yeah.' He shivered again, the fever rooting itself deep in his body.

'I don't know why you pretend it's what you want,' I said.

Raul closed his eyes and lifted his face to the sun. 'It's Carolina who wants to go to Imperatriz. I lie to myself for her.'

28

Daniella waded back to the *Deus e o Diabo* with me and we unfastened the smaller boat from the back, returning to the shore to collect Leonardo and the old man. Raul insisted on wading out to her as usual, but he looked frail and was already sweating. Leonardo, on the other hand, refused to enter the water. He said he didn't want to ruin the dressing on his leg, but the pistol never left his grip, and he scanned the water as we rowed out. I didn't blame him for being afraid. When Daniella and I had returned to collect the smaller boat from the *Deus*, we had moved quickly, fearful of whatever might be lurking below the surface.

Usually the old man would have gripped the gunwale and hauled himself up, but now his muscles were racked with pain. His fingers were weak and I had to help him, taking his hands and dragging him up onto the boat.

For a few moments, Raul's pride was gone and he stayed on his knees, dripping onto the deck, catching his breath. Rocky circled him, licking at his face, trying to encourage him to pet her. It was as if she knew he was sick.

In the time between losing Sofia and coming to Piratinga, I'd had nothing to care about other than myself, and seeing the old man on his knees, his breath coming in sharp gasps, was like a weight on my heart. The old man and I had been up and down this river many times, and our lives had both been threatened more than once, but I had never considered his mortality so much as I had these past two days. He seemed to be dying before my eyes, wasting away, and there was nothing I could do to prevent it.

Everything in my life had slipped beyond my control.

Eventually the old man looked up and forced a smile. 'Can't even climb onto my own damn boat,' he said, but the effort of those words was so great that he immediately lowered his head and went back to breathing in wheezing gasps.

'We need to go,' Leonardo said, hauling himself up onto the boat. He limped past us and dumped his pack on the deck. 'Or do you three want to waste some more of my time?' He winced and lowered himself onto the box seat he had been using yesterday.

'What's the matter with you?' Daniella turned on him. 'Can't you see he's sick?'

'And I just got bitten by a fucking monster,' Leonardo snapped. 'All I care about is making this delivery on time.'

'We'll make your delivery,' I told him. 'Just give him a minute.' I crouched beside my friend, waiting for him to look up, but he remained that way, forehead pressed to the deck, eyes closed, sweat beading on his face, running along the bridge of his nose.

I put my arm around his shoulders and brought my face close to his, so I could feel his bristles against my own skin. The heat was coming off him like he was burning up, the smell of sweat and sickness heavy on him. 'Stay strong,' I whispered. 'We'll get you home soon.'

Raul nodded and started to stand up. I helped him, gave him something to push against as he found his way to his feet.

'Do you want me to take the wheel?' I kept my voice low.

'No, Zico. You just watch him.'

'You sure?'

'Uh-huh.'

'Daniella.' I raised my voice. 'Help him to the wheel. Stay with him.'

I watched them go, then took a spanner from the housing at the back and reached down into the hatch to reconnect the fuel lines. Rocky stayed with me for a moment, pushing her nose into the compartment, then went back to the old man.

'You stay here,' I told Leonardo as I threw the spanner back into the toolbox.

Leonardo reached for his backpack and pulled it up onto his

lap. He laid the pistol on the bench beside him and started to open the pack. He took out a scrap of folded newspaper and, for a moment, my heart lurched. It reminded me of the scrap in my shirt pocket, and my hand went to my chest, feeling for it. Had Leonardo somehow taken it from me?

I felt the familiar stiffness of it against the cotton of my shirt, though, and it crossed my mind that Leonardo and I might be going to Mina dos Santos for the same reason. Perhaps he too was looking for Sister Dolores Beckett. But when he unfolded the paper on his lap, I saw a different kind of problem arise for me.

Leonardo took a pinch of the fine white powder and, blocking one nostril, snorted the drug hard into his other.

'Cocaína?' This explained his behaviour yesterday. The wild look in his eyes. The eagerness to use his weapon.

'For the pain.' He grinned and noticed the way my eyes went to the pistol on the bench beside him. 'You thinking about trying to take it from me?' he asked.

I watched him, saying nothing.

'You had your chance on the beach.' He refolded the paper and slipped it into his pocket before taking hold of his pistol once more. 'You won't get another.'

Raul started the engine and took the boat away from the bank. He steered it into the river and watched the water ahead.

I went to my usual spot on the bow, sitting on the gunwale on one side, leaning back against the railing and removing my flip-flops so I could find purchase on the other side with my toes. With my legs up like that, Daniella sitting below me and to my right, I could see the river ahead, and I could watch Leonardo.

Seeing him taking the drug reminded me of the boys in the *favela*, and it annoyed me that I hadn't recognised it. I knew how unpredictable it made them; I'd seen the way their mood could swing from god to devil in an instant, and now Leonardo had become even more of a liability to us.

I cleaned both pistols and then removed the knife which I always carried at the small of my back. Seventeen centimetres of

Brasilian steel, narrowing to an upturned point. I spat on the flat of the blade and wiped it with my shirt, running the pad of one thumb across the cutting edge, checking its sharpness.

'Don't understand how you can do it.' The old man took me by surprise and I looked up to see him sitting in the wheelhouse watching me. 'Seems like you're two different people.' His voice was quiet and weak.

I knew what he meant. He was using his boat to deliver guns but he didn't pull the trigger, so he didn't consider himself guilty of much more than illegal trafficking. He didn't think about the reality that every bullet on his boat could be used to take a life.

I was a killer, though. The old man knew that I worked for Costa and he knew what that work involved, so it was difficult for him to understand how I could do it.

All I had to do, though, was think about the day Sofia died. With that in my mind, it was easy to kill a certain kind of man.

I closed my eyes and remembered how I had been on the hillside that day, away from the *favela* houses that piled over one another in a jumble of corrugated iron and wood. I had gone there to get away from the other boys and the drugs and the guns; to look out across the sea, to feel the forest behind me and wonder what it would be like to turn in every direction and not see another person or building.

I was eating steak and fries with my hands, taking them from the paper wrapping, licking the salty seasoning from my fingers between each mouthful. I could almost taste them now.

Below me, outside a café, a group of young men were practising *capoeira*. Someone had a drum and the sound of the beat was drifting up to me, coming to my ears a little later than it was made, mingled with voices of the men singing. I could see the movements of the *jogadores*, like dancers twisting around each other, in and out, their legs and hands touching the ground and lighting off again, their bodies fluid and lithe. They cartwheeled and moved about like animals and I admired their dedication and their ability.

When the steak was finished, I ate the last of the fries and drank the last of my beer and leaned back to look up at the trees. The faint rhythm of the music from the street and the gentle breath of the wind in the trees washed over me and I thought about taking my sister and leaving the *favela*.

On my way home I saw Father Tomás and asked him to pray for me before I left him sitting on the church step, smoking a cigarette. It was late afternoon, Sofia would probably be back from work and I smiled, thinking how she'd nag me about my job for a while, telling me the same things that she always did. She'd tell me that what I was doing was wrong, and I would tell her it wasn't so bad, and I would put some money on the table to pay for our food. After that we would eat, maybe play cards with the old dog-eared deck our father had taught us to play with. We had a tin of plastic counters that he had collected, and we used them for money. Maybe I'd even go out and buy us a couple of beers.

Except there wasn't going to be any good-natured argument that evening. No cards. No beer.

My friend Ratinho was waiting at home for me, his face bruised, his lip bleeding. He was sitting on the front step, the door open to the cool darkness inside.

He looked up as I came to him, standing to meet me.

'Sofia,' he said.

It was all he had to say.

Now, on the *Deus e o Diabo*, I opened my eyes and wiped them with my forearm. I saw the old man watching me and wondered; if he knew what had happened to Sofia, would he understand then?

'You all right?' he asked.

'I'm good.' I nodded.

Daniella was staring at the deck in front of her and I wasn't sure if she was listening or not, but I narrowed my eyes at the old man, telling him this wasn't something I wanted to talk about. Not here, not now, not in front of Daniella. If the old man wanted to question what I did, how I could do it and still sleep at night, that was his right, but not in front of Daniella.

I stood and went to him, leaning on the wheelhouse for support.

Rocky looked up from her seat next to the old man, then went back to sleep.

'So what was it that Costa wanted to see you about?' Raul asked, looking at the knife in my hand. 'What kind of job did he have for you?'

Without thinking, I touched the shirt pocket over my heart, where the folded piece of newspaper carried an imprint of the nun's face. 'I told you I said no to him.'

'And I told *you* that you don't turn down a man like Costa. You're here either because you need to be or because his job is to be done later.'

I bit my lip and stared at the shining steel in my hand. I thought about how it would feel to tell the old man what Costa wanted me to do; to tell him the price for doing it and the price for not doing it. Perhaps between us we could think of a way out of it, but I swallowed my words.

I couldn't tell him.

'Who's Costa?' asked Daniella, looking up at me.

'No one.' I took my hand away from my pocket as if it would betray my thoughts. As if the soft paper were a seething ember. I went to my backpack, lying right in the bow, where the boat came to its tip, and I stuffed the newspaper cutting inside. I didn't need it reminding me who I was.

'He's a man who asks people to do things for money,' the old man said.

'What kind of things?' But she didn't need to ask. Even if she didn't want to admit it to herself, she knew what kind of things.

'Nothing.' I studied the smudges of newsprint on my fingers. 'Take no notice of him, he's being a devil. A sick old devil.'

'Tell me,' she said, but I shook my head at her, wondering what she would think of me, what Raul would think of me, if they knew the other reason why I was here on this boat.

Daniella pursed her lips at me, pouting like she did when she wanted something. It was a look I liked; the kind of look that promised me something physical if I gave her what she wanted.

165

Raul laughed. 'Now you're in trouble. There's always something a woman can hold back if she doesn't get what she wants.'

I smiled at my friend. He could make me angry, be full of mischief like a *saci pererê*, but he was the best friend I had ever had. I knew why Raul found it hard to understand what I did.

I tested the edge of my knife once more before putting it away, and an image of Sister Dolores Beckett came to mind as I did it. This would be the blade that killed her.

Just one more life.

29

'We came this way yesterday.' Leonardo spoke as he came past Raul, joining Daniella and me, his pistol in his hand. 'That old mining place is over there.' He pointed to the abandoned operation where we had seen the Indians fishing from dugout canoes yesterday.

It was quiet there now. Not another soul on the river.

'What's going on?' Leonardo persisted. 'This some kind of trick? We're going back the way we came.'

'Why don't you put that away?' I asked him. 'You don't need it here.'

'We're going back the way we came,' he said again, standing midway between Raul and me, the pistol hanging limp, looking first at the old man, then settling on me. 'Why?'

'You want to be on the Rio das Mortes, right?' I said, watching his hands.

'Yes.'

'Then this is the way to get there.'

He looked blank.

'The Rio das Mortes meets the Araguaia about fifteen kilometres south of Piratinga. We have to head back to get to it.'

Leonardo stared at me. 'The old man's getting worse,' he said. 'You wouldn't be thinking about taking him home, would you?' He lifted the pistol to waist height and my blood ran cold for a moment, despite the heat.

I forced myself to soften my expression. 'Maybe that wouldn't be such a bad thing. He needs a doctor,' I said. 'And so do you.' I motioned a hand at his leg. 'There's a hospital in Piratinga.'

Leonardo began to shake his head before I had even finished my sentence. 'Not going to happen.'

'You need help.' Daniella joined me. 'Your leg could get infected.'

'There'll be a doctor at the mine,' Leonardo said.

'Not the kind of doctor you'd want,' she told him.

'Then I'll wait until I get back to Piratinga.' The pitch of his voice was heightening. His eyes were flicking from Daniella to me and back again. 'Those crates have to be at the mine tomorrow.'

'Look at him.' She lowered her voice and pleaded with Leonardo. 'You want him to die on this boat?'

'I couldn't care less what happens to him.' Leonardo waved his pistol as he spoke. 'All I care about is getting my delivery to Mina dos Santos in time.'

'All you'll lose is a few hours.' I kept my voice even and calm, despite the fear that was building in me as my eyes watched the pistol. 'Half a day at the most.' And I was beginning to think that Daniella would be safer in Piratinga too. Luis and Wilson seemed far less of a threat right now than Leonardo was. I should have shot him on the beach instead of the *jacaré*. I should have let the creature drag him away. I should have taken his pistol. There were so many things I should have done.

'We're not going to Piratinga.' Leonardo looked right at me and sniffed hard. 'If the old man dies, then he dies.'

Now I stood up, taking my feet off the gunwale and turning to face Leonardo full on. 'We'll lose half a day.' I put up both hands and adopted a pleading tone. 'That's all. Is it really worth a man's life?'

'You tell me.' Leonardo shrugged and raised the pistol to point it at Raul. He cocked his head to one side and raised his eyebrows as if inviting me to take his challenge. 'I could just kill him now and finish the conversation. There'd be nothing more to talk about. Now I know you can take us to Mina dos Santos, it wouldn't matter.'

'No,' Daniella said. 'No you can't—'

'It's all right.' I stopped her without taking my eyes off Leonardo.

'It's OK. Have it your way. We'll go straight on. No stopping.' I had to put him at ease. Perhaps there was still time to deal with this situation. I lowered my hand, began to move it towards my waist. My revolver was close. All I needed was for him to drop his guard for a moment, long enough for me to slip my fingers beneath my shirt and ...

'And while we're talking,' he said, 'why don't you hand over those pistols you've got? The rifle in the box up there, as well.'

Leonardo emptied my pistols onto the deck, the brass casings rolling towards the stern where the boat was heaviest. Satisfied that I was disarmed, he took my empty weapons and my backpack and stowed them along with his own in the box seat he'd been using. There was an open padlock hanging from the catch, so he snapped it shut and put the key in his pocket, smiling at me as he patted his thigh. I watched him strut despite his limp, the usurper king of this small floating wreck, and I wondered how I had let him take advantage of me. Perhaps I was no longer suited for this environment. I had grown soft.

When I thought about it like that, looking back at Daniella, I realised maybe it wasn't so bad to have something to care about. Something for which you can commit an extreme act or, as in this case, something for which you need to *not* commit that act. If Daniella had not been here, I might have taken more of a risk. Leonardo might now be dead and overboard, or things might not have turned out so well for me. I might have tried to stop Leonardo and ended up dead myself. Either way, I'd never know and I had to satisfy myself with biding my time. I was not as harmless as Leonardo might think. I still had my knife, tucked in the small of my back, and there was always the old man's revolver, stashed in the wheelhouse.

Once Leonardo had stowed my weapons, he came back to me, waving his pistol, indicating that he wanted me to go and sit with Daniella.

I turned around to comply, but as I did so, something else caught my eye. Inside the wheelhouse, Raul was stepping away from the wheel. He seemed about to say something, but stumbled and collapsed to his knees.

Rocky yelped as he fell against her, and she darted out of the wheelhouse where she had been lying on the seat beside him. Once on the deck, though, she stopped and turned, coming back to rub her nose against her master.

The boat, without a pilot, drifted to one side, the prow now aiming towards the bank.

'What now?' Leonardo said, raising his pistol and aiming at the old man as if he suspected a trick.

Daniella and I went straight to Raul. I put a hand on his shoulder and squatted down to look at my friend. 'Take your time,' I told him. 'I'll sort the boat.' I knew the way from here; I'd been on this part of the river enough times by now. I wasn't as good with the channels and the currents as Raul was, but I was sure I could get us home. And that was what I had to do. I had to get him to Piratinga.

My friend was dying and I had to do whatever I could.

I looked over my shoulder at Leonardo and saw him standing behind us, aiming his pistol, and my whole body screamed with the frustration of being so helpless.

'Don't do anything to annoy him,' I said to Daniella. 'He's in pain and he's snorting *cocaína* – it's making him edgier than hell.'

'*Cocaína?*'

'Yeah. He's probably itching to kill someone, so just... just don't piss him off, OK?'

Daniella nodded.

'Stay with the old man and keep an eye on Rocky. Keep her with you.' I left them kneeling on the deck and went to the wheel. I wanted to help him, put him somewhere more comfortable, but without a pilot, the boat would drift onto a sandbank or hit something worse.

'You sure you know what you're doing?' Leonardo asked, keeping his weapon trained on me. 'This isn't some kind of trick?' He was uncomfortable with the way things were going and I tried to put myself in his position, wonder what I would do, but none of the scenarios played out well in my mind. They all ended with someone dying, and in none of them was it Leonardo. For the time being, he was in charge.

I turned the wheel, the *Deus* chugging out into the deep water again, and set her straight before going back to Raul and helping him to his feet. I placed my hands under his armpits and dragged him up, throwing his once powerful arm over my shoulder to support him as he struggled to the bow where he could sit with Daniella and catch his breath.

Raul stopped and nodded, telling me he was strong enough, he could walk on his own, but as soon as I loosened my grip, he stumbled, his knees giving in. 'Let me help you, old man,' I said. 'We'll get you over here. Sit down and rest a minute. After that, you can take the wheel again if you want.'

Raul resigned himself to my insistence and allowed me to take the weight of his body and help him to the bench. He slumped onto the hard, unfinished wooden surface and leaned forward, resting his elbows on his knees. 'It's getting worse,' he said. 'Every part of me hurts.'

'You look like shit,' said Leonardo.

'I'll get you some water.' I went to the cool box, a bright red plastic chest, the outer casing cracked down one side. The ice was long since melted and the bottles were warm, but they would do, so I brought one back to Raul. Leonardo followed all of my movements, so I tried to ignore him as I opened the top and handed the bottle to the old man.

Raul sat up to take it, feeling it, tasting it before it was even in his hands.

'Did you hurt your arms when you fell?' I asked.

'Hm?'

'Your arms. You hurt them?'

'No.'

'So what about the bruises?'

The old man turned his arms over so he could look at the soft underside. Two large marks, one on either arm, had appeared just below his elbows. They pointed away to his wrists. He rubbed them against his damp shirt and looked at them again, but the yellowish-black marks were still there.

'They're bruises, old man, they're not going to come off.'

Raul continued to look at them, trying to work out how they might have got there. 'Must've been when I was climbing onto the boat. Maybe I bumped them or something.'

'Maybe.'

'Well. Doesn't matter.' He took a deep drink from the bottle of water and kept his head back as the liquid went into him. 'I've had bruises before.' He wiped his mouth with the back of his hand.

'Sure you have.' I nodded.

'*Filho da puta*,' I heard Leonardo say. 'You want to control this damn boat?'

I looked up and saw that we were, once again, drifting towards the bank where it cut straight down into the water. A wall of hard red dirt, baked until cracked, tufts of yellow scrub and tree roots breaking through. The river was easing into a gentle curve and the *Deus* was nosing straight towards collision.

'Do it now.' Leonardo's voice carried more than a hint of fear.

'Look after Raul,' I told Daniella as I got to my feet and went to take the wheel, seeing that we were almost at a right angle in the river, heading directly for a sandy bank protruding from the water.

I straightened the *Deus*, but kept one eye on Raul who was sitting up now, sipping the water.

My old friend was the strongest man I had ever known. His powerful body, his thickened skin, his easy temperament made him the perfect creature for this life. I had never seen him unwell or weakened, but the fever that plagued him now was worsening, and the bruising on his arms worried me. It was possible he had knocked himself climbing into the boat, but that only happened a short while ago, and I'd never seen bruises appear so quickly. Seeing him deteriorate like this, his body marking and bruising, I felt a tightening in my stomach. I'd seen dengue fever cause bruising like this before, and the outcome for those people was never good. I had to get him home. I had to do whatever it would take to return him to Piratinga where someone could take care of him.

'Thought you'd keep this to yourself?' Leonardo leaned across me and slipped his hand beneath the wheel.

Disturbed from my thoughts, I started to move. Not so much thinking as reacting, I knew what Leonardo was doing and I tried to block him. My body acting before my mind was telling it to, as if the two were separate, each protecting the other. I understood that Leonardo had seen Raul's revolver beneath the wheel and I tried to reach it before he did, but I felt the jab of his automatic in my ribs and I looked down to see it there, the hammer already back, ready to drop down.

'Too slow, Zico.' Leonardo made a tutting sound and pulled Raul's revolver from its securing. 'Just in case, eh? I should have known there'd be another one somewhere.' He tossed it over the side of the boat so it landed in the water with a hollow plop and was gone, then he pushed his pistol hard enough to take my breath away. He forced it against my ribs as if trying to push it between them and leaned his sweating face close to mine. 'Anything else I should know about?'

'No.' I could have told him that I had forgotten about the pistol, that I hadn't known it was there, but there wasn't any point.

'You sure about that?' He pushed the pistol harder.

'Yes.'

'Well, just so you know, if I have to shoot someone today, the first person is going to be your girlfriend over there.' He nodded his head at Daniella who was watching the old man with concern. 'The old man, I think he's going to die without my help, but her I could assist. It would be a shame, though, she's very pretty.'

'You don't have to shoot anybody.'

'We'll see,' Leonardo said, standing and going to sit beside Daniella, the gun still in his hand.

She didn't look at him as he sat down beside her, but he smiled at me and used the barrel of his pistol to brush some of her loose hairs aside.

As he did it, though, something in Daniella changed. I saw it on her face, right away. Her fear for Raul changed in an instant, and her fiery temperament got the better of her. She shoved Leonardo's gun away and pushed to her feet, startling Rocky who leaped up in surprise, baring her teeth and growling deep in her throat.

'Daniella ...' I started to say, but Leonardo was quick. He grabbed her wrist in his free hand, pulling her round so she was facing him. But something in Daniella had snapped and her fire had risen to the surface. She struck out with her right hand, punching Leonardo across the jaw. It was unfocused but took him by surprise, turning his head, a loud slap of flesh on flesh.

Confused, Rocky didn't know what to do. Her loyalty was to the old man, but she knew Daniella and me and she sensed the threat from Leonardo. Her growl deepened and she lowered her head and began to bark at him.

Ignoring the dog, Daniella drew back her hand to hit Leonardo again, but he raised his pistol and jammed the barrel under her chin, forcing her head back. 'I'll blow your fucking brains out the top of your head,' he hissed.

I had started to stand, my fingers reaching for the handle of my knife, but now I stopped, paused halfway between sitting and standing.

Rocky continued to make that noise; somewhere between a bark and a growl. It was a savage, primal sound and it raised the hairs on the back of my neck.

'And shut that dog up.' Leonardo's pitch heightened. His eyes were wild, his muscles tensed.

The old man was speaking to Rocky, but his voice was weak and she was working herself into a frenzy.

'Make it stop. Make it stop!' Leonardo was losing control of himself, too, the drugs and fear and anger reaching bursting point.

Rocky's lips were curled back, her vicious teeth clicked together each time her mouth snapped shut, and her eyes were rolling back in her head. Her attention was focused on Leonardo and she looked as if she might attack him at any moment.

'It's all right, girl,' the old man was trying to say. 'It's all right.'

He put his hand on her, but she was only agitated further by Leonardo's shouting and the smell of his fear.

With the pistol pressed under Daniella's chin, I couldn't let this continue. The slightest twitch from Leonardo would kill her.

'Rocky!' I shouted at her. 'Stop!'

But Leonardo had already decided to take action. He turned his pistol on Rocky and shot at her.

Daniella had sensed the loosening of his grip, though, and she moved against him, disturbing his aim so the bullet went wide, clipping the top of the gunwale and zipping out across the river. As Leonardo corrected his balance and levelled the pistol once more, the old man called Rocky's name and tried to stand. His muscles were racked with the pain of his fever, though, and his joints burned from whatever demon coursed through him.

He fell to his knees on the deck as Rocky rushed to him, startled by the gunshot. Her ears were flat against her head and her tail was tucked between her legs. Gathering her in his arms, the old man touched his head to Rocky's and spoke her name over and over again. He held her tight and looked up at Leonardo. 'Please,' he said. 'Don't.'

Daniella tugged her hand from Leonardo's and went to the old man, going to her knees beside him.

'Stay where you are,' Leonardo ordered as he stepped back and turned his gun on me.

'I'm not going anywhere.' I put out my hands, fingers spread. 'Just calm down. No more shooting.'

He turned the gun on Daniella and the old man once more, before bringing it back to bear on me, as if he were deciding who to kill first.

'No more shooting,' I said again. 'You're in charge; we'll do whatever you say. Let them go back to the wheelhouse. The dog will stay there.'

Leonardo thought about it, the gun still switching from me to them and back again.

'Daniella can tie up the dog,' I said. 'Please. Just don't kill her.'

Leonardo took a deep breath and clenched his jaw tight before nodding once. He turned to Daniella and spoke through gritted teeth. 'Do it. If it gets loose, I'll kill it.'

'Thank you,' the old man whispered as Daniella helped him to his feet. She kept the dog close as she brought him back to the wheelhouse and settled him on the seat behind the wheel. Rocky jumped up beside him and Daniella tied one end of a piece of narrow rope around her neck, securing the other end to one of the struts holding the canopy in place. Once that was done, she took the wheel and steered us straight in the river.

When I turned to face Leonardo, standing on the opposite side of the bow, he sniffed hard and pointed his pistol at me.

'If you shoot me,' I said, 'there'll be no one to pilot this boat for you.'

Leonardo thought for a moment, then shrugged and shifted his aim so the pistol was pointing to the wheelhouse. 'Come and sit beside me, Daniella.'

She looked at me, then rose to her feet and came back to the bow.

'Sit,' Leonardo said.

Daniella sat on the box seat, hatred clear in her eyes.

Leonardo put the gun against her ribs. 'Are we going to have a problem about this?' He stared right at me.

I looked over at Daniella and then at the old man sitting behind the wheel. The two people who meant more to me than anything else on earth. More, even, than my own life.

Leonardo knew my weakness just as Costa knew it.

'No,' I said. 'No.'

30

Approaching the mouth of the Rio das Mortes, the sky began to darken. The sun was shimmied from the sky by brooding clouds building behind us, their shadow falling over all below them.

Raul was slumped beside me, useless and weakened by his fever, as good as dead, as far as piloting the *Deus* was concerned. His eyes were closed as though sleeping and I could only imagine how he must be feeling. Beside him, Rocky stayed quiet as if she understood how ill her friend was.

Daniella watched the old man, shifting her gaze to look at me from time to time, and whenever our eyes met, I smiled at her, nodded or winked or found some other way to reassure her that we were going to be all right. Beside her, leaning back against the gunwale, watching her like a snake, Leonardo kept his pistol to hand.

I felt confident that I could take us onto the Rio das Mortes, manage at least a few kilometres before nightfall, but the sky was blackening as if a storm were approaching, and with rain over our heads, I wasn't so sure. The way it came down out here was like nothing I'd ever seen anywhere else. Sometimes it was so hard, it was impossible to stay outside, the water driving down like nails. If the rain came as hard as it had the day before yesterday – and I was sure it would – then I was certain it would stop our journey. Even Raul, with all his experience, took the boat to the shallows when he sensed the rain coming.

In weather like that, the water would chop, stirring all kinds of debris from the depths, eroding sections of the shore that would slip into the river. Small sandbanks could rise where there had once been none, visibility would be reduced to almost nothing, and it would be easy for the *Deus e o Diabo* to become marooned on a newly grown formation or drift from her course and veer towards land.

'We'll have to stop if it rains.' Mine were the first words anyone had spoken for some time. 'If we push hard, we might make it to Piratinga before the rain hits us. We don't want to get caught out here on—'

'Just keep going,' Leonardo told me.

'We're going to *have* to stop if it rains,' I said, sensing the wind pick up around us. 'Better to stop there than anywhere else.'

'We're not stopping.' Leonardo stood and came towards me, reminding me that he was in control now.

'If the rain hits us, it might as well be dark. We're not going anywhere in the kind of rain that's coming.'

'This another one of your lies?'

'No. Maybe I should even stop here, where it's safe.'

I didn't want to stop, though, and I didn't want to press on to the Rio das Mortes. Piratinga was within range now. Just another hour or so and we could be there.

The old man was sweating and shivering. A bead of blood had trickled from his nose and trailed to his lip where it had welled in a single ruby tear and dried the colour of rust. It looked like he had a rash coming too.

'Shit.' I banged my fist in frustration and set the boat straight down the centre of the river before leaving my seat.

'Where do you think you're going?' Leonardo asked as I pushed past him.

'There's nowhere for me to go. We're on a boat.' I moved to the side of the *Deus*, sensing Leonardo's suspicion. I could almost feel him tensing, finding the reassurance of his pistol.

'Don't do anything you—'

'I have to see where it is,' I said, looking at the sky and leaning out around the housing at the back, where the rifles were snug in their cases. The river was taken from sight by the bend we had just rounded and above it, where everything was blue just a few moments ago, things were beginning to change. I watched the bruised sky behind us, seeing the transformation as torment built in the distance.

'Well, at least we know which way it's coming from,' I said. 'Straight up our arse. And it's coming fast.'

Leonardo came to the stern, keeping a safe distance from me, but leaning out to see the thunderheads gathering. Together we watched them swell and I tried to make a guess at how long it might take for the rain to reach us. I could see it a long way off, like a sheet of haze cutting my view.

'It's close,' I said, going back to the wheel and looking at Raul and Daniella. 'We're going to have to stop soon. At least this cool air should make it a little easier on you, old man.' But with the breeze pushing on us already, it wouldn't be long before the rain caught up.

I turned the boat in towards the bank, searching for a spot where it would be safe to anchor.

'I told you; no stopping until—'

'Shut up.' I turned on Leonardo. 'Shut up and let me get on with this. If we stay out here, with rain like that, we'll be blind. You saw it, too. You've seen what's coming.'

Leonardo hesitated, looked at me, glanced down at his gun. 'You're lying.'

'If you want to shoot me, you're going to have to shoot me.' I was sick of him now. Sick of this whole trip. 'If I don't put this boat in, we're going to get caught out here and we're going to be screwed. I'm not going to be able to see and, at best, we're going to get beached. At worst we're going to hit something and the boat's going to sink. Either way I hope you can swim, and both ways you're not going to get your guns to Mina dos Santos on time.'

And then the boat lurched as the hull came into contact with something in the water, something smooth like a raised hump of sand. The engine sputtered as we passed on, the boat groaning as it ground over the obstruction.

Leonardo put out a hand to steady himself on the gunwale and stared at me as if I had drawn a gun and shot him.

I grabbed the wheel and took us away from the shallows, and when I looked back at Leonardo, he had pulled Daniella close to him and was holding his pistol to her waist. 'Don't do that again.'

'I didn't do anything other than take my eyes off the river. Now do you understand? In a few minutes I won't be able to see anything. We need to stop.'

'Keep going.'

'I saw your face just then. You were afraid. How much worse do you think it will be when the storm is here? You're frightened by a small bump like that, think what it will be like in the rain.'

He didn't reply.

'You're afraid of the water, aren't you?' I released the wheel. 'You can't swim.'

'Watch where you're going.'

'Oh, you mean you want me to steer the boat?' I took advantage of his fear. 'You want me to watch where we're going?'

'Yes.'

'Then let her go.'

Leonardo thought about it. He looked to the bank, then at the unmanned wheel.

'So,' I said, lowering my hands, letting the boat find her own course. 'What's it going to be?'

Leonardo shook his head and forced himself to smile as if this was going to be his decision. He was telling himself he was still in charge, that he could laugh it off. Truth was, though, none of us was in control any more, not as long as that weather was bearing down on us.

'OK,' he said, pushing Daniella away from him. 'Do what you have to do.'

I guided Daniella past me, indicating that she should go to the bow. There was fear and anger in her eyes, her hair falling forwards around her face, her shoulders hunched as if something wild were trying to inhabit her. Her usual poise was forgotten, and I squeezed her hand, hoping that it would instil just a little reassurance. When emotions like fear and anger mix, they can blind people into taking risks. Daniella had already struck out at Leonardo once, and I didn't want her to do anything else that would endanger her.

'Stay calm,' I whispered. 'Save your anger.'

Once she was out of Leonardo's reach, I turned back to the wheel, putting my hands on it and giving my attention to the riverbank. 'You made the right decision,' I said to Leonardo as I scanned the shoreline for something with a little shelter – perhaps a small inlet, a sandbank behind which I could tuck us – but on this side of the river there wasn't much. 'A few more minutes and we'll be blind. You thought that bump we just had was bad? That's nothing. In the storm, I reckon you'd shit yourself.'

'Don't try to play me,' Leonardo said. 'You won't win.'

'Why don't you just sit down,' I replied. 'This isn't a competition.'

And then, over the sound of the *Deus e o Diabo*, I heard the engine of another boat. A higher-pitched drone, coming from behind, growing louder by the second.

A smaller, faster boat.

31

I stopped the engine and hurried back to the gunwale, leaning out and waving to attract the attention of the smaller vessel.

'What the fuck are you doing?' Leonardo gripped my shoulder, dragging me away. 'What now? Get back here and control this damn boat.'

'They can take the old man,' I said to him. 'Take him back to Piratinga for us.'

I raised my arm to wave again, but Leonardo grabbed it, pulling it down. 'No one's getting off this boat. Let them pass.'

'They've seen the rain, too,' Daniella said, coming to stand with us, keeping away from Leonardo. 'They're trying to outrun it.'

'They stand a better chance than we do,' I agreed. 'They'll be in Piratinga in no time. Let them take the old man. Please.'

The boat was gaining on us and, for the second time in two days, we could see two men, both sitting near the back. One of them was controlling the outboard, the other holding onto his hat with one hand, his shirt open to the wind. I knew that Raul would be better off with them. Their boat was much smaller, and it would skip across the water. It would take us close to an hour to reach Piratinga if we were going that way, but they would be there in half that time. They'd probably get there before the rain.

'You're not making the decisions,' Leonardo said. 'We keep moving.'

But he was too late. Both men had noticed us and turned their boat towards us, slowing the engine.

'Jesus Christ.' Leonardo raised his pistol a touch more, as if he was considering putting it to use, then he kicked the gunwale and swore.

'Try not to kill anyone this time,' I said.

'I will if I have to.'

'You won't have to,' I said. 'Let them take the old man. Daniella, too. After that, I'll do whatever you want.'

'No one's getting off this boat. And don't you forget – I'll kill her.' Leonardo moved to stand beside Daniella. He put one arm around her waist and pressed his pistol against her hip so I could see it, but it was shielded from the approaching vessel. 'Or maybe kill you first and have some fun with her. She's pretty. Maybe enough to make me forget about the guns altogether.' He stared at me for a moment, listening to the sound of the motor coming closer.

'Let them take the old man,' I said. 'Please. He's of no use to you. After that I'll do whatever you want.'

'Get rid of them.'

The outboard sidled up to us, and the man at the front took hold of the tyres while the one operating the outboard dropped the engine to an idle and picked up a rifle which he set across his lap.

I recognised the man at the front, but couldn't place him. He was tall and dark, sinewy like a labourer, with a distinctive mark on the cheekbone under his right eye, where the skin was much darker. And then it came to me: I'd seen him drinking in Ernesto's a few times, talking with the others. I wasn't sure what he did, but I'd seen him hanging around with the men who worked over at the soya factory, so I guessed maybe he was a worker from there, too. He wasn't a *pistoleiro*, but I found myself looking at his clothing, searching for the tell-tale bump of a concealed weapon. Leonardo would be doing the same.

The only thing I could see was the hunting rifle, lying across the second man's lap. It was a standard twenty-two, the type of gun people used for hunting *paca* in the forest, maybe shooting a caiman, but if he was a good shot and he raised it quickly enough, he could protect his friend from where he was sitting. There were other things too; some lines, hooks, three good sized *tucunaré* wallowing in the inch or so of water which slopped in the bottom of the aluminium boat.

'Marcio, isn't it?' I said, aware of Leonardo watching me.

'*Marco*,' he replied, standing up and putting his hands on the gunwale so he could look into the *Deus* and survey our boat.

'Yeah, Marco. Sorry.'

'You're Zico, right? Raul's friend.' His eyes lingered on Leonardo for a moment, before he looked at Daniella. 'And you're the girl from the shop?'

Leonardo nudged her and Daniella nodded. 'Yes.'

'You I don't know.'

Leonardo smiled as if he were the luckiest man on the river. 'I'm her boyfriend.'

Marco considered his words, looking from me to Leonardo. 'What happened to your leg?'

'Bitten by a *jacaré*.'

'For real?' Marco didn't look convinced.

'Sneaked up on the beach last night and grabbed him in his sleep,' I said.

Marco whistled and shook his head, then looked at Daniella. 'You OK? Need some help?'

Beside me, Daniella grunted as Leonardo prodded the pistol into her.

'No,' I told him. 'We're good.' I was desperate to ask for Marco's help, but it might lead to something unspeakable, and I couldn't let that happen.

Marco came to the front of their outboard, climbing up onto the tyres so his face was level with my chest. He brought a rope with him and tied it off to one of the cleats on the *Deus*.

Leonardo shifted, keeping his gun hidden.

The man in the boat sat up a little straighter and rested his hands on his rifle.

'This is Raul's boat. Where's Raul?' Marco eyed me with suspicion.

'He's sleeping.' I hated saying it. I was betraying the old man instead of helping him.

'Sleeping?' Marco hesitated for a moment, maybe wondering if I was trying to trick him, then he took his eyes off me and leaned over to see along the boat. 'Is that him there? He looks sick.'

I turned towards the old man as if I hadn't known he was there. He was slumped in the wheelhouse, his head resting on the dashboard, one arm dangling down. Rocky was tied beside him, looking forlorn.

'He's fine,' Leonardo said. 'A little fever is all.'

'What kind of fever?' Marco asked. 'Dengue? There's been dengue in Piratinga, you know.'

'We'll get him home soon enough,' Leonardo replied.

'Not as fast as I can,' Marco answered. 'Storm's coming. You want me to take him?'

Beside me, I could feel Leonardo's tension. He was losing control of this situation and his temper was rising. These two men were not as easy a target as the two he had killed yesterday. Those men had been close together, lined up below him, easy to pick off. These two were separated, and suspicious. It would take seconds for the man in the boat to pick up his rifle, so Leonardo would have to shoot him first, but that would leave three of us for him to control and he didn't know whether or not Marco was armed. Even for a man like Leonardo, those odds were not good.

'We'll make it,' Leonardo said, struggling to keep his tone level. 'We'll get there in time. Before the rain.'

'In this shit heap?' Marco said. 'Come on, you know how slow this is.' He looked at me. 'We put him on my boat, I can get him to Piratinga in no time.'

Marco studied Leonardo for a moment, as if he didn't quite trust him, then hauled himself up onto the *Deus*.

I took the opportunity to show Leonardo a discreet and questioning look.

Are we going to let them take him?

Leonardo clamped his jaw tight and blinked hard in frustration. There was a pause, then he nodded once, almost imperceptible, but enough to give me the tiniest sense of relief. As soon as he had done it, though, he dug his pistol a little harder into Daniella's ribs, making her wince in pain.

Marco heard the sound and turned to look at them. Leonardo smiled at him and the two watched each other before Marco turned back to the old man.

'How long has he been like this?' He was barefoot, his feet wet from the water in his own boat, and he left prints on the boards of the *Deus*.

'A while,' I said.

'And why is Rocky tied? She's never tied.'

'He doesn't like dogs.' I tilted my head in Leonardo's direction.

The air was growing darker and cooler now. It was a strange grey-blue light, with the sun still above us, and the black, brooding clouds in the distance, rumbling and flashing. The breeze was picking up and carrying the smell of the forest across the water. It was damp and earthy, as if being brought from the centre of the storm, rushing along the course of the river, swelling around the *Deus* and moving on towards Piratinga. It would be on us soon and, judging by the smell and the speed of the wind, it would be bad.

I followed Marco, but Leonardo hung back where he could see the man with the rifle. He tried to appear relaxed and sat on the bench seat, bringing Daniella down beside him, keeping his arm around her so his pistol was blocked from view.

'Some kind of fever,' I said. 'Been getting worse, but he's been like this for an hour or so.'

'Looks like it could be dengue.'

'I still say he'll be fine.' Leonardo shifted on the bench.

Marco watched him for a few moments then squatted beside Raul. The old man was drenched with sweat, despite the cool breeze leading the oncoming storm, and his face was flushed bright red.

'He's not fine.' Marco scratched Rocky's ear when she stood to greet him. 'He needs a doctor. Shit, he looks really bad. You want him to die because you can't get him to a doctor in time?'

'You're probably right,' I agreed. 'With that rain coming up behind us, we're not going to make it back to Piratinga. This boat's not fast enough. We're going to end up stuck out here.'

'So you want me to take him?'

'Yes.'

Marco lowered his voice. 'Is everything OK here?'

I considered asking for a different kind of help, but I thought about what Leonardo had done yesterday, and how he had shot at Rocky, and I remembered the gun in his hand and where it was pointed.

'Yeah. Everything's fine. I just need you to help the old man.'

We remained still for a beat, Marco with his body facing Raul, his face turned back towards me, then he spoke. 'Of course I'll take him. Raul's a good man.'

'Yes he is.'

'Then we're wasting time. Come on, help me.'

'He'll slow you down,' Leonardo interrupted. 'Leave him here.'

'Let him go,' I said to him. 'Rocky too. That way we'll have no more problems.' And I looked him right in the eye, letting him know that if he did this for the old man, I would do what he asked of me. I would get him to Mina dos Santos.

The muscles in Leonardo's jaws tensed. I could see them bulging and working, his upper lip lifting a fraction so that a wrinkle appeared beside his right nostril. Then he sighed and waved with his free hand. 'Take him. For Christ's sake just take him. And take the damn dog too.'

Marco and I pulled Raul to his feet. He was conscious and his eyes opened, but he was feverish and delirious and weak. He was unable to walk without our help, and he was barely able to speak. 'What's going on?' he asked, his voice quiet and dry.

'Getting you home faster,' I said. 'Marco will take you.'

Raul turned his head, his neck moving like it was on a ratchet. 'Marco?'

'Sure.' Marco patted Raul's shoulder. 'We'll get you home, old man. Don't you worry.'

Raul nodded and allowed us to guide him to the edge of the boat, where we helped him over the side. Marco and I took most of his weight, while the other man came over and held onto the *Deus* with both hands, pulling the smaller boat against it.

'Take him to Ernesto's,' I said, grunting with effort as we finally manoeuvred Raul into the smaller vessel. 'Ernesto will call his wife, take him to the hospital.'

'Sure,' said Marco. 'I'll make sure he's OK.'

'Thank you.'

I went back for Rocky, untying her and lifting her down into the outboard where she went straight to be close to the old man.

Marco was sitting beside Raul, keeping him from collapsing into the water, while the other man revved the engine, preparing to leave. 'You want to come, too?' Marco looked up at Daniella. 'A storm's no place for you.'

'She's fine right where she is,' Leonardo told him. 'Just take the old man and get the hell out of here.'

Marco narrowed his eyes at Leonardo before turning to me. 'By the way,' he said. 'You seen another boat on the river? Anyone passed you?'

I shook my head. 'No one.'

Marco nodded. 'My brother was out fishing for a couple of days.' He glanced back at the approaching storm. 'I saw him yesterday but there's been no sign of him today. I don't want him to get caught in the rain. You sure you haven't seen any one?'

'Sure,' I said.

'He's a little taller than me, wears a red cap. He and his friend were in a boat like this one.'

'Maybe he already made it back to Piratinga,' I ventured.

'Hmm. Maybe.'

32

'You killed his brother,' I said as the small boat became nothing but a trail of disturbed water.

'You do something like that again, I'll kill *you*,' Leonardo said. 'Or her.' He pushed Daniella away from him. 'And you'd better hope we get to Mina dos Santos before the old man sends someone after us.'

'He won't send anyone, he hardly even knew where he was. Anyway, we're here to make some money and that's what we're going to do. He knows it and I know it. And you don't need that.' I inclined my head towards his gun. 'Not any more. I'll do what you want now.'

'Well, I'll keep it handy all the same.'

'You can trust me to make your delivery if that's what you're thinking. We *will* make it to Mina dos Santos. There's no way it's not going to happen now. We're going to make your delivery and your people are going to pay me. The old man needs that money.' And I needed to get there before Sister Dolores Beckett. I had to be waiting for her, but any more delays and I might end up having to chase her up the Rio das Mortes after leaving Leonardo and his cargo. It would be difficult to explain that to Daniella. And thinking about the nun reminded me I had another weight on my mind; another tough choice to make.

'The Rio das Mortes is up ahead,' I told him. 'We'll get on it and stop. After that...' I shrugged. 'After that we wait for the sky to clear.'

Behind us, the rain was a stampeding herd, unstoppable in its advance, so I took the wheel, guided the *Deus* to the mouth of the

Rio das Mortes, and took us as far upriver as I dared before steering us well inshore. The course was wide where the two rivers met, but narrowed as we headed deeper, as if the world was closing in on us. With the darkening sky and the thick forest reaching up on either side, there was a very different sensation to be had from being on the Rio das Mortes. There was still the loneliness and isolation, but there was a more imposing and threatening feeling. The openness was gone, replaced by the dark embrace of the wilderness. It was as if the country was gathering itself around us in the way the shadow gathered itself around me. The beaches were fewer and smaller, just tiny strips of white sand. Some were marked with the tracks of turtles that had pulled themselves ashore at night, others were untouched, but all would soon be drowned by the rising water. There were shallow inlets, but in most places the forest grew right up to the edge of the water and the undergrowth was thick and impenetrable. The air was different here, too; it carried a darker, earthier smell as the odour of living trees mixed with the decaying detritus that lay at their roots.

I brought the boat as shallow as I could, and once the *Deus* was secured, I helped myself to a Coke from the cool box and retook my seat behind the wheel, leaning back, putting my feet up on the dash.

Daniella came to sit with me, Leonardo staying at the bow, watching us.

'Not much for us to do now except wait,' I told her. 'And Leonardo should be more relaxed – there's no reason not to just go straight to Mina dos Santos and finish the job.'

'Raul will be all right,' she said, understanding that I was worried about him. She knew what he meant to me. 'I'm sure of it. It's good they took him.'

'Yeah. I'm glad he's gone. He's safer – *we're* safer – but there's something about seeing him go,' I said, 'that doesn't feel right. He should be my responsibility. I should be taking him.'

'You know that couldn't happen.'

'No. But still ...' I shrugged. 'It feels wrong. Final, somehow.'

'Don't say that. You'll see him when we get back.'

'Yeah.'

'Shouldn't we get to shore?' Leonardo called to me. 'You said we shouldn't be out in the storm.'

'We're safe here,' I told him.

'You sure about that?' He looked worried, but I turned away from him and spoke to Daniella. 'The water might chop a bit, give him a scare, but it shouldn't be too bad. And there's more shelter here. We should stay under the canopy and wait for the rain. If it's gone before dark, we'll move on. If not, we can sleep on the boat tonight.'

I went to the side, leaned over and looked out to see how far off the rain was. 'They'll be well on their way to Piratinga by now,' I said. 'Maybe the old man is feeling better, looking forward to being home with Carolina. She'll make him right.' Or he might be lying face down between the slats, his cheek in the water that wallowed in the bottom of the boat.

I shook my head at Daniella. 'I'm sorry. I shouldn't have let you come.'

'What?' she said. 'And miss this? Not for the world.'

I smiled at her strength, and looked over at Leonardo watching us. Forever watching us.

'Is it always this exciting?' Daniella asked.

'Usually it's boring.' I turned away from Leonardo, knowing I'd have to shut him out. There was nothing to be done with him right now, and if I brooded, I'd eat myself from the inside out. I would take him to Mina dos Santos, we would deliver his guns and then he would pay me.

Then I would set my mind to the other task I had to carry out.

I hadn't thought about Sister Dolores Beckett for some time, but now she appeared to me once more as that black and grey image. Monochrome dots floating in my consciousness, merging to form her likeness, and I wondered what Sofia's advice would be. What would Daniella say? I watched her and thought about how it would feel to explain my dilemma to her. I had a sense of relieving the weight of my choices, but also of burdening her. And what would she think of me, that I was even *considering* Sister Beckett's death?

'Maybe we should press on a bit further,' I said feeling a sudden eagerness to reach the mine and be done with all of this. The sooner it was finished, the sooner I could get home and put it behind me. 'Perhaps the rain won't be so heavy, or maybe it'll take a while to get here. I could at least push us a little further upriver. That way we'll get there quicker. Get back to Piratinga faster.'

'He'll be OK, you know.' Daniella put her hand on my face and turned my head so I was looking at her. 'He'll be fine. Carolina will make sure of it.'

'Yeah.' I nodded. 'But I can't help worrying about him he's ...' I shook my head.

'Like a father,' Daniella said. 'I know.'

I turned and leaned on the gunwale, looking back at the approaching storm. 'I want to get back to him. To do something for him. I feel so weak.'

'What would Raul do?' Daniella asked. 'Go further or stay here?'

I stared at the gathering storm, the dark clouds like pursuing beasts spurred on by the thunder that bayed at them. Outlined from time to time by the flickering whiteness of lightning, forcing them closer. Before long, that turmoil would wrap itself around us, taking our senses. If I lost our way because of the poor visibility, our journey would take even longer. And if I damaged the boat, my friend's livelihood, I could never forgive myself. After all, Imperatriz might not have been Raul's dream, but the *Deus* and this delivery were his way of trying to make it happen for his wife.

'He'd stay here.' I sat down and gripped the wheel, my mind divided between starting her up or staying where I was. Whatever I did, I didn't want to let my friend down. But even as I thought about it, the first rain began to fall. Tiny ripples and splashes in the river that grew with each passing second, and as it became heavier and harder, I knew there was no way I could take the *Deus* into it.

It came at us as a wall of water, a hazy force advancing over the forest, then reaching the Rio das Mortes and beating the surface to froth. One moment it was beyond our reach, just the sound and the rush of cool air coming at us, and the next it was on us and over us and around us. The nails of water were driving into the canvas above, pounding the exposed deck at the bow of the *Deus*, and battering the tin roof of the covered stern section. It was like the staccato rattle of gunfire that had been my childhood lullaby.

There were many times in the *favela* when rival gangs exchanged shots over the rooftops, muzzles flashing in the night. Some even used tracer rounds that flickered like fireflies as they spat back and forth. As a child, the crackle and stutter had frightened me, and Pai would sit with me, stroking my head to soothe me. Voices would shout in the streets, but he would reassure me. When he was dead and buried, though, I was already twelve years old and accustomed to the sounds. Instead of cowering in our beds, Sofia and I would sit up and play cards or listen to Pai's old tapes, turning up the volume and singing along with the words. Sofia even taught me to samba, telling me that when I was older, the girls would love it that I could dance.

Leonardo ran for cover at the stern as the rain vented itself upon us, penetrating everything, splashing back from the deck, driving in at an angle. We were little protected under the canvas awning. My legs were quickly soaked and I drew myself inwards, huddling as small as possible. Daniella crushed herself against me as the cool wind rushed around us, making the rain feel cold on our skin.

I reached for a poncho that was on the floor under the wheel and pulled it over us. We drew our feet up onto the seat and hugged our knees, keeping our heads low beneath the waterproof.

Daniella smiled as if the downpour had come to clean it all away. Everything that had happened on the boat since leaving Piratinga, it all came to a stop when the water fell from the sky. Even Leonardo was silenced into insignificance behind us as the rain cascaded onto the canvas, beating out its own rhythm of nature.

And somewhere not far away, the sky rumbled and cracked as if it were being torn apart.

33

The rain came down and down through the afternoon. We ate cold rice left over from the day before, and the last of the beef strips that Carolina had prepared for the old man and me. We barely interacted with Leonardo other than to exchange a look from time to time. Had it not been for the constant and unnerving threat of his presence, it would have been as if he were not on the boat at all.

I hoped the rain would let up before dark, allowing us to push further west before nightfall. Raul was off the boat and we were set towards our destination, an unavoidable path now that Leonardo had taken control, so my instinct was to move on and get this over and done with.

The problem I would then face was how to make the nun disappear. Alone in Mina dos Santos, it would have been easy for me to find the right moment, but Daniella made everything more complicated. The gold mine was a wild and chaotic place, full of the worst kinds of people, and I would not want to leave her side. Finding the opportunity to be alone with Sister Beckett would be difficult, but if I missed that opportunity, I would have to follow her upriver to find another chance. Santiago's boat could put three times as much water behind her in a day than the *Deus* could, and it would be close to impossible to catch them, but I couldn't return to Piratinga without having completed Costa's job. Daniella and the old man would suffer for that and, of course, five thousand dollars would slip through my fingers.

I stared out at the rain, my head spinning with all the obstacles that had fallen in my path, and I wondered if the nun had more influence than I had first imagined. Perhaps someone up there was trying to stop me from completing my task. Maybe she had more protection than I thought. I had talked with Costa about bodyguards, and when he said she travelled without them, I thought it would make my job easier, but maybe she had protection of a more heavenly kind.

'If this doesn't stop soon,' I said, 'we're going to have to spend the night here.'

Beside me, protected beneath our tarpaulin, Daniella shivered. 'It's cold. I should have brought something warmer to wear.'

'Nothing in your bag?'

She shook her head. 'Just another skirt and top. And I need to pee.'

I looked over at the shore, squinting through the haze to see the bank just a few metres from where we were moored. In the sunshine, it would be easy, but now, in this rain, it would be like going into a war zone. The water was boiling, as if it flowed through hell, and the rain pelted the trees with a terrible vengeance. In a storm like this, I believed even Corpo Seco and Anhangá would stay hidden.

'I don't want you going back there. I'll have to bring the bucket.'

I shrugged.

'Great,' she sighed. 'Get me the bucket then.'

So I left her huddled under the waterproof and went to the back of the boat. As soon as I was out of the wheelhouse, the rain that drove in at the exposed sides of the boat soaked my shirt and trousers. I pulled my cap low and cursed the weather, heading towards Leonardo who was sheltered in the rear section of the *Deus*, the door wedged open so he could watch us. He was sitting on the floor, leaning against the boxes of rifles, his legs outstretched. The bandage was still tight around his right calf and it looked clean. No blood had soaked through.

At first, the rain had angered Leonardo. He had leaned on the gunwale and cursed it, shouting into the grey that surrounded us. But nothing out there was impressed by his threats, and when he fired his pistol at the trees, nothing had changed. As the hours passed, he grew more irritable, and then more calm as if resigning himself to helplessness as the storm stayed over us. From time to time, though, he fished the folded paper from his pocket and took a pinch of the *cocaína*, so we kept as far away from him as possible. I had seen how the drug could overload his mind and I didn't want to be close to him if that happened again.

'You enjoying the rain?' he asked, pushing back his cap.

I leaned down and took the bucket from beside the store.

'Did you hear what I said?'

'No, I'm not enjoying the rain, but I don't see there's much I can do about it. And I bet you're glad we're not out there, like you wanted.'

I thought about the knife under my shirt. I considered reaching for it; bringing out that steel and leaning down and ...

'Don't look at me like that, Zico, it makes me nervous.' Leonardo lifted the muzzle of his pistol just enough to angle it up at me.

Without another word, I backed away, returning to the wheelhouse and passing the bucket to Daniella.

'You're not going to stand there,' she said as it disappeared beneath the cocoon of the waterproof. 'I don't want you watching me.'

'I can't see you.'

'I don't want you listening, then.'

'Oh. Right.' I nodded. 'Sure.'

I moved towards the middle of the boat, and Leonardo laughed as I came closer to him.

'Nature,' he said as he gripped the side of the doorframe with one hand and pulled himself up, trying to keep his leg straight. He winced as if it might be giving him pain, but I saw the flash of irritation in his eyes too.

Once he was standing, Leonardo looked out at the river, and for a fraction of a second, there was something boyish about him. Young and fit and good-looking, I wondered what it was that had brought him to this moment in time.

'You can't stop nature,' he said.

'Maybe.' I watched the water, seeing a million drops hitting its surface like scatter gun pellets, ripples merging and fighting one another for space in the vast river. The insistent hammering on the tin roof and the canvas over my head marrying in a numbing harmony that became a single sound in my skull. Patches of brown-white froth whipped up around the banks and broke free and floated out into the river like small islands, and although I cursed my luck and I cursed the weather around me, I could see there was a terrible beauty in it.

'Whatever we do, it's always stronger than us,' he said. 'You can't stop it.'

'Tell that to the bulldozers.'

Leonardo nodded as if he hadn't thought of it like that. 'That's true. Maybe some nature you *can* stop.'

'Mina dos Santos is like a hole in the ground,' I said. 'I don't see nature winning there. Unless there's nothing left for them to mine, I can't see people wanting to leave. If there's nothing left, maybe people will move on, find somewhere else, and then the forest will grow back like that other place we saw, but otherwise...' I shrugged and clicked my tongue, a melancholy mood coming over me, brought on by the hypnotising beat of the rain.

In that second, I could believe that neither of us was in charge now, there was no captain on this boat. The weather had levelled us. Now we were just two men, equal on the river, and perhaps it meant that for a while we could behave as men should.

'Maybe the owners will push out,' Leonardo said. 'Make the mine a whole lot bigger.'

'Too much Indian land round here,' I told him. 'That mine's not getting any bigger. There are too many people trying to stop it.'

I put a hand round as if to scratch my back.

'I heard there are landowners, *big* landowners who own that place. Everyone else, they just work for *them*.'

'Of course there are. There's always someone bigger.' I looked at the water and slipped my hand beneath my shirt, reaching for my knife. 'There's always a bigger fish. Someone at the top taking their cut.'

'And maybe they're looking to expand,' he said.

As my fingertips brushed the handle of my knife, I looked round at him, beginning to see a connection between the rifles and Sister Beckett. Landowners and activists and guns weren't a good mix and I wondered how they all fitted together. 'Yeah? I haven't heard anything. Where d'you hear that?'

Leonardo shrugged. 'Around.' He leaned to one side so he was facing me. His right arm rested along the gunwale, the pistol still in his hand. Three or four steps and I would be right beside him. If I could knock his hand, or run my blade across it, the gun would fall into the river and he would no longer be dangerous. But all he had to do was move that barrel a few centimetres to one side and he could shoot me as dead as he had shot the fishermen.

I glanced back at the wheelhouse, where Daniella was huddled beneath the waterproof, and once more imagined what would happen to her, alone with Leonardo in the storm.

I withdrew my fingers and took a deep breath. 'You know this was an important place for the Portuguese?' I said. 'They used to mine gold here. The old man told me that.'

'Yeah?'

'He said they took a lot of gold back then. There's supposed to be treasures hidden somewhere out here, too, buried by a slave. Jose Maria dos Santos.'

'Sounds like shit to me.'

'Yeah, well, maybe these landowners are hoping to find it.' I watched for another reaction, thinking he knew more than he was saying, talking about expansion. 'Find gold, at least. But they're not going to hose for small flakes, they'll blast it out. Blow the place to hell.'

'It's the kind of thing they'd do.'

'And it sounds like you know something no one else does.'

He couldn't help himself, the way his eyes flickered and he glanced at the cases we had unloaded from the plane. A quick look, almost too quick to notice, but it was there. And that look gave a lot away. He knew something was going to happen.

'What are they for, Leonardo? What are the guns for? You starting a war?'

'You really want to know, don't you? The old man said he never wants to know, but you do, don't you?'

'What are you?' I asked. 'Some kind of fortune hunter?'

'I don't give a shit about digging for gold. Do I look like a worker to you? It's money I'm interested in.'

'A mercenary, then?'

'I'm just a guy who gets paid for doing a job others don't want to do.' He watched me. 'And I'm guessing that's a lot like you.'

'I already told you, we're nothing alike.'

'We both—'

'No,' I said. 'You like it too much. The things I do ... I do for money. You do it because it gives you a thrill. And you know what, Leonardo? For people like you, it never ends well.'

'For people like *us*,' he replied.

I shivered and folded my arms at my chest as an image of Sister Beckett filled my mind. She was intruding into my thoughts more and more; as constant a presence as my fear for Daniella and the old man. But it was not excitement that I felt when I thought about her. It was guilt and shame and loss. The same feelings that filled me when I thought about how I had failed Sofia and how Antonio had been dragged into my feud with Luis and Wilson.

'I'm not like you.' I said the words through gritted teeth.

Leonardo stepped towards me, his pistol practically moulded to his hand it had been there so long. I don't know what he was going to say or do, but he was distracted by movement from the wheelhouse.

Daniella was emerging from the waterproof like a butterfly breaking out of its chrysalis. The cover opened wide and she stepped out, going to the edge of the boat and throwing the contents of the bucket overboard before she rushed back under the cover. She barely even glanced at us before she returned to her cocoon and disappeared.

'Nice,' said Leonardo. 'I like to see a girl throwing her piss overboard.'

'Don't even look at her,' I said without thinking.

'Or what? What will you do?'

'Nothing,' I said, nodding at the weapon in his hand. 'As long as you have that. But remember – I'm not just stuck on this boat with you. *You're* stuck on it with *me*.'

34

It rained for a long time and the sky was bleeding light when it finally let up. The clouds broke apart and moved on, the falling sun showing its last as the day faded from us, a blood-red marbling staining the sky over the trees. The river settled and there was relief from the attack on our canopy. The perpetual sound of driving rain was gone, leaving a tranquil emptiness that was accompanied only by the music of rainwater falling from the trees and draining into the river.

'So what now?' Daniella threw off our cocoon and stood to stretch in the damp evening. 'We carry on?'

'We'll have to stay here,' I told her. 'We can't go any further in the dark.' Tendrils of steam rose from the deck, hanging low in the air, breaking in the occasional draught, swirling and vanishing.

Daniella made a tutting noise and went to the side of the boat, taking a breath of the fresh air that's always left when the rain moves on. She stared out into the remaining light. 'It looks beautiful,' she said. 'You know, in all the time I've lived here, I've never been on the river when it got dark after a storm.'

I went to stand beside her. 'It would be even more beautiful if *he* wasn't here.'

'Hmm,' she agreed.

'I was angry before. About you being here.'

'I know.'

'Not just because I thought it was dangerous, though. You were right when you said I'm like another person sometimes. I didn't want you to see that. But now? Now I'm glad you're here. Maybe we should come out on our own sometime,' I said. 'When this is all done with, I mean. We can spend a few days together. Leave everything behind like we're the only ones left in the world.'

Daniella smiled and raised her eyebrows. 'Imagine my mother's face if I told her we were going to do that.'

'You're here now, aren't you? Anyway, she'd have no choice if we were married.'

Daniella turned to me, a quick movement. 'Are you asking me to marry you?'

'I can't afford you at the moment.'

'You don't have to afford me, Zico. You just have to love me.'

'I do.'

'So *are* you asking me?'

'Would you say yes?'

'Try me.' She put her hand on mine, her skin warm. There were faint impressions across her fingers, from the stitching at the edge of the waterproof under which we had retreated.

'When the time is right,' I said.

Daniella sighed. 'If he wasn't here ...' She let her words trail away, taking another deep breath.

'Don't,' I told her. 'Don't say it. Don't even think it. I have to focus. I shouldn't have said anything.' There were times, like right then, that I felt she was all I needed. We could be together, have a good life. Not a rich one, not a *wealthy* one, but a good one. Other times, I thought I wasn't good enough for her, that maybe her mother was right. After all, I was aiming to finance our marriage on the proceeds of Sister Beckett's death. Our relationship was to be based on a murder that I couldn't avoid.

She smiled and squeezed my hand. 'We *are* going to get out of this, aren't we?'

'Of course we are.'

From the store at the back of the *Deus*, we took a black and white spotted hammock that had seen better days, and I strung it between two of the supporting poles as close to the wheelhouse as I could. I guessed that Leonardo was going to stay at the stern, protecting his crates and keeping his watchful eyes on us.

When Daniella asked if one hammock would be enough, I told her I didn't expect to sleep much that night. 'I'm going to watch him. Keep you safe.'

We were close enough to the bank to hear the cicadas, and now that the rain had passed, and the lull in its wake had settled, they were singing louder to make up for lost time. The other insects had come out in force, too, flickering across the surface of the river. From time to time there was a sharp splash in the water as *tucunaré*, or one of the other wide-mouthed surface feeders, leaped for an insect which strayed too close to a hungry fish. And, as the evening darkened, bats emerged from the forest, flitting across the river and taking the insects from the air.

'You'll need a net,' I said to Daniella, as I tied off the first end of the hammock. 'To keep the mosquitoes away.'

'Dengue fever,' Daniella said. 'You think that's what Raul has?' She pulled the strings tight at the other end, waiting for me to take them from her.

There'd been an outbreak of dengue when I was in Rio, in the dirt of the *favela*. Many people had been ill with it, headaches, fever, aching muscles and joints, the fever lasting not much more than a week. There were those who had bruised like the old man, and others who had been much worse. I'd seen people bleeding from their eyes, blood oozing through the pores in their skin. They weren't so lucky. They died slowly, the blood leaking out of their bodies.

Some of the old women said it was evil spirits in their bodies making them sick; that there was nothing they could do to stop them. Sofia told me that the Candomblé priests and priestesses said it was destiny. Not good or evil, just destiny. Either way, they believed there was no hope for the sick – that those who were going to die were going to die. But I had to believe Raul would be all right. I had to.

'With treatment he'll be fine,' I said, as much to convince myself as to convince Daniella. I forced a smile and took the hammock cords from her hands, tying them off, making sure it was safe.

'I hope they got to the hospital in time.'

I stayed where I was, both hands on the hammock, staring at the black and white design. Like dots on a piece of newspaper. 'They did,' I told her. 'I can feel it. The old man will be fine.'

'What makes you so sure?'

'Because ...' I tried to find the right words. 'Because I can't imagine life without him.'

There was rice and *farinha* left in the tins, but they were dry and dull on their own, so I put a lure on one of the old man's lines and fished in the place where I'd seen *tucunaré* surfacing for the insects.

Leonardo watched from a safe distance as I pulled the lure across the water, close to the shore, where the river was littered with sunken forest. Above us, bats skittered and dived in the final moments of dusk, small black shapes flickering like old movie pictures, their movements spasmodic and unreal.

'You're not much of a fisherman,' Leonardo said after twenty minutes of fruitless attempts, the sun finally sliding away, the river lit only by the winking cataract of a crescent moon on the blind face of the night.

But even in the darkness, I continued to cast, telling myself that if I caught a fish, then the old man would be all right. If I landed us something to eat, it meant the old man was in the hospital with nurses around him and Carolina at his side.

'It's too late,' said Leonardo. 'They won't bite in the dark.' But, as if to prove him wrong, I felt the line tug and I landed a good fish with plenty of meat on it.

I took it as a lucky sign.

The old man would live.

'So now what?' Leonardo asked as I took the fish from the hook. 'We going to eat it raw?'

'Who said anything about we?' I looked up at him. 'You want to eat fish, *you* catch one.' I dropped the roll of fishing line on the deck for him and went to the covered section at the back of the boat.

'You're not going in there,' he said, making me stop and turn.

'All I want is something to cook with.'

He thought about it, then nodded and raised his pistol as if I might have forgotten he still had it.

'You know, we all just want the same thing,' I said. There was enough light to make out his shape, the outline of his features, indistinct like a child's drawing. On a moonless night, the darkness would have been complete, but tonight the sky provided a candle.

'And what's that?' he asked. 'What do we all want?'

'To get you to Mina dos Santos, drop your cargo and never see each other again.'

'All the same...' He lifted the pistol again.

'You don't need to shoot anyone.' I went to rummage in the store at the back of the boat. When I returned, I was carrying a lamp and an old can of cooking oil, much like a jerrycan, that had been split down the middle, from top to bottom. The edges were rough where it had been ripped in two and there was a grill to place across the top.

'Can't always get ashore,' I said. 'And you can't exactly light a fire on the deck.'

Leonardo gave Daniella a knife to gut the fish while I tended the barbecue. When the coal was hot enough, we laid the fish on the grill, and soon the air was filled with the smell of its cooking flesh.

Daniella and I ate it with cold rice, sitting by the barbecue for its warmth. Leonardo took his knife and his share of the meat, a handful of rice, and limped back to his cave like a wounded and dangerous animal. He sat in the doorway to the storeroom, blocking our path to anything that might be used to cause him harm.

'You should have let him starve,' Daniella said.

'What good would that do?' I squinted and looked down the length of the boat. The moon was little more than a wink, but combined with the glow from the barbecue, the light was just about good enough for me to see Leonardo's dark shape sitting alone. 'All it would do is piss him off. We need to keep him happy. Happy people make mistakes, they get lazy, they forget to do something, watch something...'

'And then what?'

'And then I don't know,' I said, thinking about my knife.

'Would you ...' She stopped with her fork halfway to her mouth and looked at it before putting it down on her plate.

'I'll do what I have to do. But for now, all that means is getting him to Mina dos Santos.'

'What he did to those people yesterday,' she said. 'How can he do something like that?'

'It happens all the time.' I stared into the embers that glowed and weakened.

'I know ...' she sighed. 'But those people did nothing wrong.'

'Leonardo doesn't care about that.' I watched her face, seeing nothing but shadow and shape, a glint of orange where the coals reflected in her eyes.

Daniella and I sat together, talking and watching the night, keeping our voices low to exclude our captor. And when she kissed me, I allowed myself to be lost in her taste for just a moment before dragging myself back to the boat and the reality of our situation. Eventually, she rested her head on my shoulder and became quiet.

'You're tired,' I told her. 'You should sleep.'

'Not sure I'll be able to. I never liked sleeping in a hammock.'

'You should try.'

'What about you?'

'I already told you. Not tonight.' I took her hand and pulled her to her feet. 'Tonight I watch over you.'

'You promise?'

I held both her hands in mine. 'I promise.'

For a while it felt as if we were alone and I had to remind myself that Leonardo was still there, like a ghost, sitting in the darkness.

35

I waited until Daniella was settled in the hammock, then I went to the side of the boat and sat on the deck, positioning myself so Leonardo couldn't get to her without passing me.

'She's asleep?' he asked.

'What does it matter?' I spoke quietly so Daniella wouldn't be disturbed by our words.

'It doesn't.' Leonardo came to sit near me. He settled on the box seat, a couple of metres away, taking the high ground.

Clouds had formed above us, covering much of the sky including what there was of the moon, and I assumed that the pistol was still in his hand, probably pointed straight at me. Now the only light was from the remains of the barbecue, and everything outside the boat was black. The world had ceased to exist beyond the weak orange glow of the charcoal; everything had been erased and only we remained, surrounded by the alien sounds of the night forest coming to life. As if demons were pushing at our small barrier of light, waiting for it to fade before they could storm our last defences.

It was enough to drive a man insane.

'I looked in your pack.' Leonardo leaned forward to spit into the fading embers. 'I thought it was mine at first, it's hard to tell the difference in the dark.'

'Did you find anything you like?'

'Uh-huh.' He fumbled for a moment, then a match flared and I saw his face in the brilliance of the flame. The smell of phosphorus floated to me, a sweet and pleasant odour that faded almost as quickly as it had appeared. He flicked the match overboard and dragged on his cigarette.

'What's this?' He clicked on the torch from my pack. The beam was directed at the newspaper clipping Costa had given me yesterday morning.

I fought the urge to sit up and snatch it from him. I couldn't let him think it was important. I didn't want him to mention it to Daniella.

'Who is she?' he asked.

'Can you read?'

'Of course I can read.'

'Then read it.'

Leonardo turned the clipping so he could look at the words. He shone the torch at the black print, then shook his head and threw it to me. 'You read it. My eyes are tired.'

'You can't read.'

He didn't reply.

'Don't be ashamed,' I told him. 'There are worse things about you. And I can't read either. How about that? Two illiterate gunmen struggling over a piece of newspaper.' I looked at the typed words and wondered what they said about the small woman surrounded by people. 'But I'll learn.'

'You won't.'

'What makes you say that?'

'Because there's no reason for it. You are what you are.'

I turned the paper over in my fingers, staring at the picture of Dolores Beckett. 'Maybe I want to change,' I said. 'Be something else.'

'Impossible.'

'For you maybe.' I folded the clipping along the creases that were already there, the soft paper closing in on itself, hiding the doomed nun from sight. I slipped it into my shirt pocket, back where it had been before, as if it were its rightful place.

'So who is she?'

'She's no one.'

I watched Leonardo finish his cigarette and light another one from the firefly stub of the first. His face appeared in the glow every now and then when he took a long drag, and I could hear the faint crackle of the tobacco, the inhalation of breath. Somewhere out in the darkness, life surged. The simmering blackness, completely devoid of light, was filled with the electric hum of peeps and flutters and croaks and chirrups. An endless assortment of life, each with its individual voice contributing to an orchestra of sound that was almost tangible; as if I could reach out over the side of the boat and touch it, draw it into the light with my fingertips.

'It's so damn dark,' Leonardo said.

We might have been suspended over oblivion, the last remaining people on earth. He shivered and drew himself closer to the embers.

'You afraid of the *mapinguari*?' I asked. 'Maybe the *boitatá*?'

'I don't even know what that is.'

'It's a giant headless snake with horns and burning eyes. Blind during the day, but at night it sees everything. Comes out to look for food.'

Leonardo snorted and spat overboard. 'Sounds like something for the *camponêses* and *pescadores*.'

'Well, they believe it,' I said. 'And looking out there it's hard not to believe there's something in the darkness. There's worse things than *jacaré* out there.'

He straightened his injured leg in front of him and leaned back, glancing over his shoulder. The pistol was visible now, hanging limp in his hand, the coals glinting on the steel.

'There are places where it's like the forest goes on for ever,' I told him. 'You'll see it yourself when we go upriver. It gets narrow, the trees close in on you and it feels like something's watching you from in there. You see things.' I stared out at the darkness of the trees. 'And if you're not superstitious,' I said, 'how come you have the *figa* round your neck?'

'Someone gave it to me.'

'The same person you were thinking about yesterday? Someone important?'

Leonardo said nothing.

'They say it blinds you if you look into its eyes,' I told him. 'The *boitatá*. They say it's there to punish the people who threaten the forest. It punishes the ones who burn the trees, just like *Curupira* punishes the ones who kill the animals. Is that why you're here, Leonardo? To threaten the forest?'

'I didn't think this was going to be such a pain in the arse. I thought I'd come out here, collect and deliver.'

'So where're you from?'

He looked at me as if deciding whether or not to tell me. 'Vila Rica.'

I stretched out my feet and propped myself back on my elbows. 'How come a man from Vila Rica is so scared of the water?'

'I'm not scared of—'

'You didn't know what a *boto* is. You've got city written all over you, Leonardo. Where're you really from? Goiânia? Brasilia?'

Leonardo shook his head and looked at the deck, hanging his head so his hair fell down across his brow.

'So you're running away from something. Came down here to get away – not that long ago, I'd guess – and you're earning money the only way you know how.' Maybe we had some similarities, after all. 'So what did you do? You get angry and kill someone? Find out you enjoyed it and came down here where there's not so much law, is that it? This got anything to do with that person you were thinking about back there on the river after you shot those men?'

Leonardo's head moved and although I couldn't see his eyes, I sensed he was watching me through his fringe. 'You can't judge me. You think you're different from me, but you're not. You think you're better than me, but I can see the things you've done.'

'You don't know what I've done.' My thoughts went to the picture in my pocket. I considered not what I had done but what I was going to do.

'Not the details,' he replied. 'But I can see it in your eyes.' He took a long drag on the cigarette and exhaled into the cool air that still remained after the storm. 'Others don't see it,' Leonardo went on. 'They only see that you're different somehow. Maybe they're afraid of you but they don't know why, or maybe they can't put their finger on the reason why they don't like you, but I know why. It's the way you smell. You smell of death.'

'Only thing I smell of is fish and sweat,' I said, but my mouth was dry. 'Don't pretend you're some kind of witch doctor. You know what my job is on this boat. You know that I was armed. It doesn't take a witch doctor to guess I may have done things I'm not proud of.'

'You're not armed now.'

'No.'

'And are you afraid of me?'

'No.'

Leonardo nodded as if my words had confirmed something, then he took a last drag and flicked his cigarette overboard. 'You thought I was wrong to kill those men yesterday, but is it *always* wrong?' he asked. 'To kill a man?'

I looked at him, his face in half shadow. I couldn't see his eyes but I knew they were looking for mine.

'You see, you can't judge me,' Leonardo said. 'Only God can do that.'

'Is that what you really think?'

'No,' he laughed. 'There's no God.'

'So when you die—'

'When I die, I die.'

'And you know it will be violent.'

'I won't die of old age,' Leonardo said. 'Or of some disease like your old friend. I won't die like an old animal stinking of sweat and piss.'

'Oh, I think you'll die like an animal,' I told him. 'And there'll probably be sweat and piss. Blood, too.'

Leonardo made a quick sound, coming through his nose in a blast of air that was gone almost as soon as it began.

'I've known people like you,' I said. 'I've seen them die, too. Probably more men than you've killed I've seen die in their own blood, screaming like girls and asking for their mothers. People like you never die in a good way. They never close their eyes and fade. And they never go out like heroes. Always like losers.'

'Don't you mean people like *us*?'

'It's never too late to give it up,' I said. 'Never too late to get out.' But even as I said the words, I doubted they were true. I wanted to believe it. For a while I *had* believed it. Since meeting Daniella, since stopping the work I did for Costa and the people who used him as their messenger, I had left that life behind me. And yet here I was, heading towards another beginning for that life, as if my time without killing had been a lull, like an alcoholic in a dry period, and now I was going back to it. I was returning to death to pay for a marriage and a life beyond that.

The shadow darkened and I wondered if, perhaps, I was even worse than Leonardo.

36

Leonardo and I both knew the penalties that might be suffered if we allowed ourselves to sleep, so we struggled to keep awake. We willed ourselves through the darkest hours, listening to the night living around us. There were the usual sounds of cicadas creaking, accompanied by the frogs and the splash of fish in the shallows and the bump of debris against our hull. But there were other sounds. Unidentified sounds. The calls of unknown creatures somewhere out in the forest. The flicker of lights among the trees that could make a man think the *boitatá* might be real after all.

Late in the night, when sleep's assault was most difficult to withstand, I found myself drifting in a haze of fatigue. My mind meandered like the waters of the River of Deaths, bringing phantoms into my thoughts. Sister Beckett, Sofia, the old man and Antonio swam through my exhaustion, mingling into one, their faces merging. Leonardo and Daniella were there too and I fought hard to keep sleep at bay. I forced my eyes open, slapped my face and stood up, taking deep breaths.

Leonardo was gone.

He was no longer sitting against the box seat that had been his territory since he had taken control of the boat. Another day, another journey, my first thought would have been to retrieve my weapons. There was a padlock, but it could be broken. Perhaps I could get to them before ... not today, though. Now my first thought was for Daniella.

My breathing quickened as I snapped my head round in her direction. The shape of the hammock was there, hanging deep, heavy with a person's weight. But there was another shape there, too. Beside the hammock.

A figure in the darkness.

For a second I was frozen, watching the dark shadow that hung over Daniella like a malevolent, brooding spirit, paused for a heartbeat in the process of doing evil. Perhaps the old hag Cuca had come to take Daniella while she slept, or some other obscenity had slipped from the forest to torment us.

When the figure reached out to touch her, its arm extending towards the darkness that was Daniella, an image of Anhangá came to me, as if the spirit were reaching out to touch her and plant its evil visions in her mind.

But there were no hags or demons on this boat; we shared this space with only one source of wickedness.

'What the hell are you doing?' I started towards him, balling my fists. The edge of my vision glowed white then red as my body and mind prepared themselves for the imminent fight.

The unmistakeable click of a pistol being cocked.

'Relax.' Leonardo's words were quiet. Almost whispered. 'Stay there.'

'What's going on?' I hissed.

'Sh. You'll wake her.' He came back down the boat, passing me on the other side, never coming too close, and returned to his usual spot. 'She was making noises.'

'So you thought you'd check on her?' My heart was thumping hard. My voice cracked in my throat. Sofia's name was shouting through my thoughts. What had happened to her couldn't happen to Daniella. Please don't let it happen. *Please.*

'Relax, Zico,' he said again. 'I won't do anything unless you make me.'

My eyes didn't close for the rest of the night. Seeing him standing over Daniella, watching her that way, was like a shot of electricity right through me. My stomach turned at the idea of what he might have done had I not awoken. After what he had said before Marco took the old man back to Piratinga, I knew the kind of malignant thoughts in his head

I paced the deck close to Daniella for the rest of the night, never stopping, always watching. I wouldn't sleep.

I *couldn't* sleep.

Leonardo stayed still, commenting from time to time, taking the occasional pinch of *cocaína* to invigorate him or kill the pain, or both, while I had only my determination to keep me awake.

And my fear.

Every time he rummaged in his pocket, I squinted into the darkness to see what he was doing. Every time he snorted his drug, I became a little more anxious. Every time he moved, my muscles tightened and my heart quickened.

'You're like a dog,' Leonardo said sometime in the early hours. 'Circling round to find a comfortable spot, always coming back to guard her like a loyal animal. Like that damn dog I almost killed today. Or was it yesterday?' His voice was low and menacing, as if his mood was falling into a dark place, driven there by fear and pain and drugs. 'All the days are the same out here.'

'That *damn dog* saved your leg,' I said. 'If it hadn't been for her, you might even be under the water now, rotting down for some hungry *jacaré*.'

He must have smoked his whole packet of cigarettes now because he hadn't lit up for a while, and his supply of *cocaína* would not be endless. I didn't know how it felt to be hooked like that, but I knew he'd always want the fix and would be trying not to think about how little he had left. It would be another reason to make him desperate to reach the mine, and that worried at me. This was no place for a man with paranoia. The trees and the river can close in on a man like that, especially at night when the forest is alive with the sounds of unseen creatures moving in the dark.

'You know why this is called the Rio das Mortes?' he asked me. 'You know why they call it the River of Deaths?'

I checked the barbecue, the metal cooling now, the carbonised wood nothing more than grey ash scattered with a few last embers glowing like the eyes of the *boitatá*. I went to the side of the boat and tipped the ash into the water.

There was a hint of light in the air and it wouldn't be long before the sun started to raise its face.

'Hey, Zico. I asked you something.'

'One story is that there was a massacre somewhere on this river,' I said. 'A long time ago. Soldiers killing missionaries. Another story is that it's because the Xavante killed any settlers who came here.'

'So which is it?'

'I don't know.' I shook the tin, letting the grey dust float across the surface of the river like the ashes of a good friend. The still living embers died with a chorus of hissing. 'But I guess I wouldn't blame them for getting pissed off, people coming in here and taking their land. I've seen how it works.' I banged the tin with the palm of my hand.

'I bet you have.'

I looked at Leonardo, sensing the meaning in his voice. He was the kind of man who would put a match to a man's home if the price was right, and he thought I was the same. But he was wrong. I'd killed men, but I'd never burned a man's home. Never done that.

'There's always someone pushing for their land,' I said. 'Always something to dig up or pull down, so they steal it from them day by day. The mine at Mina dos Santos is a pain for them; it's dirty and killing the river in places, but it's not too big. As long as it stays that way, it should be OK, but if the miners want to expand ...' I shrugged and glanced at Leonardo. His features were becoming clearer as the day brightened and chased away the horrors of the night. 'You know something about the mine?' I asked.

'I don't know anything.'

I dusted the ash from my hands and took more charcoal from the bag in the store, refilling the barbecue. 'I heard there's soya farms, too, pushing right up to the boundaries of their land. Miners from one direction, farmers from the other. And there's loggers out there, bringing down their trees.'

'*Their* land? *Their* trees?'

'Those people have lived there for who knows how long.' I relit the fire as I spoke. 'Who else does it belong to?'

'I reckon it belongs to whoever wants to take it.'

'Whoever has the most guns, you mean?' I looked up at Leonardo. The light was growing in the sky behind him, the rising sun already warming the land. There was an ethereal mist lifting from the trees, seeping among the shrubs and grasses, rolling out across the bank and touching the surface of the water. Soon it would burn away to a dry heat and the sky would clear.

Leonardo smiled at me in a way that told me he knew something about those guns we were carrying, but I wasn't going to give him the satisfaction. I pretended not to notice.

'Another story,' I said, 'is that it's because of all the piranhas in the water.' I watched the flames dancing in the barbecue.

'Well, we know that's true. Plenty of *jacaré* too.' He reached down to touch his bandaged leg.

When the barbecue was hot enough, I filled a pan with clear water from a five litre plastic bottle and put it on the heat to boil.

I looked over at Daniella. She was awake in the hammock, lying on her side, watching the two of us talking in the early morning light. I went to her and ran my hand across her forehead, showing her my smile. 'Did you sleep OK?'

'Not much. You?'

'Not at all.' I left Daniella alone and she used the waterproof for privacy again, Leonardo taking too much interest when she re-emerged, and came to sit with me.

The way he watched her made me feel like tiny spiders were crawling over every part of me, and each time he slipped his eyes over her, I wanted to twist them out.

I poured coffee into three small cups, filled it with sugar and we drank in silence, chewing dry bread and washing it down with sips of hot coffee. On another day, in other circumstances, it would have been a perfect morning. The gentle sound of the water slopping against the hull, the soporific sway of the boat as she moved in the eddies of the river.

'We need to refuel,' I said aloud, shaking myself awake and throwing the dregs of my coffee overboard. 'Then we can get going again. You'll have to help me.'

217

'Help how?'

'Lift the barrel...' I shrugged.

He thought about it, knowing he'd have to get close to me. Leonardo always kept a safe distance – the kind of distance that a bullet could cross much faster than a man – but this would bring me close enough to be a threat.

'You try to screw me around,' he said, 'I'll kill you and make her suffer long and hard.'

'I understand.'

Together, Leonardo and I hauled a barrel from the store, him trying to hold it with both hands while keeping the pistol close.

'Where does it need to go?' he asked, panting with the exertion of it. Neither of us had slept, and we were both exhausted. He was limping a little on the bandaged leg.

I stopped and pointed to the hatch where I accessed the fuel lines, so Leonardo waited while I pulled it open and looked in to see the opening to the boat's fuel tank.

'How d'you get it in there?' he said. 'The hole's at the side.'

I held up a coil of clear plastic hosepipe. 'No pumps out here. Just a pipe and gravity.'

'What the fuck is gravity?'

I shook my head at him and mimicked putting the pipe in my mouth.

'You siphon it in?'

'We used to do it to cars back in Rio. Use the petrol for ... Well, you know. Sometimes it went into bottles, sometimes we used to sell it.'

'You're from Rio? I always wanted to go to Rio. Carnival and Copacabana.'

Sofia and I used to go down to Copacabana with Pai and play in the surf when we were little. By the time I was ten years old, though, he didn't do much other than drink and lie in bed so we used to go down there on our own. We would buy a few warm *pão de quiejo* from the bakery, made fresh that morning, and eat them on the sand. There were always boys hanging around Sofia, but she was too busy looking after me and Pai to take much notice.

Another two years, though, and we didn't go to the beach any more. By then, Sofia gave all her time to cleaning and Candomblé and I had my responsibilities to the gang.

'You didn't say where you're really from,' I said to Leonardo. 'It's not Vila Rica.'

'Belém.' He sniffed and took off his cap, scratching the top of his head with the butt of his pistol. His features were drawn and bags had formed under his eyes. He still had the soft looks, but the stress and lack of sleep was taking them away.

'You're a long way from home,' I said.

'You, too, *Carioca*. So, what are you doing out here? Why would a man from Rio want to live in this shit-hole?'

'Looking for something better. You?'

'And this is better?' Leonardo looked around us. Water and trees and land so scorched by the sun it was red and baked hard.

'Yes.' A kind of realisation for me. 'Yes, it is.'

Leonardo sighed and shook his head. 'No. This is a shit hole.'

'So why are you here?'

'For the money. I do this job and then—'

'And then you'll have enough? It'll be the last one?'

Leonardo looked at me as if I'd seen right through him. As if, in that moment, I understood everything there was to know about him.

'Then you'll go back to whoever it was you were thinking about, right?' I said.

He didn't speak.

'So who is it? A girl? Mother? Father? Brother?'

Leonardo's eyes flickered and he looked away for a fraction of a second before coming back to stare at me.

'You have a brother?' I asked.

'It's none of your business.'

'In Belém? Older or younger?'

'We going to fuel this thing or not?' he said. 'I want to get moving.'

He put his cap back on, shifting the weight of the gun in his hand, reminding me who was in charge.

*

I was rolling the empty barrel back to the store when I heard a grumble somewhere in the sky. I stowed the barrel, then went out to the bow of the *Deus*, where I'd get the best view of a sky that was as brilliant as I had ever seen it. Pale and with no hint of cloud to sully it. There was no indication that it had rained so much yesterday, except for a freshness in the air and a sweetness in the scent of the river.

I held a hand to my brow and squinted into the clear expanse of blue, as the grumble grew louder.

'What is it?' Daniella came to my side. She sounded groggy, her voice still lazy from sleep.

'A plane,' I said. 'Right there.' I pointed to the sky, where the tiny smudge of a plane moved north-east of our position.

'It looks low,' Daniella said.

'It's going to land.'

She looked at me. 'At Piratinga?'

'Mm-hm.'

'It's too early for the *Bandeirante*.' She was talking about the small passenger plane that hopped from town to town twice a week.

I nodded and watched it descending, the sound of its engines becoming louder, and then it was out of sight behind the trees.

I stared at the empty sky for a while longer, then turned and sat down, taking off my cap and running a hand over my short hair.

'Something wrong?' Daniella asked.

'No, I'm just tired, that's all.' The plane bothered me, though. It had to be Sister Dolores Beckett, and that meant I didn't have as much time as I needed to get ahead of her on the river. Piratinga was only twenty or thirty kilometres away and if her meeting with the bishop was short, she could be on the river soon. Santiago's boat would catch us quickly, I had no doubt about that, and if they passed us, Sister Dolores Beckett could get to Mina dos Santos and leave before we even reached there. If she left the main river and headed deeper inland, finding her might be impossible.

'We should go,' I said. 'We have to leave now.'

I couldn't think of any circumstances under which Costa would be pleased to see me return, knowing that the nun was still breathing.

37

The course narrowed as we pushed deeper up the River of Deaths. In places, it was as wide as five hundred metres, but in others it closed around us like the shadow that always followed me. The trees drew in, the branches reaching over the water, and the world was filled with the warm, damp smell of the forest.

'It's strange here,' Daniella whispered, scanning the jungle that pulsed just a few metres from the boat. 'It's like ... we're in a different world.' She shifted in her seat. 'I can imagine the *mapinguari* out there, right now, hoping we'll get off the boat.'

'There's no such thing,' I told her. Two metres tall, ferocious, clawed and impervious to bullets and arrows, the *mapinguari* was one of those forest legends that sounded incredible during the hours of daylight. Once the sun was down, though, and the haunting cries of the wild began, almost anything seemed possible. 'And we're not getting off,' I told her. 'You don't get out of the boat here.'

I took my eyes off the river and scanned the forest before looking at Daniella sitting beside me. Her hair was not combed and cleaned like when she was working or ready to go out. It was not tied back in the usual careful fashion, and she wore no make-up to hide her true face.

'You look beautiful,' I told her. 'Natural.'

'Really? I thought I'd look like shit.'

'No.'

'I have a mirror in my bag,' she told me. 'I could—'

'You don't need it. Not here. Not on the river.'

I could see every pore on her face. The shine on her nose. There were tiny beads of sweat on her upper lip. Her skin glowed with the sun and the air and the reflection of the water, and I studied her as never before. I noticed the faint hairs on her forearms, the tiny half moons on her fingernails, the veins in the back of her hands. I liked it that she had no make-up. It was like a mask that hid what she really was.

'It suits you,' I said. 'This place makes you even more beautiful.'

She smiled, a hesitant look, uncertain if I were teasing her or not.

'I mean it.'

She put her hand on my knee. 'Ask me. Ask me now.'

'Ask you what?'

'What you almost asked me yesterday.'

'It's not the right time.'

'It's the perfect time.'

'Not yet.'

Daniella sighed and looked away to hide her disappointment.

'Take the wheel,' I said to her.

'What?'

'It's important for you to know how to control the boat. It makes sense if something happens to me.'

'Like what?' she asked. 'What's going to happen to you?'

'I don't know,' I shrugged. 'Anything. Nothing. I was just saying it. Come on, this will help to pass the time, that's all.'

She nodded slowly, narrowing her eyes in wariness before taking the wheel in both hands, and I set about showing Daniella the rudiments of how the *Deus* worked. How she sat in the water, where she was able to go, how deep the water needed to be. I pointed out the signs of the river and how to read them best.

Giving my attention to teaching Daniella took my mind off what I was really here to do, but a festering nervousness grew with every metre of river we left behind us. My future was clouded and I couldn't see anything there other than Sister Dolores Beckett. Her face was beginning to haunt me, the black and grey dots swimming in my mind, swirling like smoke, forming an image of her face. Never before had such a thing affected me and deep down, deeper than all the murder and the sadness and the darkness that lay in the furthest corner of my soul, there was a light that had been crushed and hardened like a diamond. And in that place of light, I knew this was wrong; that no amount of money or threats could make it right.

I glanced back, as if I might see my future creeping up on me, and I didn't know if I was ready to meet it.

After an hour or so, Daniella was able to take control of the *Deus*. Leonardo hovered about with an uneasy expression because someone inexperienced was controlling the boat.

He was growing more agitated with the passing of every minute, and I felt his tension like electricity charging the close and humid air around us. He moved about the boat, pistol in hand. His limp was more pronounced and he winced in pain from time to time, so I guessed the *cocaína* had run out and he was missing the effect it had on him.

'We haven't got time for this.' He waved the pistol in Daniella's direction. 'She's too slow. If we're not in—'

'It makes no difference,' I told him. 'We couldn't go any faster if we wanted to. *All* we have is time.'

Eventually he moved up to the bow so he could spot the river and warn of any possible danger. He was a nuisance, calling out the slightest ripple, and I tried to ignore him, glad that he at least had something to do.

'It's getting hotter,' he called back. 'Does it feel like it's getting hotter?' His face glistened with sweat, and dark patches had formed on his shirt.

'It's hot,' I agreed.

'If I've caught that old man's sickness...'

I watched Leonardo and swallowed my anger and frustration. 'Dengue isn't contagious,' I said.

'Maybe it wasn't—' He stopped and leaned over the bow, squinting at the bank to our left.

'You see something?' I asked, standing and trying to see what he was looking at.

'There.' He pointed. 'Is that *jacaré*?'

About fifty metres upriver, on a narrow bank, three or four objects lay stretched out on the blazing white sand. As we approached and the shapes came into focus, Leonardo straightened and set his face firm. 'Fucking monsters,' he said, then turned and hurried along the side of the boat, limping on the bandaged leg. He kept one hand on the gunwale to steady himself as he went to the box seat. His movements were quick and agitated as he unfastened the padlock and yanked it from the fixture, throwing open the lid and grabbing the old man's rifle. He stuffed a handful of cartridges into his pocket before looking back at me and snapping the lock shut again, then he hurried to the gunwale and checked that the weapon was loaded.

'I'm going to kill the bastards.' He raised the rifle to his shoulder, took aim and fired.

The sound of the small-calibre rifle was like the crack of a whip. Anywhere else, it might not have sounded so loud, but here it was intrusive and out of place. A scattering of birds broke from the trees and came out over the water, fluttering in confusion before returning to the darkness. Others made a break across the river, heading for the other side.

Leonardo's first shot splashed into the water half a metre in front of the largest of the *jacaré*. The creatures snapped their jaws shut and lifted off their bellies as they raced for the safety of the river. Leonardo worked the bolt and fired again. His movements were quick and angry, and I could see a real need in him to kill something.

'Don't say anything,' I said to Daniella. 'Don't do anything to make him angry.'

'He's already angry.'

Leonardo fired a third and fourth shot, but the *jacaré* were too quick for him. They might look like slow beasts, but they moved like lightning and could be just as dangerous on land as in the water.

When they were gone, Leonardo kicked the gunwale and slammed his hand on the edge of it, glaring back at the place where the animals had been sunning themselves. He stood for a long moment, breathing deeply, composing himself, then turned and came back to the bow.

'Tell me if you see any more,' he said as he passed us.

I tried to ignore him, like I tried to ignore so many other things, but his voice intruded into my thoughts, asking, 'You smell that? Is that burning?'

When the bow cut through the first of the smoke, there were just a few wisps of it, accompanied by the gentle scent of burning wood. The coils of grey twisted in the air over the river, shifting and merging, flattening to hang across the surface like a sheet stretched from one bank to the other.

'Where's that coming from?' He scanned both sides of the river, each no more than a hundred metres from us, but there was no clear indication of its origin.

Once we had pushed around the gentle curve of the river, though, we were able to see what the closeness of the trees had concealed.

Ahead, fingers of smoke curled from between the dark trunks on the bank to our right. They slipped through the vines and the undergrowth, coming together to form a mist that drifted across the water in a grey haze. Beyond that, the clouds darkened to a dense black, billowing and moving like a living creature. Forming and deforming. It rose from the treetops, filling the sky, touching everything.

'What is it?' Leonardo asked, glancing back at me.

I shook my head. 'We're still a long way from the mine. Maybe it's Indians clearing land for planting.'

'Do they do that?' Daniella asked.

'Maybe it's something else,' I said, taking the wheel and wondering about those guns we were carrying. Perhaps this was all connected. When profiteers opened the forest, fire and guns were a major part of it.

Coming closer to the thick of the smoke, I slowed the engine and moved towards the far bank to keep away from the worst of it. But there was no avoiding it. If we were to go on, we would have to head through it.

'Can we go around?' Daniella asked. 'Is there another way?'

'Maybe, but I don't want to get lost out here.'

'Do we need to stop, then?'

'As long as we can see a couple of metres in front, we'll be all right,' I said, hoping she didn't hear the doubt in my voice. 'It'll take longer, but it's possible.' I slowed the engine even further and we chugged on into the blackness of the Devil's heart.

38

The smoke shrouded us, splitting at the bow and swirling in our wake. It filled the spaces between us. Only the water immediately in front was visible, and I slowed the *Deus* until she was almost at a standstill.

'We can't stop now.' I coughed as the hot, harsh smoke slipped into my throat and stung my eyes. 'Not in here.'

'We should have stayed back there,' Daniella said.

'Too late now.'

I told her to wet some cloths so we could hold them over our faces, and we pressed on and on, deeper and deeper into the dreadful, dense smoke. It was pushing in on all sides now, closing around us and blocking out the glare of the sun, as if we were moving through dusk and heading into night.

Leonardo propped the rifle in the bow and leaned over the edge, holding a damp cloth to his face and watching the river. Every now and then he would call back in a muffled voice to warn us of any hazards. An hour ago, his warnings had irritated me; now they might save our lives.

'What happens if we run aground?' Daniella asked as I guided the *Deus* around a sandbank.

I looked at her, seeing the worry in her red-ringed eyes and knew it had been a mistake to head into the smoke. I was in a hurry to reach the mine and return home to my friend, and I had allowed it to put us in more danger.

'We have a shallow draught,' I told her. 'We should be fine.'

'But if we do?'

'Well, it wouldn't be impossible to get out, but it would take time.'

'We'd have to get out and push?'

'On this sand? The stuff under the water? Uh-uh.' I shook my head. 'We'd need another boat. Maybe two. You can't stand on this sand; it shifts and moves all the time. And you don't want to be standing on it when it shifts; it'll slip away under your feet and suck you down. People have disappeared like that.'

I looked over at Leonardo who had turned to listen. His eyes were red, too, and there were dark circles under them. I would be the same. Both of us with raspy stubble piercing the skin on our faces, stale breath, stomachs that tumbled with the lack of good food and sleep.

There is a surreal edge to the world when you haven't slept; a dreamy quality to everything. Like treacle is flowing through your veins instead of blood. And with the smoke billowing around us, killing the day, it was as if we were living through a nightmare.

Leonardo touched the *figa* that hung from the chain around his neck. His lips moved as he muttered a few silent words, then he went back to watching the river. The rifle was still propped beside him, close but out of my reach.

'I see it,' he said after a few minutes. 'There.' He raised a hand and pointed into the thickest black of the smoke.

'I see it too,' Daniella whispered, and when I squinted through the tears I also saw the flames, flickering in the trees on the far right.

The temperature rose and rose. The air glittered with sparks that danced and frisked in the blackness. They leaped at us like devils, stinging our faces, then swirled away to flicker around the *Deus*. They settled on the gunwale and the canopy and the deck, glowing and dying, or lingering for a moment, hoping to find something to burn.

Something like fuel drums.

'We need to watch the boat!' I shouted to Leonardo.

'What?' He looked back at me from his position in the bow as if not understanding, then his eyes widened. 'Fire!' He pointed behind me and I turned to see the canopy smouldering over the middle of the *Deus*.

At first it was a glowing patch that spread outwards, consuming the canvas as it moved, then the flames sprang to life, growing as the fire took hold of the old, dry material.

'Take the wheel,' I yelled at Daniella and jumped from my seat, hurrying from the wheelhouse. 'Listen to Leonardo's directions.'

I grabbed the bucket Daniella had been using and, leaning over the gunwale, I filled it from the river, then hurried to where the flames were devouring the canopy over the *Deus*. The thick smoke was filling my lungs, tightening my chest and stealing my breath. I could breathe only in short gasps as I tossed the water up at the canvas.

Already the flames had spread and were beginning to take hold in other places, so I ran back and forth, refilling the bucket and tackling the fires rising above us. The embers flickered around me as I worked through the heat, and Daniella kept the boat on course, taking us slowly though the river, while Leonardo called out any visible dangers in the water.

It was as if we were journeying through hell. The smoke was at its blackest and the temperature was at its hottest. The flames flickered and the embers danced like devils. My skin stung with the pinpricks of their attacks, sweat poured from me, my eyes streamed and my lungs shrank with every metre of river. Blinded and choking, we had to escape this nightmare before we were overcome and left to drift into the bank as we slipped into the abyss.

There was something else too.

The horrific smell that lay within the smoke.

It was the ugly smell of barbecued meat and burning fat, thick and cloying, filling me with its fleshy, yellow stink. Feeling sure I knew its horrific origin – what it was that was burning – I was desperate not to breathe it in. I was sickened that it was inside me and tried taking shallower breaths, forcing the stench from my lungs, wishing I couldn't taste it in my mouth. But it was as inescapable as the dense smoke, so it invaded me, tainted the precious air I needed so desperately, and made me feel like an accomplice to its awful existence.

Deeper into the smoke, and surrounded by that monstrous smell, I began to tire. My lungs shrivelled, my chest tightened and my arms and legs grew heavy as I battled the persistent fires, coughing and hacking, wondering when my body would fail me.

Our eyes were burning and our faces were black when we finally broke through into the lighter smoke. Daniella pushed the engine harder, taking us into the fresh air, and I had never felt relief like it.

I leaned against the gunwale, sucking the clean air into me, expelling the darkness I had swallowed. There was a greasy, lingering taste in my mouth, and my whole body ached, but we were free of the fire.

'You did well,' I said, tossing the bucket aside and returning to the wheelhouse. 'You were amazing.'

'Did you smell that in there?' Daniella asked. 'What was it? Was that animals?'

'Yeah,' I said. 'Animals. Probably.' But I couldn't help thinking about the guns we had on board, and what Leonardo had said about expanding the operation at Mina dos Santos. If a land war was brewing there, perhaps the violence was spreading and territory was being reclaimed from settlers. It wasn't unusual for landowners to use fire as a cleanser. The smell that had mingled with the smoke would be the stink of their animals burning. And it would be them, too.

The people.

I was starting to see how everything tied together – Sister Beckett, the gold mine, the guns. In a place where big business was encroaching on small lives, local people needed whatever help they could get, and it seemed likely to me that a woman like Sister Beckett would come here to offer that help. I wasn't aware that the Branquinos had operations this far out, but perhaps they owned the mine, and this was why they wanted the nun to disappear – not because she deserved it, as Costa had said, but so they could manage their land war without her interference.

The guns might be here for either side of such a dispute, but it was more likely that the mine owners would have the resources to buy them, and Leonardo's comments led me to believe that was the case. The Branquinos hadn't asked me to collect them, but that didn't mean they weren't the mine owners; perhaps even Costa knew nothing about them. They might want to keep the guns and Sister Beckett separate, to give them some deniability, and would never have imagined that Leonardo and I would end up travelling on the same boat.

In the bow, Leonardo had turned to lean against the gunwale. His head was back and his mouth open. The pistol was still in his hand, the rifle propped beside him. I considered asking who he was working for, but knew he wouldn't tell me. And I was afraid to give away my own purpose. No one could know I had another reason to visit the mine. No one could know about my intent for Sister Beckett if I were to keep my friends safe.

Costa had been clear about *that*.

I collapsed onto the seat beside Daniella and watched her concentrating on the river ahead. 'I'd take you with me on the boat anytime,' I said to her.

She turned to look at me, her eyes burning red, her skin streaked with dirt and sweat. 'I don't *ever* want to do that again.'

Before I could answer, though, I heard the sound I had been waiting to hear all morning.

Over the chugging engine of the *Deus* came another noise, a virtual echo from somewhere in the terrible inferno we had just endured. Another boat was pushing through the nightmare.

One that might be carrying my destiny.

Leonardo had heard the engines too, and he came to stand a few metres away from me. 'Another boat,' he said. 'Ahead or behind?'

'Behind, I think.'

'How far?'

'It's hard to tell.' Sound travelled well out there, funnelling up and down the river like cattle herded along a corral.

So we watched and we waited.

And, just after midday, we saw it.

39

A shimmer of white and silver appeared round a distant bend in the river. It nudged out from beyond the line of trees, and within a few minutes I knew it was the *Estrella do Araguaia*.

'The old man,' Leonardo sneered and came close to touch the muzzle of his pistol to the back of my head. 'He sent someone after us.'

'No.'

He pushed the pistol into the soft place at the base of my skull with enough force to make me lean over the edge of the gunwale. I gripped the wood to stop myself from toppling over.

I would be nothing and Daniella would be alone.

'Please,' I said. 'It's not the old man. They're not after us. They're going to ...' I stopped myself. I wasn't supposed to know where the boat was going, nor who was on board.

'Going to do what?' Leonardo asked keeping the pistol tight against me. 'Going where?'

'I don't know. West. That's all I was going to say. There's a few places on the river. They could be going to any one of them. That boat, it's always up and down this river.'

'You know that boat?' Leonardo leaned in so his mouth was close to my ear. He was sweating hard, his skin slick with it, and his face was streaked black from the smoke. His breath was stinking and hot.

'I know it.'

'It's Santiago,' Daniella said. 'Please. Leave him alone. Haven't we done everything you wanted?'

'Not everything.' He stood back and jammed the muzzle harder, as if he wanted to push it right through me.

I stared at the water and waited, wondering how Daniella must feel to see me like this, so close to death. The murky river slipped by, the ripples washing out towards the bank as the *Deus* cut through it, and all it would take was one small movement – one quick twitch of the finger – and my life would empty into it.

'Please,' Daniella said again. 'Don't.'

The pistol remained in place.

'If you kill him we'll be lost. I ... I don't know where to go. I don't know where the mine is. Without Zico, we'll be lost.'

The pressure on the back of my neck eased a touch. Leonardo took a deep breath, and then the pistol was gone. He grabbed the back of my shirt and pulled me around to face him, then stood away, out of reach.

His eyes were livid. There was almost no white visible they were so bloodshot from the fire and the drugs and the lack of sleep. But they were wide with anger and frustration.

Behind us, the *Estrella* came closer and closer every moment, the sound of her engines growing until they overpowered our own.

'If they stop, get rid of them.' Leonardo left me and went to Daniella. He sat close behind the wheel, pushing himself against her and tucking his pistol into her ribs.

The *Estrella* slowed as it came up the river behind us and cut into our wake. The boat was smaller than the *Deus*, a good ten metres shorter, and its lines were sharper, but its condition wasn't that much better. It wasn't a sophisticated boat, and in a few years it would look as dilapidated as the *Deus* if Santiago didn't do something to tidy her up.

There was a small section at the bow of the *Estrella* where passengers could sit at the railing and enjoy the fresh air, but other than that, the entire boat was enclosed. The window at the front of the wheelhouse was cracked, and had been that way for as long as

I could remember, but the windows on either side, running back to the stern, were intact.

As the *Estrella* pulled alongside us and slowed to our speed, I could see Santiago sitting behind the wheel, his bare chest matted with thick hair.

I stayed at the gunwale and lifted a lazy hand, watching him return the gesture before he spoke to Matteus, the man beside him. For a moment, I thought Santiago was going to stop, but instead the two men laughed and ran their hands down their faces, reminding me how dirty we must look. Inside their boat, the smoke would not have affected them the way it did us.

When they finished laughing, Santiago raised his middle finger to me and throttled his engines.

As the *Estrella* picked up pace and slipped past us, I looked into the windows, seeing a number of faces turned in our direction. I didn't have time to count how many passengers were on board, but I had my first glimpse of the presence I had felt since leaving Piratinga.

Sister Dolores Beckett.

There was little to see of her other than her head and shoulders just above the line of the window, but I knew it was her. I saw the same curly hair, the same glasses she was wearing in the photograph. No longer just in grainy shades of grey, an image on a piece of folded paper, but a real person, flesh and blood.

Just one more life.

She was sitting by the window, face angled towards me, and I caught her eyes as they passed. Our gaze locked and I felt, for one moment, as if she knew my intention; as if my dark purpose betrayed itself in the muddy brown iris of my eyes, visible only to those who knew how to read such design.

It was only distance that broke the contact, and I watched the *Estrella* gather speed and pass beyond us, its stern low in the water, a Brasilian flag flapping in the breeze the boat created for itself.

So now I had seen her. She was real.

Sister Dolores Beckett; the woman I was going to murder.

I went to the bow and watched the *Estrella* move away from us, leaving a wake of white water behind it, and I pulled the newspaper cutting from my pocket and opened it out so I could look into Sister Beckett's eyes once more. On the paper, they were already dead. Lifeless. The photograph captured nothing of the woman I had just seen. Small and not outstanding to look at, but her eyes had seen right through me.

I couldn't shake the feeling that settled at the back of my mind like a cancer. I knew of nothing that Sister Beckett had done; nothing to warrant the bloody death that was planned for her. If I had something to latch on to, something that turned her from a saint to a sinner, perhaps I would have better reason to kill her.

I stared at the picture a moment longer then folded it away and turned to look at Daniella behind the wheel of the *Deus*. My life was taking a different course and I needed to find a way to fund it, but this wasn't the way to pay for it. Sister Beckett's life for my own. For Daniella's and Raul's. I couldn't help feeling it was going to be a bad deal for all of us.

But maybe everything was going to change because Santiago had passed us and was already moving out of sight, heading towards the next turn in the river. For us, Mina dos Santos was still several hours away, and we wouldn't be there until nightfall, but the *Estrella* would be there in half that.

By the time we arrived at the small mining town, Sister Beckett might be long gone, heading deeper into the country, making for the reservations along the Rio das Mortes.

For a while, we watched the *Estrella* hurry ahead, but soon the boat was gone and we were alone on the river once more.

Within an hour the course narrowed further and the banks closed in on us from either side. This stretch of water was in sharp contrast to the wide expanse of the river we had travelled yesterday. Here, the trees leaned out to touch the *Deus*, trapping the heat. The air was still and scorching, keeping us ever reaching for the water bottles and bringing beads of sweat from every pore. Beneath us, the water ran faster and clearer, and in the thick vegetation along the banks, *tucunaré* and piranha flashed back and forth, startled by our progress.

'Maybe you should take the wheel,' Daniella said as we brushed past the overhanging branches, showering leaves and insects onto the canvas over our heads.

'You're doing fine.' I glanced up at the holes burned by the embers. This felt like a different world from the inferno we had endured a few hours ago, but it was equally dangerous. 'I'll watch the water.'

Daniella bit her lower lip and nodded, so I showed her a smile and moved up to the bow. 'We don't want to get lost out here,' I said.

'We could get lost?' Leonardo asked.

'It's possible. There are turns you don't want to take. Some of them lead round and round and you'd never know it because everything looks the same. People have come in here and never come out. That's worse than not delivering your guns on time, eh?'

As if to prove my point, Daniella steered us past the remnants of a wreck protruding from the water by the bank. The boat must have gone down backwards, perhaps dragged by the weight of its outboard, because it was two metres of the bow that broke the surface of the water while the stern was sunk deep into the bed of silt. Any paint was long gone, and the wood was bleached white by the sun. A colony of ants had made it their home, lines of them hurried in and out of holes.

I lifted my eyes to the bank, where the undergrowth grew dense. 'There are things out there I reckon no one has ever seen before,' I said.

'Like what?'

I looked at Leonardo and shook my head. 'If I knew that, then someone would have seen them.'

'Corpo Seco,' Daniella said. 'Mãe used to tell me he lives in the trees.'

The dry corpse. A man who beat his mother and whose heart was so black he was rejected by both God and the Devil. Even the ground spat him out, so he was left to wander as a corpse, hiding in trees which eventually died from his touch.

'Cuca,' Leonardo said, making us both look at him. 'My mother used to tell me Cuca would get me in the night if I didn't go to sleep. Said the old hag would take me away.'

'Where is she now?' I asked without looking at him. 'Your *mãe*?'

He didn't reply. Instead, we lapsed into silence as we slipped through the afternoon, feeling a sense of relief when we reached a more open channel and the course widened to give us a little more space. The forest still grew dense and forbidding, but at least there were a few metres on either side of the *Deus* and Daniella was able to push us a little faster upriver.

'That woman on the boat,' Leonardo said after some time. 'You know who she was?'

I shook my head.

He narrowed his eyes and stared at me. 'I've seen her somewhere before.'

He looked like a man returning from battle. His shirt, open almost to his navel, was black with soot, the bandage around his calf was dirty, and his skin was streaked from the fire. As he watched me, he lifted his hand and wiped his forearm across his brow, the pistol coming close to his face.

'How much longer?' he said.

'Four or five hours. We'll be there just before dark unless...' I shook my head and glanced back at Daniella.

'Unless what?' Leonardo asked.

'I don't know.' I shrugged. 'Unless we have to get through another fire, I suppose.'

Daniella took her eyes off the river to watch me and, in that brief moment, Leonardo was forgotten. Sister Beckett was forgotten.

I was so afraid for Daniella, and yet I was so proud of her. She had been strong for me, shown me a determination I would never have expected from her – perhaps that she would never have expected from herself. There was no doubt in my mind that I wanted to be with her until I was old like Raul.

'I should have taken that other boat,' Leonardo said. 'The one that just passed us. Or something else. Why didn't the old man say this boat was so damn slow?'

'I guess he wouldn't make too much money if he told everyone that. Anyway, Santiago wouldn't let a man like you on board. He wouldn't carry the things the old man does. You want to carry guns, you get a man like Raul to do it. You want to carry something more respectable, you get Santiago. Who are these guns for, anyway? What's happening out here?'

Leonardo shook his head and closed his eyes in exasperation. 'Five hours?'

'Maybe four. Maybe more. Depends on the river.'

'And for them? For the other boat?'

'Less.'

'How much less?'

'A lot less. An hour maybe. They're much faster.' I shrugged and turned back to watch the river snaking around yet another bend. 'Keep it straight coming into the curve,' I said to Daniella. 'Slow her down, too. See how the water changes colour on this side? It's shallow here.'

Her face was a mask of concentration as she slowed the *Deus*, sitting further up in her seat to better see the shade of the river. Despite the reflection of the sun shimmering on the surface, the contrast of light and dark beneath was just visible as we approached the bend.

'You hear engines?' she asked.

I tried to shut out the sound of the *Deus* and listen to the river. Something ahead. Engines, perhaps, or some kind of echo. 'Maybe.'

The sound became clearer as we moved on and I felt a prickle of nervousness. 'Could be the *Estrella*,' I suggested. 'Sound carries well out here.'

'Isn't it too loud?'

Daniella was right; it *was* too loud. The engines sounded as if they were just around the next bend in the river, but the *Estrella* should have been well ahead of us now. There had to be another boat on the water. I wondered if someone knew we were here, carrying a valuable cargo.

40

Rounding the bend, keeping in the deepest channel, we saw the boat a hundred metres ahead. Its engines were revving and the water was churning behind it, but it remained motionless in the river.

'Is that Santiago?' Daniella asked.

Seeing the *Estrella* perched on the sandbank, struggling like a turtle flipped on its back, brought a relief of tension and I couldn't help a smile coming to my lips. 'Still wish you were on that boat?' I said to Leonardo as I took the wheel from Daniella and slowed the *Deus* to a near standstill.

Leonardo came forward and to the left side of the boat, looking out at the beached *Estrella*. 'What happened?' he asked.

'Took the bend too fast, I reckon. Didn't see the shallow water until it was too late.' I thought about Santiago and Matt sitting in their wheelhouse when they sped past us, Santiago raising a finger at me.

I thought about *her*, too. Sister Dolores Beckett. Our eyes had met across the dark water of the River of Deaths and I had felt as if she were looking right into my soul. From the light that shrouded her, she had seen the shadow that clung to me.

And now she was close again.

'The *Estrella* has a deep draught,' I said, trying not to think of the nun. 'Her hull is like a knife. She must've cut right through and wedged herself in there. She'll never get off on her own.' I kept the engine slow as we approached, seeing Matt lean out of the window, spot us and then disappear again. Almost at once, the

Estrella's engines stopped churning and Santiago came through the door on this side. He walked back to the stern to wait for us.

'Can we tow them?' Leonardo asked. 'Pull them off the sand?'

'Maybe, but why would you want to do that? I thought you were desperate to get to Mina dos Santos. We stop now, it'll take us even longer.' On another day, I would have tried to persuade Leonardo to let us help them, but today was different. Today I had a job to do and, with Sister Beckett delayed, I could get to Mina dos Santos before her.

'How long would it take to pull them out?' he asked.

'I don't know. Half an hour? An hour? It's hard to say.'

Leonardo grabbed Daniella's arm and pulled her close, reminding me that he still had the pistol. 'Here's what we're going to do. You're going to drive and she's going to stay close to me. We're going to pull that boat from the sand, then we're going to move the crates and finish this journey in half the time it's taking right now.'

'And if we can't do it?'

'We'll give it an hour. That's all.'

'He won't let you put that stuff on his boat,' I said. 'I already told you Santiago doesn't do that kind of job.'

'Santiago won't have any choice. If he doesn't like my cargo, he can sit on your boat and wait for you to come back. Or I can shoot him in the head and—'

'You think they won't be armed?' I replied, looking at Daniella. She was staring at Leonardo's hand, her eyes fixed on the pistol as if she were planning on taking it right out of his fingers and using it to gun him down.

I hoped she would do nothing.

'It doesn't matter,' Leonardo said. 'I can deal with that.'

'You sure?' I wondered how many people were on the boat. Costa had said Sister Beckett didn't take security with her, but there was that other woman in the photograph to consider. It was hard to believe she would come to a place like this and not have someone with her to keep her safe. She would know she was a target. I was also certain that Matt would be armed. He

243

was my counterpart; did for Santiago what I did for the old man. If Leonardo ended up shooting the nun, it would save me the trouble – I could tell Costa it was me and he'd pay up without me ever having to fire a shot – but I didn't want anything to happen to Santiago and Matteus. They were good men and they deserved better.

'You just talk to Santiago,' Leonardo said. 'Everything's normal until we get that boat out of the sand. After that, leave everything to me. And don't forget to be careful ... anything happens, your girlfriend is the first one to get hurt.'

Daniella and I exchanged a glance before I nodded to Leonardo.

'Good.' He forced a smile as we pulled closer to the *Estrella*.

'You forget how deep your boat is?' I called to Santiago, keeping us away from the sandbank. Where we were, the river was deep, the water dark, but just a few metres away, the bank was protruding. The nose of Santiago's boat was wedged firmly in the dry sand. 'Or maybe you forgot how fast it is. Speed's not always the answer, you know.'

Santiago shook his head and puffed his cheeks. He was still shirtless, displaying a chest that was black and grey with coarse hair, and a belly that swelled around the top of his brown shorts. On his head he wore a *gringo*-style cowboy hat, beaten with age and use, the felt faded, the rim dark with sweat. He tilted his head to one side and smiled at me. 'So it seems.'

'I wish the old man was here to see this,' I said, scanning the boat, finding myself hoping not to catch a glance of Sister Beckett.

'Raul?' Santiago said, the smile falling from his lips. 'Where is he?'

'Piratinga. Some kind of fever. You haven't heard anything?'

Santiago shook his head, coming close to the side of his boat and leaning against the railing. I heard the squeak as it moved in its fixings, betraying the *Estrella*'s failing health. 'Some kind of fever, you say?'

'That's right.'

'You know there's dengue in Piratinga?'

'So everyone keeps telling me.'

He watched me, reading the worry in my eyes, then took off his hat and looked inside it before replacing it on his head. 'Raul will be fine; that old man is made of iron. He's probably at Ernesto's right now, drinking beer and smoking Carltons.'

'I hope so.'

'He won't like what you've done to his boat, though. That fire back there singed a few holes in your canopy, eh?'

'We can't all sit inside,' I said. 'So where you headed?'

Santiago let his gaze wander to the far bank, maybe twenty metres away. There was a tree that would have been on dry land a few weeks ago but was now reaching from the surface of the river. Leafless, it rose from the water like the bony arm of Corpo Seco, with narrow branches at the top spread like skeletal fingers. From the crook of one of those branches an *acauã* surveyed the land beyond the trees. It preened its feathers, then opened its beak and let out a cry that people said was like human laughter.

It sounded to me more like it was in pain.

'Rain's coming again,' Santiago said. Many of the boatmen believed the *acauã's* call signified the approach of wet weather.

'So, where are you headed?' I asked again.

'Nowhere,' Santiago shrugged, still watching the bird. 'Not now, anyway.'

'Maybe we can help?'

Santiago looked over at Daniella and Leonardo standing close together. 'Do I know him?' He knew that Daniella was my girl-friend, and he'd be wondering why she was so close to Leonardo.

'This is Leo,' I said. 'He's a friend. Heading to Mina dos Santos.'

Santiago nodded as if he wasn't quite sure whether he believed me.

'Who've you got on board?' I asked.

He looked back at the windows, but no faces were visible. The people inside must have moved away from the glass so we couldn't see them. 'Tourists.'

'Fishermen?'

He half smiled. 'Kind of.'

I nodded and throttled the engine a touch because the river

was taking us away from the *Estrella* once more. 'So, you want some help?'

'You think you can help?' Matt asked as he came onto the deck beside Santiago. His hair was short, his shirt open to the waist to show bony ribs, and there was a scar that ran around his neck from one ear to the other. Matt was not as violent and ruthless as he looked, but he was capable of the brutality needed for his job and his mind worked in a particular way. Santiago might believe Leonardo was a friend, but Matt was not so easily convinced. He watched our passenger with a keenness that matched that of the *acauã* sitting on Corpo Seco's bony hand. He would be looking for something he couldn't immediately see. Something that Leonardo's closeness to Daniella might be hiding.

'Maybe we can tow you.' Leonardo forced a smile again and put his arm around Daniella, drawing her closer as if giving her a hug.

'Who are you?' Matt asked, coming forward so he was hidden behind the gunwale from the waist down. His hand dropped out of sight behind the peeling sides of the *Estrella*.

'I'm a friend,' he said, and I could hear the anger welling inside him.

'Not *my* friend.'

Leonardo's smile slipped. 'Daniella's friend.'

'And you think you can tow us?' Matt asked, his hand still out of sight, just as Leonardo's was. The two men locked in a stare like animals daring each other to attack. Matt sensed something in Leonardo just as I had sensed it the first time I saw him.

'We can give it a try,' I said, hoping to distract them both. 'Daniella, why don't you throw that rope over? I'll keep the *Deus* steady.' I pointed to a coil of thick rope that was slumped at the stern. It would be heavy for her to lift, but she'd manage.

Without waiting for a reply, I took the boat forward, bringing our stern in line with that of the *Estrella*, sweat making my hands slick on the wheel. As I did it, I looked at the rifle, still propped in the bow, then at Leonardo and Daniella standing behind me. I wondered if I would be able to reach the weapon before Leonardo could react, but I knew he would notice the moment I left the controls. I couldn't take the risk.

Leonardo held onto Daniella for a moment before letting her go and following her to the coil of rope. He kept his hand behind his back and stayed with her so he was out of Matt's line of sight.

I throttled the engine backwards and forwards, keeping us as stationary as possible, while Daniella struggled with the rope. Eventually she took a step back and, with both hands, threw it out towards the *Estrella*. On the other boat, Santiago leaned forward, arms outstretched.

The rope remained coiled, making it no more than halfway between the boats before it dropped into the river and began to sink.

'Shit.' Daniella started to pull it back in. It was heavier now, the water having soaked into it, and I could see the spray as she coiled it back onto the deck and made ready to throw it again.

The second attempt fell short just as the first had done, but the distance between the boats wasn't great and I knew Daniella was strong. It wasn't until she bent down to pick up the coil for the third time that she turned back to me and I saw the look in her eyes.

She was up to something.

I shook my head. No. It wasn't worth it. If something set Matt and Leonardo off, there would be violence. It would be quick and cruel and she was between them. If anything caused them to trade bullets across the water, Daniella would be caught in the middle.

'Let me try,' I said, thinking I could stop her from doing whatever she was planning. 'You take the wheel.'

'No,' Leonardo said a little too quickly, making Matt narrow his eyes. Leonardo caught the change in Matt's expression and tried to soften his demeanour. 'She's doing fine,' he said.

'No she's not,' Matt called back. 'Why don't *you* do it?'

'Me?' Leonardo looked surprised. 'No, I—' But even before he could finish his sentence, Daniella had thrown the rope again, this time only managing to get it over the gunwale and drop it into the water.

247

'What kind of man are you?' Matt said to Leonardo. 'You let a woman do the work? What's the matter with you? Pick up the rope.'

I could see the indecision in Leonardo's eyes as Matt provoked a reaction from him. He didn't know whether to insult the man, help with the rope or do what came most naturally to him – use his pistol.

'I'll do it,' I said as Daniella began drawing in the rope again. 'You take the wheel.'

'Just throw the damn rope,' Matt called to Leonardo. 'You want to be here all day?'

And so Leonardo finally moved. As soon as he did, though, Matt tensed and took a tiny step back from the gunwale.

Leonardo dipped down, out of sight from the other boat, and Matt waited, every muscle in his body preparing to react if Leonardo stood up, weapon raised.

I could see that Leonardo was going to throw the rope, though. He squatted and gathered it into his arms, pistol still in his hand. The coil of rope hid the weapon from view when he stood and braced himself close to the gunwale, ready to throw.

He twisted his body, calling on all his strength and hefted the rope out towards the *Estrella*. The strong movement threw his weight forwards, and as soon as he was unbalanced, Daniella reacted.

She dropped into a squatting position, wrapped both arms around Leonardo's legs as if she were embracing them, and thrust herself upwards, tipping him head first over the side of the boat.

Daniella's plan was to disarm Leonardo and gain the upper hand, and she executed it to perfection. Leonardo grabbed at the gunwale, but he was too far gone to help himself. His weapon tumbled away, and he fell head first into the water with a clumsy splash.

41

As soon as Leonardo was overboard, I threw the engine into reverse and took us away, leaving him to flounder in the water, arms beating the surface a dirty white.

While Daniella pulled the rope on board, whipping it through Leonardo's grasping, empty fingers, I hurried back to the bow and snatched up the rifle. Within less than a minute I had checked the weapon and was pointing it down at the man who had made me fear for Daniella's life.

Leonardo was harmless now, though. Daniella had seen to that. His pistol had fallen into the darkness of the river, and it looked as if I had been right about him not being able to swim because he struggled, arms thrashing and face pointed skyward, as he coughed and gasped for air. His panic at the fear of drowning was increased by the thought of what was in the river with him. Perhaps another *jacaré* – this time one large enough to drag him under and roll him like vermin until he was dead.

Beside me, Daniella looked shocked at what she had done. Surprise and fear in equal measure in her eyes. 'I did it,' she said with disbelief. 'It worked.'

'That was a risk,' I told her, 'but I'm not going to say you shouldn't have done it. Even though you *shouldn't* have.' It might have ended in a different way, but the result here was a good one. We were back in charge of the *Deus*.

In the water, Leonardo's instinct drove him to the nearest shallows – the sandbank upon which the *Estrella* had run aground – and his progress was slow and painful, his exhaustion clear.

I looked over at Matt, standing with his weapon pointed down at Leonardo, eyes on me. 'Zico? What's going on?'

I held up a hand. 'Looks like we've got everything under control now.'

Beside Matt, Santiago was crouched low, half hidden behind the gunwale of his boat. Now he stood up, his face a picture of confusion. 'What is this?' he called. 'Who *is* this guy?'

I kept the rifle trained on Leonardo as he made it to the shallower water, putting his feet on the fine sand.

'Leonardo thought he could take control of our boat,' I said. 'Daniella had other ideas.' When I glanced at her, I had that feeling of pride once more. She had done what I hadn't been able to do. She had overpowered Leonardo. Outwitted the gunman.

Daniella was leaning forward, with both hands on the gunwale, glaring at Leonardo. She was shaking, and I understood how much courage it had taken for her to tackle him. Three days ago she had been behind a shop counter, reading a beauty magazine.

'You were great,' I said.

She turned to look at me and nodded with a small, sharp movement. The way her eyes stared out from the sweat and grime covering her face gave her a savage look, but she was as beautiful then as she had ever been.

I could not have loved Daniella any more than I did right then.

Taking a deep breath, I closed my eyes and allowed myself the briefest moment to enjoy the rare sense of certainty of my feelings, then I pushed those thoughts away. 'Hold this,' I said, handing the rifle to Daniella. 'If he tries anything, shoot him.'

She nodded and I ran back to the box seat, talking a crowbar from the store and wedging it behind the padlock. One swift pull and the metal tore away from the wood.

When I returned to Daniella a few seconds later, I was reloading my pistols as I watched Leonardo begin wading across the shallows, and by the time my revolvers were tucked away in their holsters, he had stopped moving and turned to stare at me. His eyes were wide, his mouth open, a look of panic on his face.

'Shit,' he said. 'Get me out of here. Pull me out.'

I took the rifle from Daniella and aimed at him. 'Sand getting soft?'

Leonardo looked down at the water and began moving from side to side, trying to free himself from the sand that was sucking him down. 'Get me out,' he said again. 'Please.'

'I'm trying to think of a reason. I mean a *good* reason, why I shouldn't just let you drown. Let the sand take you right down and make you a part of the river.'

'Please.' He had the same panicked tone I had heard when the *jacaré* tried to take him.

'Bring us closer,' I said to Daniella, lowering my voice. 'You can do that, right?'

'Sure.' She stared down at Leonardo. 'Are you going to help him?'

'I'm not sure yet.'

She nodded, staring for a moment longer, then went back to the wheelhouse.

Within a few seconds, the engine was burbling and we were edging closer to the sandbank.

'Thank you,' said Leonardo. 'Thanks.'

'I'm coming to help *them*,' I pointed at the *Estrella*, 'not you.'

'*I* need help,' Leonardo shouted as his panic mounted. '*I* need pulling out. What about *me*?'

'What *about* you?'

'Surely you're not going to let this man die,' said a soft, lightly accented voice.

I didn't need to look up to see who had spoken.

Over on the *Estrella*, Matt had lowered his pistol and his head. He almost seemed ashamed to be armed. Santiago was turned away from me, looking back onto his own boat. And there, framed in the open doorway of the housing, was Sister Dolores Beckett.

Our eyes met, as they had done when the boat had passed us earlier that day, and once again the woman looked into my soul. Perhaps it was a trick they taught nuns; they didn't carry any weapons other than a soulful stare and the word of God.

Her face was not calm, not serene, but neither was there any urgency or panic. She was stern like a schoolteacher demanding something of a child. She kept her expression fixed and hard, but her voice calm and confident.

I stared back, hoping to see some darkness in her. I wanted there to be a reason for her death. I would kill her to protect those I loved, and I would take the money for her blood, but I wanted there to be something more. A reason. There had to be *something*.

'You must help him,' she said.

'Must I?'

'Yes. Of course.'

'Please.' Leonardo's voice was constricted by fear. 'Make him help me.'

But no one else knew how he had terrorised us. How he had threatened and murdered.

'Don't let him kill me.' He must have thought he was dead for sure, and yet here was a chance at life.

I broke eye contact with Sister Beckett and glanced round at the others. There were some strong personalities here, but everyone was turned towards her, submitting to her.

'He's not a good man,' I said.

'It's not up to us to judge who is good and who is not.'

In Candomblé they taught people there is no good or bad, only destiny. Some of the boys in the *favela* used it as an excuse to do whatever they wanted, but Sofia told me that even though there might not have been good or bad, everything we did was returned to us, one way or another. Perhaps this was how Leonardo's evil should be returned to him; by being sucked down beneath the River of Deaths.

'If you leave him there he will die,' Sister Beckett said.

I nodded. 'Yes he will.'

'And we will have murdered him.' She was still standing in the doorway, another figure just visible behind her.

'Yes,' Leonardo spoke again. 'Please don't murder me. Help me. Please.' The sand was pulling him in slowly. He was at least knee deep in it, the water close to his chest. A few minutes longer and he would be gone. 'We're *not* alike,' he said. 'You're *not* like me.'

'Because you would let me sink?' I looked down at him and wondered if it was a good time to remind him of the people he had shot two days ago. 'And it's not *we*,' I spoke to Sister Beckett. 'It's *me*. *I* will have murdered him. And I don't have any problem with that at all.'

'I dare say you don't,' she replied. 'But if I stand here and let you do this' – she looked around at the others – 'if *we* stand here and let you do this, then we will have all killed this man. And I do not plan to let that happen.'

'And how are you going to stop me?'

'I'm going to appeal to your better nature.'

'What if I don't have one?'

'Everyone does.' She showed me a sad smile. 'Some of us just need to dig a little deeper to find it.' Then she spoke to Santiago, saying, 'Captain, please help that man.'

Santiago made a move but I stopped him. 'No.' I pulled the rifle tight to my shoulder, closed one eye and trained the iron sights on Leonardo's forehead. 'He doesn't deserve your help.' I dropped my finger over the trigger, beginning to squeeze.

'Zico.' Daniella put a hand on my back. 'Don't.'

'But after everything he's done?' I spoke quietly. 'After Rocky and the old man and how he threatened you? You put him in there, Daniella and—'

'He doesn't need to die. He's not dangerous now.'

'As long as he's alive, he's dangerous.'

'I don't want you to ...' She shook her head. 'I don't want you to be like that.'

Perhaps she didn't need to see every side to me.

I sighed and turned back to Sister Beckett. 'All right. I'll help him. But, trust me, you don't want this man on board your boat.' I put down the rifle and picked up the rope to throw to Leonardo, seeing his hopeful, smug face looking up at me. It would have felt good to let him drown out here. Watching him die would not have given me any difficulty at all. I hardly knew anyone who had deserved it more.

'Zico?' asked Sister Beckett. 'Is that your name?'

I looked over at her and nodded.

'Good,' she said, keeping her eyes trained on mine. 'Pull him up, Zico. You'll be glad you did.'

I took a deep breath and threw him the rope.

I was saving a man's life, but nothing about it felt good. If it hadn't been for Sister Beckett and Daniella, standing firm like pillars to support my conscience, I might have forgotten the money and let him sink below the surface, watch him suck the silt-laden water into his lungs with his last, gasping breaths.

Daniella had asked me to save him, but I knew she was torn between letting him live and letting him die. She was struggling with her own mind, knowing it was wrong and yet wanting it at the same time.

I, on the other hand, was saving Leonardo so that Daniella didn't have to suffer any more guilt than she already was. She had put him in the river, so she would feel responsible for his death, and she would be struggling with the thought that part of her wanted him to die. I also told myself the money was a good reason to keep him alive. Without him, we might never be paid for this trip, and the old man's effort would have been wasted.

The muscles in my back strained as I pulled on the rope Leonardo had tied around his waist. My biceps burned and my forearms tightened into cords. I braced my feet square against the gunwale and put every effort into dragging Leonardo to safety.

He didn't come out of the sand like a cork from a bottle. More like finally sliding a splinter from your finger. It wasn't a sudden movement, but a gradual release as the river let go and finally gave him up.

Once he was free, I hauled him towards the *Deus*, taking no regard for how he spun in the river like a fishing lure, his head bobbing below the surface, water invading his mouth and gritting his eyes.

As the others watched in silence, I pulled him hard against the hull of our boat, banging his face, drawing blood, and then dragging him up. Leonardo clung to the skirt of tyres, trying to take more control over his rescue now that he was out of the water, but when he finally climbed up onto the gunwale, I took a step back and tugged hard, toppling him onto the deck. I immediately went to him, crouching out of sight of the others and drawing one of my revolvers. With my left hand, I grabbed Leonardo's chin as he gasped for a deep breath of air, and with the other, I pushed the barrel of my gun between his teeth.

'Zico?' Daniella said. 'What are you doing?'

'Making him safe.'

'You're not going to—'

'No,' I assured her. 'I'm not going to kill him.' I felt Leonardo relax beneath me, so I pushed the pistol harder and looked into his eyes. 'Unless he makes me.'

Leonardo shook his head. Much of the soot and grime was gone from his face now, but there was blood around his nose and it seeped between his lips and created a film across the top of his upper teeth. It filled the narrow gaps; a stark crimson against the yellow-white enamel.

With the barrel in place, I frisked my free hand across his body, looking for any sign of other weapons, but there was nothing.

I leaned close to his face and looked into his bloodshot eyes. 'The only reason you're alive is because I want it to be that way. Don't fool yourself into thinking anything else. The only reason you're still on this boat is because it's where I want you to be, you understand?'

Eyes wide. Mouth wide. Chest hitching up and down, his breathing rasping around the barrel of my revolver.

'Nod your head.'

He nodded.

'Good.'

Daniella watched with interest. Not disgust. Not fear. *Interest.*

'So we're going to be nice to the people on the *Estrella*,' I said. 'Do what we can to help, then we're going to go to Mina dos Santos, OK?'

He nodded again, teeth grating on steel.

'We're going to deliver your guns and we're going to get the rest of our money, OK?'

Nod.

'I could kill you right now, put you in the water for the fish, but you owe the old man money. Fuel costs money. His time costs money. *My* time costs money. I could try to make you tell me who the guns are for, but you're not going to give that up easily. It's the only thing keeping you alive and things would get messy before you tell me; I don't want to get into that in front of all these nice people. So for now, you have some value to me. You're going to make your delivery, make your payment and then, *then*, I'm going to decide whether or not to kill you. If you try to screw me before any of those things happens, I will kill you. Do you understand?'

I took the gun away, raking the foresight against the roof of his mouth and crashing it against his teeth. '*Do you understand?*'

'Yes,' he managed. 'I understand.'

'Zico?' I heard Santiago's voice. 'Everything OK over there?'

'Fine,' I called back, still out of sight. Then I lowered my voice again. 'In a second I'm going to let you stand up. When you do, you're going to remove your shirt and your trousers.'

'What—'

'Don't talk. Just do it.' I untied the rope from around his waist and grabbed the scruff of his shirt. I hauled him to his feet and stood him straight, dripping onto the deck, so that Sister Beckett and the others could see him.

'He's safe,' I said. 'Unharmed.'

'Are you going to shoot him?' Sister Beckett asked me.

'Wouldn't I have done it already?'

'Are you going to shoot him, Zico?' she asked again, wanting a different answer.

I glanced down at the weapon in my hand. 'I thought about it,' I told her. 'But no, I'm not going to shoot him. Not yet, anyway.'

'You've done the right thing,' she said.

'Take off your shirt and your trousers,' I told Leonardo.

He looked at me as if deciding whether or not I was serious, then started to unbutton his shirt. He removed it with a little difficulty because it was wet, then he wiped his face on it, the blood spreading into the checked pattern, soaking into the lighter parts, making the injury to his nose look worse. He made sure everyone could see it before he dropped it on the deck at his feet.

'Trousers.'

He unfastened the button and wriggled out of the wet trousers, struggling to pull them over the bandage around his calf.

'What are you doing?' Santiago asked, turning to his friend. 'Why is he taking his clothes off?'

'Zico's making him safe,' Matt replied for me. 'The guy must've done something bad.'

'Like what? What did he do, Zico? What did this guy do to you?'

'It doesn't matter.'

When Leonardo was finished, he stood beneath the canopy in just a pair of cotton shorts. Shafts of sunlight cut through the singed holes in the canvas and rested on his skin like birthmarks.

I ordered him to the seat where he had kept my belongings and took a couple of cable ties from my pack, the kind electricians use to keep things tidy.

'I didn't want all this,' Leonardo said.

'You should have thought about that before you pointed your gun at us.'

'Please, *Carioca*. Zico. I just wanted to make you get there on time. I just—'

I took his chin in one hand and lifted his face so I could look into his eyes. 'You killed two men, and you tried to kill my friend's dog – you were going to kill him, too.'

'No.' He tried to shake his head.

'You pointed a gun at my girlfriend, and I saw the way you were watching her last night. I know what you are, Leonardo.' I raised my other hand as if to hit him, clenching my fingers into a tight fist around the handle of my revolver.

Leonardo flinched away, turning his head, but I stayed my hand and straightened up. 'Put one round his wrist.' I handed the ties to Daniella and pointed the gun at Leonardo. 'Make it tight.'

She did as I asked, putting the tapered end through the locking section and pulling it closed with a clicking sound.

'Put another one through it and round the post,' I said, indicating the roof support bolted to the deck beside the seat.

When Daniella was done, Leonardo was, more or less, handcuffed to the boat. 'Now he's not going anywhere,' I said to her. 'Now he's safe.'

Leonardo pulled once at the plastic ties and slumped his shoulders in resignation. If he struggled too much, the plastic would tighten and cut into his skin.

'So what do we do now?' Daniella asked. 'We can't just leave them.'

I looked over at the *Estrella*, Sister Beckett and Santiago waiting, and I considered my next move. I knew Daniella wanted me to help them and I didn't see that I had any other choice.

'Right, then.' I went to the side of the boat and looked across at the others. 'Let's see if we can pull you off the sand.'

42

Sister Beckett watched me throw the rope over to the *Estrella*, stepping back when the coils landed with a thump near her feet. She glared at me as if I had aimed it at her, then moved back into the cabin and disappeared from view. I knew she was there, though, disapproving, and already we had made a connection I had not wanted to make.

Santiago and Matt grabbed the rope before its weight could drag it back into the water, and they tied it off to the railing at the stern of the *Estrella*. Any cleats that might have once been there were long gone.

'Will it work?' Daniella asked me.

'Who knows?' I put the engine into reverse and slid backwards over the water until the rope tightened, but the *Estrella* didn't budge from the sand.

'That woman?' Daniella said over the sound of the engine. 'You know her?'

'No. Why?'

Daniella shrugged. 'Don't know. The way you looked at her. The way she talked to you. It's like there was something going on.'

'Something like what?'

'I don't know. Nothing, I suppose.'

Beneath us the engine grumbled, and behind us the River of Deaths churned into foam, but we remained stationary and the *Estrella* remained on the sand.

'It's not working,' I said, looking at Daniella sitting beside me.

'And if we do this too long we'll damage the *Deus*. Then we'll *all* be stuck out here. We don't want—'

'Stop! Stop!'

I looked up to see Santiago and Matt waving their arms, but it was too late. With a sudden release, and the sound of shearing metal, the railing came away from the stern of the *Estrella*, ripping out and flicking out into the water.

The *Deus* lurched and began trawling backwards, dragging the metal railing like an anchor.

I stopped the boat and went to the bow to pull the rope back in, straining against the weight of the railing until I could pull it no longer. 'It's stuck,' I shouted to Santiago. 'Caught on something.'

'Time's running out,' Leonardo said.

'I'll have to cut it.' I ignored him and lifted my shirt, taking the knife and sawing at the thick rope.

'You had that the whole time?'

I stopped sawing and turned to look at Leonardo. He was leaning back on the seat, trying to find a comfortable position. 'You had a knife the whole time and you never tried to use it?'

I didn't reply.

'There must've been times,' he said. 'Times when you could've done it. How long has it been? Two days? And in all that time you never saw a moment to use it?'

'Maybe I should use it now.'

'Now that I'm tied here, you mean? You'd like that? To kill me like a pig that has its feet tied? You said you're not like me, Zico, and you know what? I think you were right. But the difference is that you're softer than me. You don't have the same edge.' He smiled as if he knew something that made him better than me. 'I know why you didn't use it.'

I turned back to the rope, cutting through another strand of it.

'It's because of her,' he said. 'That's why you didn't use it. Because you were afraid of what might happen to her.'

I continued to cut.

'Me?' Leonardo went on. 'I *would* have used it because I was afraid of what might happen to her. You chose to protect her by doing nothing. I would have chosen to do *something*.'

The blade went through the last strand of the rope and I let it slide overboard and sink into the River of Deaths as I turned to Leonardo and put the knife to his throat. 'Then you should be glad I'm me and not you,' I said. 'Otherwise I'd be pushing this through your neck right now and dropping you in there for the piranhas.'

Leonardo tried to back away, but the ties prevented it, and the most he could do was turn his head. He raised his free hand in submission. 'But I didn't harm you, did I?' he said. 'I didn't touch her. I could have, but I didn't.'

'Not so tough when the knife is at your throat, are you?'

'Zico.' Daniella stood up behind the wheel. 'Don't—'

'I'm not going to.' I released pressure on the knife. 'I'm not going to.'

'Everything OK over there?' Santiago's voice.

I stayed where I was, wavering with the blade at Leonardo's throat, my face turned towards Daniella, then I relaxed and took it away, wiping it once on my trousers before slipping it out of sight.

'I don't think this is going to work,' I called back to Santiago, noticing that Sister Beckett was in the doorway again, like she was a guardian angel for the killer I had seized. She had no idea what the man had done. She knew only that I had threatened him. 'We're never going to pull you out of there.'

Santiago nodded in agreement.

'You're too deep,' I said. 'You were going too fast.'

He rolled his eyes at me. 'The sand will shift. It'll let us go when it's ready.'

'And if it doesn't?'

'Where are you headed?'

'Mina dos Santos. We can send help from there. A couple of other boats should be able to pull you free.' It was just as I had

261

wanted it. We'd have time to get to Mina dos Santos, go ashore and wait for Sister Beckett to come to us.

The nun leaned close to Santiago and spoke to him. I could hear the sound of her voice carry across the hot, still air, but I couldn't make out the words. Santiago seemed to think about something, running his eyes over the *Deus* as if assessing her, then he spoke to me. 'You'll be in Mina dos Santos by nightfall?'

'Probably. Depends how long we stay *here*,' I said.

'By the time you get there it'll be too dark. No one will come,' Santiago said. 'Anyway, there's never any boats there, just a few canoes.'

'They'll be fast,' I said. 'And they can come right into the shallows. Maybe they can dig you out.'

'No. When are you coming back?'

'Tomorrow.'

Santiago spoke to Sister Beckett and she pursed her lips, looking across at us, her eyes on Leonardo. She thought for a while, then stepped forward to the gunwale where the railing had been. 'We'll come with you,' she said. 'You can take us to Mina dos Santos. Help Santiago on your return in the morning.' She made it sound like she was giving us permission to take her further on her journey; as if it would be a privilege for us to have her on board.

It was a strange moment. Almost dreamlike. The woman who had been my obsession for these last few days was standing in front of me, wanting to board my boat. Until this meeting, she had been a pervasive presence, but now she was a reality, coming closer and closer, as if to test my nerve.

'I ... No. He's a dangerous man.' I pointed my thumb over my shoulder. 'You won't be safe.' I didn't want her on board; I didn't want any connection to her at all. When she disappeared, someone would come looking for her, and I didn't want them to come to me.

'He doesn't look so dangerous,' Sister Beckett replied.

I turned to Leonardo, pathetic and fearful, trussed like an animal waiting to be slaughtered. Half naked, bleeding and bandaged, he presented a beaten image, but when I caught his eye, there was a twinkle under the false exterior, and the corner of his mouth turned up in the tiniest hint of a smirk. He was taking a small victory from his defeat.

'Time's wasting,' he said.

I put a hand to my pocket and felt the folded paper that nestled in the darkness, softened by the warmth of my chest and the sweat from my body.

'I need to get to Mina dos Santos,' Sister Beckett called. 'Will you take me or not?'

I withdrew my hand as if it had touched something living, and stared at my fingertips. 'I need to get there too. *Today*. And if I waste any more time—'

'Then let me come aboard now and we'll be away.'

I rubbed my fingers on my trousers and looked at Sister Beckett. It should have been easy for me to refuse her. I had to do nothing more than take the wheel and move on. I would have to explain to Daniella why I'd made that choice, but I could lie. I could tell her it was because I wanted to make Leonardo's delivery, secure his pay. I didn't have to tell her I wanted as little to connect me to the nun as possible.

'Well, Zico? Are you going to take me?'

'We'll take you,' Daniella said, making me look round at her in surprise.

'What?'

'Come on, Zico, it's the right thing to do.'

Sister Beckett nodded. 'It is, but I need to hear it from Zico.'

'All right,' I said, shaking my head in exasperation. 'We'll take you.'

I looked up at the sky and wondered, once again, if someone was watching over Sister Dolores Beckett.

The nun stood on deck, hands on her hips, and watched me approach in the smaller boat.

When I reached the *Estrella*, I stretched out to take hold of the fixed ladder, and Matt leaned over and looked down at me. 'Who's the guy?' he asked. 'The asshole on your boat.' He made a circle with his forefinger and thumb.

'We're doing a job for him.'

'What kind of job?'

'Delivery.' I pulled the boat against the *Estrella*.

'OK, OK,' he said, 'I get it. Too many questions. One of Raul's special jobs, eh?'

'Something like that.'

He lifted a bag over the edge of the *Estrella* where the railing had once been. 'You look like shit, Zico, you need anything? Some kind of help? That fire back there was tough going.'

I glanced down at myself, seeing the dirt and sweat patches on my shirt. My face would be pale from lack of sleep, and streaked with soot. My bloodshot eyes were tired, my muscles ached and I needed some sleep.

'I'll be fine. You know who this woman is?' I asked him.

Matt shook his head. 'Dolores is all she said. Speaks good Portuguese but I think she's a *gringo*.'

'Yeah, why?'

Matt grunted and lifted another bag down to me. 'Just one of those things. Accent maybe, not sure.'

I took the second bag and put it beside the first. 'Is that everything?'

'Apart from the passengers.'

'More than one?'

'She has a friend with her. Quiet woman.'

'Yeah?'

'Mmm.' Matt leaned towards me and beckoned for me to come closer. 'There's something about her "friend". She has a look about her.'

'You mean like they're *together*?'

'No, I mean like she *watches*. She doesn't talk much, she stays out of the way, but she watches. *Everything*. It's like, maybe this woman is someone important pretending not to be.'

I dismissed his comment with a wave of my hand. 'Well,

whoever she is, she can stay on the *Deus* until we get to Mina dos Santos. After that she's on her own.'

'You know what?' Matt said, glancing behind him and lowering his voice further. 'I thought you were going to let that guy drown. Just let the river suck him right down.'

'So did I. For a moment that's exactly what I thought, but...' I let my words trail off. 'So where's this damn woman then? I need to get going.'

'I'm here.' Sister Beckett leaned over beside Matt. 'Are we ready to go?'

'Just waiting for you.' I let her see my false smile. She needed to know we weren't going to be friends.

'I'd better get down there, then, hadn't I?' She put her hands on the ladder, about to climb down, when another face appeared at her side. The woman Matt had spoken about. She put her hand on Sister Beckett's shoulder, looked her directly in the eye and Sister Beckett moved to let her climb down first.

I waited as she descended the four or five rungs and stepped into the vessel. She nodded once at me, then stood to one side so she would be between me and Sister Beckett who now put her feet on the ladder and came down. Before she joined us, though, the nun motioned to her companion, asking her to step aside so that she could confront me herself.

The boat rocked in the water, but neither woman showed any sign of worry. They allowed themselves to sway with the motion, as if they had done it all before.

'Zico,' Sister Beckett smiled. 'I'm so glad you agreed to take us.'

She was much shorter than she had looked either on the *Estrella* or in the clipping I had in my pocket. The top of her head reached no higher than my chest and, close as we were in the small boat, she had to crane her neck to look me in the eye.

She was not a woman who was concerned with appearances. She had a mess of grey hair that looked as if it had never found any particular style. Her glasses were thick, her pale blue eyes magnified behind them, giving her a constant stare. Thin lips, lined with the wrinkles of a woman in her late fifties who had spent little time pampering herself or caring for outward things. She was wearing loose trousers, beige and unremarkable, a shapeless T-shirt which fell to her waist and had a FUNAI slogan across the front in green lettering. The official agency for protecting Indian interests and culture, the FUNAI shirt was the only thing that gave any clue as to who or what she was.

'You did the right thing, helping that man out of the water,' she said.

'For your sake, I hope so.'

'Why for my sake?'

'Because you're coming on board with him.'

She narrowed her eyes. 'What did he do that was so wrong?'

'You don't want to know.'

'I doubt you could say anything that would surprise me.' Sister Beckett studied me from behind those thick glasses and I could see a slight squint on one side, as if her right eye wasn't quite looking at me. 'I'm Dolores,' she said, extending a small hand.

'Dolores.' I repeated the name, telling myself to think of her only as 'Dolores'. Nothing else. She was *nobody* else. I wasn't supposed to know who she was.

I glanced down at her hand, extending my own more from habit than from wanting to shake hers. She had a loose grip, her hand not quite fitting into mine, so only our fingers came together. She leaned forward, offering her cheek for me to kiss. I made a show of unwilling participation.

'And her?' I asked, still holding her hand but watching the other woman. Young, hair the same colour as Daniella's but cut short. She was almost as tall as I was, her long legs in olive coloured trousers, the kind with pockets low on the thigh. A T-shirt like Sister Beckett's. She was the same woman who was in the background in the photo in my pocket. I hadn't recognised her immediately, but now I was sure. I was also certain that there was more to her than met the eye. She was security.

Sister Beckett *did* have protection; and not just the holy kind.

'Kássia,' she said. 'My travelling companion.'

'Is she armed?'

Sister Beckett made a strange sound, as if clearing her throat, or perhaps it was a noise of amusement, I couldn't tell for sure. She smiled her honeyed smile. 'Zico, we are armed only with our words and our smiles.'

'Well,' I said. 'I reckon you might need more than that where *you're* going.'

43

Trying to find some inner peace with my frustration at having the nun on board, I had waved farewell to Santiago and Matt and steered the *Deus* away from them.

Dolores, on the other hand, had gone straight to Leonardo.

She spent a few minutes with him in quiet conversation, checking him over and speaking with subdued concern. All the time she was with him, she had cast glances in my direction. Then she had introduced herself and her companion to Daniella. I half expected Daniella to be pleased to have them there – it would make a change from old men and *pistoleiros* – but she said no more than a few words to them before coming to rejoin me behind the wheel.

The river was hazardous here, and I kept my eyes on the water so we didn't end up as Santiago had done, but I glanced back at Dolores from time to time, ensuring that she wasn't involving herself too much with Leonardo. I had seen his false look of subjugation, and I had seen the gleam that lay behind it. I knew how to read a man like that, but Dolores would see only what Leonardo wanted her to see.

Beneath us, the *Deus* kept moving, her engine beating hard, thrumming in the loneliness of our location. To my left, the white sands of the shallows gave way to a narrow beach that may never have felt the tread of a man's foot. Two or three *jacaré* lay like driftwood, their mouths open to the day, and I glanced over to see Leonardo watching them.

Beyond the beach, a wall of dried mud had baked hard in the sun, and beyond that, a line of vegetation hid anything else from view. A toucan, bright-orange-billed, black-tipped and white-chested, moved amongst the branches searching for berries.

I kept to the right side of the river, where the water was dark and deep, where we were closer to the twisted, forbidding trees that wound their way around each other, standing in unity, uninviting and dense. From time to time, somewhere in the forest, a screaming *piha* announced itself to the afternoon.

'How long before we get there?'

I turned to see Dolores standing beside us. She wasn't looking at me directly, but staring at the trees as they crept past.

'If the river stays like this, we should be there by sundown,' I said, wiping my brow. 'Otherwise ... I suppose we'll get there when we get there.'

'It's inconvenient.'

'It's the best we can do. It's a slow boat, but—'

'That's not what I meant,' she said. 'I mean us being here. It's inconvenient for you.'

I shrugged.

'I'd like to thank you for helping us.'

I lifted a hand and let it drop, in a brief acknowledgement of her thanks.

'Do you have any water?' she asked after a moment in which we both kept our eyes ahead, as if afraid to look at each other.

'I'll get some for you.' Daniella pushed up from the seat and I couldn't tell if she was eager to offer help or if she just wanted an excuse to escape an uncomfortable situation.

'A fresh bandage, too?' Dolores asked. 'For Leonardo.'

Daniella gave me a questioning look so I nodded and she headed down to the supplies.

When Daniella was gone, Dolores came closer, and I thought she was going to sit down beside me. 'She's pretty. Is she your girlfriend?'

'What difference does it make?' It was no business of hers. I didn't want to talk to her. I didn't want to be her friend or find anything to respect in her. If I were to kill this woman, I wanted it to be without care and without regret. I wanted to find a reason to hate her, not a reason to like her.

'It doesn't make *any* difference,' she said. 'I was just making conversation.'

'I don't have much use for conversation.'

'What else is there on a boat like this?' She sat down beside me, and the shadow that cloaked me recoiled. It clung to me and whispered in my ear.

You're going to kill her.

Dolores smelled of cheap soap and body odour. 'Does he have to be tied like that?' she asked, and I caught a hint of something on her breath. Peppermint. She had been eating mints. 'It's cruel. I don't like to see any man treated like that, no matter what he's done.'

'Everyone can be saved?' The words of Father Tomás came to mind and that brought an image of Sofia.

'I think so,' Dolores said.

'What if he's a murderer?' I asked.

'Is that what Leonardo is?'

I sighed and wished Daniella would hurry up with the water. Maybe Dolores would be shocked if I told her what Leonardo had done yesterday. Maybe she would be glad he was tied up if she knew the violence of which he was capable. But if I told her, I would have to reveal my part in it. I would have to tell her how I helped to cover it up, and if I didn't, then I was sure that Leonardo would.

'*Is* he a murderer?' she asked again.

'It doesn't matter what he is or who he is,' I told her. 'He's staying right there.'

'I'll take responsibility for him,' she said. 'Release him and I'll make sure he does no harm.'

I laughed. 'You think you could control a man like him? Have you ever met—'

'I have met many men,' she said, 'of many different types. Men like you, Zico, and men with far harder hearts. Some who behave as if they have no heart at *all*. I've been in places and met people even a man like you wouldn't believe, and not one of those people has ever raised a hand to me. Not one.'

'Then you've been lucky,' I told her.

'Please. Release him.'

'No.'

'At least give him his clothes.'

'He's safer as he is.'

'Let him have his dignity, if nothing else. Let him have his clothes, Zico.'

'That man deserves no dignity,' I snapped. 'If you had been on this boat as long as I have, you'd know that. Stop pestering me and let me get on with taking you, and *him*, to Mina dos Santos. When you get there, and you're off this boat, you can give him all the dignity you like.'

She didn't even flinch. Her face remained calm, her voice measured as if she were talking to a child. 'Zico, it's inhuman to—'

'Water,' said Daniella, holding out a clear plastic bottle. The label had long since gone and the contents were nothing more than boiled water that had been left to cool. It wouldn't be cold, but it would quench her thirst.

'Thank you.' She stood and took the bottle, holding it in both hands and smiling at Daniella before turning to me again. 'Think about it, Zico. Think about what I said.'

'I don't need to.' I watched her go back to Kássia, but she didn't sit down. She spoke to her companion as she unscrewed the top of the bottle, then she went to Leonardo and lifted it to his lips. He drank, the water dribbling from either side of his mouth, and as he tipped his head back, his eyes moved in my direction.

'I was thinking about before,' Daniella said, sitting beside me. 'About when he was in the water and you were pointing your rifle at him.'

'Uh-huh.' I shook my head at the foolishness of the nun and returned my concentration to the river.

'I thought you were going to shoot him.'

I glanced down at the flesh of Daniella's thighs on the seat beside me. There were faint bruises there among the smudges of dirt and soot. A few tiny hairs beginning to show on her smooth skin.

'I wanted you to do it. Right at that moment, I wanted you to kill him for shooting those men and for making me so afraid and for ...' She shrugged. 'Is that wrong?'

'No.'

'I wanted you to *kill* him, Zico.'

'No you didn't. It crossed your mind to want it but you didn't really want it. That's why you stopped me.'

'She stopped you. Dolores.'

'No. It was you. *You* stopped me. Later, too, when I had the knife at his throat.'

'I feel dirty for wanting him dead. For seeing those other men like that, all that blood.'

'It'll pass. Give it some more time.'

Daniella nodded and glanced back at Dolores. 'She thinks you should untie him.'

'That's because she thinks she can control him.'

'Control him? Why? Who does she think she is?'

'God knows,' I said.

'You have to admit, though, she's got something about her.'

'Maybe.'

'I mean, she seems nice, but strong. The way she looks at you ...' She was still watching Dolores, seeing how she offered the water to Leonardo like he was a condemned man. 'It's like she's *some*one. Does that make sense? The way she treats people, it's as if she's someone *important*.' She paused. 'You know anything about her? Who she is?'

'Dolores,' I replied. 'That's all I know. She said her name is Dolores.'

For a while, Daniella took the wheel and I dozed beside her. I allowed my eyes to close and I let my mind drift into a numbness, knowing that Daniella was competent to do what she needed to, and that Leonardo was safely bound.

There were no dreams for me. Just the overwhelming heat

beneath the canopy, snatches of images and conversations, and then, somewhere in a place of darkness, splashed with patches of almost blinding brightness, I heard the rolling drums of thunder. I forced my eyes open and rubbed them awake with rough fingertips.

'More rain?' Daniella asked.

'How long have I been asleep?'

'Half an hour.'

I shook my head and stood, going to the gunwale to look out at the sky. There was a light cover of grey clouds, but they blackened over the forest a few kilometres south. Perhaps Santiago had been right about the *acauã* sitting in the skeletal hand of the tree. Maybe it had seen the bad weather approaching.

'Something the matter, Zico?' Dolores called.

The heat didn't seem to affect her much. There were no sweat patches on her shirt, no perspiration on her forehead. For some reason that annoyed me, but it was no reason to kill her.

'The rain,' I said. 'If it gets too hard we'll have to stop.'

She nodded once, but continued to watch me with those intense, pale blue eyes. Again, I couldn't help feel that she was reading my thoughts, or seeing the shadow that cloaked me. It was as if she knew who I was; that she had seen my dark intent. Beside her, Kássia watched too, but her scrutiny was different. Her look was one of loyalty to Dolores and warning to me.

It was clear that when the time came for me to take Dolores's life, I would also have to take Kássia's.

Breaking eye contact, I moved past them, going to the store for a bottle of water. There were two empties on the deck as if they'd helped themselves while I'd been sleeping and I cursed my tiredness. I couldn't afford for them to hijack the *Deus* with sincerity and good intent in the way that Leonardo had hijacked it with murder and mania.

'We can't stop.' Leonardo leaned forward and spoke with urgency. He kept his voice down so that his new guardian wouldn't hear him. 'My contact might have left already. If he's not there, there won't be any money.'

'He'll wait. He wants what's in those crates.' I took a bottle of water from the warm interior of the store and went back to sit with Daniella.

'At least you managed to get some sleep,' she said. 'That's good.'

'Your breath smells of mint.' I took a swig of the water, rinsed my mouth and swallowed. 'You been talking to that woman?'

Daniella stood up to stretch her legs. 'She came over before, when you were asleep. She asked me to talk to you, get you to let Leonardo have his clothes. Said he has no dignity sitting there like that.'

I shifted over and took the wheel. 'What else did she say?'

'Not much. She asked about Piratinga, about me, about you.'

'What did you tell her?'

'Nothing.'

I nodded and put a hand on the back of her thigh. It was warm and damp with sweat. 'Do you think she's right?' I asked. 'That I should give Leonardo his clothes? Maybe even cut him loose?'

'No.' She looked back at me with a serious expression. 'Don't let him go. I didn't listen to you before when I should have. You said he was trouble and you were right.' She let her gaze linger, then she turned and watched the river once more. 'She's OK, though. Dolores. I think she means well.'

'Hm. Sometimes people who mean well end up making the biggest mistakes,' I said. 'If I cut him loose he'll try to kill us all. How much dignity will she think he needs then?'

Daniella sighed. 'There's something about her, Zico. She's so sure of herself. Who do you think she is?'

'I don't know. Someone from FUNAI, I suppose.'

Footsteps on the deck and Dolores came to stand beside us. 'I'd rather not stop—'

'And me.' I looked up at her. 'But if we have to, then we have to. No one ever listens.' Beside me, Daniella moved away so my hand was no longer on her leg. She smiled down at me and walked to the bow, reaching her arms over her head and arching her back.

'We can't travel in heavy rain,' I said. 'If we can't see the river properly, it's not safe. Why does no one ever believe me when I say that?' I watched the line of trees slipping past on the southern bank and remembered the nightmare we'd had when we were smothered by the smoke. I didn't want to be blind like that again. 'But Mina dos Santos is close now. Not far at all.'

'Do you have business there?' she asked.

'Do you?'

Sister Beckett looked at me. 'I have the feeling you don't like me, Zico, why is that?'

I shrugged.

'I was talking to Leonardo,' she said. 'He told me he recognised me. From a photograph you have in your pocket.'

I was surprised that Leonardo had made any connection. He had seen the clipping late last night, an hour that seemed so long ago now. He had seen the grainy picture only by torchlight and yet he had put the faces together.

'Why would you have a picture of me in your pocket, Zico?'

'You don't want to believe everything he tells you.'

'So he's lying? You don't have a photo?'

'Leonardo is not a good man,' I told her. 'I know you think he's suffering and that it's your duty to release him, but he's not a good man.'

'I can see what kind of man he is. I can see what kind of man you are, too.' She stared at me with those pale blue eyes that didn't quite look at the same place on my face. Her glasses magnified her pupils, dark circles dilated wide to take in as much of the fading light as possible. 'I've met many men like you.'

'So you said.' I took a drink of water and turned away from her. I leaned back and listened to the gentle spots of rain falling on the canvas above me.

'Do you know who I am, Zico?'

'You said your name is Dolores.' I stared at ripples on the surface of the river. The rain was light, but there were circles appearing on every inch of water, emanating outwards, never-ending.

'And that's all?'

'That's all.' I watched Daniella lift her face to the rain, making no attempt to come under the shelter. 'It's not getting any heavier,'

I said. 'We should be OK. We'll be in Mina dos Santos soon.' I looked at Dolores. 'It'll be almost dark when we get there. I hope you have somewhere to stay tonight.'

'There's a hotel. Fernanda's.'

'More like a brothel.'

'We can't be too proud,' she replied. 'As long as there is a spot to lay my head, I will be fine.'

We looked at each other, our eyes searching for something that might not even be there.

'Your journey is almost at an end,' she said to me.

'Yes,' I replied. 'It is.'

As I watched her, the shadow that cloaked me ruffled in the breeze, and I tried to not to feel Sofia's judgement when I thought about what I had to do. I tried only to see that I was saving Daniella and the old man. Somewhere in my heart, though, I wondered if they would ever be free from threat; if a devil like Costa would ever release us.

Perhaps we could never be saved.

44

It was Daniella who first saw the figure stumble onto the shore.

The storm hadn't fallen over the *Deus* like it had the day before. The sky darkened and thunder growled somewhere far away and unseen, but the worst of it had stayed over the forest and the savannah beyond.

The light drumming on the canvas continued for half an hour or so, but the sound was gentle and hypnotic. The soft patter mingled with the thrum of the engine and the wash of the river in our wake. Circles formed in the water before us; a million perfect rings that grew and grew until they became nothing. Clear droplets bulged and dripped from the holes left in the canopy by the fires, and in the places where the rainwater evaporated on the warm deck, steam lifted like spirits rising from the depths of the River of Deaths.

When the rain stopped, the clouds remained, hanging grey and low, taking the light and colour from the sky. It was an awkward atmosphere that gave the world a grainy hue, but Daniella took the wheel and pushed us on and on, deeper and deeper.

That was when she noticed the figure appear from the foliage, and called out to me, pointing.

I came to her side, followed the angle of her finger, then went to the bow to see the ghostly silhouette standing on the raised bank to our left, no more than fifty metres away. Behind, a band of trees stood tall against the dim sky, and above them a haze of black smoke thinned in the air. The smell of the wood smoke came to us as we nudged westwards, bringing the apprehension of another nightmarish journey through fire.

The shape stood like a ghost in the grey gloom, almost seeming to hover, like it might break up at any moment and disappear.

'What is that?' Sister Beckett spoke in my ear, her voice gentle and quiet as if there were some reverence required in this place. 'Is that a person?'

We were coming closer now but the figure was still no more than a hazy outline against the trees, the shape shifting and moving with the shadows of the forest.

'*Mapinguari*,' Daniella whispered.

'There's no such thing,' Dolores replied.

'They say it killed a hundred cows on De Sousa's *fazenda* last year,' Daniella went on. 'Ripped out their tongues and drank their blood.'

I watched the dark shape and couldn't help shivering at the thought of a creature that could blend with the trees or move through the forest without making a sound. Something that could make you dizzy and disorientate you in the chaos of leaves and vines.

'Take us closer,' Dolores said.

'Closer?' There was fear in Daniella's voice. 'No, we should—'

'It's moving,' Dolores said, and we all watched as the figure that blended so well with its surroundings put a foot forwards and became real.

More than just a momentary vision at the forest edge, it stepped out towards the wall of the riverbank. It hesitated, then lost its balance and twisted, falling a metre onto the strip of white sand below.

'It's a person,' Dolores said. 'Someone who needs help.'

'Maybe.'

The figure moved again. Shifting, crawling, sitting upright, pushing to their knees, then falling flat again, arms to the side, face down, prostrate in the sand.

'We should help.' Sister Beckett was like an irritating insect in my ear, always with something to say. 'They need our help. We have to stop.'

'I thought you wanted to get to Mina dos Santos before nightfall.'

'That is a *person*,' she said. 'And they need our help. If that means we're late getting to our destination, then so be it.' She stared at me, defiant, daring me to contradict her. 'For God's sake, Zico, I know you're better than this.'

'You don't know anything about me,' I said, both hating and respecting her at the same time.

'But you have a heart. Anyone can see that. It's in your eyes when you look at Daniella. We have to help. It's the right thing to do.'

The right thing.

I turned to Daniella and drew a finger across my throat. 'Cut the engine.'

There was an odd stillness that hung over this part of the river. No birdsong, no breeze. Even the insects were quiet in the unsettling stillness as we cut silently through the water.

When we were stationary, and the anchor was in place, I handed the rifle to Daniella and told her to keep it pointed at Leonardo the whole time I was off the boat. If he looked like he was a threat, she was to shoot him.

'Where?' she asked, taking the rifle and resting it across the back of the seat to aim it at Leonardo. 'Where should I shoot him?'

Leonardo twisted in his seat, tugged once at the plastic cuffs and raised the middle finger of his free hand at me. '*Punheteiro.*'

'Wherever you like.'

She nodded once and turned away as I went back to the bow, drawing my pistols.

'You don't need those.' Dolores gave me a disapproving look.

'You don't know that.' I held them high and climbed down into the river. The water was chest deep and I kept my pistols over my head as I waded ashore, holstering them once I was there, and going straight to the body on the sand.

The naked woman did not react to my approach.

She did not make any sound when I knelt beside her and spoke. There was no resistance from her muscles or her flesh when I touched a hand to her shoulder. And when I put my fingers to her neck, there was no pulse beneath the dark skin.

I put both hands under the dead woman and braced myself before rolling her onto her back.

Then I saw the horror of what had been done to her, and I reeled away from it, drawing my pistol.

Sofia's face leaped into my mind, searing itself in my vision like hot iron sears an image onto cattle hide. For a moment, it was my sister who lay on that beach, and I saw with a terrible clarity the things I had seen so many years ago in the *favela*.

'No.' The word escaped me before I could stop it.

'What is it?' Dolores spoke from the boat.

I shook the vision from my mind and pointed my pistol towards the trees. I held up my spare hand, making rapid movements, encouraging the nun to be quiet.

'What?' she asked again. 'Is everything all right?'

I turned in her direction and put a finger to my lips, then stood and backed towards the river.

Closer to the *Deus*, I spoke without turning around. 'We should leave now.'

'What's going on?'

'She's dead. We should go.'

'We have to do something.'

'There *isn't* anything we can do.'

'We can't just leave her there,' she said. 'And maybe there are other people who need our help.'

'He's right.' Some of Kássia's first words. 'We should go.'

'Listen to your friend, Sister Beckett. Whatever happened to this woman, it wasn't an accident. You don't want it to happen to you.'

As if to punctuate my remark, a dull, flat report came from somewhere amongst the trees.

A single gunshot that started a rush of activity in the forest.

45

The birds panicked. Unsettled from their perches, they spilled upward with a flurry of wings, and the grey sky was clouded with the darting movements of *coleiro*, *uirapuru*, woodcreepers and flycatchers. They hung in the air for a moment, then descended on the trees once more, searching for safety. Other unseen creatures were startled, too, breaking for deeper cover, crashing through the forest in a sudden explosion of sound and movement.

Then nothing.

Numbed silence.

Everything was still.

Daniella was first to fracture the spell, calling my name from the boat. 'Zico.'

'I'm coming to check on her,' Dolores said, close to the gunwale behind me.

'I've checked her,' I said, 'and I've seen enough dead people to know there's nothing you can do,' I kept my eyes on the line of the trees. 'I'm coming on board and we're leaving.'

I backed into the river, moving to where the water reached my knees before I realised Dolores was behind me. She had climbed over the side of the *Deus* and was wading past me, coming ashore.

'Christ, woman.' I grabbed at her T-shirt, halting her progress. 'What don't you understand? We have to leave. It's not safe here. Not by a long way.'

Dolores whipped around to stare at me. 'Get your hands off me, Zico. Right now.'

I hesitated, then made a show of releasing the cloth that I'd bunched into my fist.

'You may not care for other human beings, Zico, but I do. I intend to help this woman and see to any others who may need it. If you wish to stay aboard the boat, then so be it.'

I gritted my teeth and watched her walk onto the sand, Kássia following close behind.

'She wants to get killed,' I said, but Kássia ignored me.

I stayed where I was, watching them go to the woman, then I continued back to the *Deus*, climbing the tyres and telling Daniella to start the engine.

'We can't just leave them, Zico. You have to stay with her.'

'No, we have to get away from here. We don't know who did this or how many of them there are.'

I could feel my own sense of urgency building. I wanted to bolt, like the animals and birds of the forest had bolted from the gunshot. I had to keep Daniella safe, and that meant taking her away from here as quickly as possible. This was why I hadn't wanted her on the boat.

'What if something happens to them?' Daniella left her place at the wheel and came to where I was climbing aboard.

'It's not our problem.' I jumped over onto the deck and headed for the wheel.

'You don't mean that, Zico.' Daniella stood in my way.

'Yes I do.' I put out a hand to move her aside. 'If she wants to get herself killed, that's not our problem.'

Daniella resisted me, saying, 'Zico, you can't—'

'Why do you care so much about her? You don't even know her. My job is to protect you and this boat, not them.' I tried to pass around her but Daniella grabbed me, pulling me so I had to look at her.

'*You can't just leave them.*' Her expression stopped me dead. She couldn't believe I was going to abandon Dolores and Kassiá on that remote beach. It was a monstrous and cowardly thing to do. I could see it in her eyes.

'Zico's right,' Leonardo said. 'We should leave them. *I* would.'

I tore my eyes from Daniella's and looked down at Leonardo.

'Don't listen to him,' Daniella said. 'You're not like him.'

I looked over at Dolores and Kássia on the beach.

If I left them, there was a chance they would disappear just as Costa wanted. I would have my money and my land. Daniella and the old man would be safe.

All I had to do was leave. Right now.

But it didn't feel right. It didn't feel right at all.

I *wasn't* like Leonardo.

When I turned to Daniella once more, I knew I was going to do the right thing. That's what Dolores had said. *The right thing.*

'Start the engine,' I said, taking Daniella to one side so that Leonardo couldn't hear us. 'Keep it running. I'll go bring them back. And pick up that rifle. Don't take your eyes off him again.'

Daniella nodded. 'I promise.'

'You're making a mistake,' Leonardo said as I returned to the gunwale and swung my leg over. 'I would leave them.'

'I'm not you,' I told him as I climbed back down into the water.

Daniella started the engine and the *Deus* coughed into life as I waded through the shallows and went to where Sister Beckett was kneeling in the sand.

Kássia stood beside her, watching the line of trees.

The naked woman was lying exactly as before, white-eyed to the sky, mouth open, tongue back in her throat. Grains of sand decorated her lips like tiny jewels, catching the flickering of the falling sun that managed to pierce the cloud from time to time. The wound in her neck was not a clean cut, but ragged as if someone had sawed at it with a blunt blade. Her arms bore angry scratches that broke the skin from shoulder to elbow. Her fingernails were broken, her thighs ripped and bruised.

Behind her, from the path that opened onto the bank, a trail of blood marked the journey to where she now lay.

Dolores had a hand to her mouth, her eyes closed, and was muttering an inaudible prayer while Kássia stood sentry.

I looked away from the dead woman, not wanting to see the images that were trying to fill my head. My sister's face burned through everything.

'We need to go,' I said as I tried to push the visions away. 'It's not safe here.'

Kássia nodded, but refused to take her eyes from the line of trees.

'Someone is going to come looking for this woman,' I said. 'Whoever did this is still in there. We heard the shot. They're going to come looking.'

'Yes.'

'We have to go.'

Sister Beckett sat back on her haunches and pushed to her feet. 'This woman is Xavante.'

'What does it matter?' I asked. 'We need to leave. *Now*. You don't want to end up like—'

'No,' she said. 'We must see if anyone else needs our help.'

'No way. Definitely not.'

But Dolores ignored me. She headed straight to the wall of dirt that bordered the beach, and hauled herself up amongst the shrubs. Kássia followed.

I looked back at the *Deus*, raising my hands to Daniella in exasperation, then I, too, followed.

'Wait,' I said, trying to keep my voice to a whisper. 'Sister Beckett; wait a second.'

She stopped. 'I'm not leaving without—'

'Yeah, yeah,' I said. 'Sure. Fine. But let's not stomp in there like a startled tapir, OK? Let's be a little quieter. You heard that shot right? A *gun*shot? That means someone has a gun and they might shoot at us.' I tried not to sound as if I were talking to an imbecile. 'You don't want them to know we're coming.'

She thought about what I'd said. 'OK, Zico. You're right.'

'Well at least that's something. And you,' I asked Kássia. 'You're really not armed?'

'Only with our words,' Dolores answered for her.

'But you know how to use a weapon, right?' I took the smaller of my two pistols and held it out to Kássia. 'Otherwise why are you here?'

'No guns, Zico. Kássia is my companion,' Dolores said.

'Sure,' I replied. 'And we all need a companion who looks like she's trained.'

'Kássia does not need a weapon, Zico.'

'I say she does.' I tried to press the pistol into her hand.

Dolores opened her mouth to speak but I cut her off saying, 'Let her speak for herself. She has a tongue, right?'

Kássia shook her head and refused the weapon.

'Fine.' I held out a hand. 'After *you* then.'

Sister Beckett remained where she was, sizing me up. 'How do you know my name is Sister Beckett?'

'What?'

'Before, coming off the boat, you called me Sister Beckett. And again just a few moments ago.'

'Did I? You must have said. Look, we really haven't got time to—'

'I told you my name is Dolores.'

'We shouldn't be standing here,' I said.

Sister Dolores Beckett looked into me again, as if she knew exactly who and what I was; as if she knew my intention. Then she adjusted her glasses and stepped to one side.

'Lead the way, Zico. I am in your hands now.'

46

A worn path cut through the trees and emerged into a small, planted area of corn that had grown almost to head height. The stalks were in neat rows, and were well tended, but there was something menacing about the way they stood straight and still, with only the slightest breeze rustling through them. The leaves buzzed in the waft of warm air, creating an unnerving hush, and even the insects paused as we entered the plot. Their humming and creaking stopped, the silence ringing in our ears, our footsteps soundless on the red earth.

Once we were moving among the plants, though, the insects began their song once more, stopping as we reached them and restarting when we had passed. Their music washed around us like a wave, just as the water cut and washed around the bow of the *Deus*.

On either side of the small cornfield, manioc grew in lines, and beyond that, a meagre collection of primitive buildings was huddled in a clearing. There were six in all, three on either side of a track which cut to the edge of the clearing and disappeared among the trees at the far side.

Behind the shacks to the left of the track, a large cleared area was strewn with ash and the charred remains of trees which hadn't been consumed by the burn. Weak wafts of greenwood smoke rose from that place, spinning, spiralling, thinning and disappearing as they met the air above where vultures waited in the treetops.

The sombre creatures hopped from one foot to another, opening their wings like storm cloaks and screeching to one another. Their calls echoed in the still and overbearing heat of the dull afternoon, reminding me of the day Costa forced this job on me; the day the old man had chased the vultures from his roof, telling me it was a sign of death to have them there.

I had laughed then, but I wasn't laughing now.

'Smallholding,' Sister Beckett said to herself as we watched the settlement from the edge of the cornfield.

Already, the shadow closed around me. Ahead, there was the unknown, and behind, there was Kássia.

I hadn't felt her as a threat before, but I was beginning to think that Sister Beckett knew my intention towards her. And I was certain that Kássia was more dangerous than she appeared.

'We have to go and look,' Sister Beckett said, and I stepped deeper among the corn, forging a route towards the buildings.

Some of the plants were bent towards us, broken off and trampled, and there were traces of blood on the ears, their trailing silks like brushes dipped in crimson.

'She came this way.' Kássia spoke to me, her eyes going to the pistol in my hand. 'Bleeding the whole way. She was strong.' She leaned close to my ear. 'I hope you know how to use that thing.'

We emerged from the corn and came to a stop, standing at its periphery, three of us in a line, Sister Beckett in the centre.

Five metres away, the closest of the buildings on this side of the track stood with its door swung open to the flattened dirt in front of it. A crude construction of mud bricks baked dry in the sun. Young trees had been cut from the forest to provide roof beams and supports, and palm fronds had been laid over them for shelter. The door was designed with some expertise using similar saplings, cut to exactly the right size and shape, then bound with a weave of palm leaves.

At our feet, the spots and sprays of blood led to a grisly pattern of deep red that was soaked into the earth on the track. Its dark, uneven shape was etched into the ground as a grotesque reminder of what had happened here.

On the shack itself, a rope was trailing over the roof support on the near side of the door, pulled taut, its tail tied off to a sturdy tree. On the other end of the rope, a bare-chested man was hanging by his neck so he was just centimetres from the ground.

His arms were tied behind his back, his dry toes brushing the dust, his chin pulled up and to the side. His face was a palette of blood and bruises and his eyes bulged in the indignity of his death.

He was dressed only in a pair of shorts, emerald green with a white stripe on the side.

There were others there, too. Other bodies that were defiled and brought together on the patch of land that had recently been cleared.

I could see now that not only charred trees lay scattered in the fresh burn, but a tangle of limbs, both male and female, lay there too. And there were limbs that belonged to neither man nor woman. Childish hands that were yet to grow but were now reduced to lifeless skin and bone and flesh.

It was obvious to me that the bodies were to be burned, and that whoever had perpetrated this slaughter was still here, finalising their massacre.

I put my hand on Sister Beckett's shoulder and whispered. 'Are you ready to go *now*? Have you seen enough?'

As I spoke, though, a man stepped out of the building in front of us, with a rifle in one hand and a blood-etched machete in his belt. He stopped to look down at the stain before him. '*Caralho.*' He kicked at the mark. 'Where the fuck did she go?' And he saw the trail on the ground, followed it with a turn of his head, looked up, eyes dark under the brim of his hat, and saw us, standing in a line, watching him.

Sister Beckett took a sharp, involuntary breath.

We all remained still, as if frozen. Wondering, calculating. The cicadas continued their indifferent chorus.

Then the man shifted his rifle, taking it in both hands and turning it on us.

So I raised my pistol and shot him through the heart.

The report was startling in that place of death and darkness. A hollow and intrusive sound, accompanied by a wisp of powder smoke hanging in my face before breaking up and vanishing.

The man took a step back, confusion in his eyes, and released the rifle, which clattered to the dirt. He stood for a second in the ringing silence, blood beginning to show on his shirt, then his legs weakened and he fell to his knees, tottering as if in prayer, before falling forward on his face and lying still.

Then a voice called out into the grey afternoon.

'Edson!'

Kássia pushed Sister Beckett to the ground, taking her low, making her small, and crouching in front of her as a second figure stepped out of the building, straight into my line of fire. This one didn't have time to take his eyes off his dead partner before I shot him in the chest, knocking him back against the doorframe, his body turning as he crumpled to the ground.

And then came more.

Two men appeared from behind the other buildings, running out into the path and spotting their friends. I fired on them too, but they weren't so close and my first shot went wide, kicking dust.

I dropped to my knees, aiming along the sights, wishing I had one of Leonardo's rifles, and I fired again as they ran to find cover.

'We have to get out of here.' Kássia spoke now. 'We have to get her away.'

'They'll follow,' I said.

'Then we'll have to make sure they don't.' Kássia took hold of Sister Beckett and pulled her to her feet as the men took their first shots at us. She kept hold of the nun and ran her to the side of the nearest building, taking cover behind its thick wooden and brick walls.

I fired another shot and followed, hitting the wall at a run, putting my hands out to stop myself.

Now everything was silent except for the regular gasp of our breathing.

Sister Beckett was white, all colour drained from her face, and she was shaking her head, staring at me. 'You killed that man.'

'I wouldn't have had to if you hadn't come up here.'

'But—'

'What else could I have done? Should I have let him kill *you*?'

'No, but—'

'Well, of course I killed him. What world do you live in, dragging us up here to get shot at, thinking you can just walk in and talk to these people?'

'We had to do something.'

'We should have *left*. You should have done what I told you and we should have left.'

Sister Beckett stared, open mouthed, flinching when another shot cracked somewhere close and wood splintered from the corner of the building, the lead whistling as it altered course and crashed somewhere amongst the trees.

'Take this.' I handed my pistol to Kássia. 'Just *take* it. Two shots left. I want you to let them know you're still here.'

'What are you going to do?' She looked at it.

'Go round the back.' I drew the other pistol. 'If they think we're still here ...' I shrugged. 'It's the best we can do. We can't wait for them to come and get us.'

Kássia nodded, taking the pistol.

'I'm guessing you don't need me to tell you how to use it.'

Kássia took a deep breath and wrapped her fingers round the handle. 'Go.' She leaned out from the edge of the building and fired into the street. 'Only one left.'

Circling the house, I made my way along the rear of the buildings, watching for the *pistoleiros*, expecting to meet them at any moment. It wasn't until I heard Kássia fire the final shot from my pistol, though, that I leaned around the wall of the last shack to see the two men taking cover with their backs to me.

Without any warning, I shot the first through the back of the head, blood spraying the second man who flinched away in surprise. My second bullet caught him in the cheek, tearing through the thin flesh. He howled in pain and I fired again, this time hitting him behind the ear, his noise ceasing immediately, his head jerking to the side and banging against the wall, leaving a glistening patch against the dark wood.

I had seen only these two men taking cover, but I couldn't

assume they were alone, so I returned the way I had come, finding Kássia and Sister Beckett just as I had left them. 'Let's go,' I said taking my pistol. 'Pick her up and let's get out of here.'

Kássia and Sister Beckett led the way through the corn, and I followed, walking backwards, keeping my eyes on the settlement, watching for movement but seeing nothing.

'You killed those men,' Sister Beckett was saying behind me. 'You killed them.'

'Yes I killed them,' I said, without looking at her. 'And if I hadn't—' I heard a loud cry and whipped around to see a man come from behind a tree at the side of the path, swinging a machete.

Kássia raised her arm to protect herself and the blade caught her high on the bicep, slicing through her skin just below the sleeve of her T-shirt, drawing blood and peeling flesh as it glanced away and the man retracted, ready to strike again.

I raised my pistol, but Sister Beckett and Kássia blocked my angle, so I moved into the trees looking for a shot as the man raised the machete for a second strike.

As he lifted the blade, though, Kássia pushed Sister Beckett away from her and grasped the man's arm. She held it firm as she slipped round behind him, raising her left hand to his throat.

From where I was standing, there was no shot to take without risking Kássia's life, but I could see that she was more than capable of defending herself, for her left hand was not empty. She had produced a blade of her own from somewhere – narrow and no more than ten or twelve centimetres of bright steel – and she slipped it, point first, into the hollow of the man's neck. In and out, like she had slid it into wet sand, and then the blade was gone and she was stepping away from him as he reeled, hands to his throat, blood bubbling from his lips.

Kássia didn't wait, didn't watch, she went straight to Sister Beckett, pulled her to her feet and continued along the path, coming out to the beach where Daniella was at the gunwale of the *Deus*.

'What the hell's going on?' she asked as we reached the boat and I pushed Kássia ahead of me, urging her to climb. The wound on her arm was superficial, but a flap of skin was hanging, folded back, and blood was coursing down her arm into the water.

I could hear Leonardo calling out, saying, 'Cut me loose and give me a gun, *Carioca*. I can help.'

'Get to the wheel,' I shouted at Daniella as Kássia climbed over the gunwale and turned to take Sister Beckett's hand. 'Get us moving.'

I put my shoulder under Sister Beckett's backside as she climbed, and found a hold on the *Deus*, pushing her up ahead of me.

As soon as we were on the deck, I went to Daniella, taking the rifle and leaning it across the gunwale, pointing it at the beach while she throttled the engine and took us away from the shore.

As we headed out into the river, I waited like that, ignoring Daniella's questions, ignoring Leonardo's calls for me to arm him, and braced myself for further shots until the beach was out of sight.

When we had finally left that place of death behind us, I came away from the gunwale and went to Kássia. I had intended to dress her wound, but already her upper arm was wrapped in a bandage. She was sitting with her head in her hands, while Sister Beckett stood over her, speaking in quiet but harsh tones.

'You're lucky to be alive,' I told her, but she didn't acknowledge me other than to sniff her disapproval.

'What happened?' Leonardo was shifting in his seat, struggling to be free from his bonds. He looked back at the shore. 'Someone going to come after us? Cut me loose, for Christ's sake. Don't let me die tied up like an animal.'

'No one's dying.' I shook my head and went to Daniella, sitting beside her behind the wheel, ignoring Leonardo's calls until he finally gave up.

'You going to tell me what happened now?' Daniella asked.

'Stupid woman.'

'What?'

'Not you. Her. She wouldn't listen to me, and look what

happened.' I told Daniella what we had seen in the settlement, and about the men I shot.

'You killed them?'

I could feel Daniella watching me and wondered if she was judging me.

'I had to.' I took out my pistols, reached for the spare cartridges I'd left beneath the dash.

Daniella was silent beside me as I reloaded the chambers. She kept her hands on the wheel, moving them only when the river required it. I could feel her breathing, the rise and fall of her chest close to mine, squeezed together as we were on the seat. My fingers were trembling as I replayed the incident in the settlement. The men I had killed, the bodies I had seen. How many people were dead in that place? Ten? Twenty? Children, too. Maybe I would be dead if the men had been carrying weapons like the ones in the boxes at the back of the boat. Those boxes were as full of death as they were full of guns.

'How did it feel?'

'Huh?'

'How did it feel?' she asked. 'Killing those men?'

I snapped the cylinder shut and looked at her.

Those men had deserved it. The things they had done to the people in that village had earned them the deaths I had given them. 'I did what I had to do to protect us.'

And I had protected Sister Beckett.

'Then you feel like you did something right?' Daniella asked.

I glanced back at Sister Beckett and remembered my mistake when I had called her by name. Did she know my intention? 'God knows why I bothered,' I said, still watching. 'God knows why I didn't let them just ...' I thought about Costa's money, and in my mind I saw Sister Beckett lying dead by another man's hand. I could have earned the money without ever having to harm her. But I would have been instrumental in her death, and back there, I had acted without thinking. I had saved Sister Beckett's life.

That had been my instinct. To protect, not to kill.

Perhaps she was the key to casting off the shadow.

'No.' I turned back to Daniella. 'It doesn't feel like anything. I did it and it's done. But for her, though, for *Dolores*, it's not like that. For her it's like someone opened her eyes to the real world, thinking she could float through it with words and good intentions. I had to kill four men to protect her life. And her friend killed a man, too.'

'Kássia?'

'Cut his throat. So much for being armed only with words and smiles. The way she did it, I'd say she's done it before. I've seen experts slaughter animals in the same way.' I put a finger to the hollow in my neck. 'She took her knife and...' I saw the distaste on Daniella's face and realised I had been lost in my own thoughts. She didn't need to know the detail. I cleared my throat. 'She dressed her wound better than I would've done and she didn't lose her nerve. Not once. I reckon she's carrying more than a knife, too.'

It was Daniella's turn to look at the two women sitting opposite Leonardo.

Sister Beckett was leaning back, her face to the sky.

'She doesn't only have to deal with what I've done in her name,' I said. 'She has to deal with what her companion has done. And she has to deal with being wrong.'

Daniella took a cigarette from the packet on the shelf under the wheel and put one between her lips. She lit it with a plastic lighter and took a drag. I wished I smoked, seeing the pleasure it gave her. The calming effect.

'You had cigarettes all this time?' Leonardo called from behind us. 'Are you going to let me have one?'

'No.'

'Are you going to tell me what all the shooting was about, then?' Those women won't tell me shit. Did you have to shoot someone and show them what a bad man you are? I told you we're not so different.'

I left the wheelhouse and went to where Leonardo was secured. 'The difference is that you would have been one of *them*.'

'*Them*? You mean the kind of people who would do what I

saw on that beach back there? The kind of people who would kill women? You saying you've never done something like—'

I grabbed the scruff of his shirt and pulled him close. 'I'm nothing like you, Leonardo. *Nothing.*' I pushed him back against the gunwale and pulled him forward again. 'Who are they for? Who are the guns for?'

Leonardo shrugged.

'Who?' I banged him against the gunwale once more.

'I'll die before I tell you that.' He grinned. 'But you know that.'

I pushed him back against the gunwale and released him, turning to walk away before I did something worse.

'You've got bad things in you, Zico,' he called after me. 'Bad things.'

47

There was almost no light left in the sky when we reached Mina dos Santos, and it would've been easy to glide past and not notice it, nestled in the dusk.

There was very little on the riverside to suggest there was any kind of community hiding just half a kilometre onshore. A cleared area of trees, a permanent beach, a small wooden jetty of no more than a couple of metres. There were two outboards moored there, the engines tipped forward to lift the long propeller shafts from the water, and there was a dugout canoe pulled up onto the sand.

Nothing else.

I cut the engine and slid the *Deus* towards the bank, keeping her to the darker water. All was quiet.

'This is it?' Daniella said to me. Her voice was close to a whisper. 'I expected more boats. People.'

'Most people come by road.'

'Unless they're carrying weapons, right?'

'Something like that.'

'So what about *her*?' Daniella asked. 'Why is *she* coming here? And why by boat?'

'Why don't you ask her?'

'I did. When you were asleep.'

'And what did she say?'

'FUNAI work.'

'Then that's all she wants you to know.' I looked at the shore and changed the subject. 'We'll let them leave and we'll go later; get some supplies for the return journey.'

'Why not now?'

'We can be alone for a while,' I said. 'We'll have the boat to ourselves. There's no hurry to go ashore.' Sister Beckett wouldn't be going anywhere tonight, and Leonardo would need to find his contact.

I took her hands and put them on the wheel, saying, 'Guide us in.'

Once we were close enough, I jumped down onto the cracked and crooked planks of the jetty, and tied the *Deus* off before climbing back on.

'Well, you got us here in one piece,' said Sister Beckett.

'Not a very comfortable ride, though, was it?' Leonardo grumbled from his seat. 'It's starting to get cold, you know.'

She ignored him and came closer to me. 'I should be grateful to you. I should be grateful but I can't find it in myself. It's wrong for me to be glad to be alive when another has had to ...'

'It's OK.'

'You understand?'

'Those men deserved everything I did to them but you don't know how to deal with it. I understand *that*.'

'I wouldn't be alive if it weren't for you.'

'And for Kássia.'

'Yes.'

'Maybe you'll listen next time. Even to someone like me.'

'I misjudged you.'

'I don't think so.'

Sister Beckett took off her glasses and cleaned them on her T-shirt. 'I learned something today,' she said, 'but I'm not sure what it is yet.' She replaced her glasses and stared at me with magnified eyes. 'I just want to be away from here now.'

'That's what we all want.'

While Sister Beckett and her companion collected their belongings, I went to Leonardo and squatted in front of him. I leaned close and spoke quietly. 'Who are the guns for?'

'You know I'm not going to tell you that.'

'For the kind of people who do things like we saw back there in that settlement? Is that who?'

'What do you care? You'll get paid, that's all that matters. You want to come all this way for nothing?'

I watched him, wondering if it *was* all that mattered. Those guns could kill a lot of people. Would all those lives lie on my conscience?

'I'm going to cut you loose,' I said, 'so you can make contact with your people.'

'You coming?' Leonardo looked past me, watching Sister Beckett and her companion.

'No. I'm staying here with your guns. You come back to this jetty tomorrow morning, bring the money, and you can have the guns.'

'You're a smart man, Zico. Smarter than I thought.'

'Hmm. We'll see about that.' Maybe a smart man would have let Sister Beckett die out there in the settlement. Take Costa's money for nothing. But, instead, I had protected her.

'That woman,' Leonardo said. 'Who is she?'

'Her name is Dolores.'

'Yeah, but who is she? I mean, why do you have a picture of her in your pocket?'

'Mind your own business.'

'I've seen her somewhere else, too,' he said. 'I've seen her before.'

'I'm going to cut you loose now. Don't give me any reason to take out my weapon. No one wants that.'

'What about my clothes? You're not going to make me go into Mina dos Santos in just my shorts?'

I took out my knife and leaned across to cut the cable tie that kept him connected to the upright. He then offered me his hand so that I could cut the other tie, and I slipped the blade under the plastic and looked at him. 'Don't give me any reason to kill you.'

He stared at me. 'If I were you, I would do it now. You don't kill me now, you'll be looking back every day.'

'You don't frighten me,' I said, pulling the knife upwards and cutting the tie.

'Yes I do. Not because you think I might kill you, though, but because you think I'll do something to her.' He looked over at Daniella standing by the wheelhouse.

I dragged Leonardo to his feet and followed him to the gunwale, waiting for him to climb over before I threw down his clothes and backpack. He didn't offer to help with Sister Beckett's bags, so I dropped them onto the jetty for her and Kássia and I helped her down.

Leonardo pulled on his shirt and trousers and waited for the two women, as if his intention was to go with them into Mina dos Santos and hide behind their respectability. I might have been wrong, but Sister Beckett didn't seem to look at Leonardo in the same way as she had when she'd first come aboard. There was an edge of suspicion in her eyes now. She had seen something she never expected to see, and she had learned a new lesson.

Words were not always enough.

As they were about to walk away, Sister Beckett came back to me and looked up, beckoning with one hand.

'Are you not going to come ashore with us? Send help for Santiago?'

'No one will go out in the dark,' I said. 'He knows that. For now, Daniella and I are going to have some time alone.'

'Don't you think she needs to get off the boat?'

'What she needs is a bit of calm.' I nodded my head at the path into the trees. 'And there's not much calm to be had in there.'

Sister Beckett smiled. 'I was looking at the name of your boat and thinking it's appropriate. God and the Devil. Which one lives in your heart?'

'Maybe both.'

'Can I ask you something, Zico?'

I nodded.

'Why do you have a photograph of me in your pocket?'

Without thinking, I touched a hand to the place over my heart. The cotton under my fingers was soft and I could feel the outline of the folded newspaper. 'I told you, I don't have—'

'Are you sure? Is there something you want to tell me? In all the time I was on your boat, you never once asked me why I was here or who I was.'

'Daniella asked. You told her you work for FUNAI.'

'That's right, Zico, I do. But you know a bit more than that, don't you? You called me by my name.'

'I must have recognised you.'

'From the photograph? The one in your pocket?'

'You shouldn't be here alone,' I told her.

'I'm not alone. I'm *never* alone.'

'Kássia won't always be able to protect you. Not on her own.'

'Even without Kássia,' she said looking up, 'I am never alone.'

'*He* can't help you. Not from bullets.'

'But that's just it, Zico, don't you see? He can. He provides his own protection. He sent *you*.'

48

Daniella and I climbed down onto the jetty and sat on the sand
for a while, positioning ourselves so we could see the cut into the
trees bordering the narrow strip of beach. The barrier of forest
that hid the mine from view was deep and thick and impenetrable.
If anyone were going to come, they would have to use the path.

Two hundred metres upriver was a tributary, too small for any
boat to navigate, flowing from the mine. That small stream was
poisonous with the pollution running down from the operations,
contaminated with mercury and sure to kill everything that lived
in the water there. If the mine were to expand, that tributary would
be widened and the volume of spoiled water would increase. It
was just the kind of thing someone like Sister Beckett would try to
fight. But maybe the Indians would fight too, and it might require
a lot of guns to keep them down.

Beyond the narrow inlet, the approaching night had swallowed
the river and the trees.

It felt good to be off the boat, to be alone. My mind was still
burdened with countless worries, but at least Leonardo was gone
and Sister Beckett was out of sight.

'You don't think he'll come back?' Daniella asked.

'Leonardo? I don't think so, not tonight. The light's almost gone;
it'll be too dark. He won't be able to see if he comes back.' I sat
up and moved so I was behind her. I slipped my legs either side
of her and reached out to loosen her hair, arranging it around her
shoulders. 'Anyway, he'll be tired and sore. If I were him, I'd want
to rest, think about what I was going to do.'

'And what would that be?' Daniella tilted her head back towards me.

I watched the line of trees as I ran my fingers through her hair. 'Exactly what I told him; come back tomorrow with the payment. It would be the easiest thing for him.'

'You're not worried he might try to—'

'No,' I said, moving her hair to one side and kissing the back of her neck. 'He's got no reason to do anything. He just wants his stuff. We're safe tonight.'

'So who do you think all those guns are for?' she asked.

'It doesn't matter.' But my mind went back to the settlement. If those men had been armed with rifles like the ones on the *Deus*, they would have cut us down. 'We have to take the money and leave. The old man deserves to be paid for this, otherwise we came all this way for nothing.'

And there was another job left to do; for Costa. Sister Beckett was still alive and I had to change that.

Just one more life.

'Maybe we should—'

'Don't think about it,' I said to her. 'Just don't think about it. Forget them. It'll make you crazy. Think about something else.'

'Like what?'

I turned Daniella's face so our mouths were close together and pressed my lips to hers, soft and warm. She put a hand to the back of my head and pulled me against her, kissing me hard before she broke away and looked at me. Our eyes were close, and I could feel her warm, heavy breath on my mouth. She pursed her lips, still tasting our kiss, then smiled.

We washed upriver from the creek, away from the mine's waste, keeping our movements soft as we scrubbed away the grime of the past days. I had reassured Daniella, telling her we were safe, but I wasn't going to lower my guard too far. We stayed quiet so we wouldn't be heard, but would hear the movements of others if they chose to approach in the darkness.

'We should get back on board,' I told Daniella when we were clean. 'Come on.'

As the last light left the sky, I dragged my trousers over my wet legs and collected my pistols while Daniella stepped into her skirt and pulled on her top. I watched her struggle with the cotton on her wet skin, the vest rolling and sticking.

When she was done, we climbed back onto the *Deus* and loosened the rope that moored us to the jetty.

'There's still a few things to eat in the back,' I said. 'I'll get us moving, you see what there is.'

'Where are we going?'

'Not far. Somewhere we won't be noticed in the dark.'

'But you said—'

'Don't worry. We're going to be safe.'

'You promise?'

'Yes,' I kissed her. 'I promise.'

I went to the wheelhouse and started the engine, taking the *Deus* away from the jetty and out onto the water. We drifted to the far side of the river, about a hundred metres from bank to bank at this point, and nosed west past the poisoned tributary.

By the time I cut the engine, the light had completely gone, and the moon was already hanging in the cloudless sky.

'This should do,' I said, leaning over the gunwale to release the anchor. 'You all right back there, Daniella?'

I tugged at the rope, checking it was secure, expecting to hear Daniella reply.

The night was silent but for the insects.

'Daniella?'

No answer.

'Daniella?' I released the rope. 'You find anything to—'

'Not yet.' She spoke from just behind me, making me turn around with a start.

Daniella was standing naked on the deck. In the minimal light from a crescent moon, I could see little of the detail of her body, but her shape was outlined and there were places where the shadows rose and fell.

303

'Something we need to finish.' She stepped forward to kiss me, running her nails down my naked back, sliding her hands into the waistband of my trousers. 'Take them off,' she said, still kissing me, and I fumbled with the button, breaking off only to stoop while I kicked the trousers away.

'That was fast.' She moved closer, backing me against the bench seat where Sister Beckett had been sitting earlier that day.

'No time to waste.'

Daniella smiled and pushed me down onto the seat.

She came forward, stopped, slapped at her arm.

'What?'

'Mosquito,' she said.

'Oh.'

She squatted in front of me and ran her fingers across my thighs, down to my calves and back up again, then she stood and watched me for a moment.

'What's wrong?'

'Nothing,' she said. 'I'm just looking at you.'

'You never look at me like that.'

'I do now.' She put her legs either side of me, her knees on the seat, and reached down to take hold of me, put me inside her before lowering herself. We held our breath together for a moment, and then she began moving, putting her hands on either side of my face.

'You need to shave,' she whispered.

I ran my hands along her thighs. 'So do you.'

'Cheeky.' A gentle slap on my shoulder, then she let her head hang back and she smiled, her long hair falling around her shoulders. I could feel her tightening around me, her muscles contracting and loosening as she moved, and in that instant everything was forgotten.

Leonardo. The guns. Sister Beckett. The old man.

All of it was gone.

My mind was nowhere else but right here in this tiny fragment of time.

I pulled Daniella towards me and kissed her once before she

broke away and stopped moving. She had the remnants of the smile on her face and she looked alive with it. Her eyes sparkled, her mouth was still turned up at the corners.

'Ask me now,' she said. 'It's the right time.'

I stared at her, the moment even more arousing than before. I was inside her, a part of her now. Her warm flesh around me and on me. I could taste her on my lips, feel her on my skin. But the sensation was beyond physical now. She was asking me to give myself to her. Lay myself open and give everything.

'Ask me,' she said again.

I swallowed hard and looked into her eyes. 'Marry me,' I whispered.

'Yes.' She began moving again. 'Yes.'

Night had settled beyond the weak, cocooning light of the barbecue, and the wilderness made its music around us. The insects sang and the frogs chorused, creating a single sound that seemed to have a shape. Within that sound, though, were a thousand million individual flutters and creaks that laced through the night.

Above us, the moon and stars winked in the passage of the clouds as the world moved on regardless of our concerns. And, in the trees, burning lights flickered as if the *boitatá* patrolled the forest. They were not the smouldering eyes of the protecting snake, though, they were the encroaching lights of human progression. They were the lamps that glowed in Mina dos Santos.

'Where will we live?' I asked Daniella. 'I can't live with your parents.'

'Their house is big enough, you could be best friends with my mother ...'

I looked at her and saw the smirk so she nudged me and leaned over to kiss me. 'Don't worry, I'd never make you live there. *I* don't want to live there.'

I stirred the rice, taking out a few grains on the tip of a wooden spoon and testing them.

'We could live at your place,' Daniella said.

'It's small.'

'It's good enough.'

'I want you to live in something that *belongs* to us. Not some room I have to rent.'

'We don't need much,' she told me.

'I need to find work. *Real* work, I mean, not spending my whole damn life on the river for just a few notes in my pocket.' An image of Sister Beckett came to me. I had missed one opportunity to do Costa's job, but I could do it tonight. I could go to the mine once Daniella was asleep and I could put my steel to the nun's throat. The thought of leaving her alone on the boat, though, made me shudder. We had moved away from shore so we were hidden, but I wouldn't risk leaving her. If I went into Mina dos Santos, I would have to take Daniella with me.

I would have to find another way.

'I can work in the shop,' Daniella said. 'Between us we'll have enough for what we need.'

'I always thought you'd want more. Nice clothes, I mean, make-up... like in your magazines.'

Daniella tilted her head to one side, her body half turned towards me. 'Dreaming is for dreaming. It's not real. Maybe, if you get all the things you dream of, it turns out you don't really want them. Does that make sense?' Her legs were crossed beneath her, one of her feet touching mine. 'Dreams are for in here.' She tapped the side of her head. 'You're not supposed to get everything you want. I like *this*. Right here. Now.'

I couldn't help myself from reaching out and running my hand through her hair. 'This isn't for you,' I said. 'This life.'

'Isn't it? Didn't you say before that it suited me? I like it out here, Zico, I think I could get used to it.'

'You deserve more. I want to give you *more*.'

'I don't need any more. I only need you. Together we'll find a way.'

Neither of us was hungry, so we left the rice in the pan, thinking we could eat it tomorrow for breakfast. It was still early, maybe eight o'clock, but it felt late. The sun was down and so much had happened over the past few hours that my watch could have told me it was after midnight and I wouldn't have been surprised.

We sat in the darkness together, taking warmth from each other when we lay on our backs on the boards at the bow of the *Deus* and looked up at the stars.

'That one there.' I pointed. 'The brightest. That's our star.'

Daniella followed the line of my finger, bringing her head closer to my shoulder. 'Why is it ours?'

'On the flag. Every star on the flag represents a state. That one, the brightest in the sky, that's for Mato Grosso. The old man told me that.'

'It's beautiful.' She took a deep breath and let it flood from her body. 'You know, when you're out with Raul on the river, I think about you when I'm lying in my bed. I felt sorry for you having to sleep on the boat.'

'Not always on the boat,' I said. 'Sometimes on the beach.'

'I like the way the boat moves. I don't feel sorry for you now. What could be more beautiful than lying here, looking at the stars? It makes you forget everything.'

'It gets colder,' I said. 'Can't you feel it already?'

'You have sheets to keep us warm, and a net that keeps out the mosquitoes. And a fire,' she said to the stars, 'to keep warm, *and* to keep the mosquitoes away.'

She was right. There was a poetry to living like this, but there was also a need to be realistic. 'It can get tiring,' I said. 'And do you really want to pee in a bucket every day?'

She smiled and a whisper of breath escaped her. 'I can do without that, but sometimes,' she said, '*some*times we can live like this.'

'And have a home to go to.'

'Yes.'

We looked at each other for a long while before I went back to staring at the stars.

The air was growing cooler and I subdued a shiver. Daniella was right about how this felt. It was good to be here with her, to share this part of my life. I considered what it would be like to marry her, to live with her every day. I closed my eyes and pictured us together in my small, rented room. I imagined myself going to work every morning, maybe as a labourer on a soya farm.

It wasn't quite how I had imagined it when Sofia and I talked about it. We had talked about owning our own land, having our own farm, and I hated the idea of being another man's slave, I wanted to be free, but it would allow me to be with her. We could come on the river at weekends, work with the old man when he needed us – or I could do what Costa had asked of me. I could provide more for Daniella without ever having the life of a worker.

The push and pull of the possibilities battled in my thoughts and I struggled to see a winner, but there was one thing that swayed the fight. *Two* things.

Daniella and the old man. Costa would take them from me and leave me to be alone, and I was afraid of that more than I was afraid of anything else.

To lose them and be alone.

'Zico?' Daniella broke into my thoughts. 'Can I ask you something?'

'Sure.'

'If I wasn't here ... I mean, if I hadn't been on the boat ...'

'Yes?'

'Would you have killed Leonardo?'

I didn't see the stars now. They were still there, still bright in the sky, but I no longer saw them. 'I don't know,' I said.

'Have you *ever* had to?' she asked. 'Someone like Leonardo?'

'Like the men at the settlement?'

'No, not like that. You were protecting yourself. Protecting Dolores and Kássia. No, I mean just for ... I don't know ... for annoying you. Or maybe for someone else; for money.'

I didn't answer. I didn't know *how* to answer. I didn't want to lie to Daniella but it would be hard for me to tell her that truth. She already suspected it, otherwise she wouldn't have asked, but the idea of admitting it to her felt shameful.

'No,' she said, understanding my hesitation. 'Don't tell me.'

I sat up, putting my hands on my face, covering my mouth. 'Those days are behind me—'

'Stop. I don't need to know.' Daniella sat up, too, putting her arm around my shoulder. 'I know as much as I want to. You carry pistols, Zico. A knife. You know what to do with them; I've seen that. The old man brings you on his boat to protect him.'

'Not just for that,' I said.

'I'm not a fool, Zico, I know what kind of man you are.'

I stared at the deck and waited for her to go on.

'You're a good one, Zico. A good man. If you did a bad thing, I know it would be for the right reason.'

I fixed my eyes on the dry boards, not knowing what to say, not knowing if I was good enough for this woman.

We sat in silence for a while, Daniella with her arm around my shoulders, both of us enveloped in our own thoughts, and I wondered what the right reasons were. I wondered if I had really done those jobs for money or if I had been looking for some kind of justice.

For Sofia.

And would she really have wanted that?

'I don't know if I *am* a good man,' I said. 'Not good enough for you, anyway. I've done things—'

'I don't care what you've done. I *know* you, Zico. I *know* you.'

'And you want to be married to me? To live with me?'

'To have children and grow old with you.'

'Children? I hadn't thought about ... We'll need money to look after them. Give them—'

'Stop saying we need money.' Daniella put her mouth against my ear. 'We have each other. That's enough.'

'Not in this world. In this world, that isn't enough to feed ourselves and put a roof over our heads.'

'What about the guns, then? Can you make Leonardo pay you more? Or get the buyers to pay you instead?'

'I've thought about that,' I said. 'Every way I can. But there's nothing that won't put you in danger.'

'Then we'll manage,' she told me. 'We'll survive.'

'Yeah,' I said. 'We'll survive.' But I was thinking about Sister Beckett again; about the sharp edge of my knife. I stared out into

309

the night and let the sound of the insects wash over me in a sheet of grey noise. The shadow was there too, draping its arm over my shoulder and whispering in my ear.

Marriage? it said. *Children?*

Just one more life, Zico, just one more life.

All I had to do was make Sister Beckett disappear.

'Are you all right?' Daniella's voice was soft.

'Fine,' I said as I turned to look at her. 'You want to go and visit a gold mine?'

49

'If we're going into Mina dos Santos, that skirt and top aren't a good idea,' I told Daniella. 'You really haven't got anything else you can wear? No trousers?'

She shook her head, so I went to the store and pulled out a pair of jeans and a T-shirt that belonged to Raul.

'They stink,' she said, lifting them as if they were diseased.

I put them to my nose and smelled the mixture of diesel and fish and sweat. 'Perfect. You'll just smell like everyone else.'

'I can't wear them.'

'Sure you can,' I told her. 'There's not many women live here and by this time of night all the men will be drunk. Trust me, you'll be glad you stink.'

Daniella made a tutting noise and pulled on the trousers.

'You really *do* smell bad,' I said, wrinkling my nose. 'But the trousers fit fine. The old man must have good legs.'

'I feel disgusting.'

I smiled to myself and sat down on the deck, switching on my torch and taking out the two revolvers. I opened the cylinders, checked the load, then tested the action on each one, thumbing back the hammers, watching the cylinders revolve and the cartridges coming into position. The ticking and clicking was loud and comforting in the quietness.

Daniella sat in front of me and crossed her legs.

'I want you to take one of these,' I said.

'Why?'

'I don't know. I might have to leave you for a few minutes or ...

Look, I just want to make sure you'll be OK if anything happens to me. It's not like Piratinga in there.'

'What would happen? What are you talking about, Zico?'

'Just take it.' I put the smaller pistol in her hands for her to feel its weight. 'But don't let anyone know you've got it unless you're prepared to use it.'

I watched Daniella's eyes move from the pistol in her hand so that she was looking straight at me. 'OK.' And then her eyes were on the weapon again.

Together, we unfastened the smaller boat and dropped it onto the water. I helped Daniella climb down, then jumped over the gunwale and lowered myself beside her.

'I'm glad you're coming with me,' I said, taking the paddle and dipping it into the river.

'Give me one of those.' She reached for the second paddle and copied my movements, sinking it deep into the water and pushing us forward.

The cloud had thickened so there was barely a glow from the sliver of moon. The beach was just about visible because the white sand reflected what little light there was, but beyond that, the world was a wall of black.

'I want to be around when Leonardo comes for his guns, so we won't be long,' I said. 'We'll get some supplies, maybe have a drink, then come straight back.'

'You sure there isn't another reason for going?' Daniella asked.

'Like what?' I concentrated on paddling and tried to hide the stress in my voice. She couldn't know about Sister Beckett.

'You're not going to find Leonardo? To ...' She looked down at the black water.

'You mean to kill him?' I said. 'No. I need him to collect his cargo and pay us. Leonardo is just ... Leonardo. After tomorrow we can forget about him.' I watched her using the oar, admiring her stamina. She was no longer just the beautiful shop-girl. Now she was much more than that. She seemed bigger, somehow, more filled with life. 'It's good you've liked being on the river,' I said, my breath keeping time with the paddle and the sound of it dipping into the water. 'I don't mean Leonardo and all ... that.' I tried to find the right words to express myself. 'But just being on the water, out here ...'

'I know what you mean.'

'It suits you.'

'It's peaceful.'

I stopped paddling, surprised that she had found anything peaceful after all that had happened. In that moment, my heart was overwhelmed with the way I felt for her and, for the first time, sitting in the dark on the river, I allowed myself to accept that we were no more protected from Costa and his people than Sister Beckett was.

It didn't matter what I did tonight; I would never be free of him.

But there was something else worrying at me. A whispering voice at the back of my mind, speaking unformed words. I had overlooked something.

'What is it?' she asked, resting her oar on the side of the boat.

'We don't have to live in Piratinga.'

'What do you mean?'

'We could go somewhere else. Just leave Mina dos Santos now and keep going. Go wherever we want.' The voice prickled at me and, though I didn't quite know what it was saying, I understood the tone, and I understood that it was telling me to run. It was warning me that something was close.

Something bad was lifting its head.

'Like where?' Daniella asked. 'Where would we go?'

'Wherever we want.' It was the perfect solution. We could just run away from everything. Leonardo, Sister Beckett, Costa. The shadow. The whispering voice that refused to be whole. I could make it all go away. 'There are other places. Think about it. We could—'

'Piratinga is our home, Zico, we've talked about that. We can live at your place and I'll work in the shop, remember? We can't just run away. What about my parents? What about Raul and Carolina?'

Raul and Carolina.

My heart almost stopped beating and a sliver of guilt needled at me. I hadn't thought about Raul in a while. 'You're right. I was just thinking out loud. Caught up in the moment.'

I couldn't leave the old man.

'Is this about my mother? Because you think she hates you?'

'No,' I said. 'Not because of that.'

'What then?'

'Nothing. It was just a thought. Just a stupid thought.'

'We can't just leave everything behind for no reason.'

She was right. I couldn't just leave. I had the old man to think about. I didn't even know how he was, whether the fever had left him. Maybe he had recovered and was at home with the wife he loved so much.

Or maybe he was still sick, dying in the hospital.

'Come on,' I said. 'Let's get this done.'

We left the boat hidden in the undergrowth away from the jetty and kept close together as we made our way through the sombre gloom, following the orange circle of weak light cast by my torch. The path was straight, carved right through the trees, a passage through living darkness where no lights could pierce. Neither the half-winked eye of the moon nor the brightest star could break the arching canopy that spread over us.

Half a kilometre on foot and we emerged into the immense clearing, but there was no sign of the moon or the stars now. In the time it had taken for us to walk from the river, the sky had lowered and grown thick with cloud. Among the trees, the air had been warm and strong with the musky smell of the forest, but out here the breeze whipped about the vast emptiness of the mine, carrying the unwanted smell of rubbish and human waste.

Here we could see the first of the scant illuminations of Mina dos Santos. Naked bulbs sparkling like gold dust in the sun. The orange and yellow flickering lamps were mostly filtered through half-open windows, but some were outside, hung to highlight a path amongst the ramshackle buildings that huddled as shadows in the night.

'That's it?' Daniella said, coming to a stop at the end of the path.

'You expected something else?'

'I don't know what I expected.'

There was barely enough light to make out the buildings littering an area that had been mined sometime in the past. Any life which had been here was stripped away and the red dirt pounded with power hoses until the ground was cratered and wrecked as if it had been carpet-bombed. Mud walls were shored up with logs, so gnarled and rotten they might collapse under a heavy rainfall.

Among the potholes and trenches and wide spaces of hollowed ground, a series of walkways crawled amongst the dilapidated wooden buildings. The paths were made from all kinds of material, whatever was to hand at the time. There was no order to the planks, logs, pieces of packing crates, cardboard and sheets of plastic that provided routes over the cloying dirt.

'How many people live here?' Daniella asked, still trying to take it all in.

'Hundreds. But this is just small. I've heard of places that have thousands of people, all hosing the ground, trying to make a living.'

'Trying to make a fortune.'

'No one makes a fortune in a place like this, unless they're the one taking a cut off the top.'

'Hm?'

'There's always someone taking a cut off the top. Someone who says the land is theirs. Someone who takes a percentage.'

Daniella shook her head at what she saw before her. 'It's ugly.'

'This is nothing. You should see it beyond the houses. During the day, it's like Hell.'

Past the lights and further into the darkness, the ground was a wasteland of mud beds and craters. Within minutes of the sun rising, the noise would be like a thousand souls screaming as the hoses worked all day, cutting the ground with water pumped from the river. There would be men and women everywhere, working the main holes, panning in the *igarapes*, the streams that run off the main river. Like busy ants, all of them searching for that one unobtainable nugget of gold. And there were those who would kill for just the tiniest flakes of panned metal.

'Come on,' I said, shifting the pack on my shoulder. 'Let's get this over and done with.'

We filtered among the primitive shelters on the outskirts of the mining town, as the sky flickered in the distance, followed by the low rumble of thunder.

'Another storm,' Daniella said. 'Coming this way.'

As if in confirmation, the sky lit up over the far side of the mine, like a camera flash, bathing everything in a silvery light. It lasted only a fraction of a second but in that instant the full nightmare of the mine was revealed. From the dilapidated buildings caked with mud and grime, to the heaps of rubbish, teeming with rats and insects. Then the light was gone and the weather let out a long and threatening growl.

'Walk faster,' I told Daniella. 'It's coming.'

Once past the outskirts of this growing town, we came to more substantial buildings, constructed with more care and ability. These were the homes of the miners who had been here longer, and they were built to last. They had roofs and doors and windows. Some of them even had mosquito netting to repel the insects and keep disease at bay. Many of these buildings had been expanded with additional rooms and porches and outbuildings which split the paths and forced them into a warren of alleys and lanes through the mud.

It reminded me of my home in Rio; the never-ending maze of the *favela* built into the hillside. As if the place itself were alive, always seeking to swallow new people and stretch itself out. Fat and bloated, like a diseased creature whose appetite can never be satisfied.

Our footfall was light on the wooden walkways that snaked among the buildings.

'You know where we're going?' Daniella asked. She kept her voice to almost a whisper, but if I'd asked her why, she wouldn't have been able to explain it. There was just something about this place that made her want to feel unnoticed; something unpleasant and threatening.

'It's changed since I was last here.' I stopped to check my bearings, identifying a route to the building we were aiming for. 'It's bigger. More houses. More paths.'

'When were you here?'

'Six months ago. Maybe a bit more.'

'And it's changed that much?'

'Places like this are always changing and ... That's where we're going.' I pointed to a large building built higher up, on a rise. 'Fernanda's. That's where she'll be.'

'Who? Where who will be?'

'No one. It's where we'll get supplies,' I said. 'There's a bar there, too.'

'That's the shop?'

'Shop, hotel, bar, brothel. The woman who ran that place last time I was here was doing everything.' I took Daniella's hand and started walking again.

We navigated the slippery catwalks, heading towards and then away from the building as we followed the pathways. We passed one or two people still sitting outside their shacks despite the approaching storm. People drinking, talking, arguing, playing guitars or listening to music on old tape players. Some watched us, following our progression with suspicious eyes, but most smiled, raised a hand and wished us luck.

'Why do they wish us luck?' Daniella asked.

'Luck that we'll find gold. They think we're miners like them. Your disguise must be working. Maybe they can smell you.'

Daniella nudged me hard in the arm, feeling more relaxed now that we were among people, knowing they were not hostile towards us. I had warned her about this place, made her fear it before she came here, but it was best to keep her on her guard. These were not bad people, they were here to earn a living just like anyone else, but when gold and drink and drugs come together, lead and steel and iron are never far out of mind.

I felt the first spots of rain on my shoulders and took Daniella's hand. 'Come on,' I said, picking up my pace, knowing the storm would be on us soon.

As we went, I looked out towards the place where the miners would be working tomorrow. Hell had not been an unfair description for it. Further away, though, beyond that area of activity, there were countless abandoned and water-filled holes; the perfect place for something to disappear.

From Fernanda's, I estimated it would take a fit man no more than ten minutes to walk out there in the dark. Perhaps twenty if he were carrying a heavy burden.

Just one more life, the shadow whispered.

50

Fernanda's was central to the whole mining community. Set on the top of a rise, along with some of the older buildings, it was where the original *garimpeiros* had settled. The hotel had started out as just a small shack, but Fernanda had been here as long as anyone, and she had expanded her empire in the mud.

Without the sophistication to build on two levels, Fernanda's had sprawled outwards as far as it could, devouring the neighbouring plots when others had moved away, given up, or died. Maybe Fernanda had bought some of them out or even pushed people away. She was a resourceful woman.

The rain was falling hard by the time we reached her place. It was rattling on the tin roofs and pounding the wooden walkways, becoming harder with every step we took. When we made it under the roof that covered the exterior of Fernanda's place, we were both soaked through.

There was music here. Louder than we'd heard elsewhere, and there were many voices to compete with the white noise of the insects and the rain that hammered at the covering over our heads.

A generator thumped somewhere in the background, providing power to this outlandish community, and the damp earth was littered with a nest of cabling running in every direction. Sometimes the snaking wires were lifted from the ground by crude telegraph poles, sometimes they ran across the roofs of the buildings, but they always found their way back to lie in the mud, waiting for an opportunity to split and let loose their deadly current.

Straight in front of us, as we came up the walkway, one end of Fernanda's complex was given over to a store. Not a shop, like we had in Piratinga, because the people of Mina dos Santos couldn't be trusted in a shop. Here, everything was sold through a hatch in a wooden wall, beyond which dim orange lights lit the goods that lined the shelves. There was everything a miner could need, from biscuits to rice and ammunition to alcohol. And if Fernanda didn't have what you wanted, she would get it for you.

At a price.

A dog, crouched between bony paws, lifted its nose and sniffed the air as we approached. Seeing nothing of interest, it rested its chin again and followed us with sad brown eyes.

Inside the store, two women broke from their conversation as we came close, and one of them shuffled over to lean on the counter, looking bored. 'What you need?'

I wiped my face and scanned the shelves, wondering what Santiago might want for his stay on the sandbank if we couldn't get him free in the morning. Something cheap that would last him. Something I could use if it turned out he didn't need it any more. Rice. Beans. Some beer, maybe, a bottle of *pinga* to keep them going. I glanced down and spotted the shotgun by the counter before looking the woman in the eye and telling her what we needed.

She scribbled it all down on a pink pad and then jabbed the prices into a calculator.

'You want to have a drink while she puts it together?' I said to Daniella as I placed the notes on the rough counter. 'See some more of this place?'

Daniella pushed back her wet hair and glanced around looking doubtful, but she nodded her head. 'OK.'

I couldn't tell if she was being brave or inquisitive, but it was a good opportunity for me to do what I had really come here for. I didn't want to leave Daniella, but I couldn't see any other way, and if she was alone inside Fernanda's for a while, she'd be fine.

'What time d'you close?' I asked the woman behind the counter.

'We never close,' she said.

'I'll come back for it, OK?'

The woman shrugged and scooped the notes from the counter. 'You paid for it. It's your stuff.'

'You'll remember me?'

'I'll remember you.'

I nodded and put a hand on Daniella's arm, guiding her to walk beside me.

We moved away from the store, keeping under cover along the boarded path, passing a group of women standing outside part of Fernanda's complex.

The women here were working, two of them standing together, leaning against the wall, talking and laughing loudly. One of them, an Indian girl, no more than fifteen or sixteen years old, stood straight and stepped towards me when she saw me coming. Her flat stomach and discernible ribcage were naked, while her developing chest was barely covered by the faded yellow bikini top. Tight blue shorts hugged her hips so closely that almost every contour of her was visible. She had tattoos around her calves, crude flip-flops on her feet and she flicked her hair from her face as she approached, backing away when she spotted Daniella beside me. She smiled anyway, just in case she caught my eye and I decided to use her services later.

As we passed, a man came out from the doorway beside which the women stood. He had his arm around a girl, but the moment they were outside, she disentangled herself from him and went straight to the other women. She adjusted the crotch of her shorts before lighting a cigarette and joining the conversation. The man who had been with her stumbled in front of us and headed for another drink.

We followed him, coming to a large boarded area, open at the sides but roofed with a combination of foliage and sheet plastic that amplified the sound of the rain. The heavy drops battered it with a hollow discord, attacking it from all angles. It pounded the ground outside, splashing mud in all directions, and thrashed the paths with such force that it broke into a mist and sprayed the boarded area, but no one took any notice of it.

The original building was set back from where we were standing now, and to get to it we had to pass through the throng of people. It seemed as though almost the whole town congregated here at night, there was a lot of noise and people, and I guessed that Fernanda didn't have to do too much of the conventional gold digging to earn a fortune in this place.

To one side of the large, open area, a band of four men provided something close to music. An accordion, some drums and a couple of guitars hammered out a samba rhythm that was as disjointed as Mina dos Santos. Around them, miners were dancing, shuffling their feet and twisting with the women.

Beside the band, almost central to the boarded area, stood a pool table with pieces of cardboard wedged beneath its feet to keep it level. There were players around the table, a few balls still unpocketed. At the back, along the edge of the main building, two women stood behind a bar built from brick, the whitewash now stained a dirty brown. They were serving drinks – mostly beer and *pinga* – to the men who crowded round them.

'We'll head inside,' I said to Daniella, raising my voice and leaning to speak closer to her ear. When she looked at me, I pointed to the main building, at the far end of the covered area. 'There's another bar inside. It should be quieter.'

Daniella nodded and showed me a thumbs up.

Away from the music and the weather and with the door closed, it was calmer in here. There were tables, all of them occupied, and there was a crowd at the bar, but the people were quieter, and while there was still the rain on the roof, it was softer. The windows still allowed the breeze to enter and the lightning to illuminate the room in flashes, but there was a different atmosphere.

'That's Fernanda,' I said to Daniella. 'The woman behind the bar.'

We picked our way through the busy tables and found a space among the drinkers.

'Two beers.' I held up two fingers as Fernanda came over.

She nodded once, stopped and looked me up and down. A big woman – strong, not fat – Fernanda looked like she was used to hard work. Her broad shoulders were those of someone who was used to carrying heavy weights, and her arms and neck were thick with muscle. She was wearing tight jeans around her ample thighs, an old pink T-shirt to cover her large breasts and a floppy sun hat that was printed with a jungle camouflage design. She reached up and pushed back the hat, narrowing her small eyes and putting her fingers to her chin.

'I've seen you before,' she said.

'Yeah, I—'

'No wait,' she cut me off. 'I never forget anyone. It'll come to me.' She took two bottles of Brahma from a fridge behind the counter and flipped off the tops with two quick flicks of her wrist. 'It must have been a while ago,' she said, putting the bottles in front of us. 'There's a lot of new faces here right now. It's getting harder to remember them all.'

'A lot of new faces?'

'Mm.'

I waited for her to go on, wondering if the new faces were anything to do with Leonardo and the crates of guns he was bringing to the mine. Hadn't he said something about landowners and the expansion of the mine?

Fernanda remained as she was, though, mouth held tight, eyes narrowed as if she were deciding what she thought of me.

I handed a bottle to Daniella and took a long drink.

'You weren't together,' Fernanda finally said, pointing at Daniella. 'I'd definitely remember a beautiful girl like you.' She glanced at me for second, saying, 'You were with an older guy but I haven't see *you* before.' She leaned over the counter and looked at Daniella's clothes. 'Those aren't yours, are they?'

Daniella smiled, pleased that someone thought she deserved better.

'Good idea, though. Pretty girl like you, dressed nice, there'd be men round you in a flash. Like flies round a dog's arse.' She studied Daniella's face. 'You're a pretty girl. People would pay good money for you. You want a job?'

I opened my mouth to say something, but Fernanda saw the

look in my eyes and held up a hand. 'Sorry. Habit. I didn't mean
to insult her. She's beautiful, maybe too good for you ... um ...' She
snapped her fingers and stood up straight. 'You bought supplies
from me six, eight months ago. There was a brawl that night and
you helped to calm things down. The old man who was with you ...
I liked him. How is he?'

'Bad,' I said. 'Fever.'

'We get plenty of that round here. Every day someone gets fever.
Mostly gold fever, but there's other types too. The kind you get
when you end up living like pigs.' She leaned forward and put
her forearms on the bar, muscles bulging like a boxer's. 'People
get cholera when you live dirty, so I'm going to start piping clean
water.'

Daniella watched for my reaction when Fernanda mentioned
cholera. She would be thinking about how my mother died, so I
shook my head, letting her know I was all right.

'That's my next project.' Fernanda saw the exchange but chose
to ignore it. 'Clean water. I do what I can to make life better.'

I nodded, thinking maybe she did whatever she could to make
her own life better, not other people's. She'd lighten their pockets,
help them spend whatever gold flakes they panned that day, keep
them right where they were. That's what happened in places like
Mina dos Santos – people found gold, sold it and spent the money.
People never left because they made a fortune. They left because
they were sick or tired or dead.

'So what brings you to Mina dos Santos tonight?' she asked.

'We brought passengers. Two women. They staying in your
hotel?' I tried to sound conversational.

At the far end of the building there were rooms, but 'hotel'
was too grand a word for it. It was more like a shed that was
partitioned with flimsy boards. It was stuffy, dirty, full of bugs,
and the noise from the bar stopped anyone from sleeping. Turn
off the lights in one of those rooms and the place was alive with
roaches. No one ever slept with the lights off in Fernanda's.

'They might be,' she said.

'You're looking for Dolores?' Daniella asked me. 'Why are you looking for *her*?'

'I'm not. Just making conversation.' I looked up at the clock behind the bar. Half past nine. It would be a while before it was quiet enough to sleep, but she might be in bed, watching the bugs climb the wall.

'You know who they are?' Fernanda asked, glancing behind me. 'Your passengers? You know why they're here?'

'No.' I shook my head. 'Do you?'

'Well, I'm pretty sure they're not fortune hunters.' She continued to gaze over my shoulder.

'They're here, aren't they?' I said. 'Behind us.'

Fernanda nodded once, so I turned and put my elbow on the bar, leaning to one side to look through the crowd. In the far corner of the room, in the quietest and darkest place, Sister Beckett and Kássia were sitting at a table.

They were both looking at me and Daniella.

'OK.' I turned to Daniella and lowered my voice. 'Stay here a moment, there's something I need to do.'

'What? What do you need to do?' she asked. 'What's going on, Zico?'

'Please.' I put down my drink. 'Just stay here.'

I turned to look at Sister Dolores Beckett, and steeled myself for what was coming next.

51

It was as if Sister Beckett had somehow poured something of herself into me, and the closer I came to her, the stronger it worked in me.

The pistol was heavy on my belt. The knife pressed against the small of my back. The shadow darkened and tightened around me. *Just one more life*, it whispered, but I had already chosen.

Coming towards the table, Kássia made a move to stand, but Sister Beckett lightly touched her elbow and stopped her. The younger woman looked at the nun, but Sister Beckett was watching me. When I reached the table, she allowed a smile to touch her lips, then she opened her hand towards an empty seat.

'Join us,' she said.

Kássia's expression tightened and I could see the violent intent in her eyes. Despite our shared experience in the settlement, and our remaining time on the *Deus*, she now saw me as a threat. Something must have happened since I last saw them. Or perhaps she and Sister Beckett had talked about the photograph in my pocket.

When I pulled out the chair, scraping it on the wooden floor, Kássia half pushed to her feet. I didn't know if she was going to reach for her knife or if she intended to spring over the table and beat me, but either way, she was ready to do something.

I held out my hands to indicate I meant no harm and waited for her to relax. After a moment's consideration she nodded once and I sat down opposite the two women, putting my pack on the floor beside me.

Kássia dropped one hand beneath the table, perhaps clutching the knife she had used to kill the man at the settlement.

'You've made a decision,' said Sister Beckett, as if she could see my thoughts.

'Yes. I have.' I put my fingers into my top pocket and Kássia bristled.

Sister Beckett put a hand out to calm her, so I removed the folded newspaper clipping and opened it out. I put it flat on the table, turned it around and pushed it towards the nun. She looked at herself in the picture.

'Are you going to kill me now?' she asked.

I glanced at Kássia who was coiled like a snake ready to strike. 'No.'

'I didn't think so. But it was your intention?'

'Yes.'

Sister Beckett removed her spectacles and placed them on the picture in front of her. She pinched the bridge of her nose and looked across at me, her lazy eye not quite matching the other. 'Are you sure it was your intention?'

I said nothing. I was considering the truth that before I had even set foot on the *Deus*, I had known I wouldn't kill Sister Dolores Beckett. Something in that thought made the shadow's grip slip a little. I had never intended to kill her. I had come on this journey for the old man, not for Costa.

'You could have left me at the smallholding,' Sister Beckett said. 'Those men would have killed me.'

'I almost *did* leave you.'

'What stopped you? Why did you help me?'

'Because Daniella wanted me to. Because Leonardo thought I should leave you. Or maybe because someone like you once helped me and when I had the chance to help him, I ran away.'

'So it was because you knew it was the right thing to do,' Sister Beckett said. 'I don't think you ever believed you would leave us behind. You were never going to kill me, Zico, I could see it in your eyes when we first met. The way you looked at me, I knew something was troubling you. And when Leonardo told me about the photograph ...' She leaned closer, as if about to share a secret. 'I knew then what was bothering you. It wouldn't be the first time someone wanted to kill me, you know.' She stared. 'Did they offer you money?'

'A lot of money. Enough for ...'

'For what, Zico? Enough money for what?'

'It doesn't matter,' I said. 'Not now.'

Sister Beckett nodded. 'And will you be in trouble? For not doing as you were instructed?'

'Yes.'

'They threatened you?'

'They threatened Daniella, and a very good friend of mine.'

Sister Beckett nodded as if she had known it all along.

'And now I don't know what I'm going to do. I'll have to think of a way to deal with them.'

'You could leave. Take the boat and leave.'

'It's not my boat. It's my friend's boat and he's back in Piratinga with his wife.' Maybe even dying from the fever that burned through him.

Sister Beckett watched me. 'He's the other one they threatened?'

'Yes.'

'But if you do what they've asked, you would probably be in trouble anyway, am I right, Zico?'

It was the truth I'd had to face earlier, on the boat. Daniella and the old man would never be safe from Costa. As long as he lived and I lived, he would always use them as a threat. He was a devil and he would do anything he could to keep the dark shadow around me. He had found a way to control me, and he would never let it go.

'Now you see it, Zico. Now you understand. The people you work for, they intend not to pay you. You think they'll let you carry a secret like this? Entrust it to a man like you? Whatever you planned to do here tonight, or on the boat, on the river, the people you work for couldn't risk you telling another soul.'

I stared as her words arranged themselves into thoughts. I was quicker with my hands than I was with my mind, but now I began to see the truth that had eluded me. This was the voice that had prickled at me when Daniella and I were coming ashore. This was the thing I had overlooked. The unformed thoughts.

Costa would not keep me and use me. He would discard me.

Sister Beckett must have seen the horrible realisation in my eyes. 'I'm sorry, Zico, but what's to stop them from hiring another man like you? A man with *your* photograph in his pocket. And what's to stop them from shooting you dead the minute you step off that boat in Piratinga? Maybe hiring someone to kill *that* man, bury you and me under a line of bodies that no one would ever trace back to them. I've been around long enough to know how these things work.'

I leaned back, heart sinking and mind reeling under the weight of her words.

Why hadn't I seen it?

Costa did not intend to control me; he intended to kill me.

The nun had opened my eyes to the reality of my situation. She had revealed the true intent of the devil who had used me.

It was maddening that Costa had tricked me into believing he would pay for Sister Beckett's life, but that wasn't what troubled me most. The worst mistake I had made – a terrible, *terrible* mistake – was that I had allowed Daniella to come on board the *Deus*. By doing so, I had not been keeping her safe from Costa, I had been sealing her death.

If she had remained in Piratinga, she would have been safe; she would have known nothing about Sister Beckett and there would have been no reason to harm her. By bringing her with me, I had given Costa a reason to kill her and, unless I could think of a way around this, she was as dead as I was, the moment we stepped foot in Piratinga.

I had endangered the old man, too. Costa would know I had travelled with him.

The devil would be waiting for my return and then he would tie up all the loose ends.

Me, Daniella, the old man. Maybe Carolina too.

Perhaps he'd even started already.

329

52

I clenched my hands into fists and remembered the old man as I had last seen him. Burning with fever, shivering and racked with pain. I had put him on a boat with a man he hardly knew and sent him to his death in Piratinga. Perhaps there was no reason for me to return there now, and I should take Daniella onto the *Deus* and do as I had suggested.

Just keep going.

On and on, putting Piratinga behind us.

But perhaps the old man still lived, and Costa was waiting for me to return. There was Carolina to think of, too. And no matter how much I disliked Daniella's mother, I wouldn't wish Luis and Wilson upon her.

I had never felt fear like this, and I didn't know what to do. I couldn't see a way out. The only thing I knew for certain was that I needed to get back to Piratinga and go to Raul. Leonardo's money didn't matter any more.

As soon as it was light enough, I would leave.

'...could do, Zico.'

'Hm?'

Sister Beckett cleared her throat. 'I said there *is* one thing you could do. Give me their names. Tell me who they are and I will have them arrested. I have some influence.'

I shook my head.

'Already we've had prosecutions,' she said. 'But if we could get to the people at the top; if someone like you were to—'

'No.' I stared at her without really seeing her. I was picturing the old man and thinking about how I had put his life in danger. 'There's nothing you can do.'

Sister Beckett leaned forward and put her hand on mine. 'Let me try.'

'There's something you should know before I leave,' I said, pulling away from her. 'I don't know why you're here, but I know your reputation, so—'

'I'm here to talk to the miners,' she said. 'Or the people who've taken over.'

'You're meeting them here? The owners?' It couldn't be the Branquinos, they did their business from offices far away and unconnected. They would never come to a place like this.

'Not the owners.' Sister Beckett shook her head. 'We don't know who they are, but we're hoping to find out. That's why I need to know who hired you. The miners found a lot of gold a few weeks ago and now they're planning to expand the mine. It's going to be huge, Zico, and the Indians are angry about the push on their land, worried it will end up like Serra Pelada. There is talk of violence. I will be going to them next – to persuade them it isn't the answer. What we saw in the settlement might be a part of this – militias pushing people out of their smallholdings. The Indians are talking about retaliation, Zico. I'm here to stop a land war, so—'

'You might be too late. The man on my boat, Leonardo, he's bringing guns. That's why he's here in Mina dos Santos.'

'How many guns?' asked Kássia. It was the first time she had spoken since I sat down. She had done nothing but watch me, seeing every twitch of my hands, every turn of my head. Every breath I took.

'Enough for a small army. And they're not just any kind of gun. They're soldiers' guns. With a lot of ammunition.'

'That's why I need to know who hired you,' Sister Beckett said. 'It could be the people who now control the mine. They have a good reason to want me dead – if I get my way, this mine will not just stop growing, it will shut down. Tell me who it is, Zico, I might be able to do something more. There has to be a connection. Who was it?'

I hesitated.

'If you tell me, I might be able to help you.'

'If I tell you, it could make things a whole lot worse for me. All I want is to get married and have a quiet life but now ...' I shook my head and hoped Raul was safe.

'Married?' she asked. 'To Daniella? I wish you lots of luck.'

'And you, too,' I said, pushing back my chair. 'But it's time for me to go.'

'Where are they now?' She stopped me. 'These guns?'

'On the boat.'

'*Deus e o Diabo*,' she said. 'Which will it be for us, I wonder? God or the Devil? Will you do something for me, Zico? Will you make sure those guns never come ashore?'

'You don't want them for your own cause? For the Indians? It could make their life easier.'

'Guns don't make anyone's life easier, Zico, they only make things worse. If you want to do something good, you'll get rid of them. Throw them overboard. Burn them. Anything to make sure they never touch human hands.'

I nodded. 'I'll do what I can.'

Sister Beckett smiled at me, but there was no happiness behind the smile. She looked tired, and I wondered what it was that made someone like her do the things she did. She had such faith in what she was doing. She really believed it was the right thing and she did it regardless of any personal threat. She lived to help others and I wondered if that was a kind of insanity.

'Who was it?' she asked again. 'Who sent you?'

'I ...'

'Please. You could save a lot of lives.'

I took a deep breath and stared at the tabletop, thinking about all the trouble it could cause me if anyone found out I had told her. But, then, if Costa was planning to kill me anyway, maybe it didn't matter. If I told Sister Beckett who had hired me, then at least someone would know what had happened to Daniella and the old man and me if we disappeared.

'Branquinos,' I said, looking up at her.

The way she nodded, I knew she had heard the name and that it confirmed something for her.

To me, though, it was like a riddle. If the Branquinos had taken ownership of this mine, it explained how Costa knew that Sister Beckett would be here. But it also meant they had hired me to come here to kill Sister Beckett while paying Leonardo to deliver guns. Both jobs could have been done by one man, but they must have wanted to disconnect everything; make everything harder to trace. There was no way they could have known that we would all end up together, but what if they had hired me to deliver the guns and Leonardo to kill Sister Beckett? If they had done that, the guns would probably have been delivered.

And Sister Beckett would probably be dead.

Maybe God really was watching over her.

'They used a man called Costa to hire me,' I said. 'That's the only name I know. He works in Piratinga.'

'Costa.' She repeated the name as if to help remember it.

'I have to go.' I put my hand on the newspaper cutting. 'Can I keep this?'

'Of course.' Sister Beckett watched as I folded it back along the creases and slipped it into my pocket, then she reached out and took my hand in both of her own. 'Bless you, Zico,' she said. 'You're a good man. I can understand now why you were so angry with Leonardo.'

I was confused for a second, not sure what she meant.

'Bringing guns—'

'No,' I said. 'It wasn't anything to do with the guns.'

'It wasn't?' She waited for an explanation, her hands still encasing mine.

'He killed two men,' I told her. 'Not long before we saw you.'

'Oh.' But she wasn't looking at me any more. There was some kind of commotion behind me, and she was looking over my

333

shoulder. Something flickered in her eyes. Something that looked a lot like fear.

Beside her, Kássia began to push out of her seat. She moved in front of Sister Beckett, raising her left hand.

I started to turn but flinched at the two loud bangs that came in quick succession.

Kássia fell back, dropping the small pistol she had hidden beneath the table. Her body lurched twice as bullets tore through her and took away her life.

I ripped my hands away from Sister Beckett's and moved to one side, ducking and reaching for my pistol as I turned, but Leonardo smashed the butt of his pistol into my face with enough force to twist my head to one side and send a white flash of pain firing through my skull.

I dropped my weapon and stumbled to my knees, both hands going to my head. Leonardo kicked me to the floor before coming closer and putting a foot on my pistol.

'Where are my guns?' It was clear he had found something to fuel his drug habit. His eyes were wild, his whole face contorted in anger. But there was something else there, too; the same glint of pleasure I had seen the day he killed the men on the boat.

He leaned forward, placing the barrel of his pistol against my forehead, tapping it hard with each word he spoke. 'Where. Are. My. Guns?'

'Don't tell him, Zico,' Sister Beckett said from behind me.

'Shut up.' Leonardo didn't even look at her. 'Where are they? I saw you at the store, you know. Thought I'd go down to the river and take my cargo while you were busy – except the boat's gone. How do you make a whole fucking boat disappear? Only reason you're not dead yet is because I need to know where you put it. Where are my guns?'

'Don't tell him,' Sister Beckett said again. 'Think of all the people who—'

'Shut up.' Leonardo raised his pistol over my head and fired two shots.

I flinched with each deafening report, the noise so close to me that I felt it reverberate in my head. When Leonardo looked back down at me, he began to lower the pistol to point it at me once more.

And that's when Daniella killed him.

53

The first shot hit Leonardo in the back of the neck and punched out through his throat.

His muscles contracted and he squeezed the trigger of his pistol, the bullet slamming into the floor just a few centimetres from my head. Wood splintered close to my ear, and the sound of the explosion numbed me. For a moment, it drove all thought from my mind. There was nothing but the noise of that gunshot and the sharp sting of the wood against my cheek.

Standing over me, Daniella continued to fire. Again and again. She worked the trigger, emptying the small pistol into Leonardo as he fell forward, stumbling to the table.

The gun popped and Leonardo jerked as the bullets entered his back, smashing his ribs, tumbling through his flesh.

Even when the pistol was empty, Daniella continued to dry fire, clicking the hammer down against the spent cartridges.

Regaining my senses, I stood and went to her, putting my hand on the pistol, making her lower her arm. 'Good,' I said. 'Good.'

Leonardo's body was hitching with the last of his laboured breaths. He uttered a quiet moan and there was a sigh as he released the stale air that had been held deep in his lungs. His blood emptied onto the table, running to the edges and dripping to the dirty floor until he became nothing.

Daniella stared at him as I scanned the room, checking for possible accomplices, but everyone was stunned into silence, stationary in their seats. No one dared move for fear they might be next.

Outside, the music had stopped, and one or two people had

come to the door to see what was going on. There were faces at the windows.

I pulled Daniella down into a crouching position, wanting to keep her low, make her a small target from anyone else who might come. Before he died, Leonardo said that he had gone to find the *Deus*, to retrieve his guns, and I was sure he wouldn't have done that alone. He would have needed help to lift those crates from the deck. What I didn't know was who that help would be. A couple of men hired just for that job would not step forward to join this fight, but the men who were here to take delivery might do anything to protect their cargo.

'We have to go,' I said, taking the small pistol from her hand and tucking it into my pocket. I retrieved my other weapon from the floor, then took Leonardo's pistol and put it into Daniella's hands. 'Take it,' I told her. 'This isn't over yet. There might be others.'

'Others?' The shock was clear in her eyes and in her voice.

'You're going to be OK, Daniella. We're going to be fine.'

She managed to nod.

'We have to get out of here, though. Do you understand? It's not safe for us here.'

The crowd was slowly coming to life around us. The first voices had begun to murmur, and people were getting out of their seats for a better look. The door creaked open and more began to come inside, edging closer as their curiosity took hold of them.

I watched them, trying to see each one, looking for any sign of threat, but it became more difficult as the number of faces grew.

'Come on,' I said, helping Daniella to her feet and then grabbing my pack. 'Let's go.'

'What about them?' she said, turning to look at the two women.

I risked glancing behind us, taking my eyes off the encroaching crowd to see Kássia with her head back, her mouth open and her eyes wide. I had seen enough of the dead to know that she had joined them.

Sister Beckett was still alive, but she was bleeding, and her breath came in palsied gasps. Her eyes rolled as she tried to focus on us.

Leonardo's bullet had punctured her beneath the collarbone, and already much of her chest was soaked and her life was ebbing away.

'We can't help them,' I said. 'We have to help ourselves. We have to go.'

Even as I spoke the words, Sister Dolores Beckett stopped moving. The rasping breaths ceased. Her eyes became still and her body relaxed.

She was with her God now.

'Stay where you are.' A voice behind me. 'Put your guns down.'

I turned to see Fernanda pointing a shotgun at us, the stock tucked into her shoulder, her eye looking along the barrel.

Two men flanked her, each of them armed.

'I didn't do this.' I wiped the blood from my face. 'You saw what happened. You have to let us go.'

Fernanda held her shotgun steady. 'Put your guns down.'

The bar was full now. Everyone who had been at tables was standing, and many of the revellers from outside had crowded in to see the drama being played out.

I kept my head lowered so my face would be less memorable.

'This is the man who killed them.' I pointed to Leonardo's body. 'You saw that. Please. Let us go.'

'I can't just let you leave,' Fernanda said.

From somewhere outside, mingled with the sound of the rain hammering the land, came the pounding of feet on the boards. Men running. Two or three, it was hard to tell, but I knew who they were. They had heard the shots and come for Leonardo. They had come for their cargo of weapons.

'They're coming to kill us,' I said, though I knew they would wait until they had their guns before murdering me and violating Daniella. 'Probably kill anyone who gets in their way. And they scare me more than you do.' I kept hold of Daniella's hand and stepped towards Fernanda. 'If you're not going to shoot us, then let us past.'

Fernanda hesitated before lowering the shotgun. She nodded to her men, and then stepped aside.

In the night beyond the bar, the footsteps grew louder and there was a heavy bang as someone slammed against the door, pushing it in. The crowd shifted and men shouted complaints as Leonardo's contacts forced their way into the large room.

'There's a way out behind the bar,' Fernanda said. 'Good luck.'

54

Daniella and I pushed through the crowd, keeping low. My back tingled in anticipation of the first shot as we ducked behind the bar and burst into the room beyond. The space was cluttered with bottles and boxes that we stepped over to reach the door in the far wall and hurry out into the night.

As Leonardo's contacts pushed through the bar, we slipped around the back, past the rear of the store and down onto the wooden walkways.

The boards were slick and the warm rain was pounding them with a thunderous beat. The worst of the storm had passed, but the last of it was still here as it chased itself out over the forest. In the distance, the sky grumbled and lightning flickered in the clouds.

'Don't stop.' I slipped both arms through the straps on my pack to secure it, and we jogged through the mine, trying to lose ourselves in the warren of shanty houses. Our progress was slow, but the mud-caked, rain-soaked boards were insecure and slippery underfoot. 'Keep going!'

We made our way down the hillside, leaving the lights behind us, heading for the darkness below. Once there, we would be hidden and could make our way to the small boat we'd left on the bank. I was confident we would be able to cross the river and find the *Deus* in the dark, but we had to make it to the boat first.

One or two people were still outside their homes, under the awnings, and they watched us race past, following our progress with a turn of the head, but none spoke to us. They could sense the danger that surrounded us. Daniella and I were marked, that much was clear to them.

We were two hundred metres from Fernanda's when we heard the men shouting. It hadn't taken them long to guess what had happened and they had come out to pursue us. They would know that our intention was to escape the mine and they would follow us down to the river.

We didn't have long.

'Faster!'

Risking a glance back, I saw the figures, silhouetted against the lights. It was a long way, and the rain blurred my vision, but it looked like three men were following.

'They're going to catch us.' Daniella's voice was filled with panic. Her breath was coming in heavy gasps, her heart thumping hard from both the exercise and the fear.

'They won't,' I said as we reached the edge of the forest and hurried into the path that led towards the jetty.

My own breathing was laboured, too, my chest bursting from the strain of running all this way in the rain, but we were still half a kilometre or so from the jetty. There was a long way to go and almost anything could happen between here and there. I had to make sure that whatever it was, it was in my favour.

The boarded walkway had come to an end now, and the ground was muddy but easier to run on. I didn't know anything about the men following us – whether they were fit or fast or whether they could shoot straight – but I did know that they were coming straight down the walkway at us. I also knew that the light from Fernanda's and the rest of the mine was at their backs.

'Get into the trees,' I told Daniella as I came to a stop. 'Right here. And keep low.'

Together we stepped off the track and into the line of the undergrowth. I pushed Daniella ahead of me and told her to go deeper, to stay inside the forest.

'What about you?' Her tense words came between breaths.

'I'm going to be close,' I said as I crouched in the darkness and then lay down in the mud with my arms outstretched, revolver ready.

I looked along the path through the trees to the place where it

341

opened out into the mine. With the lights from Fernanda's and the glittering lamps from the shacks and shanty houses, there was a fuzzy oblong of hazy yellow.

I sighted along the barrel as the three silhouettes entered the cutting a hundred metres away and stopped.

Three dark smudges.

I aimed at the one in the centre and fired.

The muzzle flash lit the ground just in front of me, killing my night sight for a fraction of a second, but not so long that I didn't see the man in the centre collapse as my bullet struck him.

Before I could fire a second shot, the two remaining men realised their mistake and parted, slipping into the darkness on either side of the path.

'Stay here,' I said. 'Don't move. Don't make a sound.'

'Where are—?'

'*Not a sound.*'

They would have seen the flash of my shot and they would expect me to move, perhaps even run, but they wouldn't expect me to move *closer*. I crawled through the mud, keeping as low and silent as possible, inching back in the direction we had come from.

Ten metres from Daniella, I stopped and shuffled closer to the trees.

Keeping the revolver in front of me, I calmed my breathing and waited.

The rain continued to fall, pattering on the leaves. The insects continued to hum.

I watched the darkness, wondering if these were the kind of men who would lie down in the mud like I had, or if they were the kind who wanted to keep their shirts clean. I stared into the blackness until it seemed to shimmer, and it occurred to me that I had left Rio under similar circumstances.

Movement.

It was almost imperceptible, but something had moved in the darkness at the edge of the trees. Upright.

So this was the kind of man who wanted to keep his shirt clean.

I raised the revolver to point a little higher and aimed at the shadow within the shadow.

When it moved once more, the faint squelch of mud reaching my ears, I squeezed the trigger.

The shot cracked into the rain and the muzzle flash illuminated the man standing no more than a few metres from my position. Even though I had only seen him for a fraction of a second, I knew my bullet had struck him in the chest. I knew he would have stumbled backwards and fallen to his knees.

I heard the slap of his body collapsing into the mud, and then the opposite side of the path erupted in a storm of gunshots and flashes.

I scrambled forwards, snaking through the thick mud, hearing the bullets thumping into the ground and trees behind me. When I reached the body of the fallen man, I turned to aim my revolver in the direction of the shooting.

One more shot gave away the third man's position. For less than a heartbeat, he lit up in the darkness and I fired on him.

'Daniella! Daniella!' I hissed her name as I crept back along the path towards the place where she had entered the forest. It was difficult to know exactly where it had been. I thought I knew how far I had crawled, but it was so dark and, though the canopy protected us from the worst of the rain, the water still came down in heavy drops, breaking through the leaves.

When Daniella didn't reply, I began to worry that a stray bullet had struck her, and I called her name louder, moving more quickly, feeling the panic rising. If she was in there, dying from a bullet wound, I would never find her. She could be just a few metres inside the trees and be lost for ever.

I alternated between peering into the dense obscurity of the tangled forest and looking back at the entrance to the path, towards the haze of lights from the mine, checking for more attackers. I moved further along the trail, calling Daniella's name, hoping she was all right.

'Daniella? Where are you?'

Thunder grumbled again in the distance and the sky flickered. The rain hardened for a moment, a sudden flurry, then faded to a gentle patter on the leaves.

'Daniella!'

'Here.'

'Thank God.' I hurried towards her voice and groped for her in the dark, our hands touching.

'I'm so scared.' She wrapped her arms around me, squeezing hard.

'We need to get away from here,' I told her as I broke away. 'We're not safe yet.'

55

We ran as if the Devil were on our heels. Despite the mud and the darkness and the tightness in our chests, we ran and ran.

We burst from the trees and onto the jetty, not pausing but dropping down onto the beach and hurrying to the place where we had dragged the boat into the tree line.

I grabbed it with both hands and hauled it into the shallows, holding it steady while Daniella climbed in. The small boat slipped through the water when I shoved it out into the river and jumped in, snatching up the paddle.

With the clouds still thick above us, it was darker now than it had been when we left the *Deus*, but I took us further out into the river, heading for the far bank. If I could keep us in a more or less straight line, we would soon see the shape of her settled in the deeper water.

Daniella was silent. The only sound was our breathing and that of the rain meeting the river and the paddle pushing through it.

Behind us, the lights of Mina dos Santos were nothing more than *boitatá* eyes smouldering in the dark now. There was no sign of anyone following us, but I didn't allow myself to believe we were safe yet.

When we finally reached the *Deus*, we climbed aboard and tied the smaller boat off to the stern. We couldn't waste time securing it as usual, so it drifted and buffeted in the current.

I settled Daniella on the seat in the wheelhouse and left her holding a cigarette with shaking fingers while I reconnected the fuel line, then grabbed the bottle of *cachaça* the old man kept in the store for emergencies.

It was dangerous to take the boat out at night, but it might be more dangerous to stay here. We needed to get some distance between us and the mine, so I started the engine and took us away from Mina dos Santos, moving slowly, squinting into the darkness and hoping the clouds would dissipate before too long. At least with a clear sky there would be a touch of light from the moon.

The engine sounded loud, but it was reassuring to hear it working well, and I spun the wheel, turning the *Deus* east and heading home, leaving the rain behind us.

Once we were on the straight, I removed the cap from the *cachaça* and handed the bottle to Daniella. 'Drink some of this.'

She looked at me as if to refuse, then conceded, taking the spirit and lifting it to her lips. She drank, swallowed and coughed.

'Some more,' I told her, so she drank again, then put the bottle between her knees, keeping one hand on its neck, while the other lifted a cigarette to her lips.

I watched her smoking and staring ahead into the night, her eyes fixed on an invisible point in the darkness. I'd seen a similar look before; in the eyes of young boys in a past I cared not to remember. It was the vacant stare of those who had made their first kill at the request of a gang leader. Boys who had passed their initiation.

'You did the right thing,' I told her.

She didn't move.

'He would have killed me. And then he would have seen you and he would have killed you, too.'

She blinked. Lifted the bottle to her lips.

'You need to think about *that*. That's the only thing you need to think about.'

'I had to,' she said.

'That's right. You had to.'

'I had no choice.'

'You did what I would have done. What *anyone* would have done.'

She turned her head in my direction, her eyes following at a different rate, as if they didn't want to be torn from the invisible point in the night. 'What you would have done,' she said. 'For me.'

'Exactly. All this time I thought I had to protect you, but it was you who protected me. I would be dead if you hadn't...'

Now she saw me. Her eyes glistened, but they were not filled with tears. This was not an emotion that brought tears. This was an emotion that brought horror and fear.

'It's not an easy thing, what you did.'

'No.' Her voice was quiet. 'It was *too* easy.'

I waited.

'You think he has—'

'Don't think about that,' I said, knowing that she was trying to think beyond the man; see family, children he might have left behind. 'There's no good to come from that. You did what you did. What you *had* to do, and you have to accept it. You can't take it back. He made you do it. Blame him. Blame Leonardo.'

'How?' she said, looking me in the eye. 'How do you live like this?'

I wasn't sure she was expecting an answer, so I stayed quiet, watching as she took another drink then turned away and looked into the night again.

Difficult though it was to judge the distance in the dark, I reckoned we were two or three kilometres from Mina dos Santos now, so I cut the engine and let the *Deus* drift. 'You rest here a while,' I said as I stood. 'There's something I need to do. It won't take long.'

'Don't leave me.' She put out her hand and grabbed my shirt.

'I'll be right here. Right behind you.'

'Then I'll come.' She got to her feet, bringing the bottle with her, and followed me to the stern of the boat, where Leonardo's crates were stacked.

Daniella sat and watched as I threw the anchor overboard then opened the first of Leonardo's crates, prising out the nails with a hammer from the old man's tool box.

I peeled away the packing and looked at the dark shapes nestled inside. The storm was behind us now, the sky clear above, and the pale light from the narrow slice of moon glowed on the weapons.

'What are you going to do?' Daniella asked.

'I'm going to put them overboard,' I told her as I took one of the rifles. 'Just like I promised.'

'Promised?' Daniella asked, sitting on the deck beside me. 'Promised who?'

Holding the rifle in my hands, feeling its weight, I remembered how the boys in the *favela* had carried such weapons. How *I* had carried such weapons. I had seen what they could do.

'Dolores,' I said, going to the side of the Deus and dropping the weapon into the water. 'She asked me to do this.'

'Why would she ask you to do that? How did she even know about them? Is that why Leonardo...' She stopped and let her words hang. 'Is that why Leonardo did what he did?'

'You ever heard of Sister Beckett? Dolores Beckett?'

Daniella shook her head. 'No.'

I took two more of the rifles, dropped them overboard and listened to the sound they made as they hit the water and went under. 'She was a pretty brave woman. Brave or stupid, anyway, I don't know which. She fights... *fought* landowners. Fought them with words. Taught Indians their rights, helped *sem terras* to occupy land.'

'*Sister?* She was a nun?'

'Yes.' I dropped another two rifles into the river.

'So why did Leonardo want to kill her?'

I shrugged and looked down at Daniella. 'I don't think he did. He didn't even know who she was.'

'But you did?'

I went to the crate and took another pair of rifles, lifting them out and going to the side of the boat. The rifles splashed into the water and slipped away, then I sat down beside Daniella and took the bottle from her.

I drank and pulled the newspaper clipping from my pocket, unfolding it and passing it to her.

She took the piece of soft paper and studied it, turning it to see

348

it better in the moonlight. She looked more awake now, more alive. The *cachaça* was doing the job I'd hoped, numbing her mind to the shock.

'It's her,' she said, looking up at me. 'Why do you have this?'

'Costa wanted me to ...'

'Kill her? For money?'

I nodded.

'And you were going to?'

'It was a lot of money. Enough for ... Well, it was a lot.' I didn't tell her the rest – that Costa had threatened her life and Raul's, and that even with Sister Beckett gone, probably none of us was safe. And I couldn't tell her that I no longer knew what to do.

'I couldn't do it.' I shook my head and stared at the decking. 'I think I always knew that – it just took me too long to realise. Too long to make a decision.' A gust of wind cut across the surface of the river, raising my skin and sending a shiver through me. 'That's why I wanted to see her. I wanted to warn her. Tell her she was in danger.'

Daniella sighed and took the bottle from me. 'It was the right thing.'

'But too late.' I had persuaded myself that I needed the money, that I could do what needed to be done to get it, but really I had never intended to kill Sister Dolores Beckett. I could no more kill her than I could have killed Father Tomás that day he found me hiding in his backroom with a gun in my hand.

I stood and returned to the task of dumping the rifles in silence, leaving the opened crates on the deck. I moved backwards and forwards dropping the guns into the river with a hollow sound, listening to them sink, their bubbles rising and bursting on the surface.

I kept the last one on board, though, loading it with ammunition from the final crate. I stored a few boxes of spare cartridges, a couple of magazines, and poured the rest into the water like heavy rain.

'You think someone might come?' Daniella asked, looking at the rifle as I slipped a magazine into its underside.

'Maybe.'

I tried not to think about Sister Beckett, but all I could see was the way she lay back in the chair, life draining out of her, and the only thing I could be glad for was that it hadn't been me who had killed her.

Staring into the darkness, I felt an overwhelming surge of emotion that tightened my throat and brought tears to my eyes. I took a deep breath and knew that despite everything, Sister Beckett's blood was still on my hands.

56

Navigating at night was dangerous and required all my concentration, but we pushed on. With Daniella at the wheel and me at the bow, we crawled east along the river, stopping only to rest, but neither of us slept. The events we had just survived were enough to keep us awake, but there was the added fear that there might be other men looking for their guns. Perhaps they were even on the river now, chasing us through the night.

I knew that every time Daniella closed her eyes, she would see Sister Dolores Beckett and Kássia lying dead in the bar. She would see herself shooting Leonardo. I saw those things too, but I also saw Costa's face, grinning at me from the shadow.

We stopped sometime after midnight, in a place where the River of Deaths was at its widest. The storm was long gone, but the river swelled under the weight of its payload. The rainy season had begun in earnest now, and soon the river would burst its banks and flood out into the forest. For now, the water moved faster, rushing against the stern of the *Deus* as it hurried on towards the Araguaia. It swept us onwards as I dropped the anchor to keep us from being washed into the bank.

The *Deus* shifted and tugged the rope taut before twisting with the current. The river washed about us, regardless of what had happened. The River of Deaths had no concern for the events played out on its edges or on its waters, and it poured eastwards as it rose to claim the white beaches and meet the sun-baked banks.

Exhausted from the intense concentration of piloting the boat in almost complete darkness, plagued by the perpetual dread of running aground or taking the wrong course, we tried to rest.

More than once, though, we thought we heard noises coming from behind us, the buzz of another engine on the river somewhere in the night, and I took a position at the gunwale, pointing the rifle in the direction of the sound.

The weak moon gave only enough light to see three or four metres from the *Deus* before the world disappeared into oblivion. There might have been a whole fleet of boats out there, bristling with guns, but we saw nothing. Not even a flicker of light. Each time I waited with my head cocked towards the sounds, my ear straining to hear engines or voices, but each time the night just settled to the natural rhythm of the forest and the river.

We were alone.

Daniella came to sit with me on the deck close to the stern, leaning back against the gunwale. She lit a cigarette, keeping the brief flare of the match out of sight of the bank. In that fleeting flash of orange light, I saw how tired and worn she looked and I felt a rush of sentiment. There was a huge burden of ugly emotions because I had allowed her to come with me, muddled with the dread of Costa's intentions, and I knew that life would have been easier for her if she had never met me. I felt a degree of guilt for loving her and for being loved by her. If not for me, Daniella would still be in the store, reading her magazines and arguing with her mother. Perhaps the right thing was for me to leave her; that way I couldn't affect her life any more than I already had. But there were other things, too; warm sentiments to combat the colder ones. My love for Daniella made me weak in Costa's eyes, and it magnified my guilt and fear, but it was also good and it gave me strength.

I understood now that I didn't need money, I just needed my friends. I needed *Daniella*; and in her own way, she needed me. As long as we could feed ourselves and put a roof over our heads, out here, that was enough.

'How did you feel the first time?' Daniella asked.

'The first time?'

'Yeah. The first time you ...'

As her words faded, I put the tip of my finger in a small puddle of water that reflected the moon on the deck, and traced a dark circle on the boards. A hint of silver light caught in the pattern like a shard of precious metal.

I thought back to the first time I had taken a life. I had lived in the midst of the shadow, but had never been the perpetrator of such unchained bloodletting as I now saw myself committing.

I remembered the chase through the *favela*, running the boy down like an animal. I was consumed by the wrong he had done and my blood raged with an overwhelming need not just to kill him but to destroy him; to wipe him from existence. There was no other thought in my head, and he knew it. He saw the fury in me and he knew fear like he had never known before.

Unarmed, alone and afraid, he had run for his life, but my desire to take it was stronger than his ability to keep it. A single shot to the back of his thigh brought him down by a rubbish heap that smelled of decaying food and human excrement, and he crawled and he crawled, raking through the waste, trying to burrow into it, to escape, to save himself.

The rifle I borrowed from my friend Ratinho held thirty cartridges. Thirty pieces of lead; each one capable of killing a man.

I put all thirty into that boy.

'I didn't feel much of anything,' I said, still tracing the shape on the deck. 'I thought it would make me feel good. I *hoped* it would make me feel good, but it didn't make me feel much at all.' It hadn't satisfied the anger of the shadow in which I had been living.

'You hoped to feel good? I don't understand. Why would you ...'

'He wasn't even a man. Just a boy really. I was seventeen when I shot him.'

'Why? What did he do?'

'He raped and killed my sister.'

'Zico.'

'And if I had never been involved with people like that, boys who sold drugs and murdered one another, maybe it would never have happened. They would never have noticed her.'

'You don't know that. You can't blame yourself for that.'

353

The patch of water was drying now, so I took my finger away and wiped it on my trousers. 'I came home one evening to find my friend sitting on the step. The door was open and when I went in, Sofia was lying on the floor. My friend told me that one of the boys had taken a liking to her but when she turned him down he took her anyway. And then he killed her.'

I had never spoken about it to anyone before, not even the old man, yet it followed me everywhere. I still felt the pain of it now, the horror at what I had found in my home.

Sofia was no saint, but she had been a good person; probably the best I knew. She was good like the old man was good; like Daniella was good. She kept away from the dark stain that blossomed in parts of the *favela*, and she always tried to make me do the same. She worked hard and she did her best for us. When the *pinga* suffocated our father's mind, she took care of him while I resented him and left him to pity himself.

All that was taken away, though, and she ended up lying twisted on the floor in the centre of the small living room, her face beaten so she was barely recognisable. She had been shot, too, but it was impossible to know how many times.

I knelt in her blood and held her and put my face to her hair while the tears came. I would never again hear her laugh, or feel the back of her hand given in chastisement, or beat her at cards, or listen to the stories she had learned about the Gods she had turned to.

Sofia had been my sister, my friend and my mother, but now she was nothing.

I stared at the deck as the memory of that evening played out in my mind – as it had done so many times before.

Eventually, I wiped my eyes and looked up at Daniella.

'I didn't know what to do. The police, they did nothing. For them it's just how life was. I was less than nothing to them. So I took a gun and I found him and I killed him.' He deserved every bullet I had shot into him, and if I could have given him back his life, I would have done it, over and over, so I could keep on killing him. And now I realised that was exactly what I had been doing ever since. I had told myself I did it for the money and because I could do it without remorse, but the truth was that every time I killed a man, I was looking for the vengeance and justice I had hoped to feel that first time. I had been killing that same boy over and over again.

'After that it was like someone had cut a part of me away. Or maybe pressed a switch that let me ... do things for money. It never felt good, though. It never made me feel better. I didn't ever do it to save a life, like you did. Not until today, anyway.'

Daniella said nothing. She put back her head and stared at the sky through a hole in the canopy, letting the cigarette smoulder in her hand.

'I left the *favela* a couple of years later. Sofia and I always talked about leaving, but not like that. I was paid to shoot a boy called Gato. A *dono da boca*. That's what we called the ones who led the dealers. He'd killed and raped and beaten and deserved to die, so when someone offered me money, I took it. I just wasn't smart enough to see it would start a war, and I ended up hiding in a room in a church when his people came after me. Can you imagine that? Me protected by a priest.'

The boat moved in the swell of the river, waves slopping at the hull. Somewhere close by, a *boto* surfaced to take a breath. It blew into the night before filling its lungs and diving into the abyss.

'They killed him for it,' I said. 'When they found out where I was, Gato's boys came and killed the priest. I heard it from where I was hiding so I climbed through a window and never looked back.'

Daniella sighed and took a drag on the cigarette. She didn't tell me if I was right or wrong because there was no right or wrong about it. It just *was*.

'His name was Father Tomás. He had this old church falling apart in the *favela*, built right on the hillside. From the front, you could look out and see the statue of Cristo Redentor, standing up there on Corcovado. When he was hiding me, Father Tomás told me that it sees all and blesses all and loves all. It was the same thing my sister Sofia had said and I told him it was bullshit, but maybe, though, maybe it *did* bless me. Maybe it chased me out

355

of the *favela* and gave me you and the old man. Not at first. Not right away. But now.'

I thought about Sofia and Father Tomás and Sister Beckett; about how everything seemed to slip beyond my control. I had chosen to turn away from Costa's demands, to warn the nun, but none of it really mattered. Now she was lying on the dirty floor in Mina dos Santos anyway, and I felt a great sadness for her and for the priest and for my sister.

'It's my fault Sister Beckett is dead.'

'You didn't kill her,' Daniella said.

'But I brought Leonardo here. I should've let him drown. When she told me to help him, I should have let him drown.'

'How much?' she asked. 'How much money were they going to give you?'

'Does it matter?'

'How much?'

The words didn't want to come out. They tasted dirty. 'Five thousand American dollars. There was land, too. A small place.' But it now occurred to me that Sister Beckett was right: the money and the land were a lie. Costa probably hadn't even contacted the Branquinos after our first meeting. He hadn't gone back to them with my terms. He had simply made something up to sweeten his manipulation. There had never been any money, just an order passed down to assassinate the nun and leave no connection.

'And now she's dead,' Daniella said. 'And the man who was going to pay you doesn't know who did it. Maybe something good can come from it.'

'We can't profit from it.'

'Can't profit from it? Why not? Maybe it's the *only* thing we can do.'

'No.' I thought about telling her that the money wasn't real and that Costa would probably be waiting to kill us anyway, but she'd had enough. 'The only good I can take from this is how it's made me feel. What it's made me understand.'

'What it's made *you* feel?'

'Yeah. About you. About us. About what's really important.'

Costa's money didn't matter to me any more. I already had the things that mattered. Daniella and the old man. They were my family, and if I could live the rest of my life with Daniella, like the old man did with Carolina, I would be happy. I didn't need to be always waiting for the next thing. I already had everything I wanted.

'What about me?' Daniella asked. 'What about how it's made *me* feel?'

Something was rising to the surface. Daniella's shock had subsided and something else was coming. I could sense it building like a storm, her voice rising in pitch and volume.

'This hasn't just happened to you,' she said. 'All this shit these last few days has happened to me too. You think I wasn't worried about Raul? That I wasn't scared having that gun pointed at me the whole time? That I wasn't afraid Leonardo was going to shoot your brains all over the boat? How do you think *I* feel?'

'I didn't mean—' I reached out to touch her but she pushed my hand away.

'I killed a man, Zico, and there's nothing good in that. What about *me*?'

'You saved my life,' I said. 'You did what you had to do.'

'Saved your life? It was your fault I was there in the first place.' She hit me on the shoulder with her balled fist. 'It was *your* fault, Zico.' She hit me again, the *cachaça* bottle tipping, spilling its contents onto the deck and rolling away. 'You took me there.' And she punched me again and again, turning now so she could use both hands to beat me. 'It was your fault.'

She was letting out her anger and her frustration and guilt and sorrow. All that emotion was boiling inside her like a poisonous broth, and she was pouring it on me and that was good. I raised my hands to protect myself but did nothing to stop her. I let her continue to punish me until she had vented her anger, and then she fell against me, wrapping her arms around me.

I responded in the same way, pulling her tight, telling her that I loved her, that everything was going to be all right.

'Show me,' she said. 'Show me you love me.' She looked up

and held my face in her hands as she kissed me. Soft at first, then harder. She took my lip between her teeth for a moment, biting hard enough to make me wince, but she held me to her and opened her mouth as a different kind of passion overcame her. 'Show me,' she said again as she ran her hands down my back, dragging her nails, before pushing the shirt over my head and then standing back to remove her own. She didn't take her eyes off me as she unfastened her trousers and kicked them away, reaching out to loosen my belt.

And when we were both naked she gripped my shoulders and lay back, opening her legs, pulling me on top of her, desperate to feel something other than what she had felt since leaving Mina dos Santos.

'Tell me you love me,' she said between breaths. 'Tell me you love me.'

So I told her.

I told her and I told her.

Afterwards, we lay together in a tangle of limbs, and I stroked Daniella's hair until her breathing deepened.

My thoughts returned to the last conversation I'd had with Sister Beckett. By opening my eyes to a truth my mind had already been trying to understand, perhaps she might be able to save my life as I had been unable to save hers.

I could not trust Costa, but nor could I kill him. He had made it clear that such an event would have consequences. I would have to find another way to deal with him. And as I watched Daniella sleep, the seed of an idea began to take hold in my mind.

57

When dawn touched the sky, I turned the engine over and headed out onto the water. Daniella stirred, hearing the *Deus*'s heartbeat. She rubbed her eyes and looked about, then got to her feet and hugged the sheet around her. She came to the wheelhouse to sit beside me, and for a while, didn't speak.

The *Deus* passed over the calm water as the day opened before us, the sun rising and the world coming to life.

'Did you sleep?' Daniella's first words.

'Not really.'

She nodded, still not looking at me.

'You OK?' I asked.

'Yes.' She edged closer to me, putting her head on my shoulder. 'Yes.'

As we travelled east on the River of Deaths, we kept watch for any sign of being followed, but there was none. We didn't see any other boats.

Coming closer to the spot where the *Estrella* had grounded, I told Daniella she needed to get dressed, so she threw off the sheet and went to the back of the boat. She found her skirt and vest, and pulled them on, kicking Raul's jeans and shirt into the store.

We rounded the bend in the river and spotted the *Estrella* in the distance, still marooned. 'There they are. The sand didn't shift,' I said. 'Good.'

Daniella looked up at the boat in the distance, a streak of white, reflecting the sun. 'Why is it good? If it shifted, they might have got away.'

I slowed the engine. 'I have to leave you now, Daniella. You have to get off the boat. I want you to stay with Santiago and Matt.'

'What? Why?'

I chose my words, wondering how I was going to tell her, but knowing I had to. One way or another, she deserved to know everything and, if anything happened to me, she might *need* to know. 'Remember what I told you about Costa? About the money?'

'I shouldn't have said it.' She jumped in. 'I was angry. I shouldn't have made ... shouldn't have suggested—'

'It's not that.' I put a hand on her cheek, making her look at me. 'This isn't about what you said, this is about what Costa is going to do.'

She creased her brow, not understanding.

I swept the hair from her face, tucked it behind her ear and thought about how much I loved her, how much I admired her now, even more than ever. There was something between us that few lovers ever have – a bond of life and a shared experience of death.

'Sister Beckett said something to me last night,' I said, 'and I can't believe I was so stupid. If I had half your brains ...'

Daniella shook her head.

'I don't think he was ever going to pay me. What he asked me to do ... his people won't want to leave a trace. You, the old man, me, we all lead back to what he asked me to do.'

'But you *didn't* do it,' she said. 'You didn't do it, Zico, everything's going to be OK. You said so.'

'No, I didn't do it, but it was still done. And whether it was done or not, I don't think it would matter. There might be people waiting for me, Daniella. Waiting for *us*. Costa will want to bury his secret with me. Hide it deep.'

'So why did you listen to him? Why did you let him ask you to—'

'I didn't have a choice,' I said. 'And maybe I was blinded by the money. I thought we could use it for ...'

'I know what you wanted it for. I understand.'

'But we don't need it; I can see that now, Daniella. We'll manage another way.'

'So what are you going to do?' she asked.

I shook my head, looking at the *Estrella*. 'I'm not sure. But I have to go to Raul and Carolina and you can't come back to Piratinga. Not yet. Costa will already know you came with me, it's not safe for you there.'

We were closer to the *Estrella* now, and Santiago had heard our engine. He was coming on to the deck to stand with his back to the sun.

'Let me come with you,' Daniella said. 'I can help. Like I did last night.'

'No. Santiago and Matt will take care of you. And if anyone follows from the mine, you just tell them I passed by without helping. You don't know me.'

'You still think someone might come after us?'

I looked back at the river and shrugged. 'Maybe Leonardo mentioned the name of the boat, I don't know, but those guns were worth something and if they had plans for them...' I took a deep breath. 'I just don't know, Daniella, but I need you to stay here with Matt and Santiago. Will you do that for me? Please?'

Daniella watched me for a long time before nodding.

'I'll send someone to help you get off the sand,' I said. 'To pull the *Estrella* out.'

'Let me come.'

'You'll be safer here.'

'I'll be safer with you.'

I remembered the last time she had said that – when we went ashore at Mina dos Santos. She had been wrong that time, and she might be wrong this time too. I couldn't take that risk.

'Can you forgive me?' I asked.

'For what?'

'For all of this.'

'Of course,' she said.

When we were close enough to the other boat, Daniella climbed down and let me row her out to the *Estrella*.

I told Santiago I had business in town, and that I would send help as soon as possible. He and Matt knew not to ask any questions.

Daniella held me tight and kissed me before I left, and once I was back on the *Deus*, I started the engine and raised a hand to her, then settled behind the wheel and guided the boat east along the river.

As I rounded the bend, Daniella was at the stern of the *Estrella*, watching me disappear from sight.

I tried not to think that I might never see her again.

58

Several hours into the morning and the sun was already scorching the land. Any sign of last night's storm was long gone and the cloudless sky gave no protection. The *Deus* chugged along the River of Deaths with me behind the wheel willing it to go faster. The current was flowing in my favour, so the journey was quicker in this direction, but it still seemed like an eternity before I reached the Araguaia and turned north towards Piratinga.

The creeping sense of dread that had settled in my stomach stirred into life. For these past few hours, alone on the river, I had thought of nothing but Daniella and the old man. I had led them into danger and my regret was dampened only by my fear for them.

I knew I couldn't take the *Deus* into town because Costa would have people watching. He would know about it, the moment I arrived. I also suspected that whoever had hired Leonardo – either the seller or the buyer of the weapons – would be planning their next course of action. I had to assume that they would know the name of this boat; perhaps they would even know my name.

There was nothing I could do if they knew who I was, but there was something I could do to prevent them from finding the boat and tracing it to the old man.

The *Deus e o Diabo* would have to disappear.

Just before noon, the sun arcing towards its highest point, I came to the final bend in the river before Piratinga. The river was more than five hundred metres wide here and at least a hundred metres deep. On both sides, the beach was receding beneath the murky waters as the season swelled the course. Soon the levels would reach the tops of the mudbanks and flood into the trees, washing through the forest floor.

It was the perfect resting place for the boat that had served the old man so well for so many years.

I took the *Deus* into the centre of the Araguaia and cut the engine. The need for urgency that had gripped me earlier had subsided now that I was so close to Piratinga. Desperate though I was to check on the old man, I was also afraid of knowing what had happened to him.

I threw the anchor overboard and sat for a while in the silence of the day, summoning the courage to move. The world seemed to be at peace, but the sense of dread grew heavier in me as I contemplated what I was going to do. I felt cold, despite the heat of the sun. When I held my hands out in front of me, my fingers trembled.

Leaning back, I turned my face to the sky and spoke a quiet prayer to whoever or whatever might be listening. I didn't know if there was a god watching me or if he would even care about me, but I asked him to make everything all right. I would cast away the shadow and live my life in the light if I could have Daniella and Raul's lives in return.

With a deep breath, I pushed myself up from the seat behind the wheel and went to the stern to drop the smaller boat into the water. I left one rope, preventing it from floating away, and it drifted in the current, lazily bumping the hull of the *Deus*.

A flock of red macaws passed by, with a swish of feathers and a shrill screech as they went. I turned to watch them glide over the forest in the distance and waited until they were tiny specks of black and then nothing, as if it were important for me to see them disappear from view.

When the birds were gone, I unfastened the first of the fuel barrels. It was only half full, but shuffling it from the stern to the main deck was difficult on my own, and I sweated hard under the sun. As soon as there was enough room, I tipped the barrel onto its side and rolled it towards the wheelhouse where I unscrewed the cap and let the diesel pour out and wash over the planking.

It darkened the boards, soaking into the dry wood and running over them, draining between the gaps. It caught the sun and glistened in a rainbow of colours as the fumes shimmered in the heat.

The second barrel was heavier and took longer to move but I persevered, manhandling it to the deck and spilling its contents across the *Deus*, letting the fuel soak into the empty rifle cases. When I was done, the deck was awash with fuel and the air was thick with its smell.

With a heavy heart, I climbed over the gunwale and dropped into the smaller boat. I untied the rope that secured it to the *Deus*, then slid opened the box of matches I had taken from the wheelhouse. I lit one and used it to light the others, watched them flare in a burst of sweet-smelling phosphorous. The flame grew, twisting around the box, curling towards my fingers.

'Sorry, old man,' I said, then flicked the matches up into the *Deus*.

The fuel caught immediately, igniting with a hollow whoosh and a sudden rush of heat. I pushed the smaller vessel away into the river as the fire sucked the oxygen from around me, drawing it in to feed itself. Within seconds, the canvas coverings were ablaze and black smoke washed around the *Deus* like a demon. Sparks jumped as the wood took hold and began to burn. The fire danced around the boat, reaching out to every part of it, flickering and playing as it consumed my friend's livelihood.

By the time I was a hundred metres away from her, the *Deus* was alight from bow to stern. The canvas was gone, pieces of it still spiralling into the sky, glowing, smouldering. The scraps disintegrated and broke into tiny, flickering fireflies of cinders that spun in the heat and the smoke. The bow, which had been my lookout perch on so many journeys with the old man, split with a loud crack in the intensity of the inferno. Her boards popped and the planking sprung from its fixings. The tyres burned black and stinking.

Further away still, the third fuel barrel ignited. There was no loud bang or violent destruction of the boat, though. Instead, a rush of flame erupted from the stern, as if the cap had popped from the drum and the diesel had squirted up under immense pressure. The curling ball of yellow and orange rolled skywards, chased by a rising pillar of fire, up and up until it was ten metres tall. It burned bright for a few seconds, but as it rose, the flame darkened at the edges, shifting and thickening once the fuel had burned away, and was engulfed in dense black clouds.

With her anchor line burned through, the *Deus* began to drift downriver, towards Piratinga, but she would sink and die long before she reached the town.

Close to the bank, I paddled towards the place where the trees gave way to the sandy beaches, and I watched, unable to tear my eyes from what I had done. Seeing the boat burn filled me with an awful sense of finality and the aching need for reassurance. I hoped I had done the right thing.

The *Deus* released a pillar of heavy, terrible smoke into the blue sky as she washed further downriver, then she listed and began to take on water.

Within a few minutes she sank and disappeared, as if she had never existed.

Once I was ashore, I shouldered my pack and abandoned the tin boat, trudging across the sand towards the path leading into town. Walking on the sand was hard, and the sun was cruel that day. I was thirsty and tired and dirty. Sweat poured from my brow and soaked my shirt. I carried a heavy burden too, in my thoughts – Sister Beckett, Kássia, the *Deus* – but I tried to push them away. I had to keep my head clear and think about Daniella, Carolina and the old man. I was here to keep them safe. I could not help the dead but perhaps I could do something for the living. That was all I had to do.

All I had to think about.

As I came into town, I headed along the shore, passing the houses and bars, scanning the riverside, looking for anyone watching the river. Costa's people would have seen the smoke in the distance, but they would have had no reason to think it had anything to do with the *Deus*. They would be expecting me to bring the boat into town, so that was what they would be looking for.

I hoped that Sister Beckett was wrong about Costa. I entertained the possibility that he might pay me for the nun's death and leave me to live in peace on the promised piece of land, but I knew there was no chance of that. I wasn't even sure I would want it to be that way. I couldn't live in a place that had been bought with Sister Beckett's blood. Such a place would be cursed.

I slipped unnoticed past Ernesto's bar, feeling the urgency grow to an almost unbearable level. I was close to the old man's place now. I was within reach. Raul was just a short distance away. I wanted to break into a run, to get to the house as quickly as possible, but I had to stay calm. I had to control myself.

My heart quickened and my mind raced. My stomach crawled like the forest insects had swarmed inside me.

I was almost there.

Then I saw them. Two men waiting on the shore.

They were just sitting and looking out at the river. Luis and Wilson. The two men who had begun all this just a few days ago when they came to my apartment. The men who had murdered Antonio and had their lives promised to me by Costa.

I paused and watched them sitting close to Raul's place, waiting in almost the exact spot where the vultures had been the day Costa threatened my friends. I remembered coming back from Ernesto's and laughing when the old man threw rocks at the ugly bird that had perched on the roof.

I kept my eyes on Luis and Wilson as I slipped past behind them, one hand on my pistol, and went straight to Raul's house. Once I was out of sight of the beach, obscured by the building, I knocked on the door.

Somewhere inside, Rocky barked, but my heart thumped and there was a washing, swirling noise in my ears. It wasn't for fear of the men watching the river, it was because I was nervous about what I might discover right now. I needed to know if the old man was all right. I needed to see him standing in front of me, strong and fit.

I knocked a second time, telling myself I always had to knock more than once. Carolina never came straight away.

When I raised my fist to knock a third time, the door opened.

59

'Zico,' said Carolina. 'Thank God it's you.'

Rocky came out to greet me, pressing against me and thumping her tail on my legs.

'Where's Raul?' I went in, ignoring the dog, looking around. 'Is he all right? I need to talk to him.' I stepped past Carolina, took two paces into the house and stopped.

Their place wasn't much. One main room right here behind the front door, with a low table in the centre and a couple of soft chairs and a sofa. To the far side, there was another table with four chairs where we had eaten together a few nights ago. There was a kitchen and a bedroom, both doors leading off this one room.

It was dark in there, that was the first thing I noticed. The shutters were closed and I was surprised I hadn't spotted that from outside. I had been too wrapped up in watching the watchmen.

The table, which would normally have at least two cups and a flask of coffee on its glass surface, was clear.

'Carolina?' I turned to look at her.

She had closed the door behind her, guiding it back rather than letting it swing on its hinge and slam in its frame.

'Where is he?' But I knew. The pain of his loss was already growing in me. It was spreading from muscle to muscle, sinking into my soul and invading every part of me.

Carolina stayed where she was, her face almost hidden in the shadow created by the fingers of sunlight creeping through the shutters. I could hardly see her expression, but I saw her shake her head. She opened her mouth but closed it again as if she didn't know what to say.

I went to her and raised both my arms, hesitated, not knowing quite what to do. 'When?' I asked her. The word came out as a whisper. It felt wrong on my lips, as if someone else had spoken it.

Carolina took a deep breath and looked up at me. Her eyes glistened in the half-light. 'Yesterday... Early... He asked for you.'

You should have been here for him, something screamed in my head. *You should have brought him home.*

I gave myself a moment to steady my voice. 'What happened?'

'The fever never broke. And he started... he was bleeding, Zico. Everywhere.'

I turned away and wiped my fingers across my eyes before I looked back at Carolina and saw her strength and dignity. 'Do they know what it was? Dengue fever?'

She swallowed her grief and looked down, nodding.

'And you?' I asked, putting a hand to my mouth. 'Do you feel all right?'

When she looked up at me, her despair was clear, but she fought it, determined not to let it pour out of her. 'Can I get you some coffee?' she asked.

'Sit down.' I took her hand and led her to one of the soft chairs. I sat opposite and leaned forward, putting my hands on my face. 'I should have come back with him. I should have ...' My words died in my throat.

Rocky came to me and rested her chin on my lap.

'There was nothing you could do, Zico. Nothing even the doctors could do. They tried giving him more blood but there was nothing.'

I rubbed my face, pressed the heels of my palms into my eyes and tried to think, but my mind was filled with just one thing.

I couldn't believe he was gone.

The old man was gone.

'I wanted to bring him home,' Carolina said, 'but they wouldn't let me. I'm going to bury him tomorrow. Will you be there?'

I nodded and we sat in silence, neither of us looking at the other. I stroked Rocky's head and cast my eyes around the room, seeing all the signs that he was still here. His hat on a hook by the door. A shirt across the back of a chair at the table. A pair of shoes. Photographs.

'What will you do?' I asked, lowering my head to put my face against Rocky's fur. 'Will you go to Imperatriz?'

Carolina shook her head. 'What would I go there for?'

'To be with your son. Francisco.'

'I never really wanted that,' she said. 'I belong *here*. It was Raul's dream more than it was ever mine.'

I looked up at her and felt the tears well in my eyes. 'He said the same thing to me.' My voice was quiet. 'That it was your dream, not his.'

'He said that?'

'Yes.'

She smiled, a melancholy look. 'Silly old fools. We spent all our time pretending we wanted something because we thought it was what the other wanted. Don't be like that, Zico. Be happy with what you have. You don't know when it will be taken from you.'

It was as if she had read the dilemma I'd struggled with for the last few days. If she had said it to me before, though, I might not have believed her. Only now could I see that she was right. Costa's money meant nothing if I had to sell my soul to have it. All that mattered was the family I had built around me since coming to Piratinga. I had to live for what I had, not for what I *hoped* to have.

'You cared a lot for each other,' I said, wondering if it would be the same for Daniella and me. If we were meant for each other the way Raul and Carolina had been.

'So he never wanted to go to Imperatriz?' she asked.

I shook my head.

'It makes sense.' She closed her eyes and sighed. When she opened them again, she widened them as if something was clouding her vision. There was grief there, but she was proud and stubborn and wouldn't allow herself to cry. 'You were more of a son to him than Francisco ever was.'

I wiped my own tears from my cheeks. 'You can't say that.'

'I can say what I want. I can say what is true. You were *here*, Zico. You shared his life. He spoke of you like you were ...' She stopped, her throat constricting, the pain wanting to come out, but she swallowed it down, reset herself.

'But I *wasn't* here,' I said. 'Not when it mattered.'

'You sent him back to me. That's all you could have done.'

I stood again, went to the kitchen and checked the flask but it was empty. Carolina had not made coffee today. 'Let me get you something,' I said, opening a cupboard, the door loose on its hinge. 'I should fix that.'

'No.' She came through and put her hand on me. 'Let me get something for *you*.'

I protested, but she made me stand aside while she boiled water, made coffee, found some dry biscuits. But when she put everything on the table, neither of us felt much like eating, so we sipped the hot coffee and ignored the biscuits.

'When I was a boy,' I said. 'I did a thing that rotted me from the inside. Something that I did again and again until I couldn't get away from it any more.'

Carolina raised her eyes to watch me.

'It was the only thing I was good at, but it made me dirty. Raul... he made me a better person. Being with him made me a better person. Maybe not a good person, but *better*. Do you understand?'

'You were a son to him. He spoke about you as if you were his own. He loved you.'

I lowered my head once more and stared at Rocky, feeling the tears swell in my eyes.

'Some men came to the hospital,' she said, making me look up. 'They wanted to speak to Raul but he was ... he couldn't ...' She swallowed some coffee. 'He didn't even know who he was by then. I stayed with him every minute. Held his hand when he went.'

'What did they want?' I asked, feeling a pang of something other than grief. 'These men?'

'They came here last night,' she said. '*Here*. No shame, no respect. They were asking for you, Zico. Daniella, too.'

'Daniella?'

She nodded. 'Such a lovely girl, Raul always said. Maybe too good for you.' She managed a half smile. 'Will you bring her tomorrow when I ... bury him?'

'Yes.' But I was hardly listening now. I was thinking about the men who had come to the hospital. It would have been Luis and Wilson.

I tightened my hands into fists and remembered that they were sitting on the beach awaiting my return. There was no time for grief now. I had to bury it deep and save it for another day.

'There are men here now,' I said. 'Outside. Waiting. Are they the same ones?'

Carolina stood, went to the window and opened the shutter, just a crack so she could look out. 'It's them. Do they want to hurt you?' she asked.

'I think so.' I went to stand beside her and look out.

'Don't let that happen.' She took my hand and put it on my gun. 'Don't let them take you from me, too.'

60

Closing Carolina's door, I stopped to stare at the spot on the river where the *Deus* was usually moored. I thought about what the old man said to me about not wanting to go to Imperatriz, about how he and I were part of this place and that we would never leave it just as it would never leave us. That was truer for him now than ever before.

I took a few steps forward, Luis and Wilson coming into view, both of them still sitting on the shore, smoking and watching the river.

I took out my pistol and checked the load once more, looking over at the men as I rolled the cylinder in my fingers. Then I took a deep breath and began towards them, coming at them almost from behind, raising my pistol so it was level in front of me.

About five metres from where they were sitting, I stopped and called out. 'You waiting for *me*?'

Both men turned, eyes wide as if startled from a moment of boredom. They looked at one another, then back at me.

'Yes,' said Luis. He was wearing a Brahma T-shirt today, and burgundy trousers that needed a wash. The same cap was on his head, the peak still hard and crisp.

Beside him, Wilson put his hand to his waist, searching for the reassurance of steel and lead.

'That's right,' I said to him. 'Take it out.'

I could see the confusion in his eyes, dark under his straw hat, the questioning look wondering what I was doing. Inviting him to draw his weapon. He'd be deciding if I was giving myself an excuse to shoot him down.

'Do it now.' I wanted to get this done quickly. It wasn't too busy here, but someone might come. Someone who didn't need to see this. 'You, too,' I said to Luis.

They lifted their shirts with one hand and used the finger and thumb of the other to pull out their pistols.

'Now throw them in the water.'

They hesitated, looking at each other.

'You won't hit me from there,' I said. 'Not before I put two holes in each of you. Don't test me; I've had a bad week.'

They looked at each other once more, then Wilson said, 'You know how much I paid for this *pistola*?'

'Tell Costa to pay for a new one.'

Still they hesitated.

'Let me throw it over there,' he said, nodding to a dry patch of ground.

'In the water,' I told him. 'Right now.'

'Shit.' Luis grimaced and hefted his pistol out into the river where it landed with a hollow sound, like a heavy stone. A spit of the river rose in complaint, then settled into concentric rings and disappeared.

'You too,' I said to Wilson. 'Or I'm going to start shooting.'

Wilson shook his head and threw the pistol.

'Good. Now I feel much safer. Anyone else here?' I asked, keeping my distance.

'No.'

'Costa only sent you two? I'd have thought he'd send more.'

Wilson looked angry, like he wanted to make me pay for forcing him to throw away his gun, but Luis looked a little scared now he was disarmed.

'You came to kill me?' I asked. 'Like you killed Antonio. You remember Antonio, right?'

The two men remained silent.

'Are you here to kill me?' I asked again.

'No,' said Luis. 'To meet you is all. Costa wanted to know as soon as you came back.'

I went straight to him, raising my pistol higher and pressing the barrel to his chest, right where his heart was beating. 'Don't lie to me.'

Luis put both his hands out, his breath quickening, his eyes widening in fear.

'How much,' I said. 'How much was Costa going to give you to kill me? *How much?*' I pressed my pistol harder into his chest.

'Thirty,' Luis admitted. 'Thirty reais.'

So Sister Beckett had been right. Costa had been lying to me from the start.

'I'm sorry, Zico.' Luis saw the anger in my face and his fear increased. His skin glistened with sweat and his eyes darted as he searched mine, trying to anticipate what I planned to do with him.

'Thirty reais?' I asked. 'And for Daniella?'

'Thirty for each of you. For the old man, too, but he was already dead.'

'Lucky for you,' I said, pressing the gun hard against his sweat-dampened shirt. 'If you had touched him, I would have cut out your eyes. You're lucky I haven't done it already.'

Luis swallowed hard. Beside him, Wilson remained still.

'Thirty reais a piece?' I said. 'That's fifteen American dollars. Not much for a man's life.'

'I do what I can.'

'You have a family?' I asked. 'Wife? Kids?' I nudged him with the pistol and he nodded.

'And you?' I looked at Wilson.

'A girlfriend,' he replied.

I shook my head. 'He's playing you the way he played me. He's got all of us running around trying to kill each other.'

'Who? Costa? What are you—'

'Yes, *Costa*,' I said. 'He's like a devil lying to all of us. You two know who I am, you know the kind of thing I do for him. He's sent you here to cover something up. Something he asked me to do.'

'Like what?'

'Doesn't matter. What matters is that he said he was going to pay me for a job and then he sent you here to wait for me. To kill me the moment I put a foot in Piratinga.'

'So?'

'Christ, you two are even slower than me. What makes you think he won't do the same thing to you? Send other men. Less reliable men. Not family men like you.'

'That's bullshit,' Wilson said. 'Why would he do that?'

'Same reason he'd do it to me. To cover it up. Hide it deeper.'

Wilson pursed his lips, the hairs on his moustache straightening. He narrowed his eyes. 'He wouldn't do that to us.'

'He did it to *me*. And I've done work for him for a long time. More *important* work than you. You know how much he's supposed to pay me? Five thousand dollars.'

'*Caralho*. What did he want you to do?' Wilson asked. 'Kill the Pope?'

'I already said it doesn't matter.'

'Why would we believe you?'

'Because you're here. Because he's going to pay you to kill me.' I looked at both men. 'Maybe I should just shoot you now. Kick you in the river and leave you for the fish.'

Luis's fear returned. For a moment he'd been distracted, had something else to think about, but now it was real again. 'No ...'

'Or maybe we should go talk to Costa,' I said. 'See what he's up to. What do you think of that?'

Luis and Wilson looked at each other, then nodded to me.

'We'll see if those five thousand dollars are in that safe of his,' I said. 'See if it ever even existed.'

'OK.' Luis spoke quickly. 'We should do *that*. We should go see Costa.'

I took a step away from him, removing the barrel of my pistol from his chest. 'I'm going to put this away and walk behind you. Don't make me take it out again.'

We moved in silence, Luis and Wilson in front, me following. I kept my pistol hidden, so as not to attract any attention, but it was close to hand if I needed it.

377

'You didn't think this through, did you?' I said as we walked. 'Waiting for me in plain view like that.'

'Costa wanted us to talk to you, find out if you did his job for him. We didn't think you'd know that—'

'That you'd be there to kill me?'

Luis slowed his pace and glanced back at me. 'Look, Zico, it's just business.'

'And that's meant to make me feel better? Because you're doing it for money?' I considered for a moment that I had done the same thing – tried to justify my actions with the same argument. There might have been a time when I fooled myself into thinking money had been my incentive, but I knew better now. Financial reward had never been my motivation. It had always been revenge.

'Are you going to kill us?' Wilson asked.

'I haven't decided yet. But troubling the old woman ...' I shook my head. 'That's low.'

'We were looking for *you*.'

'Sure you were.' I glanced across at the hospital as we passed it, thinking about the old man lying in there on a slab or a bed or maybe just on the floor; I didn't know where they kept the dead. I didn't even know if he'd be cooled or if he'd be lying in a warm room getting higher. I spoke a silent farewell, and promised myself I would make it to his funeral tomorrow.

I would stand by Carolina's side if that's what she wanted. I would be with her when she put him to rest.

The street was almost deserted when we turned off and headed to Costa's office. The sun was high and most people were keeping to the shade, sleeping off their lunch. A single car moved slowly on the road as if it, too, was exhausted by the heat.

'Go on up,' I said to the two men when we came to the blue door on the corner. 'He'll be surprised to see us.'

It was cooler in the stairwell, no windows for the sun to penetrate, and it smelled of concrete dust, just like always. Our footsteps were soft on the cracked stairs and broken tiles, me in flip-flops and the other two in shoes that were so old the soles were soft like animal hide.

I followed them through the door at the top and into the outer office where the ancient secretary looked up, eyes peering over glasses that were now held together in the middle with a piece of tape. Her mouth opened when she saw me.

I put a finger to my lips and shook my head, raising my pistol so there was no mistake about what I was holding and what I would do with it.

She closed her mouth and sat bolt upright, putting her hands on the desk in front of her, knocking a pencil that rolled to one side and fell onto the tiled floor.

'Costa in there?' I asked.

She nodded.

'Is there a key for this door?'

She nodded again.

'Lock it and sit back down.'

The secretary took a key from a pencil pot on her desk and crept over to the front door, not once taking her eyes off me.

When I heard the click of the lock, I took the key from her and told her to sit down. 'This won't take too long,' I said. 'You'll be quite safe if you stay right where you are.' And as I spoke, the door to Costa's office opened and he stepped out saying, 'Samara, is someone—' He stopped when he saw Luis and Wilson. 'Oh it's—' And then he saw me standing behind them.

For a moment he was lost for words. I could see his eyes moving as his mind raced and his mouth floundered. He looked at the door, saw it was closed, then his eyes took in what was in my hand before he looked at my face. He shook himself. A shiver ran through him as he composed himself and forced a smile to his lips. 'Zico,' he said, stepping forward. 'You're back. I sent Luis and Wilson to meet you.'

'Yes, you did.'

'And your trip?' He inclined his head to one side. 'Did it go well?'

'Why don't we talk about it in your office? You can sit down. Get comfortable.'

Costa hesitated, looked around the room. He narrowed his eyes at Samara, a questioning look, or maybe an angry look because she hadn't warned him, then he cleared his throat and stood aside. 'Of course. Why don't you come in.'

'You first.'

Costa retreated into his room, turning his back to me, going to the window to look out, then to his desk, standing behind it. He put his hands to his chin, then dropped them, crossed them over his chest, then dropped them again, putting his hands into his pockets.

'Nervous?' I asked.

'No, Zico. Why would I be—'

'Sit down, Costa.' I looked at Luis and Wilson. 'And you two can stand over there.' I pointed at the corner of the room where Costa kept his small safe.

'I guess that's where my money is,' I said. 'My five thousand dollars. Why don't you tell them the combination?'

Again, Costa hesitated, then he swallowed, nodded and told them the numbers.

Luis keyed them in, pulled open the door and stood aside so I could see what was in there. Two shelves. A small bundle of notes on the lower one, reais. On the top shelf there was a bundle of papers weighed down with an automatic pistol.

'No way of knowing if it's loaded,' I said to Luis. 'Safety on or off. It wouldn't be worth it. You can take out the money, though. Count it.'

Luis looked at me, then slowly put his hand into the safe and took out the cash. He leafed through it a couple of times, then counted each note individually. 'Two hundred reais,' he said.

'No dollars?' I looked at Costa.

'Not in there. I have to put it together. Have to make sure you did what I asked.' He narrowed his eyes.

'How would you ever know? She was supposed to disappear, remember. No trace.'

'And did she?'

'Well, she's dead, but I didn't kill her. And there are a lot of people who can confirm that.'

'You didn't...' He lowered his eyebrows. 'Then... I don't have to pay you?'

'I suppose not,' I said. 'But then, you weren't going to pay me anyway, were you? There never was any money; it was all a lie. Maybe some clever trick to make the Branquinos think you're worth something. To make them let you leave this place you hate so much. So there was no money, no land, and you sent these two idiots to kill me.'

Costa shook his head and his mouth struggled to form the right word. 'N... No.'

'And, even worse than that, you were going to pay them to kill the old man. My girlfriend, too. Thirty reais,' I said. 'I would have thought I was worth more than that. At least a hundred. Maybe even two.'

Costa opened his mouth to speak, then closed it again.

'And these two?' I said. 'How much were you going to pay someone to kill *them*?'

'What?'

'Come on, Costa, it took me a while to catch on to it, but I know what you're planning. Someone much smarter than me worked it out. They kill me, someone else kills *them*...' I gritted my teeth and swallowed my anger. 'You want to bury this deep,' I said. 'All that talk we had about investigations, people taking an interest in the kind of things you people do – the kind of things you ask people like *me* to do.'

'No.' He shook his head, looking at the other two men. 'I mean. If you didn't... if it wasn't you who...'

'Wouldn't make any difference, though, would it, Costa?'

'Is it true?' Luis took a step towards Costa.

'No.' Costa shook his head, the sweat running from his forehead. There were dark patches under his arms, down the front of his chest.

'I can see why you'd be worried,' I told him. 'About what Luis and Wilson might do, I mean. And you'd be right to worry. I think they could be very bad men. Worse than me. Less controlled.' I leaned closer to him. 'Tell you what. You tell me the truth, and I'll let you live. I'll kill these two men and walk out of here. You can keep all your money but I'll never want to hear from you again. Anything happens to anyone I know – I so much as see someone suspicious – I'll come straight to your house and I'll kill your wife and I'll kill your children. Do you believe me?'

Costa nodded.

'So tell me the truth.'

He looked at Wilson and Luis as he weighed his options. Tell me what I wanted to hear and he would live. I would kill his two *pistoleiros* and walk away. Tell me something else and I would kill him right now. He only had one choice. Whether it was true or not, he only had one choice.

Like he had given me only one choice.

'I paid them to kill you,' he said.

'And then you were planning to do the same to them? These men right here? One of them with a family?'

'Yes.'

'Louder, Costa.'

'Yes.'

'And didn't you say to me, before I left, that if I did this job for you right, you would let me have them?'

He nodded.

'And, by that, you meant you would let me kill them?'

There was silence in the room. I looked at Luis and Wilson, both men staring at Costa like they wanted to rip out his heart.

I shook my head at Costa. 'You're so full of lies. Even your lies are lies.' I turned my pistol on Wilson and Luis. 'Didn't I tell you?' I cocked the hammer back with my thumb. 'He'd kill us all.'

Wilson took an involuntary step backwards, so he was half hidden by his partner's body, but Luis didn't take his eyes off Costa. As if he were trying to murder him with his final look.

I waited like that, ready to fire, then sighed and lowered my pistol. 'Well,' I said. 'I suppose he's all yours now.'

All three men looked at me in confusion.

Everything that had happened over these last few days had begun with them, and now it would end with them.

As much as I wanted to punish Costa for what he had done, he had already made it clear there would be consequences for me if anything happened to him. If his employers thought I'd had anything to do with his death, the crime would not go unpunished. So I would let Luis and Wilson do it for me. Let them be punished for his death.

I could kill all three of them without lifting a finger.

'We don't need to be enemies,' I said to Luis and Wilson. 'This devil is our enemy. He would have us all killed then take his money and buy something expensive for his wife.'

They both turned to face Costa and there was no mistaking the murderous look in their eyes.

There's a hundred reais each in there,' I said. 'A nice-looking *pistola*, too.'

'What ... ?' Costa stepped back and held up his hands as he floundered for the right words. 'You ...'

'You're a devil.' I looked right at him. 'Anhangá. I know it, and now these men know it.'

'But you made me say it,' Costa finally managed. 'You *made* me. I wasn't going to have them killed. I wasn't going to—'

'Sure you were,' I said, going to him and putting my mouth close to his ear. 'And it looks like you didn't know me as well as you thought, eh? When you asked me to kill Sister Beckett, I knew I didn't want to do it, not even for the money, but you forced me into a corner. Now you know how that feels.'

Walking to the door, I stopped and turned to Luis and Wilson. 'He's all yours,' I said.

Luis reached into the safe and took out the gun. He looked at Costa as he ejected the magazine, checked the load and slipped it back in, racking the slide to bring a cartridge into the chamber.

'You don't want to stay for this?' He looked at me. 'It's as much for you as it is for us.'

'No,' I said, turning the handle and shrugging the shadow away. 'I don't have the stomach for this any more.'

61

Leaving the shadow behind, I let myself out of Costa's office and stepped into the light, not knowing what was going to happen now. I headed down to Ernesto's place, staying in the open, where the sun was hot on my shoulders and felt good.

Coming into the bar, there were a few men drinking beer, not talking much because it was too hot or they had nothing to say.

'Zico,' Ernesto said as I came in. 'Beer?'

'Brahma.' I held up a finger before turning to the other men.

Marco was among them, the man who had brought the old man home. He came close to me, his eyes to the floor. 'I'm sorry about Raul,' he said. 'I did what I could.'

'You brought him home.'

And from behind Marco, one of the others spoke, saying, 'He was a good man.'

'Yes he was,' I told them.

'We'll miss him.'

Ernesto put a beer on the counter and I took a long drink before fishing in my pocket and pulling out a few notes.

'On me.' Ernesto put his hand on my arm.

'Thanks.' I raised the bottle saying, '*Saúde*,' and took another drink. I swallowed and looked at the men sitting at the bar. 'Saw the *Estrella*,' I said. 'She's stuck on the sand just at the mouth of the Rio das Mortes. Can anyone help?'

'When?' asked one of the men. Zeca, I think he was called.

'Yesterday. They were still there this morning.'

He nodded, stood, and drained his beer. 'I'll go now,' he said, looking round. 'Anyone else?'

'Sure.' Another stood and finished his beer. 'We'll get it out.' He looked at me. 'You bringing Raul's boat?'

'No,' I said. 'She's gone.' It felt right that the river had taken the *Deus e o Diabo*. She and the old man had been connected somehow, unable to exist without each other.

'We saw smoke,' Ernesto said. 'Was that—'

'That was her,' I told them.

The men nodded and left the bar, so I ordered another beer and followed them outside, walking down to the riverbank. I climbed onto Zeca's boat and sat at the bow, thinking about Raul and Carolina. I thought about Leonardo and about his brother waiting for him in Belém. It was all I really knew about him.

I took the cutting from my pocket, feeling the soft newspaper between my fingertips, and looked down at the photograph of Sister Beckett. The collection of black and grey dots didn't do justice to the woman who had died in Mina dos Santos. It illustrated nothing of her strength or determination. I considered letting the breeze take it as Zeca started the engine, but changed my mind, deciding to put it in my pack for safe keeping.

When I brought it onto my lap, though, and opened the fastenings, I realised that it wasn't my pack at all. This was Leonardo's backpack.

He must have been carrying it when Daniella shot him in the bar, and in our haste to leave Fernanda's, I had picked up his instead of mine.

I tried to remember everything I had lost, reassuring myself that it wouldn't matter who found it. Nothing could identify me and everything could be replaced. Perhaps there would even be something here other than cigarettes and *cocaína* that I could use.

What I found was an automatic pistol with a spare magazine, a knife, three packets of cigarettes and what looked like a package of *cocaína*. There was a spare T-shirt in there too, and at the bottom, a brown paper bag that I pulled out and opened.

I stopped when I saw the money. American currency bound in two bundles of hundred-dollar bills. My guess was that there was at least ten thousand dollars in that paper bag.

I scrunched it closed and stared out at the tree line, wondering if the money had always been there or if Leonardo had picked it up in Mina dos Santos. Perhaps it was down payment on the guns – the rest to be paid when he brought the weapons ashore. It didn't really matter. It belonged to Daniella and me now. To Carolina too.

Replacing the paper bag, I looked at the picture of Sister Beckett once more before refolding it and laying it on top. I closed the backpack and put it by my feet, then watched the water while I sipped my beer, thinking about the old man, and the number of times we had set out together on the river.

A slight wind picked up, throwing a cloud of sand my way.

I wiped my eye with the back of my hand and waited to bring Daniella home.

THE
DARKEST
HEART

Reading Group Notes

ABOUT THE AUTHOR

Dan Smith grew up following his parents across the world. He's lived in many places including Sierra Leone, Sumatra, northern and central Brazil, Spain, and the Soviet Union. He is now settled in Newcastle with his family, where he writes both for adults and for younger readers. His debut novel, *Dry Season*, was shortlisted for the Authors' Club Best First Novel Award 2011, and was nominated for the IMPAC Dublin Literary Award.

THE STORY BEHIND *THE DARKEST HEART*

Some years ago, I read an article about a nun who was murdered by gunmen in Brazil. The assassins, hired by a landowner later convicted for the crime, were paid a meagre sum of just a few American dollars to carry out the murder. The photograph accompanying the article, of the place where the nun was murdered, looked very much like the dirt road that led to the house I lived in as a teenager. Seeing that path, with the rainforest surrounding it, recalled memories of a time in my life that I always regard very fondly. But the article also reminded me of some of the people I knew – people who laughed, joked, played football, went fishing. People who seemed completely ordinary. But some of them, I heard, would draw their gun or knife and kill, for just a few notes in their pocket. This was something I always found difficult to understand – these were people I *liked*, and yet they were said to be killers – and it has led to a theme that crops up in many of my novels.

In *The Darkest Heart* I try to explore what might drive a person to kill without regret or guilt, and I test where that person might draw the line. My story is about a killer, and what makes him kill. But Zico, who I should add isn't based on anyone I know, is not an evil maniac with a glazed stare and a lust for blood. He is an ordinary person who has been dealt a difficult hand and has made some bad decisions. He would kill someone who, he felt, deserved their fate, but would he murder someone who is a force for good? How far would he really go?

Dan Smith, 2015

FOR DISCUSSION

....

- How does the author establish a sense of place?

- 'Human nature is human nature. We subject ourselves to things we know we might not be able to endure.' Why do we?

- Why does Raul pretend to yearn for Imperatriz?

- How does Sofia influence Zico's life?

- 'It occurred to me that maybe too much of a man's life is taken up looking for something else, something *better*, and too little is passed with the understanding of what he has, and what he really wants.' Is this the central theme of *The Darkest Heart*?

- What's the difference between Zico and Leonardo?

- 'I like it muddy . . . I like it that you can't see what's down there. It's like we're not supposed to know. There are things down there we shouldn't see.' What does this tell us about Raul?

- 'You can't stop nature.' Is Leonardo right?

- How does *The Darkest Heart* make you feel about Brazil?

- 'I'd killed men, but I'd never burned a man's home.' What does this say about Zico's moral world?

- What is Sister Beckett's role in *The Darkest Heart*?

- Do you like Zico?

IN CONVERSATION WITH DAN SMITH

....

Q How do you feel about Brazil?

A I haven't been to Brazil in a long time, but there is
something about the country that has stayed with me.
I have such fond memories of both the place and the
people. Writing *The Darkest Heart* was, in some ways,
an indulgence for me. It gave me the opportunity
to dwell on the sounds and smells of Brazil, to once
more feel the sun on my neck and the breeze on my
back, and I hope that when readers open its pages,
they will be transported to the places I remember so
well.

Q Do you treat Death as a character in *The Darkest Heart*?

A It wasn't my intention to treat Death as a character, but I can understand why some readers might see it that way. Death is certainly a constant presence, in the same way that God or the Devil might be. Of course, that idea gave rise to the name of the battered boat that makes its way along the river in *The Darkest Heart*, and also gave me the original working title for the novel – *God and The Devil*.

Q How important is the setting to the story?

A Perhaps the bare essentials of the story could be transposed to another setting, but the beliefs and behaviour of the characters are all dictated by their culture and their environment. If it were to take place anywhere else, many of those things would have to change.

Q Is Zico 'good and bad at the same time'?

A I think he is. Zico wants to be a good man, but hasn't had a lot of practice or opportunity. The only way he has ever made a life for himself is by doing bad things. When I lived in Brazil, I knew a number of people who, it turned out, were said to be murderers. To me, they seemed ordinary, just like everybody else, and it still fascinates me when I think about the things they had apparently done. They never struck me as bad people. I wanted Zico to be like them. Life is not always black and white, good and evil, right and wrong – those things can be mixed together in the most complicated ways.

Q 'We make dreams to pass the time, and we pretend that we want to be somewhere else; it's what men do. Maybe we do it for our women or maybe we do it because it's expected of us, I don't know, but we're all supposed to have dreams, Zico, we're not supposed to be content.' Why do we?

A I don't know! Maybe it's just human nature to always want something other than what we already have.

Q 'Perhaps we could never be saved.' How far is *The Darkest Heart* about redemption?

A I don't really think Zico is looking for redemption.

I'm not sure he even carries guilt for the things he has done. Zico's moral compass has been skewed by his experiences and he feels that all the people he has killed deserved what he did to them. He sees them as an extension of the boy who raped and murdered his sister. Zico isn't looking for redemption so much as he is looking for something better and brighter in his life. This is why he struggles with the idea of murdering Sister Beckett. He doesn't think she deserves to die, and if he were to carry out Costa's demands, he would certainly spend the rest of his life searching for redemption.

Q 'In Candomblé they taught people there is no good or bad, only destiny.' Is there any truth in this do you think?

A I don't think I believe in destiny. Maybe only when it suits me! I do believe there is good and bad, though, but not that people are either *all* good or *all* bad. Perhaps some people sway more one way than the other, but I'm sure even some of the most evil people in history didn't go through life without doing a single good thing.

Q 'Maybe, if you get all the things you dream of, it turns out you don't really want them.' How far is contentment, or lack of it, a theme of *The Darkest Heart*?

A It's definitely a theme throughout the book. Zico's fairly modest dream is to have a little money and a piece of land to call his own, but he doesn't pause to look at what he already has. He is, in fact, content with his lot. The life he lives is simple but good. He has found a family in Raul and Carolina, and he has Daniella. Pursuing his dream leads him to a very dark place. In a similar way, Raul spends his life pursuing a dream he doesn't really want. I'm not suggesting we shouldn't have dreams and aspirations, but I think it's important to sometimes take a moment and look at what we already have. Perhaps we already have what we want.

SUGGESTED FURTHER READING

Atonement
by Ian McEwan

Eleven Minutes
by Paulo Coelho

The Kite Runner
by Khaled Hosseini

Gabriela, Clove and Cinnamon
by Jorge Amado

Crime and Punishment
by Fyodor Dostoevsky